CROWN

OF THE

PHOENIX

BOOK ONE

C. A. VARIAN

Crown of the Phoenix

Contents

INAS

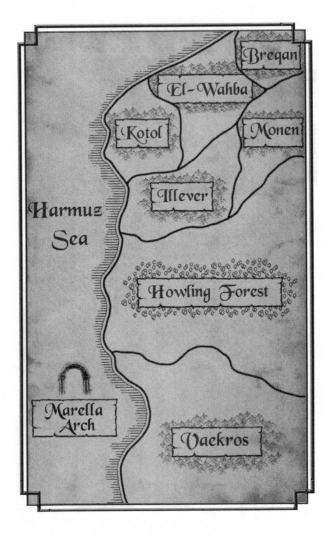

EKOTORIA

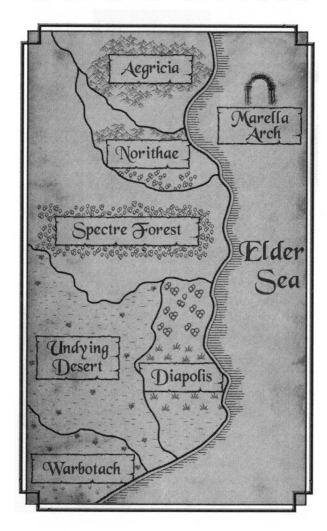

Chapter One

Vaekros

*B*lood *thrashed her veins like it wished to erode her very being, much like the sea upon the rocky shoreline. Pain unlike anything she'd ever known raged within her as she felt the call. She wanted—needed—to go to the arch. The irresistible longing was an unbearable weight on her chest, sharpening each breath, and telling her to fly.*

"Aurelia, you're going to have to try harder if you're ever going to be able to defend yourself. You hit like a girl!"

Wiping the sweat off her brow, Aurelia Vesta grasped her sword in both hands, swinging at Amadeus' larger weapon, only for him to slap hers to the ground. She grunted.

"It's not a fair fight, you know. Your blade is bigger."

Her brother snorted, bracing his feet in a defensive stance.

"Likely excuse, Lia. Likely excuse."

"Room for me?" Septima strolled across the grounds of the villa, calling out to them. Just as Amadeus turned to look at their sister, Aurelia slammed her sword into his, forcing it from his hands. It clattered loudly as it hit the grass.

"Hey!" His outraged shriek held little threat with Aurelia's blade now leveled with his gut. "I wasn't ready."

Waiting until she thought he just may piss himself, she smirked and lowered her weapon to her side. "Likely story, Amadeus. Likely story."

Dropping her sword, Aurelia ran to Septima, wrapping her arm around her sister's shoulder. "We have room for you, but I doubt you want to fight against that loser." She flipped her thumb over her shoulder, pointing at their brother, who rolled his eyes.

"I'll fight you then," Septima said as she darted for Amadeus' sword, swiping it from the ground, and wielding it in her sister's direction.

Aurelia retrieved her blade and swung it at Septima, only for her strike to be blocked. Her jaw dropped as Septima sneered at her. When her look morphed into a mischievous one, Aurelia braced herself for retaliation.

Amadeus began walking toward the house. "I'm going to head home. I'll grab my sword later. Have fun and try not to cut off each other's ears."

The sisters barely paid attention to him as their eyes remained on one another, waiting for the next move to be taken. Septima circled left, waving her weapon in arcs. Aurelia backed up, dropped her weapon on the ground, and took off running toward the gardens.

She was tired of sparring, and leading a chase was far more fun. Glancing over her shoulder, she noticed Septima in pursuit.

Once they entered the gardens, the pair fell to the ground and began giggling uncontrollably. They laid among the flowers, admiring the cloudless sky and the breeze rolling off the Harmuz Sea. The sea, ever crashing against the weather-beaten white cliffs, carved dramatic rock faces. Though the cliffs were too high to climb down for a swim, the view was magnificent. Laying in the gardens, overlooking the water below, was one of their favorite pastimes.

"It must be such a thrill," Septima said, rolling onto her side to face Aurelia. Her dark eyes shined in the sunlight and her long ebony braids shimmered like black silk.

Aurelia turned to face her sister, twirling a yellow wildflower between her fingers. "What would be a thrill?"

The longing for adventure played across Septima's features. "To fight... to be a badass warrior. I'm sick of being expected to be a proper lady who spends her time doing tedious things."

Sighing, Aurelia flicked the flower toward her sister. It landed near her hand. "Father would never allow it. You know we are to be wed. It's what is expected of us. I'm surprised he hasn't married me off yet. My twenty-first birthday will be here soon." She knew why her sister wanted to seek adventure instead of marriage, but she did not know how to help to make that happen for her. It was something she thought about often, knowing Septima did not fancy men at all. She was only attracted to women, but marrying the same sex was not allowed in Vaekros. Neither were women warriors. The options to bring her sister happiness were slim, and that was heartbreaking.

Rolling her eyes, Septima turned onto her back to gaze at the sky. "I'm not getting married to a man, expectations or not."

Aurelia's chest tightened at her sister's plight. "Marrying a woman isn't an option in Vaekros. You know that."

Septima sighed. "That may be true, but I will not be forced to marry a man, either. I'd rather die, Lia. I will not do it."

Aurelia bit her lip and turned to stare at the sky as well. They laid in silence for a while, neither knowing how to continue the conversation. Neither knowing how to solve a problem that had no solution in their society.

Aurelia stood and dusted off her clothes. "I'm going to go check on Kano. He needs to get out of the house before he shreds up everything in it. I'll catch up with you a bit later." She leaned over to give her sister a kiss on the cheek before heading toward the house. Septima waved as she walked away.

While Septima was not Aurelia's sister by blood, she was the single most important person in her life. Aurelia's father had found Septima when she was only a baby, while his army laid siege on El-Wahba. Septima's father had been killed in the attack, and her mother had been enslaved. Aurelia's parents became Septima's, although they could not have been more different in appearance.

Septima was not the only baby their father saved and brought back to their home in Vaekros. He had also given Aurelia a tiger cub. Her beautiful Kano who, aside from Septima, was her best friend. She remembered it like it was yesterday. She was less than two years old when she met her baby sister, but was ten years old when the tiny cub was placed in her arms. She named him after the Sun God, because the colors of his fur reminded her of that golden orb in the sky. No one thought he would survive—a runt they called him—but she had cared for him, and he grew and thrived. Some would shun such a pet, but Kano was far kinder than his wild kin. For ten years, he had grown with, loved, and protected her.

Aurelia approached the villa from the back door. She adored the home. It was disposed dramatically along the rocky cliff tops near the Howling Mountains and Forest. The large seaside estate, decorated with mosaics and frescoes, was built around an outdoor atrium. The external walls were covered in stones and a separate building housed the servants. A small wooden cottage on the edge of the property belonged to Amadeus, who had yet to be married.

The stone atrium was filled with a variety of potted trees, vines, and flowers. A large pool sparkled in its center—a pool the girls frequented in the warmer months since reaching the sea was impossible from the height of the house.

Inside the stately villa, sleeping chambers, guestrooms, bathing rooms, reception areas, dining rooms, and even a library filled the large, two-level home. The floors were polished marble and gleamed throughout the structure. Her father, Proteus, made sure of it. He did not allow a dirty house, and the servants knew better than to disobey him. So did his children. His decades as military commander reinforced his no-nonsense personality. There was no warmth in Proteus. Aurelia wondered if he had always been that way, or if the death of her mother changed him.

When Aurelia entered her bedchamber, Kano stretched his massive body and slinked up to her to nuzzle her legs. She dropped into the vanity seat and untangled her braid while she gazed at herself in the bronze mirror. Her large blue eyes and crimson hair were such a contrast to Septima's long midnight braids and her deep tawny skin.

Some said her red hair was a gift from Veena, the Goddess of Life and Death. Not unlike the goddess, Aurelia loved to spar. She loved learning to wield weapons, even if it was all but forbidden in her society. She had to be a respectable Vaekrosan lady and that meant never making a man feel weak in her presence. Even so, she sparred with her brother, and with Septima, to practice her swordsmanship. With as many fights as Vaekros picked, she never knew when such skills would be useful.

Aurelia turned to admire her bedchamber. Walls of rich aqua mirrored the color of the sea that always reflected the light of the sun from the floor to ceiling windows. Bright white silk drapes fluttered in the breeze. A huge four-poster bed took up a large part of the suite, large enough for Kano to sleep alongside her and keep her warm.

Her favorite view from her window was that of the Marella arch. The sea had carved an arch out of the rock that looked like a portal to a magical world. The legends of the arch were contradictory in Vaekros, so Aurelia settled on the one in her dreams. The water was too dangerous for anyone to approach it, although Aurelia dreamed of traversing the distance, of flying through the arch.

Curled up like a mountain at her feet, Kano let out a mighty snore. She reached over and caressed his sleek fur, rousing him from his slumber. Large canines gleamed as he yawned. His amber eyes were still full of sleep. Rising to his feet, he rubbed against the cloth of her pants as she rubbed his head.

"You're being lazy today, Kano. I think it's time for us to play outside."

He bobbed his head like he understood her. Leaving her chambers with the great cat trailing behind her, Aurelia took the stairs quickly to look for Septima and sunshine.

After searching the villa twice over, she found both at the same time. Septima sat on a stone bench in the rose garden, soaking in the sun and reading a book. Kano sprinted at the sight of her, nuzzling his enormous head against Septima's legs. She giggled, ruffling his fur.

"Hey there, big guy," she said, placing a kiss on his head before gleaming a toothy grin at Aurelia. "What are you two up to?"

Aurelia shrugged, dropping to sit beside her. "Kano has been too lazy today. I thought a game of hide and seek would be good for him. Do you want to play?"

Septima chuckled. "Aren't we a little old for such games?"

Rising from the bench, Aurelia straightened her tunic. "I'm older, and I still play." She shrugged. "Let's go Kano, the last one in the forest is a horse's ass."

Running as fast as she could, Aurelia darted into the tree line. The sound of Kano's enormous paws thudded close behind her.

The forest was vast, dense, and rich. Its canopy comprised pine, Buxus, and holly. Enough light shimmered through their crowns for a medley of shrubs to take advantage of the fertile grounds below. Silent vines suspended from many a tree, and a range of flowers, which grew in a sprinkled, disorderly fashion, brightened up the otherwise homogeneous scenery. A mishmash of noises, predominantly those of critters, echoed throughout, and were backed by the occasional sounds of birds of prey gliding in the air.

Aurelia laughed as she ran, climbing into an abandoned hollow just big enough for her to fit. Holding her breath, she knew he could smell her, but he seemed to pretend he couldn't, like he knew the rules of the game.

Quick footsteps paced in the distance. She pulled herself as far into the tree as she could, hoping there weren't any rodents nesting in there that would bite her like last time.

"Got you!" Septima's mane fell into the hollow, nearly slapping her in the face. They both began giggling as Kano bounded up to them as they kneeled, licking their faces.

Aurelia wiped the slobber off her cheek with the back of her hand. "I thought you were too old for this game?"

Septima shrugged as she wiped her own face. "You know I'll be playing in the forest with you even when my hair turns gray, especially with this big guy." She reached out and scratched Kano behind his ear. He leaned into her.

They played for hours. Each taking great care in where they hid, only for Kano to find them each time.

With barely enough energy to walk back to the villa, thirsty and covered in dirt and leaves, the sisters and Kano entered the back garden of their home just as the sun began making its descent over the Howling mountains.

A snarl ripped out of Kano before they cleared the threshold of the house. Aurelia looked at him to see that his ears were laid nearly flat against his head. She gently stroked his fur in an attempt to soothe him. She looked up to see her father standing in the foyer with two strange men, and her heart dropped.

Chapter Two

Aegricia

Walking back to her cell in the depths of the dungeon, Otera dragged her feet as the cloaked monstrosity of a man yanked her alongside him. It was cold—bone chilling—yet she had been pulled out of her bed with little more than a nightdress on. Her people were scared, and her military was gone. She was powerless to help even herself.

"You don't have to drag me. I can walk by myself." She tried to muster power in her voice, but it came out as a desperate plea. He grunted and tugged her arm harder, his fingers biting into her flesh.

She had rarely used the dungeons below her castle. Only the most dangerous criminals were housed there, and only if another punishment was not more fitting. Because the cells received little use, they weren't fit to house anyone, not a dog, and certainly not a person. It was the last place the Aegrician queen ever thought she would find herself.

The Warbotach cavalry had moved swiftly, laying siege to her castle and leaving her with no choice but to let them in or risk harm befalling innocent civilians. Her military had fled, not to abandon their people, but to build up strength and allies. They would then return to Aegricia, when the time was right, and reclaim their land.

That was the plan they settled on when word of the invasion of Norithae had reached them weeks prior. Her warriors would be back for her, for their people, but she did not know when. Until then, the Warbotach leader, Uldon, wanted her power and her crown. He couldn't get it by killing her, so her safety was guaranteed, although her comfort was not.

Forced back into the stone-enclosed darkness, Otera retreated to the straw bed in the cell's corner, as her escort slammed the iron door behind her. The resounding echo, highlighted only by the retreating footsteps of her captor's man, faded into an ominous silence. She had never felt so utterly alone, with only the light of one slender window to keep her company. The light of the window and her endless thoughts.

Chapter Three

Vaekros

Proteus took one look at the dirt on his daughters' clothes and frowned. Not hiding the disdain on his face, he cleared his throat, took a sip from his glass, and gestured toward the stairs. His expression was unyielding, leaving no room for argument. "Aurelia... Septima... go make yourselves presentable and come introduce yourselves to the men you will marry."

Aurelia's lungs lost their ability to expand, and she saw the same look of dread color on her sister's face. Septima wrapped her arms around her chest as they locked eyes, before they forced their feet upon the steps. The pair climbed higher, feeling as though they were walking to their deaths. Instead of heading to her own chambers, Septima followed Aurelia.

"I can't do this, Lia," Septima said, as she pulled her filthy clothes over her head. She scurried through the bathing room that separated their chambers to grab a suitable dress. "I will not marry that man."

Aurelia's heart hammered as she stepped out of her trousers, tripping over the fabric as her chaotic thoughts whirled. "I know. We'll figure this out. I promise. But we have to go back downstairs."

Septima grimaced as she tied her dress into place, ignoring her disheveled hair, and walked toward the door. Aurelia followed.

Stumbling down the stairs to the strange men who waited for their hands in marriage, both women silently begged for a way out.

As they entered the dining room, they saw their father and the two men sitting at the table with glasses of brown liquor in their hands. Both men looked to be in their late twenties, nearly a decade older than their potential brides. The sisters took the seats opposite the suitors, with Proteus at the head of the table—a king in his castle. Proteus' face held no humor or patience for their objections, and the sisters knew better than to raise any.

Aurelia glanced at the vacant chair opposite their father, where their mother sat before she passed away. Although it had been nearly fifteen years, Aurelia's heart still ached when she looked at that empty seat. She had always imagined her mother being at her wedding and teaching her to care for her children when the time came. Instead, it was servants and nannies who raised her while Proteus fought in wars and spent his time in the Vaekrosan Senate, which was days away in the capital city of Westtide.

Her mother, Messalina, had succumbed to the plague. Her father, having been away on campaign in a foreign land, was not infected. Aurelia and Septima, only children then, were also spared, kept away at the first sign of illness. Aurelia didn't have to watch her mother waste away, a fact that comforted her. She had loved her mother dearly and was glad to keep the memories of her beautiful face in her mind, not her deathly visage.

"Aurelia," Proteus said, interrupting her thoughts. "I'd like you to meet Philo."

The man directly across from her dipped his head in acknowledgement as a half-smile spread across his face. "Nice to meet you," he said.

"And you," she responded, forcing a smile of her own, although she knew it did not reach her eyes.

Philo was handsome, but he was at least five or more years her senior. Sandy blond hair swept across his forehead but was pulled back into a ponytail at his nape. His eyes, the color of summer grass, eased her nerves ever so slightly. She didn't want to marry him; she didn't even know him, but she was relieved that he at least appeared to be kind.

"Septima," her father said, motioning to the other man. "I'd like you to meet Caius."

Her sister's ashen face pinched in a nauseated grimace as she looked at Caius. He greeted her kindly, but she did not appear to be interested. Aurelia knew better. After breathing what appeared to be a hello, Septima reached for Aurelia below the table. Lacing their fingers together, Aurelia ran her thumb over Septima's trembling hand. The air in the room felt too thin as she struggled to inhale.

Caius was also an attractive man, though that meant nothing to her sister. Philo was fair like Aurelia, but Caius' complexion was bronzed. With his dark hair, rich brown eyes, and sun-kissed skin, Aurelia assumed he was from the city of Kotol.

Proteus rambled on with the men, not taking a moment to acknowledge his daughters or inquire about their wishes. He didn't bother to even ask about their day.

Dinner was brought out as Aurelia and Septima sat in silence, watching their father talk with the two men. Roasted duck and vegetables were placed in front of them as well as a tomato and cream bisque. The soup was Septima's favorite, but she did not accept the bowl when Aurelia pushed it toward her. Aurelia ate a small amount of each dish, but she had lost her appetite after being accosted at the door by their father with unwanted engagements.

Septima's hand continued to grip Aurelia's, although the tremble had subsided. Aurelia couldn't help but dwell on what her sister was going through at that moment. What would she do if forced to marry a man? Aurelia didn't want to marry a stranger either, but marrying for love in Vaekros was unheard of. Still, it was a dream she had always held in her heart, a hope for their society to change.

Most marriages in their world were arranged for purely political reasons. The potential to gain power and connections was the only thing that mattered. Fathers arranged their daughters' unions, usually as soon as they reached eighteen years of age, to someone who could advance the families' political futures. If the bride's family was of a lower class than the groom's, a dowry would be paid to entice the prospective suitor.

Aurelia did not know what arrangement Proteus had made with the two men, but he did not need money or political power. She assumed the arrangement was, at the very least, mutually beneficial to the two families. Although she couldn't imagine it would be beneficial to her or her sister. Philo caught her eye several times, smiling kindly at her. Maybe she could grow to love him, but her sister could not do the same with her own betrothed. Even if she could come to care for him as a person, she would never be able to love him as a wife should.

Their father cleared his throat loudly as they finished dinner. Aurelia frowned. Septima's dish remained untouched. Proteus noticed the full plate but allowed the servant to take it away. The scraps would undoubtedly go to Kano, who was sleeping in the bedroom upstairs.

Rising from the table, her father lowered his eyebrows and leveled them with a stern look that left no room for argument.

"Well," He reached over to shake the suitors' hands. "I have some work to get to in my study. Lydia will bring out dessert. Girls," he said, looking at his daughters. Aurelia's stomach tied in a knot as she hung on Proteus' next words. She didn't want to entertain the men, although it didn't appear she had a choice. She held Proteus' gaze as Septima dropped her head and rubbed her eyes. "Get to know these fine young men. I'll be in my study if anyone needs me."

Nodding to the men he had selected for his daughters', their father strolled out of the dining room.

Once he was gone, Septima rose from the table without warning and dashed out of the room. Proteus would be furious when he found out Septima had abandoned her betrothed at the table. There was no way he would not see her with his study being so near their chambers. Murmuring an apology to the men, Aurelia went to look for her sister.

A loud clap echoed around her as she took the stairs two at a time. Aurelia made it to the second-floor landing as Proteus entered his study.

She found Septima curled up on her bed, sobbing into Kano's fur. He looked up as Aurelia entered the room, but Septima never looked up as sobs wracked her frame. Crawling onto the bed, Aurelia laid behind her sister and wrapped her in an embrace.

"Are you okay?" Aurelia knew she was not okay, but she had no other words for her sister. Proteus didn't have to hit her, but he did a lot of things he didn't need to.

"I can't do this, Lia." Septima's voice hitched as she spoke into Kano's fur. Aurelia squeezed Septima's arm, unsure what to say or do to ease her pain.

"I know, sissy. I just don't know how to fix it."

Septima rolled over onto her back, staring at nothing while she continued to pet Kano. It was more to soothe herself than him. Tears trailed down her beautiful face as the mark from Proteus' hand had begun to turn purple on her cheek.

"I can't stay here. I can't let him do this to me. I don't know where I'll go, but it won't be here."

Aurelia swallowed thickly around the lump of emotion in her throat. "What do you mean? You can't... but..." She fell silent, although her mouth continued to move. Septima turned to face her. Unspeakable sadness was reflected in her eyes.

"I'm sorry. I have to leave. I'm not sure where I'll go. Maybe I'll cross through the forest and go to one of the towns on the other side. I don't know. I just have to get out of this marriage."

Aurelia stewed on her sister's words, trying to make sense of the situation. She couldn't lose her. It wasn't an option. They laid in silence as the sun fell behind the mountains, throwing the room into darkness. As Aurelia rose from the bed to light a candle, dangerous thoughts flooded her mind. Thoughts she was willing to entertain for Septima.

"I'm coming with you."

Septima's eyebrows rose as she lifted herself onto her elbow. "You don't have to sacrifice your own marriage for me."

Aurelia snorted, returning to the bed. "I don't even know that guy. I don't know about you, but I have always wanted to marry for love. I want to make my own way. I can't do that under Father's thumb."

A mischievous smile crawled across her sister's face. "I said I wanted adventure, but this may be more than we bargain for. How will we eat? Where will we stay? There are creatures in those woods. How will we protect ourselves?"

Aurelia glanced sidelong at Septima before reaching out to scratch Kano under the chin. "As long as we have this guy, we will be safe. As far as food, we can pack our satchels with as much as we can carry." She pulled two leather bags out of her armoire, tossing one to her sister. "We can figure the rest out as we go."

Septima sat up, grabbing the bag and pulling it against her body. "When do we leave?"

Looking at the clear night outside the window, Aurelia turned to face her sister. "Tonight."

Having never been on their own before, neither sister knew what to expect once they left the safety and comfort of their father's home. But that didn't matter. They were determined to escape the unwanted marriages that awaited them if they remained in Vaekros. They were going on an adventure. If they could avoid being caught, that is.

Chapter Four

Vaekros

Sneaking into the kitchens once the servants had turned in for the night, the sisters stuffed their bags with fruits, vegetables, dried meats, and breads. There were wild berries in the forest, and they could learn to hunt if they needed to, but they grabbed what they could to get themselves started. Both strapped their swords to their backs and a dagger around their thighs. They dressed warmly, choosing tunics and trousers and wrapped hooded cloaks over their shoulders.

After returning to take a final look at the bedroom they adored, Aurelia and Septima left the house unnoticed and entered the night air of the back gardens. Both took a fortifying breath and braced for what the forest, and the future, had in store for them. Giving each other a silent nod, they pulled their hoods before they headed for the forest, Kano following stealthily behind. The sisters crept to the tree line in silence, not wanting to chance waking their brother, who lived in the cottage at the edge of the property.

They didn't have a plan other than traveling west through the forest. They knew there were small towns that bordered the forest, as well as larger cities, including El-Wahba, which was where Septima was born. All they knew existed beyond the forest was war-torn cities, none of which sounded like a place they wanted to live. So, they intended, at least at first, to settle in one of the smaller towns, and learn what they could about what else was out there. Both women had gold and silver coins in their bags, money they had saved over the years, and money Proteus would not miss. They hoped they could support themselves, for a time, with what they had.

The dense brush of the Howling Forest took on a more ominous appearance at night. It had been named the Howling Forest for a reason. A menacing howl sounded in the distance as an owl hooted from above. Aurelia gripped Kano's leash so tightly her hand ached as she flinched at every sound. Septima's held a torch that illuminated their way as they traversed the dense branches and vines until it finally opened up to an easier path after several miles.

Knowing they couldn't stop for long, but too exhausted to go any further, they stopped in a thicket to rest. Their father would undoubtedly begin a search to look for them after he had servants scour the extensive property. They had little time to rest, but they could afford to sleep until at least first light. They built a small fire and backed themselves against the trunk of a hollowed-out tree. Septima took the first watch while Aurelia attempted to sleep. Kano remained on high alert while they sat in the darkened forest. Aurelia leaned back against the great cat, closing her eyes and waiting for unconsciousness to consume her.

Tendrils of mist recoiled in front of her, beckoning her forward like the inward curl of a finger. Its invitation was seductive, alluring, but the path was dark. Where was it leading her? She did not know.

"What are you doing here?" The woman demanded as she sat upright in the corner. Her trembling hands straightened the hem of her filthy, tattered dress. Dirt was caked under her nails as though she had tried to claw her way to freedom. "I cannot give you what you want! You're wasting your time."

The man, face hidden in shadows, huffed angrily as he stomped away. "Maybe some more time in the cell will change your mind."

The sparkle of a glittering crown faded into the darkness as the iron door slammed shut. It no longer sat atop the head of the crimson-haired woman, imprisoned in filth. Instead, it floated away in the calloused hand of the stocky man who had stolen her freedom.

Aurelia woke to hands roughly shaking her shoulders, along with the low growling of Kano at her side.

"Lia, someone's coming. Wake up." Septima crouched beside her, whispering in her ear. Rubbing her eyes and shaking off the strange dream, she sat upright and peered into the distance.

"What's going on?"

"The branches cracked, and I heard voices. I put the fire out, but I think it's too late. They'll see the smoke."

Aurelia nodded as she pulled her legs closer to her body, trying to make herself as small as she could. The faint rustling of trees could be heard in the distance and could almost be mistaken for an animal. But the voices... the muffled voices made it clear people were nearby.

The forest was still black. There was no way to know the time, only that it was somewhere past midnight and before sunrise. It was too late to run. Their footfalls and their inevitable stumbling upon the forest floor would make too much noise for them to escape unnoticed. Their only option was to sit quietly and hope the others would pass them. Aurelia's hands were slick with nervous sweat as her heartbeat thundered in her ears, but they sat still, afraid to breathe as they hoped to remain invisible.

The voices grew closer as the sisters huddled together. Aurelia cringed, clutching at her throat as she realized the people would walk right by their hiding place, and there was nothing they could do about it. Kano's own snarling lowered in volume as if he realized they were supposed to be hiding, and not drawing attention to themselves.

"Do you smell that?" A woman whispered. "Hang on, someone is out here."

The sound of dragging metal slithered through the air, setting Aurelia's teeth on edge. Someone had drawn a weapon.

"Who would be out here?" Another female voice asked. The voice spoke louder, more demanding. "We know someone is out here... no sudden movements... just come out nice and slow."

Eyes wide and with no other solution, the sisters looked at each other. Aurelia grabbed Kano by his leash, and they slowly stood from their place behind the trees.

Two women stood on the trail, only feet from them. They were tall and, although the darkness hid most of their features, the glint of moonlight showed the sword in the hands of the blond woman. Aurelia's stomach did a nervous flip, causing the meager food she consumed to rise in her throat.

"We don't mean any harm," Aurelia said, taking the slightest step back as she reached out and took Septima's hand. "We are just hiding from our father. By the morning, we will be on our way."

The woman who was not holding a weapon, tall with long black hair that draped over her shoulders, tilted her head, eyeing the large tiger at Aurelia's side. "And the beast?" she asked, as she reached toward the handle of a dagger gleaming at her side.

Aurelia gulped, glancing down at Kano before returning her eyes to the women standing before them. "He's not a beast. He's my friend... my pet. His name is Kano. I've raised him since he was a cub. He protects me."

The women looked at each other and lingered for a few agonizing moments, as though they were communicating silently. The same woman spoke. "And when we walk away, you will sic him on us? Have him tear us to shreds?"

Pursing her lips, Aurelia shook her head vehemently. "No, of course not. He's only here to protect me. He will not harm you if you do not harm us."

The other woman, the one with sword in hand, and hair that appeared white in the moonlight, spoke next. "You said you were hiding from your father. Why?"

Septima squeezed Aurelia's hand gently before responding. "Our father intends to marry us off to strange men. We refuse. We are trying to find somewhere else to create a home, to find a place where we can decide our own futures."

The woman snickered. "It's a foolish endeavor. In a world like this, in Vaekros, there is no escaping such a plan. Your father will find you. Women do not have the kind of rights you seek. Not here."

The black-haired woman shot a warning look at her companion. The woman with the sword looked at the ground in a submissive response. There was somewhere else. Aurelia felt it in her bones. She said not here as though there was another place, a place where women had more rights. She chanced to ask.

"My name is Aurelia. This is my sister, Septima." Aurelia lifted her and Septima's intertwined hands. "If you know of a place where we could be free, please tell us." She thought about explaining why Septima could not—would not marry a man—but she did not know of their prejudices, so she didn't.

The woman who held no weapon, clearly of a higher rank, responded first. "My name is Taryn. This is Exie." The woman with the sword nodded. "We knew of a place like that, a place where women had more rights, but it's no longer safe, so it doesn't warrant discussing."

Aurelia frowned. "Where are you from? Are you from Vaekros?" Although it was apparent that the women were not from Vaekros, she still felt it polite to ask instead of assuming.

"We are from a long way away," Exie responded, with no intention of explaining further.

"But you're in Vaekros," Aurelia pressed. "I don't mean to pry. Do you at least know of somewhere safe my sister and I can go? Somewhere we could survive away from our father?"

Taryn arched an eyebrow, looking them both over. "Can you fight?"

Aurelia started, eyes widening as she glanced at her sister. "Fight?"

"Yes. Can you fight? With a weapon? If you can, then I can use you. Maybe." Taryn waited for the sisters' response, shifting her weight and taking a sip of water from her canteen.

Meeting her eyes, Aurelia nodded, as did Septima, but Septima responded. "We train with our older brother. Aurelia trains more, but we both know the basics. We can learn. We will earn our keep. We don't want charity—just a chance to live free."

"There are towns through this forest, but I doubt you would ever make it, even with a tiger. If your father didn't find you first, there are enough beasts in these trees who are the things of nightmares. I do not want your deaths on my conscience. We will take you to our camp, but I'm telling you this once..." Taryn paused, scanning both sisters. "The moment you enter our camp, you cannot return to your old lives. I need to make sure that is something you can handle."

Catching her sister's gaze, Aurelia bit her lip as she weighed their options. She attempted to steady her voice, to fill it with resolve, as she responded. "We will not miss our lives in Vaekros. A part of us will surely miss our brother, but staying here isn't worth losing control of our futures."

Nodding, Taryn held out her hand to Aurelia, and they shook to seal the promise. "Very well. Gather your things. Our patrol is ending, and we must return to camp before first light. We need to move before your father's search parties scour this forest looking for you."

There was not much for the sisters to gather. They had brought barely more than the clothes on their backs and the food they'd stuffed in their satchels, but they collected it. Aurelia wrapped Kano's leash around her hand, petting him gently in assurance, before stepping onto the path to follow the two mysterious women deeper into Howling Forest.

They walked for what felt like hours. Aurelia's legs were weak, threatening to fracture beneath her. The brisk chill of the air wasn't enough to stop the sweat that coated her skin from forming. They walked until night began to fade into day. The light of the sun peeked through the openings in the tree cover, but Exie still held her sword at the ready. Braced for what attack—Aurelia did not know.

As they came upon a clearing, the previously buzzing forest fell silent. Eerie. Finally, sheathing her sword, Exie reached for Septima's hand. Septima stared as if it would bite her. She took a hesitant step back. Before Aurelia could ask what was happening, Taryn reached for her hand as well.

"If you want to follow us," Taryn said impatiently, "then you'll have to take my hand and trust me. You can't cross the barrier on your own."

"Barrier?" Aurelia asked, confusion clear in her tone. Fear of the unknown weighed on her, making her exhausted limbs heavier.

Exie smirked, waiting for Taryn to explain.

"There's more to this world than what you can see around you, Aurelia. If you want to see our world, you'll have to take my hand."

In an unspoken agreement, the sisters dropped their interlaced fingers and grabbed the hands of the mysterious women before being led through an invisible barrier into a place unknown.

Chapter Five

Howling Forest

T he air rippled as the sisters stepped into what appeared to be
a clearing in the forest. It was like entering a vacuum, and
the momentary change in pressure made Aurelia's ears pop. She
swayed slightly as she tried to regain her equilibrium.

Although the clearing had been quiet and empty before she took
Taryn's hand, once they crossed whatever invisible barrier they had
been escorted through, it was bursting with life.

Hundreds of warriors, all women, were scattered throughout
the clearing. Some sparred while others ate and chatted around the
many bonfires that burned throughout the area. Their escorts had
released their hands after they crossed over, but the sisters moved
closer to each other and stared at the scene playing out in front of
them.

The women looked nothing like those of Vaekros. They were
tall, muscular, and no one wore a gown. Dressed in trousers,
tunics, or fighting leathers with fur-trimmed cloaks of animal

skin draped over their shoulders, they looked the fiercest of warriors. Leather belts circled their waists, adorned with a variety of weapons, including short swords, daggers, and even arrows for the bows that were strung across their backs.

Aurelia reached over and touched her sister's cheek. Exie noticed their shock and chuckled. She flourished her hand in front of her and said, "welcome to the Aegrician war camp."

Septima tilted her head like a puppy who didn't understand a command. "War camp? In the Howling Forest?"

"It's in Vaekrosan woods, but it's not. The space is shielded. The humans won't be able to see us."

Aurelia's mind swirled. *Humans won't see them? They aren't human? Who were these women? What were they? Surely Exie was joking.*

"What do you mean 'the humans won't see you'? And what kind of shield?" Aurelia's voice shook as her words poured out, toppling over each other at a speed that made her incoherent. She did not—could not—understand. Exie smiled mischievously as Taryn returned. Aurelia had not even noticed she left.

Just before Taryn was within hearing distance, Exie turned to the sisters. "There is a lot you do not know, but you'll learn in time. Until then, just trust us. You are safe."

Aurelia nodded as Taryn joined them. Now that there was some illumination, she took in the warrior's appearance. Her attire mirrored that of the other women in the clearing, except for an intricate gold and jeweled pendant of a phoenix that glimmered near her collarbone. Both women were a head taller than the sisters, who weren't exactly short among Vaekrosan women. Taryn's hair was black as the night and braided down her back, ending just above her waist. Her locks had been a wild mane when they crossed paths, so the sleek braid was unexpected. Aurelia wondered at how she had tamed her hair so quickly, when she noticed something that made her breath catch in her throat. The tips of Taryn's ears were slightly pointed, a shocking contrast to the rounded tips of humans. Turning to Exie, she noticed her ears were the same. She wanted to ask them why, but did not want to sound rude or critical. So, instead of asking for an explanation, Aurelia swallowed her comments as Taryn spoke.

"Blaedia will see them now," she said to Exie, who nodded.

The muscles in Aurelia's chest constricted as she squeezed Septima's hand. Septima grimaced at the strength of her hold, and she loosened her grasp minutely.

Their new companions led them forward, toward a cluster of large tents, but Aurelia hesitated. She could not control the trembling in her body. Fear of what she had gotten herself and her younger sister into consumed her. The anxiety of the unknown was overwhelming. *What if I made a mistake?*

Septima gave her a reassuring smile and took the lead, addressing Taryn. "Who is Blaedia? What's going to happen to us?" Septima hesitated, but the females did not interrupt. "I'm sorry to sound ungrateful or like we don't trust you..."

Taryn stepped closer, placing a hand on their interlocked fingers, and said, "You don't have to apologize. We understand. Everything will be explained to you soon, I promise. Blaedia is our general. I can't tell you more without her approval. I should have spoken with her before offering you sanctuary. Just know that you are safe. Blaedia will tell you everything. She's agreed to offer you protection in our camp. Follow me, and we will get your tiger set up in an enclosure before you meet her. Then we will get the two of you in a tent so you can rest. You must be exhausted."

Without another word, Taryn turned and walked toward the cluster of tents once more.

Aurelia and Septima's heads were on a swivel as they scanned the extensive camp concealed within the Vaekrosan forest. Hundreds of tents of various sizes were erected around the perimeter of the clearing, extending back into the trees. Near the back of the camp, in the direction they were heading, there was a tent larger than the rest. Aurelia assumed that was where Blaedia was waiting for them. They passed the large tent, however, and cut between it and the structure adjacent. They came upon a large fenced-in space within the trees that was clearly meant for Kano. A chunk of bloody meat and a water trough came into view as they grew closer. Kano licked his lips as the scent of the meal met his muzzle. He pulled on his leash, eager to get inside.

"Will he be safe here?" Aurelia asked, nervous about letting him out of her sight.

Taryn nodded as she placed her hand upon the gate, causing the latch to click and the door to swing open. Kano darted inside, yanking his leash from Aurelia's grasp and tearing into the meat. Aurelia snickered. "Well, I love you too." The great cat looked up at her, gore dripping from his face, before dipping his head back down into his meal.

"Here," said Taryn as she handed a bronze medallion hanging from a leather cord to Aurelia. "There are wards around his enclosure. This will open it. Just place the emblem against the gate, and it will open for you. Only a few individuals have access, which is as much for his protection as for everyone else's."

Clutching the medallion in her hand, Aurelia placed the cord around her neck before tucking it beneath her shirt for safekeeping. She'd been given many necklaces in her life, but never a magical one, never one so important. She prayed she would not lose it.

"Ready?" Taryn asked as she strode toward the largest of the tents. She didn't wait for a response, her pace increasing as they rounded the corner. The flaps of the door were already slightly ajar, but a heavily armed woman stood guard in front of the opening. She moved to the side as they approached, allowing them entry without a word.

Shock caused Aurelia's mouth to fall open as she took in the immense space. It was so much larger than it appeared from the outside. The tent was only a single room, but furniture and screens separated it into sections. Aurelia could just make out the view of an enormous bed behind one screen, and a kitchen area in one corner. A modest throne sat before them, but it was empty. Instead, a woman with jet black hair stood at a table in the center of the room, leaning over a large map. The woman straightened as they walked in, nodding to our guide.

"Taryn," she said.

"Blaedia," Taryn responded, ushering them further into the room. She introduced the sisters to the general, gesturing to each in turn. "This is Aurelia and her sister, Septima."

The general smiled at them, although it didn't quite meet her eyes, and returned her gaze to the map. Aurelia shrunk into herself, feeling dismissed, until Blaedia covered the map with a cloth and indicated for them to follow her to a table near the kitchen. They were glad when Exie's friendly face entered the tent and joined them at the table. "I'm sure everyone is hungry," Blaedia said. Her voice was sharp but not unkind. "Exie, ask Manara to bring in some stew. Please, sit. Let's talk."

"Any fresh developments?" Taryn asked, lowering herself into one of the chairs. Blaedia rubbed her eyes with her palms, shaking her head. Her responding voice was tense.

"None. From the messages I've received from the ravens, she is still holding onto her strength. He has the crown, but that is it. However, we will need to move in closer soon. The arrival of the ravens has slowed. I suspect they are being captured as they try to bring news." Taryn slumped at the general's response. Aurelia knew nothing about these people and whatever plight had driven them to set up camp in the Howling Forest, but whatever they were discussing felt important. It was like a switch flipped within her and suddenly she knew this was where she was meant to be. Although she had no idea why.

Blaedia shifted her eyes to the sisters as a woman entered the tent with a large steaming pot and set it on the table. Aurelia met Blaedia's stare. Every instinct within her told her to lower her eyes, but she held firm.

Blaedia was exotically beautiful. Her eyes were such a bright blue they appeared almost silver. Just like Taryn and Exie, she was impressively tall, even as she sat at the head of the table. Unlike Taryn's long locks, Blaedia's hair was cut shoulder-length and shaved on one side. She also wore a phoenix pendant on her cloak. Aurelia suspected it was a symbol of authority among their people. They all waited for the general to dip her spoon into her stew before digging into their own.

"Why are you running?" she asked, catching Aurelia by surprise. Taryn nudged her under the table when she didn't respond. Dropping her spoon back into the meaty stew, she glanced at Septima before returning her eyes to Blaedia.

"Our father... he is trying to arrange our marriages to strangers, and we cannot go through with it. We ran to stop those marriages from happening."

Blaedia's eyebrows lifted as she took another bite. "I'd imagine these types of arrangements are common in your family."

Aurelia nodded. "Yes. It's a common practice in Vaekros for all women."

The general grimaced, turning her attention to Septima. "Any particular reason why you won't marry the men chosen for you by your father? Were they evil men?"

Aurelia started to respond, but Septima interrupted. "I doubt they were evil men... but I have no interest in men. My sister ran away with me because we swore to stay together—no matter what."

Nearly choking at her sister's admission, Aurelia took a sip of water. She stared at Blaedia, anxiously waiting for a response. What if desiring the same sex wasn't acceptable in their society, either? She braced herself for the worst, but Septima seemed resigned to her fate, no longer choosing to hide who she was. No matter how the general responded, Aurelia was proud of her sister.

Blaedia smirked before lifting her glass into the air. "I, also, would rather die than marry a man. Thank you for being honest with me, Septima. You'll find our society much more tolerant."

"Probably because our society is not run by a bunch of horny men," Exie chimed in. Blaedia lifted her glass in Exie's direction as well, in a silent toast.

The tension in Aurelia's heart loosened. From the way her sister's body visibly relaxed, she could tell Septima felt the same way. A society led by women sounded like a myth. She couldn't imagine what that was like, but it sounded better than where she was from.

"What brings your camp to Vaekros?" Aurelia knew it may be too bold to ask, but not knowing filled her with unease. Blaedia's grin fell, and Taryn cleared her throat. The general met her eyes.

"It's a long story, so I'll shorten it for you. Aegricia, our kingdom, was invaded. Our queen, Otera, has been captured. We are here while we plan to reclaim our lands."

"I've never heard of Aegricia," Aurelia said, chancing a glance at Septima, who shrugged. "Is it far from here?"

The general pushed her empty bowl away from her, wiping her face with a cloth. "Yes, and no."

Chapter Six

Howling Forest

"Remember how I told you that there was more to this world than you could see?" Taryn's eyes bore into Aurelia and she shifted uncomfortably in her seat. The way they stared made Aurelia feel like she was being evaluated, like they had something important to share, but wanted to make sure the sisters could handle it. Aurelia nodded, reaching for her sister's hand under the table. "Our land is not of the same realm as yours. It is close, but not everyone can cross over the threshold. It is why we are at war."

"Your realm? What threshold?" Aurelia's mind spun. Who were these women?

Taryn tilted her head toward Blaedia, who continued the explanation.

"We are not of your world, Aurelia. We are not of the human world. You may know us as ignis avis, phoenixes. We take this form, the form of a human, unless our powers are needed. But we are not human, we are fae. We enjoy the pleasures of a human-like body, the ease of having opposable thumbs, but it is not our only form."

Aurelia went completely still. Her thoughts churned too quickly to focus on any one thing.

"Who invaded your territory?" asked Septima. Her voice caught Aurelia by surprise because she had been so quiet. Blaedia turned to her.

"There are many kingdoms within our world," Blaedia began.

Aurelia interrupted, finally grasping onto one question she needed answered. "What world? Is it not of this planet?"

Allowing her interruption, the general turned to Aurelia. "Our world is called Ekotoria. It is not of your earth, or at least not as you perceive it." Although still confused, Aurelia nodded. Blaedia returned her gaze to Septima. "As I was saying before, there are other kingdoms within Ekotoria and beyond. The territory of Warbotach invaded Aegricia, our home. We, and the territory of Norithae, are the last barrier between our realm and yours. Norithae fell quickly. The Warbotach attack on them was unexpected. Their scribes managed to send a raven to us before their king fell, barely allowing our warriors to retreat here before our queen was captured." Blaedia began to twirl the hilt of a jewel encrusted dagger in her hand, digging the blade into the table. "Our queen is safe for now. Warbotach won't kill her until they manage to take her power. They want into the human realm — to conquer it."

Aurelia swallowed thickly, going rigid in her seat. "Can they get into our realm? Why did they attack your lands? What do you mean, 'they want to take your queen's power'?" Her words came out in rapid succession—full of desperation as she struggled to understand—but Blaedia was patient.

"The lands of Warbotach are dying, starving the animals and people. They want the human lands to live on because it is vast, but they are an evil people. If they find their way through the portal, the humans won't stand a chance."

Septima choked out a gasp, squeezing Aurelia's hand. "What's stopping them from coming here?" Septima asked, her voice cracking. "Can they get through the portal as your people did?"

Taryn shook her head, but the general responded. "No... well, not as yet. That is why they are trying to take our queen's power. Our people are the gatekeepers. We can cross, but only in flight, and only in the crown's favor. The people of Warbotach cannot fly and do not have the power to cross the portal, thankfully, but that doesn't mean they aren't trying to steal that gift from our crown." Blaedia lifted herself from her chair, placing her dagger back into its holster. The sound of the blade sliding into leather marked the end of their conversation. "Exie, show Aurelia and Septima to their sleeping quarters so they can get cleaned up and rest. They'll start training tomorrow."

Exie nodded and stood, motioning them toward the door. Without hesitation, the sisters followed out into the action of the clearing. They passed Kano's enclosure, ensuring he was safe, and stopped at a newly erected tent right beside it. Exie opened the flap and led them inside. "Showers are in the tent beside Blaedia's. There should be clothes in the trunks beside the beds and water on the shelf against the wall. You'll hear a bell when it's time for meals to be served. If you didn't notice the eating area when we came in, it's the large tent just beside the sparring rings. You won't miss it if you walk back the way we came. If you need anything, my tent is just to the right of yours, on the other side of Kano's enclosure. Rest and get to know the camp later. I'll see you at dinner."

Tipping her head in farewell, Exie left as the sisters shared an overwhelmed look and took in the space that would serve as their new home. Just as with Blaedia's tent, their tent was also larger than it appeared from the outside, although it was not as big as the generals. There were two double beds against one wall, with a large screen near another wall for privacy when changing. Wooden trunks sat at the foot of each bed.

Throwing herself onto one of the beds, Septima sighed loudly. "So, what is going through your mind right now?"

Aurelia, still dazed, lowered herself onto the remaining bed. "I don't know. We've always lived in a world where magic was nothing more than legend and definitely didn't exist, according to father. I'm not sure what to think. Did we make the right choice?"

Septima faced her, tucking her arm under her head. "It's hard to say so far, but I have a good feeling. I feel safe with them—even if the things they've told us are overwhelming. Can you believe their society is ruled by women? Who would have thought a place like that existed? I feel so empowered with them, or at least more excited about our futures." Her face was filled with wonder as she spoke of their saviors.

"I know. What did you think of Blaedia? I've never met a general quite like her."

Septima drew idle circles on the blanket as she took a deep breath and exhaled slowly. "I think she's fascinating. She's in a position of power, and she's like me. I think she's more amazing than I can vocalize."

Aurelia's mouth spread into a slow grin. She could almost see the moon-sized admiration growing in her sister's eyes. "Oh, you'd better make sure she isn't taken before you start making moves on her."

Septima shot a playful glare her way before throwing a pillow at her sister's face as she explained it wasn't like that. Aurelia laughed and ignored the denial. Teasing Septima gave her a sense of normalcy that had been absent since the moment her father had announced their pending betrothals. "I bet you want to see her fire, don't you, dear sister?"

Before Aurelia could brace herself, Septima launched herself across the beds and smacked her with another pillow. They fell into a fit of laughter. As their joy faded into soft sporadic chuckles, they realized how exhausted they were. Their jaunt through the Howling Forest and the discovery of a whole new world wore on them. Without bathing, they fell asleep in Aurelia's bed, the absence of Kano the only thing keeping their little family from being complete.

Chapter Seven

Howling Forest

The sisters slept the day away, waking only when the dinner bell reverberated throughout the camp. Aurelia didn't dream, which was a welcome respite. Her dreams were usually unpleasant and confusing.

Groggy from their nap but famished, the sisters climbed out of bed and staggered out of their tent. Kano trotted to the fence as they approached and gave a happy flick of his tail. Aurelia cooed at him as she passed, promising to visit soon. As they rounded the bend to where the sparring ring stood, they saw a gathering of women at the entrance of a massive tent. They approached it hesitantly, unsure of how the strangers would receive their presence. Exie spotted their uncertain approach and jogged over to them.

"I thought I was going to have to wake the two of you up!" she said as she led them to the dining tent. Aurelia was beginning to realize Exie was the easygoing one in the group. It was an unexpected revelation. The night before, she was focused with her sword at the ready as she escorted them back to camp. But within the safety of the barrier, she seemed to be a free spirit. She floated on her feet, almost skipping her way into the dinner tent. Her golden hair was just as wild as it had been when they met, but her brown eyes were a smooth caramel in the setting sun and held a softness that hadn't been there before.

Food lined the back wall of the tent, buffet-style. Aurelia's eyes grew wide at the sight, her rumbling stomach reminding her she'd long since burned off the stew they had when they first arrived. Taking their fill, the three of them sat down with bowls of stew, rice, and a variety of roasted vegetables. Chatter filled the space as it overflowed with what must have been hundreds of women. Aurelia scanned the space for men, but saw very few.

"Exie," she began. "Where are all the men? You said your society was run by women, but I would have expected more men in your warrior ranks, at least."

Exie swallowed a mouthful of stew and smiled before responding. "They're around, but most of our military is women. Men don't have the ability to fly. It's a gift born solely to females in our society, although not all are blessed with it. If a woman is born with the ability to transform, then she is usually trained to be a warrior and gatekeeper. It is what is expected of us. Many of our men remained in Aegricia. Since they cannot fly, they work in a variety of other professions and continue to assist our territory in their own ways." She motioned to the room at large. "Many of the women here are bonded, or married, as you would call it, but their husbands are back home."

"Your people are under the control of Warbotach?" Septima asked. Exie nodded grimly.

"Yes. But just because the men cannot transform, does not mean they are not strong or useful in a fight. For now, our people at home are biding their time. When we return to fight, they will be ready to help us win. We left solely to protect our forces because our army would have been the first target of their stealth attacks. Warbotach has no interest in murdering our innocents because they do not want to live in our territory. They want the human lands. That is the big prize. Our lands are not good for grazing animals or living the way they were accustomed to before their land became inhospitable. So, our civilians are safe for now. We will return—with any luck accompanied by allies. Norithae is weak right now, but we know there are still those who want to fight. We also plan to send emissaries to the kingdom of Diapolis. They are not involved in the conflict, but we hope they will help us."

Exie waved at a red-haired female at another table before returning to the conversation.

"Do the people of the other kingdoms have abilities like yours?" Septima asked. "I know your general said the Warbotach people could not fly, but what about the others? Do they have powers?"

"The land of Ekotoria contains magic, so all of its peoples have powers that humans do not. Those powers are usually based on their land, as though they developed to survive within their own environment, but not always. The people of Diapolis live on the coast. Their powers come from the water, and many of them can even live below the water if they choose. The Norithae people are fae, like us, and have wings, but they maintain their human appearance even with their wings. They do not shift as we do."

Aurelia was so focused on the new information being divulged that she'd forgotten about her dinner. She took a bite of her stew before interjecting the questions she'd been dying to know the answers to. "And what about your queen? Her crown? I don't understand how Warbotach can take her powers." Septima's gaze looked distant as she ran her fingers through her long braids. She appeared just as confused as her sister.

Exie heaved a sigh and pushed her plate away, the conversation dimming the carefree glimmer in her eyes. "They seem to think they can steal the power of her crown. The wearer of the crown is given the power to control the gateway between realms. Without it, Warbotach's warriors cannot cross through the portal. The Aegrician crown is not inherited by blood. Fate decides who becomes our queen and can wield its power. Currently, the Warbotach king, Uldon, is trying to use magic to manipulate its allegiance. He's trying to make Otera's crown choose him. Messages suggest he has tried to use oracles and witches to accomplish his goal. So far, nothing has worked. Now, he is searching for the Elemental of Spectre Forest to aid him. A man has never worn our crown, but he's not a man who gives up easily."

Aurelia rubbed the back of her neck, glancing around the almost empty dining area. The need for answers consumed her, but she had so many questions that she didn't know what to ask first. Nearly everyone else had eaten and left before she asked the most important one. "What do you think the outcome will be?"

Exie shrugged casually, but her voice hardened with a determined edge. "We will seek alliances, build up our strength, and fight until we cast every single Warbotach warrior from our cliffs. At least, that is our plan and how I like to think. We can't stay here for much longer, so I imagine we will learn of our fate soon."

"What's going to happen to us?" Septima asked. "When all of you leave Vaekros, what will happen to us?"

Aurelia didn't dare move as she awaited Exie's answer. Exie looked at them both with unwavering conviction. "We will take you with us. Both of you. Kano, too." She reached across the table, taking both by a hand. "Taryn and I wouldn't have brought you here if we planned to abandon you. We asked if you were willing to give up your old life to come with us because we intended to take you back to Ekotoria if you agreed. Have you changed your mind?"

She arched an eyebrow as she eyed the sisters warily. They both shook their heads, but Septima responded. "No. We want to come with you. We just didn't know if we'd be able to. You said only your kind could cross through the portal."

"You can cross as long as you're holding onto one of us. I'll carry you on my back and ensure you make it across."

"On your back?"

Aurelia's question made Exie chuckle. "Yes, Aurelia. On my back. The only way through the portal is to fly, remember? I can't fly in this form. I will go through it as a phoenix, so I hope you aren't afraid of heights."

Aurelia gulped in an attempt to swallow her nerves. She felt like the entire story was a trick. It was all too fantastical to be real. But just as she was about to question the legitimacy of the tale, she glimpsed bright colorful wings flare out above Exie's shoulders, stretching only once before disappearing. Both sisters sat slack jawed, their eyes the size of medallions, as Exie threw her head back and roared in laughter.

"I think the two of you have had enough adventure for one day. Blaedia said your training starts tomorrow. I'll walk you to the showers and then off to bed with you. Come now." She said as she stood from the table, stretching her long arms above her head. Aurelia couldn't help but to stare at her extended limbs as she thought of the vibrant wings that had been visible only moments before.

Septima and Aurelia showered in adjacent stalls. They washed in silence, savoring the warmth of the water in the middle of the cold forest. They dressed quickly and rushed to visit Kano. Having been made for women much taller than them, they had to hold up the bottoms of their nightclothes.

Aurelia used the medallion still hanging from her neck to enter his enclosure and say good night before bed. She hated leaving him outside overnight, although she realized how silly it sounded. He was a wild animal, after all, but he had been raised in the comfort of her family villa. He was accustomed to sleeping in Aurelia's bed, not on the cold forest floor. He seemed quite happy, comfortable even, to be outside, so even though leaving him behind made her heart ache, Aurelia placed a kiss atop his head and closed the gate firmly behind them.

They returned to their tent after visiting Kano and crawled into bed immediately, but falling asleep proved to be a challenge for Aurelia. Her mind raced as she continuously replayed the information Exie had shared with them. The wings she had seen flare out of the female's back were burned into her memory, and she imagined what the true phoenix form was like. *Phoenixes.* She pondered what other abilities they had in that form, and—more than anything—she wondered what it was like to be able to fly.

Chapter Eight

Howling Forest

Sniffles filled the dimly lit room, making her listen harder as she searched for the source. Someone was crying, and they needed help. She tripped as she fumbled around the room, trailing her fingers along the rough stone wall to guide her progression. She strained her eyes, but could hardly make out more than the mouse that skittered past. The rodent startled a gasp from her, but she continued on and called out.

"Who's there?"

The only response was another sniffle and a breathy sigh. She drew closer to the sound as a single stream of moonlight shone through a narrow window set high on the wall. But the spot it illuminated was empty.

The ancient metal door clanged as it opened, its hinges squealing in protest as it moved. A burly man, dressed in leathers and a fur cape, stood just inside the doorway. The flame of a single torch flickered, highlighting the rage that painted his sharp features. She could make out tan skin and eyes so dark they were void of color. A vicious scar ran down his cheek, adding to the sinister aura that surrounded him. His head was too large for his body, and had an odd, non-symmetric shape. Everything about him was terrifying. The muffled cries ceased the moment he entered, replaced by a frantic scrambling in the far corner.

"Reconsider yet, Otera?" His rough voice sliced through the silence. It was deep and unyielding. Though his words held the lilt of a question, it sounded like an expectation—a demand.

"No." Otera's tone was just as inflexible. Whatever the decision she was expected to change, she had no intention of doing so.

His responding chuckle was smug, a mixture between a snort and a grunt. "You will. Either you will give me what I want, or the crown will, but I will get it either way. The only question is how much you will suffer before then."

The resounding slam of the cell door punctuated his statement, and the soft cries of a fallen queen filled the room once more.

Fantasies of soaring through the sky, the breeze whipping her hair, had eventually lulled Aurelia into the unconsciousness she longed for, though it was fitful. Everything she had been told about the Aegrician queen had been enough to infiltrate her mind and invade her dreams. The thought of Otera locked away in a dungeon made her blood run cold, but she wondered which was worse: the reality of the queen's situation or her own imagination.

No light filtered through the canvas tent. As she jolted awake from her desolate dream, Aurelia wondered if it was still night or if the sun had already risen above the horizon. The breakfast bell didn't ring yet, so she knew it had to be early. Her heart continued to race. The face of Otera's captor was burned into her mind's eye, but Septima's even breathing was an anchor to reality that comforted her.

Their training was to start after breakfast, and the prospect was terrifying. They both trained with Amadeus often, but something told Aurelia that the phoenix-shifting warrior women would be more arduous than anything their pushover big brother had ever put them through. Thinking of Amadeus was like taking a knife in her gut. She knew they had made the correct choice, but knowing she'd never see her brother again left a wound that would never fully heal. The agreement they made with Exie and Taryn had been clear, but sometimes the right decision was painful.

Dwelling on what they left behind would do no good. She turned her thoughts away from the open sore that was Amadeus and began to wonder about the enchanted lands of Ekotoria. She was curious about the appearance of the different territories, and about whether leaving the human world would prevent her from getting married when she was older. In a land devoid of humans, would she be able to find someone she loved? She was running from an arranged marriage, but that didn't mean she wanted to give up on her desire to marry for love. Even so, the thought of someday marrying a non-human man was inconceivable. There was much to consider about the future, far more than she contemplated when she agreed to leave Vaekros behind forever.

Climbing out of bed, Aurelia lit a candle before quietly digging through the wooden trunk at the foot of her bed. She pulled out a pair of trousers and a tunic similar to the ones the warriors wore around the camp. The dark brown pants were a buttery leather secured around her waist with laces. They hugged her body as though they were tailored for her. The green tunic was composed of a heavy cloth that would keep her warm in the chilly temperatures. After she dressed, she checked Septima's face to ensure she hadn't awakened before slipping out of the tent and into the brisk morning air.

The sun's rays barely permeated the dense trees as Aurelia headed for Kano's enclosure. Already awake, he prowled around his space as though he were stalking prey in the wild. She admired the fluidity of his movements for a moment before crossing the threshold that appeared when the magic of the medallion met its mark.

His head shot up at her approach, and he abandoned his hunt as he darted over to greet her. He nuzzled his giant muzzle into her legs. She bent down to rub him behind the ears. "I know. I missed you too, Kano."

She sat cross-legged beside him, her fingers never leaving his fur. After the distance that they'd had between them since arriving at the camp, she couldn't bear parting with him a moment sooner than she had to. He flopped onto his back, his tongue lolling happily from his mouth, and all but begged for a belly rub. Aurelia obliged, a genuine smile on her face. Being with Kano was natural; it was easy. There were no worries about the future or fantastical lands when she was with him. Other than her sister, Kano was the only piece of her old life, her old self, she had left.

A few women passed by the enclosure, eying the massive tiger warily. Aurelia flashed them a friendly grin, hoping to ease their worries, as she wondered if the camp knew of her and Septima's arrival. Would they embrace them with open arms, as Exie seemed to do, or did they just trade one tragic situation for another? She did not know how the people of Ekotoria viewed humans. All she could do was pray they would be accepted in their new land, and not face discrimination over something they could not control, just as her sister had in Vaekros.

The bell rang throughout the clearing, signaling the start of breakfast. Aurelia tried to ignore the pit of anxiety forming in her stomach as she placed a kiss on Kano's head. Mealtime meant training was that much closer and as she stood and dusted off her clothes, her hands trembled from nerves. She left the enclosure, forcing herself to put one foot in front of the other, and went to wake Septima. To her surprise, not only was her sister awake, but she was eager to start her day. She collided with Aurelia as she rushed from the tent. All the fears that Aurelia battled didn't seem to affect Septima. Her sister was lighter, happier than she'd ever seen her—maybe that was the power of being able to truly be herself.

As she had the night before, Exie waited outside the dining tent. Aurelia hoped to make friends with more women in the camp, but Exie taking them under her wing meant the world to her. She huffed a laugh at her unintentional pun under her breath and waved at Exie, who flashed a brilliant smile as they approached.

"Morning ladies! How did you sleep?"

"Like a rock," said Septima.

"Same," Aurelia lied. Images of the dingy cell and the barbarous man from her dreams flashed through her mind. Her rest had left her feeling more exhausted than she'd been the night before.

Exie motioned for them to lead the way into the dining tent.

They grabbed bowls of porridge and eggs before sitting at one of the few unoccupied tables. Most of the camp's occupants arrived before the bell had even rung. Aurelia didn't know if she would ever be that punctual.

"Are the two of you ready to start your training?"

Aurelia gave a noncommittal shrug as Septima nodded. "I'm definitely ready to train, but I hope the trainer is forgiving. We have a long way to go before we can be considered warriors."

Exie smirked. "I'll try to go easy on you."

Aurelia sputtered, nearly choking on her water. "Wait, so you will be the one training us?"

"Yep! Very few of the warriors in this camp need a beginner's course, so I'll oversee your training." Exie seemed to puff out her chest just a little, sitting up straighter as though she were proud of her new position. Aurelia nearly giggled.

Relief flooded Aurelia, and she was sure Septima felt the same. She watched the tension in her sister's shoulders release.

"So, Exie..." Aurelia hesitated as Exie gave a high-five to a red-haired woman passing by. Turning back to the sisters, she shoveled a huge bite of porridge into her mouth and lifted her eyebrows in response. Aurelia took that as a signal to continue. "How will we be received in Ekotoria? How do the people there, and the ones in this camp, view humans? I don't know what to expect and it's been weighing on me."

Lifting her eyebrows, Exie nodded her head as she chewed her food. "That's understandable, but don't worry." Her shoulders tensed, belying the positivity in her tone. Aurelia did not miss it. "I mean... There are certainly some who are prejudiced against humans, but I think that is to be expected. There have been some negative interactions between Ekotorians and humans throughout our history, and some have not forgotten. It is the main reason the ability to traverse the portal is limited to Aegricians now and not the rest of Ekotoria or the human lands."

Aurelia's eyes widened. "You mean others used to be able to cross? More humans know of your existence? I've never heard about you, at least not in any way that wasn't a fairy tale."

Exie nodded. "Yes. A treaty was made between our people and the government of Vaekros long ago. The portal was restored, forged with the same magic as our crown. The crown chooses who reigns, and its choice is based on who will protect the security of the treaty. That is why the Warbotach leader needs our crown to favor him. If its allegiance changed to him, he could fly across the portal and conquer the human world."

Aurelia swallowed. Fear and the meager breakfast she'd eaten rising in her gut. "Can he do it, though?"

"Do what?"

"All of it. Changing the allegiance of the crown, crossing the portal, conquering the human world, can he do it?"

Exie shrugged. "I'm not sure, but he seems to think so. He will certainly exhaust all possibilities before he ever gives up. I don't think our queen can give him what he wants even if she desired to, but there is undoubtedly magic out there that he just has to find to bend it to his will."

Chapter Nine

Howling Forest

"Show me how your brother taught you to fight." Exie stood on the outskirts of the practice ring with her arms folded across her chest and a smirk on her face.

She seemed to expect the sisters to fight like court jesters putting on a show, and not like true fighters. Just the thought of it made Aurelia's stomach churn. Lifting their swords, the sisters went through some of the movements Amadeus taught them. Aurelia disarmed Septima. Her sword fell from her hand as Aurelia halted her blade inches away from slicing her sister's gut open. Exie clapped slowly, although Aurelia was not sure if she was being facetious or if she was truly impressed.

"Not bad, Aurelia. If it had been an actual fight, Septima would be dead. I'm surprised you have so much power in that tiny body of yours." She looked at Aurelia as though she were a rare zoo animal.

"I spent more time with Amadeus, otherwise Septima would kick my ass." Septima looked discouraged as she retrieved her sword. Aurelia gave her an encouraging smile and squeezed her shoulder.

Exie shrugged. "We all have to start somewhere. One thing I noticed, Septima, is that your defensive stance and footwork need a bit of help."

Exie approached Septima and wrapped her arms around Septima's back to show her how to stand while holding her sword. Septima's eyes flicked up to meet Aurelia's as Exie's arms snaked around her waist. Aurelia had to cover her mouth to stifle a laugh. She wondered what was going through Septima's mind as the beautiful warrior pressed against her. Exie was simply showing Septima how to hold her sword, but it didn't negate how close their bodies were.

Aurelia scanned the perimeter, noticing how many of the warriors were watching their training session, and felt the flush grow inside her. Just as she was feeling self-conscious about their growing audience, Aurelia realized the warriors were not watching them. Their eyes were locked on a group running toward them. Three females, weapons in tow, hurried through the clearing. One of them leaned against the others as she limped heavily on one leg. Aurelia held her breath as they approached, stepping out of their way as the group moved right past her and toward Blaedia's tent.

"What was that all about?" she asked Exie, who looked worried. Her eyebrows had drawn together while she watched the running warriors.

"I'm not sure. I'll be right back."

Before either sister could respond, Exie jogged toward Blaedia's tent. Septima and Aurelia exited the training ring and watched Blaedia's tent in silence. Taryn dashed into its entrance as well.

"What in the hell do you think is going on?" Septima asked, barely concealing the nerves in her voice.

"I don't know, but I don't think it's good."

Aurelia wasn't sure how much time had passed before Exie exited the tent and hurried back to where they sat, just to the side of the training circle. Her face no longer held the same lighthearted humor it had. She motioned for them to follow her to them. The sisters gave each other an apprehensive glance as they followed. They barely contained their questions.

"What's going on?" Aurelia asked as soon as the tent flap fell shut. Her voice came out higher pitched than she intended.

"It's your father," responded Exie. Her voice was low and controlled, her tone even. "He's looking for you. We didn't expect him to happen upon our clearing so quickly since he can't see it. He must have some talented hounds. This forest is too vast for him to find you so soon. His men chased our patrol unit and injured one of our warriors in the process."

Septima gasped, and Aurelia reached out to grasp her trembling hand.

"Is she okay?" Septima asked in a small voice that hitched as she choked out her question. "Do we have to go back?" Her fear was palpable. The idea of returning to their seaside villa was quickly becoming their greatest fear. Life with their father had never been easy, but after running from him and their intended husbands, there was no telling what the hell he would make them pay.

Exie's eyes softened as she moved forward to embrace Septima, but hesitated, her arm hovering awkwardly in the air before she lowered it to her side. "No, don't worry. There are wards that prevent humans from seeing our camp. He's found the clearing, but he hasn't found us. And she will be okay. Our bodies heal quickly. Blaedia is concerned because your father's people have set up camp near the clearing as well, so our scouts barely made it past without being noticed. We have groups who go out throughout the day to look for food and make sure our perimeter is safe. They cannot do that with your father's people so close by."

"So, what are we going to do?" Aurelia asked. Her sister was still quivering against her hand.

"We're going to leave. Blaedia is coming up with a plan for where we will go next."

"Our father will keep searching," said Septima. "I don't think we will get away from him if we stay in the Howling forest."

Exie nodded. "Blaedia is considering that in her decision. I don't think we will stay in these woods much longer because of that. We will have to cut training short today but standby for Blaedia's decision."

Aurelia nodded, her heart pounding in her chest. Just the thought of Proteus finding them, of what he would do to them for running away, chilled her to the bone.

"Should we pack?" she asked, not knowing how to pack their tent and all of its contents. She had no idea how they had gotten all the tents and furniture into the encampment to begin with.

Exie shook her head. "Don't worry about any of that. It'll be moved for you."

Septima's eyebrows drew together as she glanced around the space. "How?"

A mischievous grin spread across their companion's face as she wiggled her fingers playfully. "Magic."

The sisters remained in their tent awaiting the general's orders

With hunting dogs as skilled as his, they would be tracked down no matter where they were in Vaekros. If there was even a trace of their scents, Proteus would find them. A lump formed in the back of Aurelia's throat as tears of fear and guilt for endangering the camp threatened to spill.

There was no escape as long as they remained on the continent. Blaedia must have come to the same conclusion because when Exie returned a few hours later, they were informed that the entire camp would leave the Howling Forest in seven days.

Blaedia planned to return to Ekotoria. The warriors would regroup in the Spectre Forest and continue plotting to dismantle Warbotach's hold over their territory. Once they received confirmation from their allies on the other side of the portal, they would leave Vaekros behind for good.

Knowing their father was near made Aurelia uncomfortable, but Blaedia was confident in the wards that obscured the camp. The general did, however, restrict her forces from leaving the safety of the protective enchantments to patrol the forest. Everyone was ordered to stay inside the protected space, and the magical wards were reinforced regularly.

Now that the camp was mobilizing, everything felt more concrete than before. Traveling to another world was no longer a fantasy, but an impending reality. Aurelia was admittedly terrified of journeying to Ekotoria. She was frightened of flying through the enchanted portal on the backs of a fairytale creature. Once they arrived, they would encounter countless magical beings she'd never imagined truly existed. Everything frightened her. Even the idea of increasing the distance between them and their home was a scary concept, but she would follow through with her choice for her sister. While Aurelia's inner turmoil ceaselessly rampaged inside her mind, Septima appeared unbothered. It was as if anywhere was better than the life their father had planned for her.

Blaedia announced a mixer would take place after dinner. She would share her plans with the other warriors then. The sisters did not know what kinds of shenanigans went on in a mostly female warrior camp, but Exie promised that a night of foolishness and revelry would follow. Aurelia was simply looking forward to meeting more of the people she would live with for the foreseeable future.

After receiving word of the event, Aurelia went to spend time with Kano while Septima napped. Someone delivered a deer just before she arrived, and Kano was buried headfirst in the carcass when she approached, not even lifting his head to acknowledge her. She stifled a gag at the sight of the gore and found a tree stump to sit on, as far away from the carnage as possible. Even with the grotesque view of Kano's mealtime, she opted to enjoy the outdoors versus remaining in the darkened tent with her grim thoughts.

After he finished eating, Kano perched next to her seat and enthusiastically groomed himself. With the sun's rays warming her, Aurelia dozed off in the forest beside him.

The dinner bell woke her from her slumber. She kissed Kano atop his head, careful to avoid any bits of deer he'd missed while cleaning himself, and returned to wake Septima. Her sister was already awake and sprawled across her bed, her blank stare fixated on the ceiling.

"What's wrong?" Aurelia climbed onto the bed.

Septima shrugged and rolled to face her. "I'm just worried father will find us and take us back. I don't know what I would do."

Aurelia wrapped her arm around Septima's shoulders. "Don't worry about that. Blaedia promised we would be safe. They can't be caught here by the humans either. Seven more days. After that, we will be where he can't find us, no matter how many hounds he has."

"Aurelia... Septima..." Exie called from outside of their tent.

Climbing out of the bed, they wrapped their capes around their shoulders and exited the tent.

"Sorry," Septima said as they approached Exie. The blond warrior leaned casually against a tree, cleaning her nails with a dagger.

"It's okay. I was just hoping the two of you hadn't changed your minds and left the camp."

"That's not happening," Septima responded as she patted Exie on the back. "Sorry to say that you are stuck with us."

Exie smiled and wrapped her arms around both sisters' shoulders, pulling them into her and leading them to the dining tent. "Good."

On this night, unlike others, they heard music playing as they approached the crowd of warriors near where dinner was served. Instead of everyone lining up inside the tent, many were standing outside and moving to the music.

As they grew closer, Aurelia could see and hear why. Three females played a festive blend of fiddles and drums. The attending warriors, most with glasses of brown liquid in their hands, watched the musicians instead of securing their meal. Tables of roasted meats and vegetables were set up outside, as well as containers of that mysterious brown liquid, which Aurelia assumed was some sort of alcohol.

Instead of leading them to the food, Exie led them straight to the table of liquor and poured three glasses. She shoved the drinks into their hands and clinked both of theirs with her own.

"Cheers!" Exie shouted enthusiastically. She finished the alcohol in one gulp and slammed her glass down on the table. Aurelia and Septima followed suit, but not with the ease their friend had. Both sisters gagged as the liquid fire hit their throat.

"What is this?" Aurelia choked out, still feeling the residual burn in her chest.

Exie chuckled and refilled her empty glass. "It's Aegrician whiskey. Don't tell me it's too much for the two of you?"

Septima forced back the rest of the liquid in her glass and failed to completely stifle a gasp as the liquor hit her throat. "It's different from the berry wine we are used to, but I can handle it."

Raising an eyebrow, Exie clanged her glass against theirs once again, nearly toppling the glass from Aurelia's hand. "To a night of fun," she said as she tossed back another glass of liquid fire. She grabbed a roasted turkey leg and tore into it greedily. Aurelia couldn't help but laugh. Exie may have been a warrior, but she sometimes seemed like anything but.

"So," Aurelia started as she reached for her own piece of roasted meat. "You mentioned other warriors had husbands at home. Do you have one waiting for you to return?"

Exie snorted and almost choked on her food. "Definitely not! Bonding up with a male is very far down on my list of priorities. I'm with Septima when it comes to a husband. Not interested."

Septima smiled down at her glass before scanning the perimeter.

"Come on," Exie said, moving toward the crowd. "Let me introduce the two of you to some of my friends."

Chapter Ten

Howling Forest

B y the time they stumbled back to their tent, the world spun
violently as the trees danced. The trek seemed far more
perilous and salacious than it should have been. Exie led the way,
but she was not much help since she, too, was heavily intoxicated.
She led them into three different tents, all belonging to other
warriors, before they found the path that led to theirs. All but the
last was vacant, thankfully. After witnessing the nude acrobatics in
the occupied tent, movements that had the trio backing out with
their hands over their eyes, they were afraid to enter the wrong tent
again. Blushes colored their cheeks as they made their way home,
hoping the occupants would forget their faces by morning.

Their giggling grew more obnoxious, and Septima's stumbling
got progressively worse as they soldiered on. Exie and Aurelia
had to carry Septima the latter half of the way, because she had
consumed a few too many glasses of the Aegrician whiskey.

Aurelia was a little more conservative with the quantity she drank, wanting to focus more on socializing than getting wasted and not remembering anything the next day. It was a decision she would be proud of by morning while teasing her hungover sister.

The night had been fun. Exie introduced them to several of the female warriors and a few of the males who traveled with the camp in other capacities. Everyone had been incredibly friendly. Still, Aurelia couldn't help but wonder if that was because of the free-flowing alcohol or if they genuinely accepted the human sisters who entered their camp and put them at risk.

From what she could tell, Exie's best friend was a silver-haired woman named Holera. They had a snarky friendship where banter laced nearly every line spoken between them. Watching them pick on each other nearly brought Aurelia to tears of laughter.

Exie explained that she and Holera met when they attended warrior training. They were in the same group because they were close in age. Aurelia did not know how old the warriors were. She thought it rude to ask, but she knew they were far older than she was. From the snippets of conversation she'd overheard around the encampment, she surmised Ekotorians had longer lifespans than humans, and Aegricians were nearly immortal. Their abilities as phoenix shifters allowed them to regenerate life in their fire. So, although they could be killed, they didn't die of natural causes as humans did, nor did they age quite as fast. While she didn't fully understand how it all worked, she assumed Exie was ancient compared to her.

At first, Aurelia thought Exie and Holera may have been lovers. They were so comfortable with one another that it was a fair assumption. The speculation was erased, however, when

Holera stuck her tongue down a man named Kason's throat. There weren't many men at their camp—not one had piqued Aurelia's interest—but clearly Holera found one worthy of kissing and seized the opportunity. He had not seemed shocked by her unprovoked advances, so it must not have been the first time. They ran off together as Exie broke out into song and dance, drawing Aurelia's attention away from the fleeing lovers.

Blaedia and Taryn did not attend the party. They showed their faces long enough for Blaedia to make a few announcements to the crowd about their plans to return to Ekotoria by week's end. There was a bit of rumbling through the crowd, mostly concerns about their collective safety, but the general did her best to put those insecurities to rest before she and Taryn returned to their tents for the night.

After what felt like a never-ending journey to their tent, Aurelia and Exie deposited Septima on her bed and tucked her in for the night. Septima did not say a word when she collided with her bed. She rolled over and fell asleep instantly. Exie patted Aurelia on the back hard—her movements rough and clumsy in her inebriated state—and reminded her of their early morning training session. She turned to leave, walking into the canvas wall before stumbling out of their tent in search of her own.

Aurelia almost followed her, to ensure she actually made it back. In the end, she decided Exie could take care of herself. Still, she peeked through the tent flap to watch Exie until she turned toward her tent. She wasn't totally a rotten friend, after all.

Unlike Septima, who still wore her fighting leathers that reeked of sweat and dirt, Aurelia changed into her nightdress. They had missed their nightly shower, which left her feeling disgusting. She promised herself she'd shower immediately after their morning training as she crawled into bed. For the first time since she'd joined the Aegrician camp, her thoughts were quiet, and she fell into a dreamless sleep quickly.

Exie did not wake the sisters at dawn, nor did the toll of the breakfast bell disturb their rest. By the time they had awoken, still groggy from their drunken stupor, the cooks were already preparing lunch. Even their trainer had slept in after the long night of drinking, singing, and dancing, and did not look for them.

After peeking into the dining tent to see when the next meal would be served, they made their way to Exie's quarters, lamenting the breakfast they missed.

When they reached Exie's tent, they heard emphatic grumbling and moaning from outside. They didn't dare barge in, but Septima called out to her, just to ensure their friend was okay.

"Come back tomorrow," Exie whined. "I'm too busy dying today. I'll never drink again." The sisters laughed, twinging at the pain that lanced through their battered brains, before they poked their heads inside. They were greeted by the sight of Exie, clothes askew with hair that resembled a rat's nest, sprawled across her bed with one shoe still on.

"Are you going to make it?" Aurelia teased. She pulled off Exie's shoe and worked to twist her until she was lying on the bed the right way. The only response she received was somewhere between a grunt and a whine. "We'll bring you food when they serve lunch."

Septima grabbed a pitcher of water from the bedside table, poured a glass, and offered it to Exie. "Here. Drink this. You need to rehydrate if you want your head to feel better."

The hungover warrior rolled just enough to take a sip before she buried her face into the bed. "How are you not suffering right now, Septima?" The mattress muffled Exie's words. "You were drunker than me last night."

Septima's cheeks flushed. She sat on the foot of the bed, slouching forward to hide her embarrassment. "Because I woke up before dawn and drank nearly an entire pitcher of water before going back to sleep. I felt just as awful as you this morning."

Before Septima uttered the last word, Exie let out a booming snore. The sisters left as silently as they could, letting their friend sleep off the alcohol.

Knowing they still had time until lunch, Aurelia and Septima took a stroll around the camp. They had yet to get a proper look at their temporary new home, nor did they get to meet many of its occupants.

It was the perfect day to explore. The breeze blew gently through the trees surrounding them. The temperature was tolerable thanks to the layers of leather, cloth, and fur they wore.

The camp was larger than they realized. Hundreds of tents spread throughout the tree line surrounding the clearing. Most appeared to be sleeping quarters for the warriors who filled the dinner tent every night. There were surprisingly only a few people out and about as they wandered. Aurelia figured the long night of debauchery had claimed many victims who needed to sleep the Aegrician whiskey off.

Although Blaedia decided they would no longer leave the protection of their wards to patrol the beyond, warriors remained stationed along the perimeter. Aurelia wondered, as she and Septima approached the outermost path on the eastern border, if her father's men were still searching nearby with the hounds. The thought sent a foreboding chill through her. She hoped he had moved on by now, though a part of her knew her father would never stop searching. Their escape was a slap to his pride and damaging to his reputation. He would hunt them to the ends of the earth. It was enough of a reason to be thankful they would be traveling to another world soon.

Septima spoke, slicing through Aurelia's inner musings. "So, what do you think about all of this? Truthfully."

"About what, specifically?" Aurelia realized what information her sister was probing for, and her stomach tightened into an uneasy knot. Septima was clearly concerned about how much Aurelia was giving up, worried there would be resentment between them in the future if Aurelia sacrificed her own life solely for Septima's happiness.

Aurelia watched Septima from the corner of her eye as she shrugged, her head hanging mournfully. She reached out and grasped her sister's hand. "I don't know. I suppose I just want to know what you think about us leaving Vaekros behind. It's a big change."

Aurelia gave her sister's hand a reassuring squeeze. "I know it is, and I'm happy to do it. Don't worry about me. I didn't have much of a life or a future back home, either. I go where you go. It's always been that way. You and Kano are my home, not the home that awaited me after entering a loveless marriage and definitely not the villa. That place stopped being home when Mother died."

"What about Amadeus?" The question was a physical blow to the gut. Aurelia swallowed thickly, trying to keep her voice from cracking.

"I'll miss him, of course, but he has his own life. He's an adult who will be married and create a family of his own soon. I'm surprised he isn't married yet."

Septima chuckled fondly as they spoke of their brother. "That's because someone would have to put up with him." Aurelia joined in on the joke. Their brother's pride was the size of a continent, but it didn't translate to cleanliness. He could dominate in a sword fight, but he couldn't seem to keep his dirty underwear and socks off the floor.

"Yes. She will need to be great at apologizing for things that were not her fault and picking up behind him. Poor woman."

"I'll miss him, too." Septima sighed loudly, catching the attention of the guards who stood along the boundary of the path they traversed.

The sisters waved sheepishly before they turned in another direction. "I'm starving. Do you think they've laid out lunch yet?" Aurelia glanced toward the clearing, barely able to see through the trees. "Only one way to find out."

Arm in arm, they dropped the conversation about their family, and any hesitation about leaving the human lands, and ventured into the trees toward the dining tent.

Chapter Eleven

Howling Forest

Septima and Aurelia approached the dinner tent and spotted a long line of people waiting to be fed. Hungover warriors trudged through the open flap, devoid of their usual chatter and energy, as they grabbed their food. The sisters picked up their pace as they saw Exie. She still looked like she was feeling the effects of the night before, but at least her hair was brushed now. She slumped against a tree trunk, shying away from the sun's rays, as she waited for them. Aurelia couldn't help but notice the smile that had crept upon her sister's face as they approached the blond.

"Before you say anything," Exie quipped. "You did not see me like that. I'm a terrifying, fully in-control warrior. Got it?"

They snickered and nodded simultaneously.

"Got it," responded Aurelia. "Well, let's get this beast of a warrior some food. Shall we?"

Exie arched a skeptical eyebrow before she threw her hand out in front of her, motioning for them to lead the way.

The tent was still packed, but there were a few more empty tables than usual, a sure sign that some were still sleeping off their hangovers. After snagging a bowl of stew for themselves, the trio joined Holera's table. She leaned over a bowl of stew and grunted a greeting through half-lidded eyes. Kason, the man she'd left the mixer with, shoveled food into his mouth faster than he could chew. He glanced up and raised his chin in acknowledgement before returning to his lunch.

Aurelia studied him for a moment. They were told Aegrician males held different jobs, but he certainly looked like a warrior. Aegrician women were taller than average humans, but so were the men. Not only was he exceptionally tall compared to human men, Kason's muscles were also endless. He had thick black hair that was a stark contrast to Holera's long silver hair. It was pulled back into a leather strap at the nape of his neck, accentuating his sharp jaw.

Between his size, muscles, and the intricate tattoos that covered his arms, he made Aurelia's mouth water. While he was clearly taken, she wondered, just for a moment, if her future would include a man like him. If all the Ekotorian men looked like Kason—and she hoped they did—maybe mating with someone from a foreign magical land wouldn't be so bad.

She was so lost in thought that she didn't notice she was still staring. He noticed her appreciative gaze and flashed her a wry smile. He winked at her before turning back to Holera. Aurelia's cheeks flushed a deep crimson as her eyes darted down. If she kept her eyes glued to her bowl, maybe she could avoid embarrassing herself any further.

The venison and root vegetable stew smelled rich and earthy. It was a version of the same meal they had been given nearly every day since they arrived at the camp. She couldn't complain, however, since a bit of dried meat and fruit was all they'd fled the villa with. At least they were eating hot food containing more than one ingredient.

Exie, who'd been gagging since the moment the smell of food hit her nose, forced down her first bite. For a moment, Aurelia was certain the stew would work itself back up, but Exie's will seemed to win the internal struggle for domination over her stomach. She continued to force herself to eat. "Next time I try to drink that much," she said, her shoulders slumped over the table, "knock me unconscious."

Septima laughed as she nodded and patted the warrior on the back. "I'll make it my personal mission. But I really liked that performance last night and was hoping for an encore. How did that song go? Was it something about wine and a stone wall?"

Aurelia snorted, covering her mouth with her hand to avoid spewing its contents at Kason.

Exie scowled and hid her face in her palms. "Oh, gods. Did I really sing that damned song again? Forget you ever heard that." She glared at them through her fingers. "How large was my audience? Please say it was only the two of you."

Aurelia grinned and shook her head. "Sorry, friend. You basically performed in front of the entire camp. You even danced. Did you choreograph those moves, or were they spur of the moment?"

Exie flew forward, her hair flailing wildly as she repeatedly banged her head on the table. "This is so embarrassing."

Septima snorted. "Just own it, Exie. Everyone was just as drunk as you were. I doubt anyone remembers."

Lifting her head from the table, Exie shot her an incredulous scowl. "That's highly unlikely."

"So," Aurelia interjected, to grant her friend some respite. "Are we going to train tomorrow?"

"Absolutely." Exie's tone turned serious, all thoughts of her performance forgotten. "Blaedia would probably skin me alive if she knew we skipped today."

"What would she expect with a party like that?" Septima asked as she pushed her empty bowl away. "I doubt anyone trained today."

"You're right," Exie sighed. "And that's unfortunate. The likelihood that we end up in battle soon is high. We can't afford distractions like last night. So, although it was fun, I doubt we will have another until we take our territory back."

Even though the impending war made a pit form in her stomach, Aurelia nodded. She didn't fully understand the conflict in Aegricia, but she knew enough to realize how important it was to take the crown back before the Warbotach leader found a way to bend it to his will. Not only was their success vital to Aegricians, but to the humans on her side of the portal as well. They faced certain destruction, unbeknownst to them, if Uldon and the Warbotach army crossed into their realm.

Aurelia was ripped from her slumber by the sound of barking. She knew there were dogs in the camp, but not nearly enough to make the cacophony of sounds that echoed all around her tent. Grabbing the fur cape from beside her bed, she and Septima ran out into the still darkened forest, their heads whipping around for a clue as to what was going on.

Aurelia did not know what time it was, but the full moon hung high in the sky, and there was no hint of a rising sun. Kano's ears were pulled back against his head, and his teeth were bared. Though the sisters were still confused, the tiger's reaction was enough to tell them that there was a threat.

The sisters scurried between the row of tents, holding hands for fear of being separated, and dashed to the sparring rings where they spotted a large group of wide-eyed warriors, all circling the space to figure out where the incessant barking originated. Blaedia and a pajama-clad Taryn rushed from tents on opposite sides of the clearing and joined the group.

No one dared to speak as they fixated on their general. The silence prevented the dogs from hearing them, but it also stopped any information from being shared. Several warriors, including the general and commander, ran toward the southern tip of the camp, using only hand signals to communicate.

No one followed. The vicious barks and snarls were the only sounds shattering an otherwise peaceful night. Even the air remained still, not even the slightest of breezes blew, as if it were helping to hide the sisters and their scent. Aurelia did not need to be told that the aggressive hounds belonged to her father. She could feel it in her gut, but she still feared what that meant. Exie pushed her way through the mass of giant warrior women and wrapped a hand around each sister's forearm. She yanked them toward Blaedia's tent without so much as a word of explanation.

"What's going on?" Aurelia whispered, but Exie shook her head once roughly, her eyes bugging out in a silent warning as she continued to pull them along.

Exie lit a candle as soon as they entered Blaedia's tent and sat at the table. Her face was pinched in distress, aging her youthful face by at least a human decade. She dragged her hands down her face in a slow, measured movement, as if she was avoiding Aurelia's question. After a long moment, she heaved a sigh and met the eldest sister's gaze as she answered. "Your father's hounds have scented you through our wards. They are going wild just outside of our barrier. We thought the wards would block your scent from escaping, but we were wrong. Blaedia and the others are reinforcing the boundary now, but it will not hold for long. The animals will break through, even if the humans cannot, and when they do, the enchantments will fail. We will not last five more days here. The time to leave Vaekros is upon us. I would not be surprised if we cross through the portal before sunset, maybe even before sunrise."

Aurelia's heart gave a pitiful squeeze before taking flight. Its erratic thumping overwhelmed her ears and made her head throb painfully. Exie said something else, but she couldn't understand it. Her panic was too intense, too all-consuming. Everything was happening so fast her world spun. Taking slow, deep breaths, Aurelia tried to steady herself so she could check back into the conversation. She tried to lick her lips, but her mouth was a desert. "Will it be safe to go to Ekotoria right now? Where will we go? What will we do?" The words were rough, garbled even as she forced them out.

Septima wrapped her arm around Aurelia's shoulders, giving a comforting squeeze. Exie was visibly struggling to keep her face neutral, but worry still broke through the mask.

"We'll set up camp in Spectre Forest. Is it safe? Well, nowhere is truly safe right now. But this isn't your fault... that we must leave, I mean. We aren't supposed to be here, anyway. It was only a matter of time before we returned to Ekotoria to prepare our attack. We came here first, because Warbotach could not follow. There are also more dangers in Spectre Forest than this one, but our warriors are strong. We will be fine."

Septima swallowed loudly and moved closer to her sister. Exie gave a weak attempt at a comforting smile.

"What do you mean when you say more dangers?" Septima's words were hardly more than a whisper.

"Magical beings. Some are monstrous brutes. Others are more devious, using wit rather than strength. We will shield our camp, just as we have done here, but we will be on higher alert there. It doesn't matter, though. We must get back to Ekotoria, regardless. Training is but a minor part of the plan to reclaim our territory. We need to form alliances, and we can't do that from here. We would have returned whether the two of you had crashed the party or not. Go back to your tent and dress in warm layers. Spectre Forest is frigid this time of the year. Kano will be caged and readied for transport soon. I suspect it won't be long before we leave this forest for good."

Aurelia's eyes became saucers as she let out a gasp. Her mind had finally caught up with all the information they were given, and she came to a horrifying conclusion. "Exie... won't my fath-I mean, *Proteus* and his men see us? You said we would have to fly to Ekotoria. Can the wards shield us in the sky? Vaekrosan soldiers are renowned marksmen."

Exie gave a grim shake of her head, and Aurelia regretted her decision for the first time. The Aegricians took them in, expecting nothing in return, and they'd brought an enemy to their door. If their father hurt even one phoenix, it would be their fault.

Exie, not privy to the inner turmoil that plagued Aurelia, answered. "Once we fly above the treetops, we will be visible. That's why we need to be ready to leave at a moment's notice. If we can't leave before sunrise, we'll have to struggle to maintain our wards until sunset. The dark will help to obscure us. If they see us, well, I hope we are far enough away to dodge their arrows."

On that horrifying note, the sisters followed Exie's instructions and returned to their tent to pack. They dressed in the warmest layers they could find and filled their wooden trunks with the rest of their belongings. Clad in leather pants, tunics, and sleeved fur-lined capes, they returned to the clearing and joined the gathering of warriors. Aurelia did not know how the large camp, overflowing with tents and other belongings, would be moved, but Exie had said magic was involved. She could not begin to imagine, with her limited understanding of the mystical world, how the feat could be accomplished.

The barking that penetrated their invisible barrier had reduced in volume but not in intensity, as though they had moved further away. The aggression of the sound was enough to tell her they had not left their borders, but rather the placement of new wards had been successful. Hopefully, it would give them enough of an opportunity to flee the clearing without being spotted. Blaedia and her commander approached the cluster of women, looking determined and fiercer than she had ever seen.

"Our plans have changed. The threat outside our wards has increased. We will evacuate this camp before sunrise." No one made a sound as Blaedia addressed them, not even the creatures of the forest. Her voice rang out over the masses, authority permeating her every word. It was clear she was an experienced general that expected everyone to follow her orders without hesitation. "Prepare yourselves. We'll reconvene at the rendezvous point in one hour. Lanistas, the tiger comes with us. You know what to do."

"Who is Lanistas?" Aurelia whispered. She jumped at Exie's presence, so focused on Blaedia that she missed her friend's arrival.

"Lanista is a job title, not a person. They are our animal trainers. Don't worry. He's in capable hands. They'll sedate and cage him. It'll be best if he isn't conscious during the flight."

She wasn't convinced. It wasn't that Aurelia didn't trust the lanistas, but Kano had been agitated by the barking and was on high alert. She was worried about him but nodded in acknowledgement before returning her attention to Blaedia, who was busy assigning specific tasks to the warriors.

A group of approximately twenty females and a few males left the meeting, breaking off into smaller groups as they approached the tents that surrounded the clearing. The canvas structures began disappearing before her very eyes, and Aurelia's mind struggled to understand the visual. Septima's eyes grew in size as she fixated on the vanishing act, but no one else paid it any attention.

As soon as the general finished issuing orders, the remaining warriors splintered off to complete their assigned tasks. Aurelia and Septima remained in the clearing, unsure of what to do. Exie seemed to take pity on them and hooked her arms through theirs, pulling them toward Kano's enclosure.

"Let's go get that beast of yours in a cage," Exie quipped, with forced cheer.

Exie dropped their arms as they approached Kano's enclosure and opened the fence with a medallion identical to Aurelia's. Kano prowled the area, tail twitching in agitation. He straightened out of his defensive stance when he spotted the sisters and dashed over, nuzzling his face into Aurelia's legs as she rubbed his head. He let out a rumbling purr at her touch. As Aurelia pet him, Exie laid her hands on his back. His eyes grew heavy as he laid at their feet. He was unconscious in seconds. Aurelia's heart shuddered at the sight. She knew he would be okay. She trusted Exie. Still, seeing her constant companion bend to her magic, to have his happy greeting turn into an unnatural slumber, was too much to handle. She fell to her knees and wrapped her arms around him as tears left tracks down her cheeks.

"It's okay, it's okay." Exie crouched next to her and petted the enormous cat affectionately. "He's only been sedated, so he isn't stressed during travel. This is a better alternative for him. He will wake up feeling like he had the best nap of his life." Sniffing, Aurelia lifted her head to meet Exie's gaze. She nodded, setting her jaw in determination as she fought back tears. Her heart struggled to catch up to what her head knew.

He's not dead. It's just magic. He'll be okay. She mentally repeated the mantra in an attempt to soothe her frazzled nerves as she stood, gazing down at her beloved pet. Exie waved her hand ever so slightly, and a large metal cage developed around him. The enclosure vanished, replaced by trees and foliage that fit in with the surrounding forest. Except for the three women and the great cat, it was like the enclosed area had never existed.

The forest looked natural, as though the encampment had been a figment of Aurelia's imagination. The only trace that remained were the hundreds of warriors fumbling with various sized packs and containers as they readied themselves for departure. None of the luggage was large enough to hold the camp's contents. It made Aurelia wonder if they'd magically shrunken everything down to a portable size or if they somehow teleported the bigger items. The idea of magic was so foreign still. She could not help but wonder at both the abilities and the limitations.

Her musings did nothing to calm her nervous stomach. It whirled dangerously as they waited to leave the clearing. It was almost time. Soon she would leave her home—her realm—to go to a world she never knew existed. She reached for Septima's hand, expecting it to be trembling, but it wasn't. Her sister's face was set in determination, not a hint of fear or unease in her expression. She could see a familiar look in her eyes and knew that her longing for adventure had returned. Septima's steady gaze, her unfaltering presence, gave Aurelia the strength to push forward and face her fears.

Taryn joined them and patted Aurelia on the shoulder, flashing her a reassuring smile before approaching Kano's cage and testing its security. Two others approached and connected large cables to the metal crate that would carry him as they flew.

What if they drop him? The thought of it made bile rise in Aurelia's throat and she shoved it down, unable to bear the images her imagination had begun to conjure.

Blaedia stepped forward, facing the warrior collective. The muffled whispers of the congregation ceased as she lifted her arm above her head. She gave a few silent hand signals, and the clearing burst into bright colored flames, the heat washing over Aurelia, as the warriors transformed.

Chapter Twelve

Howling Forest

The scene was magical, yet horrifying. Aurelia took a step back at the sight, unsure of how to react. One moment, she was standing amongst hundreds of warriors. While they were much taller than her, they still looked human. But now, she and Septima were the only women who remained. With the exemption of a few dozen men, they were surrounded by enormous, colorful birds—*phoenixes*.

When Exie explained their ability to shift forms, Aurelia tried to picture it. She figured they would be the size of an eagle, a small dog at most, but they were enormous. Far larger than she could have ever imagined. Most were the size of a small horse.

Exie remained beside them. Her phoenix form was stunning. Feathers of nearly every color coated her fowl form, although the plume atop her head contained accents of her blond hair. Her warm brown eyes lingered as well, the only sign that the bird was truly Exie. Her long tail feathers fluttered in the stiff breeze, a prism of colors that resembled the ribbons Aurelia had played with as a small child.

Although her eyes were familiar, the eagle-like head they were set in looked vicious. Her sharp beak and pointed features were the things of nightmares. With talons longer than Aurelia's fingers, there was no doubt her friend could tear flesh from bone as easily as slicing through butter. Her wings were primarily red and gold, and their span was wider than their tent as she stretched and shook them out.

Exie dipped her head slowly, as if she was afraid to startle them. Her eyes held theirs in a reassuring gesture. It was like she was trying to tell them she was still herself and not to be afraid.

They knew they were still safe. They trusted Exie explicitly, but Aurelia and Septima still stared at her in a stunned silence. Neither sister knew how to react.

Harsh winds whipped around them, sending their cloaks snapping against their bodies. Dust clouds formed mini tornadoes as the phoenixes took to the air in small groups. Aurelia watched her beloved Kano as his cage was hefted up, held in the talons of a bird the color of fire. He was pulled into the sky, still asleep from Exie's magic.

She was forced to look away from her feline friend as another phoenix, crimson feathered with accents of black, approached them from where Taryn had just stood. Stepping in front of the sisters, Exie and Taryn bowed their heads, giving an encouraging bob when the sisters did not move.

Aurelia had never been more unsure about anything in her entire life. But she trusted the warriors who took them in and promised them a future. The Vesta sisters looked at each other, resolve visible in their shared gaze, and climbed onto the backs of the impossibly large birds.

Aurelia slid into the groove at the nape of Taryn's neck, mounting the phoenix like she would a bare-backed horse. Reins adorned her friend's neck, and Aurelia gripped the hand hold firmly before ensuring Septima had done the same. The warriors waited until their passengers were settled and stretched their wings.

The moon had long since begun its descent, but the sun had yet to make an appearance as the flock of phoenixes flapped their enormous wings and rose into the tree canopy in a few swift beats.

Part of Aurelia wanted to vomit, but the other part of her wanted to giggle. The feeling was exhilarating. She did her best to compose herself, to project a calmness she certainly did not feel. Relief flooded her as they vacated the area surrounding the camp, placing them outside of the range of being shot. If her father's party had taken aim at them, no arrow had met its mark.

Taryn and Exie flew alongside each other, leaving only enough space to prevent their great wings from knocking into one another. Septima's face was full of joy as she leaned forward on Exie's back, closing her eyes periodically against the wind that lashed at them.

The sun peeked over the crest of the Howling Mountains as they gained speed, soaring low over the Harmuz Sea, and darting toward the Marella Arch.

Aurelia had spent her entire life marveling over the arch, dreaming of traversing the rough sea to reach it, but never did she expect to make that journey on a phoenix's back. She closed her eyes in fear as they drew nearer, expecting to crash and drown. Taryn folded her wings against her massive body and shot herself at the target. Aurelia gripped the reins so tightly her fingers went numb, but her terror was for naught. She forced herself to look as Taryn glided through the center without so much as a feather brushing the weathered surface of the arch.

She managed a glance back to ensure Exie and Septima still followed before slamming her eyes shut once more. Aurelia could feel the environment shifting around her as they traversed worlds. The air seemed to warble and shift around her. It made breathing difficult and left her disoriented.

She peeked once more before her eyes became saucers. They were so high, flying just above the clouds, and Aurelia had the urge to reach out and touch them. Shock was the only reason she hadn't attempted it. A line of colorful phoenixes flew in front of them, stealing her attention from the white tufts they soared over.

The clouds thinned as they pressed forward, and she chanced another glance down. The view was equal parts terrifying and stunning. They flew over water the color of deep sapphire, far darker and more brilliant than the Harmuz Sea that their villa overlooked. The sight, and the violent gusts that battered her, took her breath away.

While the experience was one she'd never forget, after a while, Aurelia was ready to reach their destination. Hands that had once gone numb from her fearful grip had become numb for another reason. She'd dressed as warm as possible, but the temperatures were harsh as they raced across the sky. She'd lost feeling in nearly every appendage, her eyes stinging and dry from the incessant wind, and she wasn't sure how much more she could take.

She was just about to tell Taryn she couldn't handle flying any longer when shades of dark green appeared on the horizon, getting closer with every flap of their wings.

Aurelia focused on a solitary black feather on the back of Taryn's head as they began to descend. The quick change in elevation made her ears pop and stomach flip violently. Suddenly, she was glad they had not eaten breakfast before leaving. Taryn's wings were outstretched as they glided toward the forest floor, fluttering slightly just before they landed with a soft thud. She slid from Taryn's back and took a moment to take in her new world.

At first glance, the Spectre Forest could have passed for human woodlands, but Aurelia knew its appearance was deceiving thanks to Exie. The forest reached beyond her sight, dark and prosperous. Its canopy comprised pine, juniper, and alder trees that permitted ample sunlight to shine through. A flood of ferns reigned over the moss-covered ground around her. Coiling vines clung to the occasional tree, and a range of flowers—which desperately tried to claim the last remnants of light from their taller brethren—spruced up the monotone forest floor. A symphony of sound, consisting mostly of songbirds and descending phoenixes, reverberated through the air and formed a chaotic orchestra in conjunction with the wind that whistled through swaying treetops.

Exie had warned them about the magical creatures who dwelled in the forest, but Aurelia saw nothing out of the ordinary until she looked closer. Tiny balls of light twinkled as they flittered among the trees. She didn't know what they were, but she fixated on them until a gust of wind sent her hair flying into her face and drew her attention away.

Phoenixes shifted back into women all around her. Taryn joined them and shifted back into her tall, beautiful human form.

Aurelia caught a glimpse of Exie and Septima a few yards away and ran to her sister, wrapping her in an embrace. Tears filled her eyes, overflowing and streaming down her face. She wasn't sure why she was crying. It could have been from finally being free of their father's control or from fear of the unknown, but—whatever the reason—she couldn't stop the tears from falling.

Their reunion was cut short as Blaedia ordered them to move out. Even after the long flight, they still had to walk a few hours inland to find a secure location. Kano, awake and freed from his confines, walked between Aurelia and Septima on a long leash that he tangled periodically by darting into the tree line to snag a small animal to eat.

By the time they found a clearing suitable for them to set up camp, Aurelia was exhausted. Had they given her more than a moment of rest on their never-ending trek, she would have fallen asleep in the dirt. She forced herself to stay conscious as Blaedia, Taryn, and several other warriors put wards up around the perimeter of their new camp. Aurelia didn't know the first thing about the magic being wielded, but she watched, transfixed, as the environment seemed to bend to their will with every sweep of the warriors' hands.

The clearing was not as large as in the one in Vaekros, but the phoenixes were making it work. Everyone had a job to do, except Aurelia and Septima, which made her feel admittedly out of place. Tents went up around them as the smell of food being prepared filled the air.

"So, how was your flight?" asked Aurelia as she and Septima approached the new dinner tent. After getting Kano situated in his new enclosure and visiting their new tent, the sisters had all but run at the sound of the lunch bell. After leaving Vaekros before dawn and flying for hours, they were famished.

Septima faced her and grabbed her hands, eyes sparkling with excitement. "Oh, my gods, Lia! It was so exciting! Just the wind in my face... I felt so free. I've never felt so alive. What about you?"

Septima's enthusiasm was so infectious that Aurelia forgot the complaints she'd had on the journey. They chatted about their flying experiences as they stood in line, giggling as they grabbed their stew and found a place to sit. Exie plopped down beside them and dug into her meal without a word. They all ate in ravenous silence. Her hunger was so gnawing that Aurelia did not even ask what kind of meat circled the chunks of potatoes and carrots.

"How sick did you get?" Exie asked with a wide grin.

Aurelia rolled her eyes. "I didn't get sick, but thanks for your concern."

Exie chuckled. "I'm just playing. I'm glad you didn't get sick. Taryn wouldn't give you another ride if you lost your stomach on her, and it's likely we'll have to fly again. Septima did great, just giggled damn near the entire time."

Aurelia looked over as her sister's cheeks flushed. "I heard all about it," Aurelia said, before she changed the subject. "What are we going to do now?"

Exie glanced around the camp before returning her eyes to Aurelia. Her grin was subdued, and she hesitated before answering. The warrior's usual swagger and confidence seemed to falter, as she spoke barely above a whisper. "Blaedia, Taryn, and the other officers will convene and make a solid plan. For now, we will train as we did before. Emissary groups will be sent to Diapolis and Norithae for negotiation, but I'm not sure when they'll do that. We need to form alliances, but Norithae was attacked by Warbotach before we were. Their government is in an upheaval right now. At least that's what we've heard via communications we've received so far. Their king, Orpheus, was killed. His heir is missing while a Warbotach general oversees their territory. Those remaining in Aegricia, and the Norithae people, are biding their time. They're unable to fight Warbotach on their own and unwilling to lose any more lives until they are strong enough to take their kingdoms back. Our most likely allies are them. They have more to lose than Diapolis, who is on the opposite end of the continent and not currently at risk of invasion. Diapolis may very well choose to stay out of the conflict. I wouldn't blame them if they did."

"So, we will start back with training?" Aurelia asked, fixating on the one thing they had control over in this situation. Septima stared at Exie, that longing for adventure still shining in her eyes even after everything they'd been told.

"Yes. We will start tomorrow. For today, eat up and go get some rest."

Chapter Thirteen

Aegricia

The iron door to Otera's cell creaked open. A small, hunched figure shuffled into the dark room, carrying a tray in her shaky hands. The slender window let just enough sunlight into the shadowy prison for Otera to make out the frail woman's features. *Bremusa.*

Somewhere behind the old woman, a guard cleared his throat roughly. From under Bremusa's hooded cloak, Otera could just make out the darting of her eyes as they flicked to her right hand and back to the open door behind her.

Otera lunged at the humpbacked female, wrapping her hands around the elder's gnarled fingers, and weeded out the discreetly folded sheet of paper as she pulled the tray of food into her own hands. Her heart thundered in her chest in fear for both herself and Bremusa as the paper slid into her fingers. She didn't know what was on it, but she knew what would happen if Uldon knew the elderly female had snuck a note to her queen. He would do as he'd threatened to any who disobeyed his rule. Bremusa would be strung up between two of his fire-breathing horses and torn apart.

"Hurry up, you old crone," snapped the gruff voice from the poorly illuminated hall. Bremusa squeezed Otera's hand with gentle affection before she scurried back out and closed the door behind her.

Otera rushed to the window and held the note under the solitary ray of sunlight that fought its way into her bleak accommodations.

The birds have landed.

That was all it said, but those four words filled her with a hope that had been all but extinguished.

Raising her palm, she summoned a single flame. Without her crown and trapped within Uldon's wards, it was the only power she could wield, but it was enough. Otera held the message in that single flame and watched. Paper burned, turning to ash, and that ash scattered in the breeze as she held them out of the barred windows. She hoped her people, and her land, could feel the promise of help that those ashes carried.

Chapter Fourteen

Spectre Forest

After lunch, Aurelia led the way to Kano's new enclosure on the far side of camp. She couldn't help but fixate on the little sparkling lights that floated through the trees. It was as though they were following them, watching them.

"Exie," Aurelia hesitated as one of those buzzing lights floated right in front of her before zooming away. She could almost make out a miniature humanoid shape obscured by the light it emanated. It moved too quickly for her to visualize any specific features aside from a vague outline. "What are those?"

"Sprites. They're curious, and mischievous little shits. I'd avoid interacting with them if you can."

Septima shrieked and swatted at one that nearly collided with her face.

"Well, don't smack it." Exie laughed. "Just ignore it if it talks to you. They are full of tricks. And if any of your things go missing, they are definitely to blame."

Aurelia eyed the tiny creatures warily as they passed. The tiny figures flooded the area. They clung to tree trunks, sat on branches, and hovered in the air as the trio walked by. A brave few continued to dart around them, flying between their feet like they were trying to trip them. She wondered how such little creatures, no larger than a hummingbird, could cause so much trouble. "Do they always light up?"

"No, only when they are excited or try to defend themselves. They can turn it on and off like fireflies, except their entire bodies glow and not just their butts. You will find that a lot of things glow in Spectre Forest."

Kano had already made himself at home in a fenced-in courtyard by the time Exie pressed a medallion to the gate. He dug into a hunk of meat with reckless abandon, his muzzle slick with blood. He raised his head a fraction in acknowledgement as the women approached before returning to his macabre feast. Aurelia guessed he was just as starved as she'd been.

"Your medallion will still work on this enclosure," Exie said as she gestured to the necklace that hung from Aurelia's neck with a lazy flick of her wrist. "I placed your tent next door, because I thought you'd be more comfortable in close proximity to him."

"Thank you, Exie," Aurelia said, and placed a hand on her friend's back. "Thank you for seeing after Kano for me."

"Of course." Exie nodded and smiled before exiting the enclosure and calling out over her shoulder. "I'll see the two of you at dinner later. Get some rest and get to know the camp. Don't forget to stay away from the sprites!"

Aurelia and Septima played with Kano, running around the entirety of his new abode in an intense game of tag until they were sweaty and exhausted. The forest air was brisk, just like Vaekros, but it was heavy with a humidity they were not accustomed to.

The sprites continued to fly around, watching them from a distance. Considering they'd had no problem fluttering around the sisters, Aurelia figured they were afraid of the tiger and with good reason. Kano would not hesitate to snap them up in his maw for a quick snack.

As the sun began its descent beyond the horizon, the great cat let out a yawn and stretched before curling up to take a nap. The sisters left in silence, not wanting to disturb him, and made their way to the bathhouse. They were too tired to linger. After a quick shower, they stumbled bleary-eyed to their tent and fell into a deep slumber as soon as their heads hit their pillows.

It wasn't until the dinner bell tolled Aurelia rose from her nap. The past twelve or so hours had felt like a dream. It wasn't until she walked outside and was greeted by a horde of flickering sprites she realized they were no longer in Vaekros.

"Are you ready to go eat?" Septima asked through a yawn. Aurelia looked back through the open tent flap as her sister threw her legs over the side of her bed, tying her dark braids into a ponytail at the nape of her neck.

"Beyond ready. Hurry, and put your shoes on. I'm starved."

Septima let out a chuckle as she slipped on her boots and flung a cloak around her shoulders. "Good to see traveling to a new world hasn't dampened your dramatics, Lia."

Aurelia, ever the mature adult, stuck her tongue out at her younger sister and let the tent flap fall in her face. The action incited a war of antics between the two. They bickered and joked the entire way to the dining tent, which took far longer than it should have to reach.

They took the long route, mostly because they did not know where they were going, but they didn't mind having the chance to explore the encampment. The layout was like the setup they had in the Howling Forest, but it was far from identical because of their surroundings.

The trees in the Spectre Forest were thicker and taller than in their homeland and the colors more vibrant than they were used to. Everything seemed to have a heightened level of existence, like magic poured from every surface. The moon hung high in the sky, bathing everything it touched in an ethereal silver glow, the light of the sprites accompanying them the entire way. Aurelia couldn't be sure, but she thought one of the sprites had tried to help her trip Septima as they fooled around.

The tiny glowing creatures became sparse as they reached their destination, but a curious few fluttered around the warriors gathered outside the dinner tent. Much to her dismay, Aurelia had yet to get a closer look at one. Once the novelty wore off, they would become the nuisances Exie claimed they were, but she was still curious about their appearance.

Exie waited for them, as always. Her hair was wet and slicked back, a far cry from the wild blond mane she usually had.

"Looks like we weren't the only ones to hit the showers early," Septima quipped as they approached the smiling warrior. Exie wore a layer of fur over her usual leather pants and tunic. The fur of the cloak was like a silken night wrapped around her shoulders. Exie arched an eyebrow as Septima mindlessly caressed the fur on the female's shoulder. Septima let out a chuckle, flushing in embarrassment, as she pulled her hand away quickly.

"You like my cloak, Septima?" The look on Exie's face was playful. Septima's cheeks turned a shade darker.

"I... it's a beautiful cloak," she said before she spun on her heel and rushed to the dinner tent. They followed her inside.

The trio sat joined by Holera, Kason, and a few unknown faces at their table. One of the warriors, Thaestris, was the fiery red phoenix that carried Kano through the portal. Her shoulder-length hair was the same brilliant crimson as her feathers. Her eyes were a bright emerald, and her complexion was more bronze than most of the other warriors. She was soft-spoken and kind, her subdued nature a stark contrast to her intense features.

The other female at their table, Marpesia, better known as Rockie, was introduced as an expert archer. Unlike Thaestris, Rockie was loud and lively enough to rival Exie. Her jet black mohawk was laced with blue highlights that complimented the blue of her eyes. She was shorter and slimmer than the other warriors at the table, but she made up for it in bravado alone.

Their stew and tea had a distinct flavor to it, different from the stew in Vaekros, and Aurelia wondered what plants and animals were used to create it. She had a feeling they were not ones that could be found in her native land. Although it differed from what she was used to, she enjoyed the rich, earthy flavors and she finished it quickly, just as her sister did beside her.

"Card game?" Exie asked after most of the table had pushed their empty bowls away. "We can play in my tent."

Rockie and Thaestris eagerly agreed, but Holera leaned over to consult with her lover. After a brief whispered conversation, they declined, claiming to be tired, and promised to join another night. The pair were the first to leave, and Aurelia could only imagine what they would do instead. She secretly wished she had the same excuse.

She hadn't been with a man in over six months, and she missed it dreadfully. Her last lover had been a stable hand, Savvas, who had been shipped away once her father found out. Pushing the thoughts of both him and how much she missed a man's touch aside; she placed her dishes in the dirty bin and followed the others back to Exie's tent.

Aurelia quickly realized that by card game, Exie meant getting too drunk to be able to see the cards before forgetting about the game altogether. The cards Exie had laid out on the table were completely neglected as the Aegrician whiskey began flowing. Laughter, jokes, and singing took precedence as they drank.

The sisters returned to their tent a few hours later, stumbling less than they had after their introduction to Aegrician liquor. Aurelia couldn't help but smile, as she felt her first sense of true joy since leaving Vaekros. Training began the following morning, and although she feared what this new world held for her future, she was excited to finally have a purpose in life. She was no longer expected to be a doting housewife with no rights. She was going to be a warrior, and she was ready.

Chapter Fifteen

Spectre Forest

The following week passed without incident. Septima and Aurelia trained every morning. They ate with Exie, and occasionally enjoyed after dinner get-togethers in one of the warrior's tents. They felt safe within the protective bubble of the camp and had assimilated to life in Ekotoria with ease. They were not privy to the strategic planning led by Blaedia and Taryn, and the other inner workings of the camp. They were left out of the loop, but Aurelia did not mind.

"How do you feel about your training? Are you confident in your abilities?" Exie asked at the end of their seventh session. She wiped sweat from her face with a rag that hung from her belt and took a sip of water from her canteen.

The answer was complicated. Aurelia was always a better fighter than her sister. She trained with Amadeus more often, but Septima had proved to be a natural under Exie's tutelage. They definitely improved over the past week, but they were nowhere near the level of the other warriors. It was unlikely they would ever be as skilled as the phoenixes. Confident to what extent was a better question. If that extent was remaining inside their isolated camp with no real enemies to quarrel with, then she felt quite confident in her skill.

Aurelia shrugged noncommittally, but Septima answered their instructor. "I am more confident every day, but nowhere near confident enough to face an enemy. Although, I'm not sure someone is ever ready for potential death." Aurelia watched her sister drag her sword across the dirt, drawing lines, as she avoided meeting Exie's gaze.

"It's hard to walk into a battle you may not survive. But when you're fighting for something worth dying for, it doesn't matter if you're scared." Aurelia moved in closer as Exie spoke, focusing on what her friend was saying. "This war, the one coming, is worth dying for. But I realize it isn't your fight, and I realize you aren't ready. We will keep training until we are out of time. I would never throw either of you to the wolves."

Aurelia frowned at her friend's words. It was their fight. Warbotach wanted to invade the human lands. Sure, it wasn't their queen who was captured, but they had a stake in the war just the same. However, she didn't correct Exie. Asserting ownership over the war wasn't something she was mentally or emotionally prepared to do just yet.

The sisters remained silent as she continued to address them. "Anyway, Blaedia wants me to take both of you with me on my hunts. It's not the same as killing an enemy, but it'll give you more real-life experience with the weapons. It will help familiarize you with the land as well."

Although she had never hunted in her life, Aurelia was flooded with relief. She'd much rather stalk a beast through the forest than be sent on a dangerous mission for the cause. She simply wasn't ready for that yet.

They were set to head out at dusk. They had just enough time to eat lunch, check on Kano, and rest the muscles they'd overexerted during training. It was unclear how long they would remain outside the protective barrier, but being exposed to the elements made her nervous.

The weather was vastly different from Vaekros. From what Aurelia could tell, it followed different rules than the non-magic world. The air was cool and crisp but still filled with enough humidity to make her crimson hair frizz and nearly double in volume. They had yet to see rain, or snow, yet the forest remained vibrant.

Exie advised they add a warm cloak over their usual leathers. It didn't seem cold enough to do so at the time, but they followed her instructions, nonetheless. Aurelia did not realize how much the wards controlled the weather until Exie led them through the invisible wall into the wilderness. A blast of snow smacked against her as soon as they passed through the warbling air of the barrier. She understood and was thankful for the added layers.

"Damn, Exie." Aurelia's voice was unsteady as she shivered and secured her cloak around her neck. "You could have warned us about the weather."

Exie shrugged. "I told you to bring a cloak."

Aurelia grumbled but didn't talk back as Exie continued.

"We are hunting for anything edible, really, but deer are our most likely targets. There are more threats to contend with here than in the forests you are used to. Keep your weapons ready and keep your wits about you."

The snow coated the land, glistening on tree branches, and gave the forest an ethereal feel. Aurelia tried not to let the beautiful scenery distract her, as she pulled her bow from her back and locked an arrow into place. She practiced archery with Rockie a few times, but she was nowhere near confident in her ability to hit a moving target.

The moon and the bobbing lights of the tiny sprites illuminated their path. They navigated the trees and brush gingerly, afraid to slip on the slick snow, as they made their way to the natural blind the Aegrician hunters reinforced beside a nearby stream. They waited in silence, assaulted by cold flurries, for hours until they spotted movement near the stream.

Enthused by the break in monotony, Aurelia took aim and fired. She missed the first few shots but was able to strike a snowy white deer. It took all their strength, and a good bit of Exie's magic, to carry the fallen animal. Exie congratulated Aurelia for her kill as they made the trek back to camp, but Aurelia could not join in her enthusiasm. It was the first time she'd ever taken a life, and it was not without remorse. She knew they had to hunt to survive, but she had not expected to feel such contrition. The snow cleared as they reentered the boundary of the encampment. They passed the deer off to the cooks, and Aurelia headed directly for the showers without another word. She shed her bloody clothes and stood beneath the scalding water, hoping it would wash away her guilt along with the evidence of her kill. By the time she returned to their tent, Aurelia was completely drained. Even walking had become difficult. Without so much as a word to Septima, who stood freshly showered at the foot of her bed, Aurelia laid down and closed her eyes. She fell asleep almost immediately to the crackling of the small wooden stove that heated their room.

Chapter Sixteen

Spectre Forest

The snow fell lazily, settling onto the surfaces of the forest like a fine layer of sparkling dust in the moonlight. A rabbit with cloud-like fur nibbled on a patch of grass, scanning its surroundings while it chewed. With the rustling of trees, its ears perked up, and it scanned the forest again, fluffing its already thick fur to make itself appear larger. Before the snowy rabbit had a chance to react to the danger, a snarl, followed by a black-coated beast of legend, clinched its jaws onto its prey and fled into the darkness.

Aurelia awoke with a new appreciation for the forest. She didn't know if the creature in her dreams existed, but the thought chilled the blood in her veins. Light could not infiltrate the thick walls of the tent, so she stared into the blackness, hoping the snarling beast wasn't watching her from one of the dark corners.

They were so far away from home and in a world so different from their own. She took in a deep breath, willing it to settle her nerves as she blew it out slowly. Septima was still asleep. The sound of her peaceful breathing was reassuring.

Aurelia kicked off her blankets and climbed to her feet to put another log on the wood burner. She rubbed her hands against her chilly arms.

The camp was quiet, and she wondered if the protective wards kept out the sounds of the forest as well. From the lack of light through the small slit in the tent flap, she could tell that day had yet to break. Minus the flicker of sprite lights floating throughout the camp. All that lit the blackness was the sliver of moonlight through the thick canopy of trees. Her heart tugged on her to visit Kano in his enclosure. They had spent so much time together before she and Septima ran away. It made her feel guilty to leave him in the enclosure, even if it was a perfect space for a tiger.

Pulling on her cloak and boots, Aurelia slipped out into the night to visit her loyal companion. The chilled night air smelled of pine and a floral scent she could not place. She breathed deeply as she made her way to Kano's enclosure, relishing in the crisp air. The medallion against his fence worked quickly and created an opening large enough for her to walk through.

Locking onto her approaching scent and the crunch of her footsteps, Kano had already made his way to meet her as she entered. He nuzzled her leg, as he always did. Aurelia dropped onto the forest floor with her legs under herself as Kano curled up beside her. The more she caressed the great cat's fur, the more her eyelids drooped until she fell back asleep with her head upon his. It was a similar sleeping arrangement to when they were back in Vaekros.

Holera joined their hunting party the following night. This time they were prepared for the snow and dressed appropriately for the weather that awaited outside of their bubble. Dressed in their thickest wool and leather, the sisters were ready for the journey. Even if Aurelia wasn't sure she was mentally prepared to take another life.

The sun had just started to dip behind the trees when they met up with the armed phoenixes, still in their human forms. Holera and Aurelia were to use the bows and were tasked with the hunting. Exie and Septima carried swords for protection against any outside threats. Aurelia decided not to dwell on what sort of threats they could encounter.

The sisters took their weapons from the warriors' and secured them to their person before they were led through the barrier.

As soon as they entered the forest outside, snow flurried around them in spirals and settled on the inches that preceded it. Aurelia tucked her sleeves into her gloves, her feet sinking ankle deep into the cold slush as they stepped into the tree line. The forest was quiet except for the crunch of their boots that trampled the hidden brush. The noise was a perfect warning system for their prey, and an enticing beacon for any predators. Aurelia notched an arrow as she scanned her surroundings hoping to find their next meal before they became hypothermic. Nothing stirred, and she hated the relief that flooded her. She wanted to do her part to assist the camp, but to say she was eager to kill again would be a lie.

They moved as quietly as possible with weapons raised toward the blind they'd used the night before. Their progression was halted when the sound of wings flapping flooded the air. Boots making impact on the forest floor, surrounding them. Fear, unlike any other, flooded Aurelia, making her freeze in a way the harsh weather had not. Septima remained stationary as well, but their experienced companions moved without hesitation.

Great colorful wings exploded in a burst of fire from both of their shoulders, but they didn't shift fully as they fell into defensive stances with their weapons at the ready. Holera grabbed Aurelia quickly, shoving the girl behind her as Exie did the same to Septima. The warrior women stood back-to-back with the sisters between them.

Humanoid men with leathery wings that rivaled the phoenixes' in size were joined by a handful of others that sat atop crimson horses. They completely encircled the four women, cutting off any path of retreat. It looked like a fight was imminent, their only hope at survival, but they were outnumbered five to one.

"What is this?" Exie demanded. Her great wingspan blocked most of Aurelia's view as she peaked over, but she could tell by her stance that the warrior was prepared to strike if provoked.

One of the men on horseback urged his mount a few steps closer. Aurelia had to hold in a shocked gasp as his grotesque face came into view. Nearly every inch of the tawny flesh he had exposed was covered in jagged scars. His skin looked like it was stretched too thin over his abnormally shaped skull, leaving a weird translucence that allowed Aurelia to see the outline of his veins. He had a stocky stature, far different from the tall and fit Aegricians.

Exie didn't so much as twitch as he advanced, but the tension in her shoulders was visible. The shuffle of feet broke the silence of the stand-off. Two men, one winged and one not, restrained a struggling woman. Her long black braid was disheveled, but even as she thrashed wildly in an attempt to get free, she was recognizable. Aurelia's breath caught in her throat as she locked eyes with their commander.

Taryn's gaze wasn't pleading. It was determined. She could not speak with the gag in her mouth, but the message was clear. *Do not bargain with them.* She would sacrifice herself without hesitation to protect her subordinates. Exie didn't react to the sight of her captured commander, but Aurelia had no doubt that she would not abandon one of their own.

"What do you want?" Exie demanded. The monster on horseback grinned, the feral expression further disfiguring his face.

"We knew it was a matter of time before the infamous firebirds returned." Taryn continued to struggle as he sneered at them. Aurelia wanted to reach for her sister's hand, but she didn't dare lower the bow she aimed over Exie's shoulder.

"You don't belong in this forest, Warbotach scum," Exie spat vehemently, but his grin only grew.

"This land is ours. Norithae is ours. Aegricia is ours. What did you expect after fleeing like cowards?"

Aurelia could have sworn she saw the winged captor on Taryn's right grimace at his words, but the expression disappeared so quickly that she wasn't certain.

"Spectre Forest belongs to no one, least of all you! And Aegricia is not yours. Our crown will never bow to your worthless king."

He snarled when she insulted their ruler before composing himself. Then he chuckled, the sound rough and menacing, and nodded to the stout man on Taryn's left. The man reacted to the unspoken command and pulled a dagger out of its sheath, pressing it to their commander's neck. Aurelia held her breath as the blade pierced Taryn's flesh, a tiny drop of blood pooling at its tip.

"You are trespassing, firebird. Unless you want to see this bitch bleed out, you will come with us."

Aurelia couldn't tear her eyes away from the restrained phoenix. Taryn stopped thrashing and went stock-still as soon as the steel bit into her.

"Where?" Exie shifted her weight, sword at the ready. The tiny bead of blood grew, leaving a thin trail down the column of Taryn's throat, punctuating his threat.

"You are not in a position to ask questions."

Several men moved to the front of their ranks with iron chains in hand. *Chains.* Aurelia's lips trembled as she stifled a sob. She could feel Septima's hand reach for her back, clinching at the fabric of her cloak. Before Aurelia could lower her weapon and reach for her sister, Exie threw her sword down at her feet and whispered to them over her shoulder. "We will get out of this. For now—for Taryn—we will go. Don't fight. Everything will be okay."

She held her hands above her head, palms out, as she retracted her wings and stepped forward in surrender.

Aurelia dropped her own weapon to the ground, reaching back to squeeze her sister's hand before following Exie's lead. The women stood shoulder to shoulder as they waited for the inevitable. The men approached in pairs, each flanking a side, and wrapped the irons around their wrists.

Aurelia stumbled as the men on either side of her yanked her forward. Her heart raced, her breathing frantic, as her vision blurred. Her eyes darted around, looking for a way, *any* way, out, but there was no escape.

They were thrown in a cage pulled by the same fire-red horses the deformed men rode. Aurelia, Septima, and the three phoenixes were taken deeper into the forest. The longer they traveled, the greater the distance between them and the safety of the encampment grew. They could not fight or run. They could only lay bound like animals as they were led to slaughter.

Chapter Seventeen

Spectre Forest

Aurelia did her best to study the faces of their captors while she remained trapped in the rolling cage for what felt like an endless amount of time. The men on horseback shared similar features to the monstrous creature that had ordered their capture. They were all stocky men with tawny, scarred flesh, and slightly deformed heads. She assumed they all hailed from Warbotach.

While she didn't know much about Ekotorians, she'd been told that those from Warbotach could not fly, and that Diapolis had control over water. That led her to believe that the winged men were from Norithae. She studied the guard that marched beside the mobile prison.

His leathery wings were folded at his back as he stared straight-ahead, not sparing so much as a glimpse at those he imprisoned. With jet-black hair that made his ocean eyes shine brighter, he was by far the most beautiful man she had ever seen. She tried not to stare, but she could not help it.

He'd deigned to glance at her once and caught her watching him, but she looked away immediately. He was her captor, whether by choice or force, and did not deserve her attention. Still, she wondered if he was just as powerless as they were. Her mind kept going back to the grimace she thought she saw as he restrained Taryn. Norithae had been conquered before Aegricia, after all. Maybe he was just as much a prisoner as she was.

She shook herself in an attempt to dislodge the growing empathy and looked at her companions. Septima had stopped sobbing after a few miles and now sat in silence, her eyes puffy and bloodshot. Taryn slumped against the back of the cage, the fight draining out of her the moment the others were bound. Exie and Holera sat beside each other, eyes scanning their surroundings. Aurelia could almost see their brains working overtime. She wondered what the trio of warriors were thinking as they were hauled further and further away from their people.

Their jailers did not speak as they marched forward with weapons drawn. No matter what evils existed in Spectre Forest, she had a hard time believing they were worse than the men who had kidnapped them. They remained vigilant, nonetheless. With nothing but the monotonous, snow covered landscape and fear to occupy her, the rhythmic trotting of the horse eventually lulled Aurelia to sleep.

A guttural growl, deeper than any Aurelia had heard before, startled her awake. A beast, black as night with saliva dripping from its maw, crouched just inside a thicket of trees they were passing by. Their captors continued to push forward through the forest, ignoring the threat. Their group was large enough that she was surprised the animal approached at all.

The beast, which appeared to be the mixture of a wolf and something eerily human-like, was not deterred. It stalked after them the same way Kano did when he'd locked onto his prey. Its growl intensified as they pressed on. One of the captors, a burly male with an eyepatch that boasted more scars than the other Warbotach soldiers, notched an arrow and shot at the beast. The creature dove behind the bushes, and the arrow did not meet its mark. Aurelia did not see the animal again, but she still felt its gaze as they traveled.

The horses slowed and pulled to a stop. Aurelia didn't know where they were, but it was at least several hours away from their encampment. The leader spoke in a language she did not recognize. The door to their cage was ripped open immediately after, and she was dragged out by her chains. She was thrown face first onto the wet ground, barely able to stop her head from smashing into the forest floor. Four thuds echoed beside her as her companions were dumped on the ground as well.

Most of their captors busied themselves with setting up camp for the night. Only one guard remained to watch over them—the beautiful, winged man she'd watched from inside the cage. From her spot on the ground, she noticed his ears had a slight point. He was obviously fae, like the Aegricians, but that was one of the few similarities between him and the phoenixes. Unlike the fire birds, his wings were featherless and a solid inky black. Except for being exceptionally handsome, the rest of him looked no different from the human men of her world.

"Are you okay?" Exie whispered under her breath.

His eyes shot to them at the sound of her voice, but he said nothing. They all nodded in answer as they watched the men intently.

"What's the plan?" asked Holera, her eyes never drifting from the men laying out bedrolls nearby.

Taryn's head drooped as they sat, her slumped posture full of defeat. Her guilt over getting captured was clear. It made Aurelia's heart ache. It was not her fault, and she wished Taryn knew that.

"We can't get away right now," Exie murmured. "Our people will find us. Play along and, most importantly, stay alive. Don't be more trouble than you are worth."

The winged male shushed Exie, his eyes wide almost in warning, before his face hardened once more. She scowled but did not respond.

Although the snow had stopped, Aurelia still shivered as the frigid air made its way under her cloak. The frozen slush they sat in only made it worse, but she didn't dare stand for fear of drawing attention.

Another russet-complexed, winged male took pity on them and gave them blankets made of animal fur. The sisters cuddled together, using their body heat to keep warm. The chains and shackles made getting comfortable impossible, but Septima's proximity helped to calm Aurelia's frayed nerves ever so slightly.

They did not remain stationary for long. Some men stood guard while others slept. They switched after a few hours. Once they'd all had a chance to rest, they began breaking down their camp.

The women were escorted into the tree line to relieve themselves behind the shrubbery. It was humiliating and demoralizing to use the bathroom behind the bushes in front of a guard, but—with the only option being to soil themselves—they complied. As their jailers broke their fast, the women were given a pitiful amount of water, bread, and dried meat. As soon as the men finished eating, Aurelia and her friends were stuffed back into their cage to continue the journey.

The forest's terrain became increasingly rugged as they traveled. The monstrous leader that ordered their imprisonment refused to tell them where they were headed, so Aurelia had no way of knowing how much longer they'd be trapped in their tight confines. But as the sun continued to move across the tree-covered sky, Spectre Forest gave way to mountains and plateaus. Evidence of a city emerged, the building outlines filling Aurelia with a sense of dread. As uncomfortable as the ride had been, the idea of reaching their destination filled her with fear. How would Blaedia and the others save them once they were in a Warbotach stronghold? As they traversed out of the forest and descended toward the city, all of her hopes of being rescued died.

"Norithae," Holera whispered, confirming Aurelia's fears.

Chapter Eighteen

Norithae

The city of Norithae stood proudly along the coast of the Elder Sea, the same sea they had flown over after crossing the portal. Aurelia's chest was still tight as she worried about their fate, but she could not help but marvel at the bustling city.

Tented shops lined the dirt street their cage was led down, selling everything from fresh food to tapestries. Patrons browsed the stalls, filling their wicker shopping baskets and moving on with their day. Hardly anyone acknowledged the captives as they were carted by. Most went out of the way to avoid coming into contact with the men who marched down the center of the bustling strip.

Their traipse through the town center went unhindered, and soon Aurelia caught sight of an overcrowded harbor. Dozens of ships were moored at the docks. Thick storm clouds darkened the sky, and the sea had already begun to toss violently. She doubted anyone would brave the water in such conditions, but she would gladly take her chances with the rough waves if it meant escaping their Warbotach jailers.

All thoughts of fleeing by boat fled her mind as her attention was stolen by a majestic palace in the distance. Any other time, she would have been in awe of the hulking structure. Now, it only served as a metronome. Each tick brought her closer to her doom. *Tick.* Aurelia forgot how to breathe. *Tick.* Panic consumed her. *Tick.* She needed to get free. *Tick.* Before it was too late. *Tick.*

She couldn't take it anymore. "Help us. Please." Aurelia was frantic as she whispered to the handsome winged man walking alongside them. Maybe she hadn't imagined his expression the night before. If he really grimaced at the Warbotach leader's words, maybe he would help them.

The entire trip he'd been but a foot away and had only spoken to issue commands. It was a foolish hope, but she had to try. His expression pinched, the only sign that he heard her, but he didn't respond or even glance her way. She yanked on her manacles in anger and frustration, nearly making herself bleed. He reached out and grasped her wrist, his gentle touch contrasting his hardened features. He still did not look at her.

"Help me. Please." The rage faded as fast as it had appeared, leaving only sorrow and fear behind. Her eyes burned as tears fell. She half-heartedly pulled on her manacles once more.

His ocean blue eyes softened as they met hers, and she felt hope well up inside her.

"Stop doing that. You're going to hurt yourself," he whispered, earning a grunt from the Warbotach beast who steered the cart. Her escort tightened his jaw, emphasizing the sharp lines and

angles of his handsome face, and her paper-thin optimism was torn
to shreds.

She turned her attention back to the palace that marked the end
of their journey. It was enormous, with twelve round towers linked
with small bridges and connected by thick walls of dark granite.
Rough windows littered the walls in a seemingly random pattern,
along with symmetric crenellations for archers. There was a vast
gate with giant metal doors and a drawbridge guarded by armed
men. Remnants of catapults, swords, and shields besmirched the
fields surrounding it — a painful reminder of the recent siege
that resulted in the Norithaean king's murder and subsequent
replacement by a Warbotach war leader.

Fighting was useless while they were bound and caged, so
Aurelia gave up her struggle as they approached the palace. Each
of the women was ripped from their temporary prison by a pair
of guards and forced into a line before being led toward the palace
door. Aurelia expected to be brought into the palace, to whoever
ruled over the battle torn castle, but they were escorted around
the side of the courtyard and into a narrow alleyway. The passage
was narrow, the stone walls forcing her captors to trail after her
as she walked. Her chains were held firm so that her hands were
restrained behind her. The other women were ordered to follow
suit, dashing any opportunity for escape.

They were led through an iron door on the side of the palace,
down a dimly lit hall, and thrown into an even darker chamber.
Flickering candles sat in small mountains of melted wax. The scent
of their overused wicks melded with the smell of mildew, assaulting
Aurelia's nose. She followed Exie's lead and remained quiet until
the iron doors clanged shut behind them. The sound of heavy

bolts sliding into place echoed around the musty walls of their new confines as they were locked inside.

"What are we going to do?" Septima asked as she dropped onto one of the wooden benches that lined the perimeter of the square room. Aurelia sat beside her, interlacing their fingers, as Septima laid her head upon her sister's shoulder.

"For now, we rest," Exie said. "There isn't much we can do in this box while exhausted and starved. Blaedia will find us. Our people will track us down. It's only a matter of time. Have faith."

Holera and Taryn each claimed a bench of their own, following her advice. Taryn laid down her back to the others and tucked her arm beneath her head as a pillow. Aurelia worried about the commander. She wasn't acting like herself, but it was clear she didn't want to talk. Putting thoughts of the morose phoenix out of her mind, she rested her head on Septima's and closed her eyes. Silence filled the room as they drifted off to sleep, one by one.

The metal door squealed open, pulling Aurelia from her fitful sleep. The beautiful man who escorted them to Norithae, the one she'd begged for help, entered with a tray of bread and water. His wings were tucked behind him, and his chiseled face revealed nothing as he handed her the tray.

"Can you help us?" Aurelia pleaded once more in a whisper as his eyes held hers.

Her fingers trembled as she gripped the tray, but her gaze remained steady. His response didn't come in the form of words, but the answer was clear enough when he turned and left. She slumped in defeat, staring at the enforced iron door. The heavy bolts slid back into place, locking them in. The sound was like a nail being hammered into her impending coffin.

Taryn placed a gentle hand on her shoulder and guided her back to the benches their companions sat on, waiting for the pitiful bit of food she held. It wasn't nearly enough to help them regain their strength, but it would prevent death by starvation—for now.

As they ate, they scanned the dank stone room for anything that could be used as a weapon, or a way out, but found nothing. There was no way out. They had no means of defending themselves, aside from their rapidly fading physical strength. Aurelia didn't ask the phoenixes if they could still shift or use their magic for fear of their answer.

They remained in the dungeon for what felt like days. They had no way of knowing if it was day or night, so they could only guess at the passage of time. Aurelia wondered what would become of them and if they would make it out of there alive. The only person who visited their prison was the handsome winged man who delivered their meager sustenance.

Just when she thought Warbotach had forgotten them, the door squealed open and the beastly man with the patch over his eye barreled in.

"Which one of you is the leader?" he growled, low and guttural. Taryn went to stand, but Exie beat her to it.

"I am." Exie said, pointedly avoiding Taryn's stare. Her message was obvious to Aurelia. She wanted the commander to stand down and trust her. Taryn's jaw tightened, fists clenched at her sides, as she read Exie's face. She gave an almost imperceptible nod, face grim, and leaned back against the wall.

The one-eyed man kept his eyes on the warrior who claimed to lead them, not seeming to notice their silent interaction. He advanced on her sadistic smile, fixed on his grotesque face, and dealt a vicious punch to Exie's abdomen. Septima leaped to her feet and started forward as the woman doubled over in pain. Aurelia gripped her arm and yanked her back down roughly. The sisters glared at each other. Aurelia tried to communicate with her eyes. *Don't. Just trust Exie. She knows what she's doing. We have to bide our time.* From the way the fight drained from Septima, sorrow painting her face, she knew the message was received.

The one-eyed man signaled to someone in the hall. The handsome man came in, approached Exie from the back, and placed manacles on her wrists. He led her out of the room. The door slammed behind them. That was the moment Aurelia gave up on the fantasy of him helping her. Whether or not he was voluntarily working with Warbotach, he was the enemy.

Septima dropped to her knees and sobbed into her hands as they heard Exie's grunts of pain through the door, the agonizing sound growing more distant. Aurelia dropped beside Septima, pulling her sister's head into her lap, and caressed her braids softly. Taryn kneeled beside them and placed a tentative hand on Septima's arm. Holera remained on a bench, watching them in silence. Her expression contained the same worry as the others, but there was nothing they could do. They simply had to wait and have faith that Exie would return.

"She'll be okay," Taryn murmured. "Exie is a well-trained warrior. She knows what she's doing."

That was the last time anyone spoke for what felt like hours. The iron door swung open later, startling them. Exie was unceremoniously dumped back into the room. She collapsed into a heap on the floor as the door banged shut behind her. Septima rushed to her side, scooping Exie's face into her hands. The warrior's lip was split and bleeding. One eye was swollen shut and had turned a sickly shade of purple. Her clothes were crumpled, splattered with blood and dirt. Had they been properly fed, Aurelia would have lost her stomach at the sight of what was done to her friend.

Septima held the battered warrior in a soft embrace and wept. Exie's uninjured eye fluttered shut as she lost consciousness.

Chapter Nineteen

Aegricia

The birds have landed. That was the last message Otera received. Since that time, she had received no other communications. She didn't know where her warriors were or when they would come for her. She remained in the dungeon, marking the passing days by a sliver of light that filtered through the window. The small flame she could summon remained steady, her only companion in the desolate prison.

The Warbotach leader made fewer and fewer visits to her dungeon, not that she was complaining. He probably gave up on demanding she relinquish her power and moved on to trying to change her crown's allegiance. It wouldn't work. She knew it wouldn't work. The Crown of the phoenix would never bow to such barbaric scum. But he just wouldn't see reason and cease his efforts.

Several days had passed since Bremusa's visit. Otera could not shake the fear that Uldon had discovered the elderly woman's act of rebellion. The queen had no way of knowing, but—given the level of Uldon's sadism—she knew the woman was likely alright. Had she been caught, the cruel king would have surely made her watch, helpless, as he tortured Bremusa.

Two levels above the dungeons, while Otera tormented herself over Bremusa's fate, Uldon paced the royal chambers he'd stolen. His patience had just about reached its end with his confidant, Ezio. The man fed him an endless amount of excuses as to why the crown had not yet bent to his will. He was sick of petty justifications. He wanted results.

The Marella arch taunted him as he stared out the window. He needed a way to cross through the portal. As soon as he controlled the magic, his people would dominate the human world. His horses needed land to graze on. His people land to live on. They could not continue to dally about.

"We searched, Sovereign. The Elemental of Spectre Forest cannot be found. We received word from the legion in Norithae. No trace of her was located, but they captured some of Otera's warriors in Spectre Forest."

Uldon grunted, turning on his heel to face the man. Ezio shuddered, his fear clear. The king grinned, reveling in his subordinate's terror. "How many fighters did they capture?"

"Five. They believe one is a commander."

His vicious smile grew. "Excellent. I want confirmation that it's a commander. Tell the legion to do what they must to get my answers."

Chapter Twenty

Norithae

Exie gave a violent heave from the corner of the room. Aurelia could hear the vomit splatter against the floor. She sat up from her place on the bench and saw Septima holding the warrior's matted blond hair back.

The beating Exie had taken the day before left her in terrible condition, and the lack of food did not help. Everyone gave the injured warrior a portion of the bread they were given for dinner, hoping the increase in calories would help her heal.

Holera remained stone-faced. She did not speak or move about much. It was almost as if she'd completely disassociated from their reality and retreated into the deep recesses of her mind. Taryn hovered around Aurelia when she wasn't checking on the others, which she did periodically. Septima had not left Exie's side since she was returned to the cell.

"We have to do something," Septima said from the corner. Exie's face had gone an unsettling shade of gray as she slumped against

Septima's lap. She rubbed a soothing hand over the wounded woman's back.

"Our only option is to fight when they open the door, but we don't know how many guards are out there. We don't know how many guards are surrounding this city." Holera spoke for the first time in days as she pressed her palms against her eyes. "We may break out of this room only to be struck down in the hallway."

"We have to try." The pain in Septima's voice was audible as she stroked Exie's hair away from her pallid face. The warrior had drifted off to sleep, her body positioned awkwardly.

"She can't even walk!" Holera snapped, gesturing violently at the unconscious warrior.

Septima opened her mouth to respond, but Taryn cut her off. "Enough." The commander, who had been a shell of her former self, was back in all her glory. Authority filled her voice as she stood and motioned for them to gather round.

They spent the next few hours plotting their next move. They would lay a trap for the guard when he brought their food. If they were lucky, they would be able to pilfer a weapon or two from him. Whether they could flee the city—they did not know—but they knew they would have to try. They agreed to delay their plan until the following day, so Exie recovered from the beating she had received. Phoenixes healed inherently fast, but the lack of nutrients hindered the process. They hoped that would be enough time for her. Their escape would be unsuccessful if Exie was immobile. They had to be swift and silent if they were to have any chance of success.

When the metal bolts that locked them inside the dungeon slid open later that night, Aurelia stiffened. Every part of her expected them to take Exie again. The warrior had not, and would not, give them information. If they took her and beat her again, their hopes of escape would be dashed once more.

To their collective relief, it was not the scarred face beast that entered but the winged man. His eyes darted around the room as he entered, scanning their faces, as Aurelia approached to take the dinner tray.

Her heart sat in her throat as she neared him, just as it had done every other time he entered the prison. Someone cleared their throat in the hall, the sound echoing off the damp walls. He glanced over his shoulder with a clenched jaw.

He faced Aurelia, and his eyes bore into hers with an intensity he'd never shown before. She reached to take the tray, and his right hand gripped hers. He forced a small piece of paper into her palm. She froze for a moment before she pinned the note between her hand and the tray. Their gazes remained locked for a long moment, her heart thundering dangerously in her chest, until he turned and left. She stood there, watching his retreating form, until the lock slid home.

The only person not staring at her in confused silence was Exie, who was fast asleep in the corner. The tray shook in her trembling hands. He had passed the note so covertly; she was certain not even her companions had noticed. They could not know why she was afraid to move. She was scared to even pull the paper from her hands for fear of an enemy spotting what could possibly be their only lifeline in this hellhole. The winged man hadn't spoken more than a few words since her capture. What could he possibly have to say? A part of her hoped, perhaps foolishly, that he was going to help them escape. After he'd ignored her tearful pleas for help, it wasn't the most likely scenario. Still, if he didn't intend to help them, why would he risk passing along a message? She didn't even know who he was, or what side he was on. All of her questions could be answered by simply reading the note, but she was having a hard time mustering up the courage to do so.

"What's wrong?" Septima asked. Her eyebrows furrowed as she approached her sister and reached for the tray. Aurelia hesitated, afraid of dropping the paper, but she relented and pulled the note further into her palm when the tray slid out of her grip. Septima's eyes widened as she caught sight of what Aurelia was holding, but she quickly schooled her expression.

"Come," she said. "Let's sit down and eat."

Aurelia squeezed the note so tight her nails dug into her palms. They huddled around the sleeping Exie and shared the stale bread and water, making sure to leave enough food for the healing warrior.

Leaning over the scraps that served as her portion of dinner, Aurelia let her long red locks fall forward, concealing her face. She held the sheet of paper in front of her eyes, making sure her curtain of hair hid her hands, and unfolded it carefully.

Help is coming.

That simple brief message lifted the giant weight that had crushed her chest since they were imprisoned. She didn't know what the note meant, didn't even know the man's name, but help was on the way. She wasn't sure if that meant he was bringing help or if Blaedia had located them somehow, but the promise of help did wonders to lift her spirits. They didn't need to attempt a dangerous escape. They didn't need to attack him when he brought their next food tray. As hard as it was, they needed to wait.

Unsure of what to do with the paper, but unwilling to get either of them caught, Aurelia placed it into her mouth and chewed, swallowing it quickly. She shared the contents with her companions in the quietest whisper she could manage.

The night was eerily silent as the women sat in their cold cell, huddled against each other for warmth. Exie had stopped vomiting but could still hardly stand. Aurelia did not know what they had done to her. None of the women wanted to ask and force her to relive her trauma, but it was evident that her injuries extended beyond the black eye and busted lip. Septima held Exie close—having never strayed out of the wounded woman's reach since her return—and comforted her as best she could.

Later that night, a thump sounded outside their door. It startled them, but they remained quiet, eyes wide, as the metal door squealed open. Their winged guard crept into their cell and peered into the darkness. A torch flickered in the hall behind him, making him appear celestial. Aurelia still did not know if he was good or evil, but she hoped with all her might that he was good. Her heart hammered as she watched him.

He approached them gingerly and squatted down in front of them, speaking just above a whisper.

"Follow me quietly. I'm going to get you out of here."

"Who are you?" Holera asked, matching him in volume. She stared at him, her expression disbelieving.

"Cristos. Save the introductions for later. We have to go *now*."

They looked at each other before Taryn nodded. They worked to heft Exie onto shaky legs. The warrior was too weak to walk on her own. Holera and Taryn braced her on their shoulders and led their friend out into the shadowed hallway. The guard that stood watch outside their cell lay in a gigantic heap and partially blocked their path. His dark-skinned, scarred face stared lifelessly at the ceiling. A puddle of blood formed around him, still seeping from his slit throat. Cristos had killed him. Aurelia didn't see any blood on their savior, but she knew it was true.

Cristos' slowed his brisk pace as they reached the end of the hallway. He turned to them, shadows obscuring his handsome face, and thrusted a dagger into Taryn's hand.

"In case we have to fight."

Taryn took the weapon and nodded as she stared at the door separating them from the outside—from freedom. Cristos slowly nudged it open and peered outside.

A horse-drawn cart used to carry fruits and vegetables to the market was parked a few yards from the building. He lifted the back cover and motioned for them to climb in. They obeyed his command and approached the impromptu caravan in silence. Exie turned a sickly green as Taryn and Holera helped her up, her teeth clenched against the pain she endured. But even she did not make a sound.

Once the women were settled, Cristos climbed in behind them and pulled the thick cloth down to conceal the stowaways. He tucked it around the crates of vegetables before he smacked the wall of the cart. As in response, a whip cracked, and the cart lurched into motion.

No one made a peep as the cart bumped along the rough road. With six people crammed into the tight space, Aurelia was forced to press against their savior. If she sat any closer, she'd be on his lap. His scent filled her nose, a blend of sandalwood and spices, and her face heated. She wondered how unbearable her own stench was after so many days without a bath. He didn't seem to notice. His arm rested precariously close to her right thigh.

Focusing on Cristos was proving to be dangerous to both Aurelia's rapidly beating heart and her flushed cheeks. She stopped observing him and took in their new surroundings instead. The interior of the small cart was dark, and the smell of soil and potatoes overpowered the space. They sat in the center, surrounded by strategically placed produce crates. From the outside, she had little doubt that it appeared to be a normal trade cart, and not one smuggling runaway prisoners from the palace.

After a few hours, the cart slowed to a stop. Cristos threw back the cover and hopped out, offering his hand to Aurelia as she climbed out. Her breath caught as she held onto his hand, his blue eyes locked on hers. She felt her blush return as she looked away and stepped forward to allow the others out. Once all the women had exited, he grabbed a few sacks from inside and tossed them onto the ground. He took a moment to speak with the driver and slipped something to him. Aurelia assumed it was money or some form of Ekotorian payment. The cart drove off a moment later.

They were left alone in the forest with Cristos. He returned to their group and reached for the packs. He slung one over his shoulder before offering the rest to them. Aurelia and Septima took the remaining packs, while Holera and Taryn supported Exie's weight.

"Why are you helping us?" Holera asked. The edge in her voice was hard to miss. She was clearly just as tired of Cristos' silence as Aurelia was. He had helped them escape, but hadn't uttered more than a few words to them. They did not know who he was or what he gained by helping them. Did he plan to leave them to fend for themselves? She had an endless stream of questions for him, and he offered no answers thus far.

He grabbed Aurelia's arm, tugging gently, and led them off the road into a copse of trees.

"I'm helping you because my kingdom needs Aegricia's help to oust Warbotach. They killed our king. My people have no freedom. We don't have enough power to take back our kingdom alone."

"Our own queen has been captured. Surely you know that. There isn't much Aegricia can do for your kingdom when our own is in peril as well." Taryn's tone was clipped.

He nodded and scanned the tree line before he returned his eyes to them. "I know about your queen. I plan to travel to Diapolis to speak to their king. Maybe together we can convince them to help. Neither of us can get rid of Uldon and his people separately. This alliance is our only hope."

"We can't do much until Exie heals enough to walk and shift. Taryn and I cannot fly with two people on our backs. We have to find somewhere to rest until then. How far is our camp from here?" Holera asked. She shifted her stance to better support Exie's weight. The warrior's head hung as she stood. She was barely conscious. Aurelia's throat felt too tight, her chest too heavy, but she did her best to bring air into her lungs and back out. The action was more difficult than it should have been. They may have escaped the dungeon, but they were far from safe. She felt exposed and vulnerable. There was nothing she wanted more than to be back behind the wards of their encampment, playing with Kano.

"I know of a place where we can lie low," he said. "It's a few hours from here, but I can help to carry her." Cristos set the packs he was carrying on the ground and reached one arm around Exie's back, and the other under her knees. He lifted her gently but with great ease, as though she weighed nothing. "Hold those packs. We need to get moving before someone finds us."

They headed in the same direction the cart had been traveling, still hidden within the tree line. Each step they put between them and Norithae made Aurelia breathe easier. After the time they'd endured in the seaside palace, she wholeheartedly hoped to never return. Silence was their constant companion as they traveled. They could not chance drawing attention to themselves for fear of being imprisoned once more.

Chapter Twenty-One

Spectre Forest

A familiar snarl destroyed the silence that filled the forest. The same midnight beast who followed them as they were transported to Norithae crouched several yards ahead of them, blocking their path. It watched them, unblinking, as most of their group approached. Aurelia halted, frozen in fear, as she stared back at the creature. It did not move against them, but its wary eyes tracked their every movement.

Cristos did not stop walking and appeared unphased by the ferocious-looking wolf hybrid. He carried Exie closer to the beast as he called out in a friendly tone, "Calm down, Variel. It's me, Cristos."

Its snarling maw snapped shut as its eyes flicked to him. Aurelia could see the recognition in its face. The black beast shifted from the thing of nightmares to an elderly female in seconds. Her long dark hair hung nearly to her waist, completely devoid of gray despite her obvious age. Her eyes were as dark as her fur had been, the irises blending seamlessly with her pupils. Aurelia's limbs defrosted as soon as the beast had transformed, and she stepped closer to the woman. She stared wordlessly, waiting for an explanation of some sort. She wanted to know who the elder female was and how Cristos knew her, but she was afraid to break the silence that followed his greeting.

"What trouble did you bring to me today, Cristos?" the old woman asked as she turned and headed deeper into the forest.

He flashed a smile in response. The first time Aurelia had seen him do so. He trailed behind the old woman, still carrying Exie with ease. Confused and uncertain, they followed Cristos and Variel to a clearing that opened within the dense forest. They came to a halt just outside of the vast expanse, and Variel muttered a few words under her breath. A door appeared. Before Variel muttered to herself, there had been nothing but a forest clearing, but when Aurelia went through the door, a cottage appeared. The woman obviously used wards to camouflage her home from unwanted visitors, but they were unlike the ones the Aegricians used. The air did not warble as they entered. Had it not been for the home appearing out of thin air, she would not have even realized they passed through a magical barrier.

"Let's get her inside," Variel said as she opened the door to her cottage. "What happened to her?" The last question was directed at Cristos, and all of Exie's companions listened intently. They wondered the same for days now.

"She took a beating." Cristos set Exie down on a plush brown sofa against the far wall. "I think the Warbotach general used his abilities on her and choked her aura, or something like it. I don't know much about their powers, but that's what I gleaned from their conversations."

Variel nodded curtly and leaned over to examine the injured woman. "Get these ladies some food and show them where to clean up. Give them clothes from my chambers." Cristos nodded and faced them.

"This way," he said, pointing to a door at the back of the room. Aurelia could not take her eyes off the male as she walked beside him. His face, which was so severe back in Norithae, softened and filled with kindness as soon as they entered Variel's sanctuary. She didn't think he could become any more appealing to her, but he did somehow. Her heart fluttered dangerously as his gentle expression made something blossom inside of her.

She mentally shook herself, focusing on more pressing matters—like getting clean. The door led to a bedroom with a large soaking tub in the corner.

"I'll heat some water." Cristos grabbed the two buckets next to the tub. "There are clothes in the chest at the foot of the bed. I'll be right back." He left the bedroom, and the four women stared at each other, still not quite believing the events that had led them there.

Part of Aurelia still wasn't sure their escape was real. If not for the gnawing hunger and muscle fatigue, she would have easily believed it was all a dream.

"So, what do the three of you think about Cristos?" Aurelia asked as she opened the wooden trunk and carefully riffled through its contents. She found a tunic and trousers, holding them against her body to make sure they would fit. They were a bit large, but they would have to do. She tucked them under her arm and turned to face her friends. Holera didn't answer as she approached the basin, using the cold water within to splash her face.

"It is so obvious that you have a crush on him, Lia." Septima's mischievous smile made Aurelia blush. She gave a dramatic gasp, trying to pretend her sister's observation was inaccurate. She was not wholly convinced he was their friend yet. He had been a part of the group who captured them, after all. She could not deny how she felt when she looked at him, but she was not quite ready to admit it out loud.

A light tap sounded before Cristos walked in, carrying a steaming bucket of water in each hand. Aurelia tried to force back her flush as her companions' bore holes into him with their intense stares. He crossed the room, muscles flexing under the weight of the buckets, and poured the hot water into the tub.

She could tell he was trying to pretend he didn't feel their eyes on him, but his wings tucked tighter against his back like he was trying to make himself small. When his back was to them, Septima made kissing faces in the air, providing much needed comic relief. Aurelia covered her mouth to muffle her giggle.

"I'll check with Variel for more blankets and bedrolls, and light a fire in the grate," he said as he set the buckets down. "It's best for you all to get some sleep tonight. One of you should return to your camp tomorrow to update your people. The rest of us will remain here until your friend is able to travel."

"Will she be okay?" Septima asked. Her concern for Exie was clear in her tone.

His voice softened in response to her emotion. "Variel is a powerful healer and oracle. She is more than capable of nursing her back to health, and your friend's firebird abilities will help her heal faster than a mortal would. She just needs time. Don't worry."

Septima nodded and went to wash her face in the basin.

"I'll check on that bedding and grab wood for the fire." He left the bedroom, closing the door behind him.

"I'll go back tomorrow," Holera said as she stripped off her grimy clothing. Her utter lack of concern at being stark naked in front of them caught Aurelia by surprise. She tried not to stare as the silver-haired beauty snagged a cloth from a nearby pile of towels and washed herself. It was times like this that reminded Aurelia she truly was in another world. The proper, snooty women of Vaekros would never disrobe in front of others.

Holera continued speaking as she scrubbed at her skin. "If I fly back to the sea and head there from the arch, it should be easy to find our camp. I'll let Blaedia know what's happened and hopefully prepare a diplomatic envoy to send to Diapolis."

"It's a good plan, Holera, but be careful. We don't know if Warbotach has men searching Spectre Forest or the skies. They have to know we've escaped by now," Taryn said as she used the fresh water to wash up. Septima and Holera dug through the wooden chest for clothes, pulling out matching tunics and trousers for themselves. Aurelia doubted the clothes would fit, but anything was better than the disgusting rags they were imprisoned in. Variel could burn those clothes as far as Aurelia was concerned. She never wanted to lay eyes on them—and the memories they held—ever again.

Once they'd all washed up and changed, the four women climbed onto Variel's large bed and waited for Cristos to return to light their fire. Aurelia and Septima grew impatient after a while and went to the living room to check on Exie. Variel sat on a wooden stool and spoon-fed the injured warrior who reclined on the sofa. Her eyes were barely open as she swallowed bits of soup.

"There is root vegetable soup in the kitchen, dears," Variel said, not bothering to look over her shoulder. "Cristos is chopping wood out back. He should be back soon."

Septima approached the sofa and lowered to her knees beside Exie, offering to take over spoon-feeding duties. Variel obliged and rose onto her long legs. The shifter prowled into the kitchen, her human body as lithe and graceful as her animal form. Aurelia could hear the woman readying bowls of food, but she headed for the back door instead of offering her help. She walked out into the night in search of their savior. While part of her wondered what was keeping Cristos, she honestly just wanted an opportunity to learn more about him.

A loud chop echoed through the clearing, as Aurelia closed the door behind her. The candlelight from the cottage subtly illuminated the shirtless, winged male. Cristos' tunic was tucked into the waistband of his leather trousers. He pulled it out and wiped his brow as he stood next to a pile of wood he had just finished chopping.

An ax hung loose in his grip as he wiped beads of sweat from the back of his neck. His muscles gleamed with moisture despite the chill in the air. Between the perspiration and the soft moonlight, his tanned skin glistened, causing the black swirling tattoo that extended from his chiseled pectorals all the way down his left arm to stand out.

Aurelia's mouth went dry at the view. She knew she should look away, but his body held her transfixed. Cristos turned and spotted her, his ocean eyes holding her captive. A tense silence passed between them. She didn't know how to explain why she sought him out. She couldn't very well tell him she had come outside just to speak to him and ended up gawking instead. His intense stare drifted down the length of her, returning the favor. Her entire body heated at his gaze, although She knew the borrowed clothes did nothing for her figure. She suddenly felt far too hot for such a frosty night.

Aurelia cleared her throat to break the charged tension between them. "I, uh, was just checking to see if you would like some soup," she said as she flipped her thumb back toward the door. "Variel is serving some for everyone."

The tilt of his head, the sly smile teasing at his lips, told her he did not buy her reason, at least not completely. She could feel the blush that colored her cheeks and was glad for the darkness.

"Why are you nervous?" he asked. The forest seemed to go too quiet.

"What? Why would you say that?" Her face grew hotter.

He shrugged, finally looking away as he set another log onto the stump to chop. "I can sense emotions. Smell them." He ruffled his wings as he swung the ax. The split logs hit the ground. "And you are nervous."

She hadn't been able to tear her eyes from his rippling muscles, so the sound startled her. Her mind had been so wrapped up in him, in his words, that she hadn't even noticed the wood.

"Sorry, I didn't mean to rattle you. I'm starving. I'd love something to eat."

He flashed a disarming smile and pulled his tunic back on. She watched panels on the back of his tunic fold around his wings, and she had the urge to caress the leathery appendages. Now that his enticing muscled body was covered, Aurelia could think straight again. She stifled that thought and opened the door, holding it ajar as he brought the wood inside with ease. Before they entered the cottage, she worked to calm the redness on her face. Her sister would read into the smallest expression.

Exie remained laying on the sofa, and Septima sat at her feet, eating a bowl of soup. Holera and Taryn had left the comfort of the bedroom and sat at a small table as they all but inhaled the dinner Variel had laid out for them. Variel shoved a bowl into Cristos' hand as soon as he dropped the wood in front of the fireplace.

Aurelia wondered how the winged-fae knew the shifter oracle, but she didn't feel like it was her business, so she did not ask. Instead, she grabbed her serving and slumped onto a settee by the window in the corner. She gazed out of the pane, looking at the shadowy forest, and smiled softly at the muted flicker of sprites. A rustle of wings was the only warning she received as Cristos stealthily approached from the kitchen and sat next to her.

"You seem to have calmed," he said as he swallowed his first spoonful. He was so at ease in the cottage, so much more than she had ever seen him, and the change enthralled her. "I'm glad to sense it."

She grimaced. "It's kind of creepy that you can get into my head like that."

He chuckled. "I'm sorry. It's not intentional. I can try to stop, or at least stop telling you. Besides, I'm not in your head, per se. It's more like I'm in your heart."

She giggled at his words, trying desperately to prevent her blush from returning. *In her heart.* The words should have made her cringe, but nervous butterflies fluttered in her stomach instead. "Great. Then I'll just be wondering what you're thinking about me and my emotions."

"It's not anything bad, I assure you."

His smile was sheepish, and Aurelia did not know how to respond. She did not know what he meant by his admission, and she was afraid to read too far into it. *Is he flirting with me?*

Before she had a chance to respond, Septima approached her from behind. "Holera said she's leaving tomorrow. Any idea how long we will be here?"

Aurelia's frazzled mind took a moment to realize her sister was speaking to Cristos and not her. He shrugged.

"It's hard to say. It depends on Exie's recovery time. We will leave as soon as she can travel, either on foot or in her phoenix form. Traveling by air would be the fastest, but it takes a great deal of physical strength and energy for her to shift. I doubt she will be able to do that for a few days, at least."

Septima nodded and squeezed her butt into the small amount of space between the two. Cristos excused himself, giving her more room to sit. He returned to the kitchen, where Variel and the others were cleaning up. Aurelia glanced over her shoulder at the sleeping warrior on the sofa.

"How's Exie feeling?" she asked. Septima's eyes had glazed over, and she did not know if it was because of exhaustion or sadness.

"She's weak, but not in much pain anymore. She needs to rest. I'm going to make a bed on the floor next to her for tonight. I don't want her to be left alone."

"Won't Variel be watching over her?"

"She will, but Exie doesn't know her. I don't want to leave her without a familiar face. Where is everyone else going to sleep?"

Aurelia shrugged. She had not even thought about where they or Cristos would sleep in the two-bedroom cottage. "That's a good question. The property seems heavily warded, but I assume someone will still stand watch while the others sleep. I guess whoever sleeps first will lie down in bedrolls and blankets wherever they can."

Septima patted Aurelia on the shoulder and stood up. "Well, I'm exhausted. I'm going to get ready for bed. Get some rest, Lia. I have a feeling we won't have time to sleep soon enough. We should get it while we can."

Aurelia nodded. "You too."

Chapter Twenty-Two

Aegricia

A glass vase hit the stone wall and shattered. Uldon paced angrily while Ezio cowered on the other side of the table.

"How did they lose them?" Uldon roared, spittle flying from his mouth as he yelled. The tenuous restraint he had over his temper snapped. His face flushed a violent crimson, making the scars on his face more pronounced. Ezio took a step back, trembling in fear.

"Someone helped them escape, sire. Humbert is not sure who aided them or how they managed it yet, but we believe it was a Norithaean." Ezio hated having to be the one to share such news. With the fitful state the king was in, he was just thankful it was the vase that smashed against the wall and not his head. He didn't so much as take a breath, scared to become the next target, as Uldon swiped everything off his desk in a fit of rage. An inkwell collided with the wall, splattering blood colored ink everywhere. Papers crumpled and scattered all over the floor, books fell open, faced down with crumpled pages, and a delirious part of Ezio wanted to sigh. That would not be fun for him to clean up and organize later.

"Bring me the queen." Uldon spoke in a level tone, his wrath disappearing in an instant, as he perched on his ornate wooden throne. The rapid switch in temperament was startling and made the king appear unhinged even to his own advisor.

Ezio bowed low, his eyes fixated on his feet, and left the room.

Uldon tapped his scarred fingers on the armrest. His blood boiled. Time was running out. Soon *she* would come for him. If he did not achieve her goals... if he did not find a way to cross that portal—he couldn't bear to finish the thought. A ragged breath escaped him.

The wooden door creaked open, and the crimson-haired queen was shoved inside. Otera's nostrils flared in outrage when she saw him sitting on her throne. Her emerald dress was ripped and stained, and her bare feet were calloused and filthy. He smirked, reveling in her pitiful state. It only made the fire in her eyes brighten.

"Get out of my throne," she snarled. Her voice was much fiercer than her destitute appearance.

Uldon chuckled. He slid his dirty hand across the polished wood. She watched every movement as though she could will his hand away. "I rather like this chair. I was thinking of taking it with me when I cross the Marella portal."

Heat seemed to radiate from the queen. She took a shackled step forward, but the nameless guard yanked her back by her chains, causing her to fall to her knees. She hissed. "You will never cross that portal."

Uldon gave a careless flick of his wrist. "It's only a matter of time. We captured your commander in the Spectre Forest, as well as several of her companions."

Otera's freckled face blanched at his words, but she schooled her expression. Her eyes flitted around the room, surveying her surroundings, before she laughed. "You lie. If you captured my commander, then why did you throw a tantrum and destroy my chambers?"

Uldon snarled like a ferocious beast as he surged to his feet. He barreled forward, his heavy stomps echoing throughout the room. He gripped the queen's face roughly, his fingers digging into her cheeks as he forced her to look into his eyes. "You forget yourself, prisoner. You no longer rule Aegricia. *I do*. These are *my* chambers. Your little bitch and her band of misfit warriors may have escaped, but it won't be for long. We will find them again, and when we do, my men will bring them here so I can kill them in front of you."

Chapter Twenty-Three

Spectre Forest

A *single flame blinked in and out of existence. It called to her,*
beckoning her forward, but disappeared every time she took
a step toward it. She paused and took a deep breath, blowing it out
slowly, and rubbed her palms across her eyes. How was she supposed
to reach it if it kept vanishing? The light flickered again, but before
she could attempt to approach again, a face appeared behind it.

Aurelia's sleep was restless, but everyone had managed to grab a
few hours of the rest their bodies so desperately needed. Cristos
offered to take the first watch, which he did from the roof of the
cottage. Part of Aurelia wanted to spend the watch with him, to
find out more about him and his thoughts about her, but she had
no way to get onto the roof without asking him to carry her, and
she didn't have that much nerve.

Taryn took the second watch, also from the roof. Aurelia watched from the back door as she shifted into her phoenix form in the forest behind the cottage. The burst of fire she gave off had given Aurelia a brief reprieve from the cold.

Holera had shifted and left the protective space of the cottage to return to their camp well before the break of first light. Aurelia hoped with everything she had that the warrior would find it. After being gone for so long, the protective wards would make locating it difficult, but she knew Holera would not give up until she did. She had no doubt about that.

When Aurelia left the bedroom in the morning, Exie was sitting up on the sofa. Septima sat next to Exie as they ate a bowl of what looked like porridge. The pair glanced up at her as she trudged into the living room. Taryn passed out immediately after her hours' long watch ended and was still sleeping on a bedroll in the bedroom's corner. The oracle had risen with the sun and was busying herself around the kitchen. Cristos was awake as well, seated at the table. He and Variel were deep in hushed conversation. Aurelia was not sure where the fae male had slept, but she only ever saw him enter the bedroom to add more wood to the fire.

"Good morning," he called out, as Aurelia approached. "Would you like tea?"

Aurelia regretted not checking the mirror before leaving the darkened room when she noticed Variel eyeing her hair. She passed her hands over her crimson locks and nodded. "Tea sounds great. Thank you."

She headed for the kettle, but Cristos beat her to it. He filled a steaming mug and placed it in front of the seat next to him.

"How did you sleep?" he asked. Her heart fluttered as she admired how much his face had changed since leaving Norithae. The worries of the world had melted away, taking the hardened mask he'd worn with them. Their reprieve was only temporary, but being away from the palace by the sea, and the scar-faced men who now controlled it, did wonders for his mood.

"Good, and you?" She lowered herself into the chair next to him. She could not help but meet his sparkling blue eyes. He smiled.

"I got a few hours." He gestured to the space near the side of the fireplace, across the room from Septima and Exie. His leathery black wings were tucked in tight against his back, almost as though they were too big to stretch in the limited space. She had the burning desire to touch them, but did not dare to act on it. Still, she couldn't help but wonder what they looked like in action. She had never seen anyone quite like him. He fascinated her.

Variel placed a bowl of porridge in front of Aurelia and went to check on Exie, leaving them alone in the kitchen. Aurelia's chest tightened.

"Why are you nervous again?" he asked. His expression was mischievous, with a touch of genuine concern. She didn't know him well enough to guess at what he was thinking. She blushed.

"I am not." She sounded more defensive than she intended. He glanced side-long at her, and it was obvious he knew she was lying.

"If you say so. I'm just here to help." He rose from the table and washed his dishes before he returned his eyes to her. "Well, I am going to go hunting. Variel will need help to feed all of us."

Aurelia jumped to her feet with more enthusiasm than was warranted. He had a way of making her more awkward than she had ever been. "Can I come with you? Exie taught me how to hunt. I may go crazy if I stay inside all day."

He watched her for a moment, an eyebrow arched in amusement. "Okay, as long as you stay out of trouble."

She gasped dramatically, placing a hand on her heart as she feigned offense. "I never get into trouble."

"Did I not just break you out of prison?" His smile was incredulous.

"Okay, well, captivity notwithstanding, I never get into trouble." She rolled her eyes, bringing a chuckle out of him.

"You should probably get bundled up before we set out. It's quite cold beyond the wards."

Aurelia drained the rest of her tea, washed the mug, and sauntered into the bedroom, quietly closing the door behind her. Taryn still slept soundly. Aurelia glanced at the commander as she pulled a cloak out of the wooden chest and then laced up her boots. She did her best not to wake the warrior as she left the room, closing the door as quietly as she could.

Cristos was waiting for her when she exited the bedroom. He leaned against the door frame with his hands in his pockets, a bow and quiver filled with arrows already strapped over his shoulder. A sword ran down the length of his spine, its hilt peeking out between his folded wings.

"Here you go," he said, handing her the bow and quiver. "Let's make this a competition, although we will have to negotiate the prizes. We will see who can bring home our dinner." He flashed a cheeky grin.

She reached for the weapon, and her heart flipped. He *was* flirting with her.

"Be careful," Septima said when they made their way to the back door. Aurelia promised she would, and waved to her sister before they exited.

The snow had stopped falling, but it was still freezing outside. Aurelia pulled her leather gloves higher and tucked them into the long sleeves of her tunic. Cristos' sandalwood and spice scent was carried upon the wind, caressing her nose as she walked behind him. She could not help but to inhale deeply, reveling in his scent. She was in trouble, and she knew it.

"You're being quiet today." His voice was so low she had to strain her ears to make out what he said.

"Aren't we supposed to be quiet, so we don't scare the game away?"

"In theory, yes, but I haven't been able to speak to many people since Warbotach took over my kingdom. I guess I'm just desperate for interaction."

"So, you're only talking to me because you're desperate?" Her tone was light and teasing, but his words did hurt a bit.

He stopped walking and looked over his shoulder at her. Aurelia was not expecting the sudden stop and nearly ran into his back. She may have wanted to touch his wings, but she didn't want to smack face-first into them. "That's not what I meant. It's just that... Look, you are not the only one who is nervous."

She swallowed, finding it hard to meet his gaze. "Why would you be nervous?" She was almost too scared to ask. She had some experience with men, but not nearly enough. She certainly had no experience with gorgeous winged fae.

He faced forward and began walking again, but she could see the pointed tips of his ears flush red as he spoke. "It's not every day that a beautiful woman drops into my life, and I have to risk everything to save her."

Her heart hammered at a dangerous cadence at his admission. "Well, you didn't have to save us." She wanted to smack her palm to her forehead. *Smooth, Aurelia. What a way to ruin a compliment.*

He stopped and turned around. Aurelia was prepared this time and stopped to avoid running into him. "You have no idea how untrue that is. I absolutely had to save you."

"Thank you." It was all Aurelia could say. She knew it wasn't enough to repay him, but she had nothing else to offer.

He smiled softly. "You're welcome."

They crept through the forest in silence for a while. She kept pace behind him, surprised she could keep up after being imprisoned for so long, and watched him as he moved through the trees. She focused on how his wings were folded, and how his backside filled out his leather trousers. She tried to force her eyes on something else, anything else, but it was an impossible feat. Aurelia knew she should be searching for prey, but she couldn't think about anything other than the man in front of her. His scent and the way his muscles bunched and flexed as he moved seemed to taunt her.

Eventually, she had to stop ogling and watch her footing as they traversed a denser part of the forest. Taking the road would have made for easier passage, but it wasn't safe to travel where Warbotach could easily find them. The trees continued to grow closer together until they reached a stream smaller than the one she'd hunted near before. The forest opened up, creating a small glade around the water. Cristos placed protective wards around them. Being protected from Warbotach's eyes made her feel more at ease. Remaining unseen in their blind, which was nothing more than a copse of trees and shrubs, was an added benefit. Behind the blind, they sat on the ground and fixated on the stream as they waited quietly for their prey to appear.

Aurelia chewed on her fingernails. "What you said back there... Did you mean it?"

"Of course, I did. Why do you ask?"

Aurelia's pounding heart made it hard to think. "You called me beautiful."

His smile was flirtatious as his oceanic stare held hers. "I meant that."

The thumping in her chest sped up, becoming erratic. Their gazes remained locked for longer than was proper. Aurelia glanced down at his deliciously full lips as she licked her own. Cristos dipped his head toward her, his eyes hooded with desire as he leaned in. She knew he was about to kiss her, and she was absolutely going to kiss him back. She knew little about him, but she craved him all the same. He was but a whisper away from her when a rustling sounded behind them and brought the moment to a grinding halt.

She held in a frustrated groan as he leaned back and held a finger up to his lips. Her mouth should have been there instead of his hand.

Cristos turned around and quietly peeked through the bushes. Even though the animal could not see them, they had to take care to prevent it from hearing or smelling them.

A snow-white stag gingerly approached the stream and dropped its head to the water for a drink. Aurelia notched an arrow, but Cristos held up his arm to stop her and motioned for her to take a closer look. She leaned forward, her cheek nearly touching his. When the deer turned to glance at her, its antlers burst into flames, but no harm came to the animal. The site was breathtaking. Wide-eyed, she lowered her bow.

"It's a Ceryneian deer," he whispered. His warm breath caressed the shell of her ear and her body came alive. Shivers raced through her as the desire she'd felt when he nearly kissed her reared again. "They are sacred. The antlers flame when it feels threatened."

She nodded and ducked back behind the bushes as she tried to get a handle on her lust. She fixated on the majestic creature, a stunning distraction, until it galloped away.

"It was beautiful," she said. He nodded. "Are there many of them?"

"No. Some people go their whole lives without seeing one. I think we can consider our experience to be a good omen."

She smirked. "We could use some good luck."

"I agree. Hopefully, we will get lucky by bringing home dinner tonight."

Seeing the Ceryneian deer was not precisely the way Aurelia wanted to get lucky, but she kept those thoughts to herself as she shifted away from the tempting man. She didn't know what came over her, but she knew she was toeing a fine line with Cristos. While the attraction was intense, she wanted to get to know him better before she decided she was ready to, or if she even should, cross that line.

They watched the stream for a few more hours, but had no other animal visitors. Aurelia was beginning to lose hope when a branch snapped to the left of their blind. She peeked through the brush and spotted a wild pig sniffing around a cluster of leaves. Cristos nodded, and that was all the confirmation she needed. She notched her arrow, lined up her shot, and downed the wild pig on the first try.

It was not Aurelia's first kill, but it still filled her with grief and shame. She was thankful that the animal's last breath came quick, relieved that it did not suffer, at least. They had to eat, and she needed to be able to take care of herself and her friends, but that didn't make it any easier to take an innocent life.

"Excellent shot!" Cristos cheered. He turned to crawl out of the blind but halted, his wings fluttering gently at his back. He faced Aurelia, grabbing her hand gently. His thumb rubbed soothing circles across her skin as he spoke again. "It is okay to feel sad over a kill, but don't punish yourself for following nature's rule. It's the circle of life. We must eat this pig and it will nourish us, just as the creatures it has consumed nourished it."

His words comforted her, though the fact that he could read her emotions still unsettled her. She murmured a quiet agreement, and he released his hold on her, exiting the blind. Using rope and a stick, he tied the pig up, securing it for their trek back to the cottage, so they would be able to carry it between them. Aurelia was glad they didn't have too far to go because it was quite heavy.

Aurelia stumbled under the pig's weight, but Cristos kept a slow pace for her. When they returned, Taryn perched on the roof of the cottage in her phoenix form, scanning the forest for intruders, while Variel hung clothes to dry on the line beside the home.

Although Aurelia killed the pig, she left the butchering to Variel. The elderly woman seemed to take no issue with getting her hands dirty and happily took over as soon as Cristos dropped the carcass onto an outdoor table. While she prepared the meat, Cristos and

Aurelia headed to wash up from the day's hunt and rest. After hefting the large animal all the way back, she was exhausted.

Septima still sat beside Exie in the living room. Her head lolled to the side as she napped, her uncomfortable position a sure sign that she had not intended to fall asleep. Exie was also unconscious, her head resting on Septima's lap. Neither stirred when the pair entered the cottage.

Creeping past the sleeping women, Cristos and Aurelia slipped into the bedroom and closed the door.

Aurelia's heart thundered in her chest as they entered the room. The two of them, in such close proximity to a bed, felt intimate, even though their only intention was to clean up and rest until dinner. She could not stop thinking about him calling her beautiful—twice. She was drawn to him, and he seemed to be attracted to her, but she didn't want to head down a road that would lead to heartbreak.

She was human. He was not. He lived in Norithae, and she was currently no more than a grifter. She didn't know where she would end up after the war—if she even survived. She led a sheltered life in Vaekros, one where her entire life was laid out before her by her father. Even if it wasn't what she wanted, she knew exactly what was in store for her. Now her future was in her own hands, but it was more uncertain than ever.

Cristos approached the water basin and used the cold water to clean his face and hands. He poured fresh water from the bucket for her and stepped to the side.

"Thank you," she said as she squeezed past him.

He didn't move enough for her to pass unhindered, so her shoulder brushed against his wing. He stiffened when they made contact and shifted out of her way quickly.

"You won the competition. Think about your prize and let me know what you decide on." His voice was gruff, husky, and it sent a delicious chill racing up her spine. She watched him as he crossed the room in long, power strides and grabbed a bedroll. He set it on the floor in front of the fireplace and laid down with his back to her.

What had he felt when she touched his wing? His rapid retreat was at odds with the sexy rasp in his tone. She wanted to know what was going through his mind, but she feared what would happen if she asked. Aurelia wasn't sure what she feared more—his rejection or his desire.

Returning her attention to the basin, she washed her face, and arms as Cristos had. She grabbed another pair of trousers and a tunic from the wooden trunk and changed behind the dressing screen.

A part of her, the part that wrestled with her rational side, hoped Cristos would join her behind the screen as she slid the trousers down her legs, but he did not. She watched him as she crawled into bed. His chest rose and fell in a rhythm that told her he was asleep or great at pretending. Either way, she did not disturb him. Putting the questions she wanted to ask aside for now, Aurelia pulled the covers to her chin and closed her eyes.

Chapter Twenty-Four

Spectre Forest

Aurelia had no idea how long she slept, but she was not surprised by the faces that greeted them when she and Cristos walked out of the bedroom that evening. The sun had already set, and the smell of roasted pork filled the cottage. She was not looking forward to explaining that nothing happened, and that they only stayed in the bedroom to avoid waking Septima and Exie. Both of whom were now awake and staring at her and the winged fae. She was tempted to return their accusatory looks, but refrained. She got the impression her sister was trying to hide her growing feelings for Exie, but they were obvious to Aurelia, all the same. If Septima and Exie were falling in love, she would support her younger sister and be happy for her. That did not mean, however, that she would not tease Septima mercilessly if she made so much as one taunt about her and Cristos.

Cristos went out the back door to relieve Taryn's watch without saying a word. The flush that colored the tips of his ears was the only sign he noticed her sister's intense stare. Aurelia approached Septima and Exie and dropped onto the sofa beside them, mustering the most unamused face she could manage.

"Nothing happened," she whispered before they even had a chance to comment, but her sister did not look convinced.

Septima smirked. "Sure, Lia. Whatever you say."

Aurelia bumped Septima with her shoulder. "I'm serious. I haven't even kissed him. You and Exie were asleep when we returned, so we went into the bedroom, so we didn't disturb you. He slept on the floor, and I slept on the bed. Nothing happened."

"I believe you," countered Exie. "Not that you have to explain it to us."

Septima shot Exie an indignant glare and called the warrior a traitor under her breath before addressing Aurelia again. "Don't listen to Exie. Of course, you must tell me everything. I'm your sister."

"And what about you two?" Aurelia, not ready to talk about the almost-kiss on the hunting trip, turned the tables on them. She would not lie to her sister, but she had no qualms about distracting her. Her lips curled into a sly half-smile as Septima's eyes widened. "Did you truly think I hadn't noticed?"

Septima's mouth fluttered open and shut repeatedly, too shocked to respond. Exie smiled wryly.

She rose from the sofa as her sister continued her nonsensical sputtering and left the cottage. It was best to let Septima stew on her probe—and to flee before she came to her senses enough to throttle Aurelia for asking such a question in front of Exie.

The cool night air wrapped around her as she took a moment to appreciate the view. Moonlight streamed through the canopy of the trees, creating a magical glow upon the foliage of Spectre Forest. Sprite lights flickered between majestic pines and dense shrubbery, like the fireflies Aurelia loved as a child. The only time Howling Forest held true magic was when the phoenixes inhabited it, but at night, the fireflies gave it a whimsical appearance. Drawing parallels between the world she'd always known and the one she currently occupied gave her a sense of calm. While Ekotoria differed vastly from the human world, at least she had some familiarities to enjoy.

This swish of wings cutting through the air, and the brush of wind that made her red locks stir around her shoulders, announced Cristos' arrival. She turned to face him, a shy smile gracing her lips.

"I wanted to go on watch with you," she offered in explanation after a long, silent moment. "I want to be helpful."

The corner of his mouth quirked up, his eyes brightening with a playful gleam. "You brought home dinner. That was quite helpful, Aurelia."

The way he said her name was like a verbal caress, making her ordinary name sound exotic and sexy. Her pulse quickened, but she maintained her composure as she smiled at him. "You're right. We still need to discuss my prize."

"What do you have in mind?"

Her heart continued to increase its erratic pace. She was not an experienced flirt, but Cristos tempted her enough to try. Every time she laid eyes on him, her desire grew. *I am in so much trouble.*

"I don't know yet. Take me to the roof, and I'll think about it."

Cristos looked her up and down, and she forgot how to breathe. "How will you defend us without a weapon? You will need one for watch."

That's what he was looking for. A weapon. She felt silly for assuming he was admiring her physique. Trying to hide her embarrassment, Aurelia grinned as she replied. "That's a fair point. I will be right back."

She hurried inside and grabbed her bow and quiver before returning. He chuckled at her, holding his arms out in invitation. She approached him calmly, fighting back the giddy, girlish giggles that threatened to explode out of her. He wrapped his arms around her, holding her so tight her cheek pressed against his firm chest. She could feel the heat he radiated warming her flesh as his delicious scent filled her nose. He kicked off the ground, simultaneously flapping his leathery wings, and flew up to the roof in two powerful beats.

He released her gently after she steadied her footing on the wooden shingles. "Don't get too close to the edge. I wouldn't want you to fall."

She smirked as she sat. It wasn't as if she wanted to fall off the roof, either. He settled beside her, a hair's breadth of distance between them.

"At least it's not freezing tonight." One of his wings stretched around her back, blocking her body from the breeze. She tried not to make it obvious, but she noticed.

"So," she hesitated. "What are we looking for?"

Cristos' gaze swept over the moonlit forest. Aurelia remained fixated on him as he scanned the tree line. His black hair was still tussled from sleep, and she clutched her hands in fists at her sides to refrain from brushing away the stray locks that fell upon his forehead.

"Honestly, I do not expect to see much. Variel's wards are quite secure."

"How do you know her?" Aurelia had been dying to ask, but had never found the right opportunity before now.

"She knew my mother," he said, nostalgia in his tone. Aurelia realized, without him having to say it, that he had also lost his mother too.

"I'm sorry." She chanced to grasp his hand, but he did not pull away. Instead, he interlaced his fingers with hers. Nerves made her mouth go dry, but she tried to ignore it as she comforted him.

"Thank you. It's been a long time since she passed on, but it's not something one gets over easily." She knew that feeling all too well.

"I understand. My mother is gone as well." Cristos met her gaze. Silver lined his brilliant blue eyes as he waited for her to continue. "I was five years old. She got sick, and it all happened so fast. They secluded us—Septima, our brother and I—to keep us from catching it. I never even got to say g-goodbye."

Her voice, thick with emotion, cracked. He squeezed her hand gently, his face softening even more. "I lost my mother many years ago as well. She was killed by a rebel sympathizer. A Warbotach general killed my father during the invasion, too, so it's now only me."

Aurelia's heavy heart dropped into her stomach as she covered their entwined fingers with her other hand and drew soothing circles on the back of his. He had lost both of his parents in such violent ways. A tinge of guilt hit her when she thought about how she'd left her own father by choice. It didn't matter if he tried to control every aspect of their lives. He was still her father, and she still had love for him. She didn't regret her decision, but there were moments when she missed the rest of her family.

"Cristos, I'm so sorry. I don't know what else to say."

He gave her a small smile before looking out upon the forest once more. "Thank you. Variel was one of my mother's advisors. She fled the capital after my mother's murder and has secluded herself in this forest ever since. I dislike her being alone, though I know she enjoys the solitude, so I visit whenever I can. She's always remained an important person in my life."

Aurelia thought about the elderly female in the house. She spoke so warmly to Cristos and treated him like family. Aurelia smiled. "I think it's amazing that you still have a relationship with her. She seems like a great person."

He nodded. "She is."

The conversation gave way to silence as they both watched the tree line. The fluttering sprites created patterns in the darkness with their glowing bodies, almost like they were trying to spell out words.

"They are so energetic," Aurelia giggled. A group of sprites had gathered only yards from them, dancing through the air.

He chuckled as he let go of her hand. "That they are. They are very mischievous. I think they like the attention. Watch this."

She missed the warmth of his hold but watched as Cristos held out his arm and four sprites broke away from their group.

Aurelia stiffened in surprise but watched in awe as the tiny creatures with wings like starlight landed on Cristos' arm. They looked like miniature humans with slightly pointed ears, ears just like her other Ekotorian companions. Aurelia leaned in closer as the sprites, all female, twirled their little legs, their feet tracing patterns along his arm. They stared up at him with bashful admiration.

"What are you all doing out there, Dewdrop?" He spoke to the sprite closest to his elbow. He knew them. Her tiny teeth gleamed as she smiled at him, batting her eyelashes flirtatiously. She could almost hear the sprites swooning. Jealousy surged, making Aurelia's chest tighten. Cristos did not belong to her, and the sprites were far too small to even dream of being with him, even so, the emotion reared its ugly head within her and left her feeling utterly ridiculous.

The sprite, Dewdrop, responded in the tiniest voice Aurelia had ever heard. "Dancing for you, your..." The sprite trailed off. "Dancing for you, Cristos. Who is your friend?" The sprite turned to eye her. Cristos followed the sprite's gaze, his smile joyful.

"This is my new friend Aurelia. She will be traveling with me for a while." The little sprite crossed her tiny arms over her chest. Cristos noticed, and his smile widened. "She will be traveling with me, along with her friends. Don't you worry, Dewdrop. You will always be my number one female." The sprite beamed and cupped her flushed cheek with her hands. The three sprites next to Dewdrop crossed their own tiny arms over their chests. Apparently, they all thought they were his number one female.

"You are quite the ladies' man, Cristos," Aurelia teased, the sprites' reactions too adorable for her envy to last. She watched the angry faces of the other sprites. He just continued to smile at them. "Are you going to introduce me to your girlfriends?"

All four sprites giggled at her, but Dewdrop spoke. "Cristos, you said I am your female, but Dragonfly said she was your female yesterday. And Ash," she pointed to the golden-haired sprite to her right, "Ash said she was your female last week. Flora even had the nerve to say she was going to be your female next week! Tell them it isn't so, Cristos! Tell them I'm your one and only female. I'm your true mate, Cristos."

He watched Dewdrop in pure amusement while Aurelia stifled a chuckle at the amount of times she said his name. He used his fingertip to smooth back her auburn hair, which had become ruffled in her monologue. "I could not fit in your tiny house, Dewdrop, so we cannot be mates. But you are all my special girls. Can you ever forgive me?"

Aurelia nearly lost the tenuous hold she had over her giggles. The sprites stared at him as he forced a sad but contemplative look on his face. They huddled together in a heated, whispered discussion before turning their angry eyes back on him, their tiny arms crossed over their chests in solidarity.

"We will think about it," huffed Dewdrop before they flew off and darted back into the forest. Aurelia's giggles escaped as soon as they disappeared into the darkness.

"They are so mad at me." There was little more than amusement in his tone. "I guess I will have to find a new female." He stared at Aurelia, a flirtatious grin in place, but she leaned back and grimaced at him.

"Don't look at me. You have too many females for me to join your harem. I do not share well with others." He looked offended, but he let out a roar of laughter after only a few seconds. It was a belly laugh Aurelia had not heard from him yet, and it warmed her inside.

"Will you be okay if I fly down and grab dinner for us? I'm starving, and it's probably ready now." Aurelia nodded, and seconds later, he spread his wings and hopped off the side of the cottage. She waited in silence while he was gone, watching the remaining sprites dance across the darkened tree line. She wondered if Dewdrop and her friends were still angry, but hoped they weren't. They were by far the cutest things she'd seen since Kano was a cub. Just thinking about her feline friend was enough to dampen her spirits, but Cristos returned before she could wallow too much.

He landed with two bowls in his hands, and a fur blanket draped over his shoulder. He wrapped the blanket around her and set a steaming bowl of pork, vegetables, and rice into her hands.

"Thank you, especially for the blanket. It's colder than I realized."

He reached his wing around her back again to block her from the wind. "I thought you may have been colder than you were letting on."

"I think Dewdrop and her friends abandoned the party." She pointed toward the trees, where only a few sprites remained.

"Yep. I think I lost her love for good."

Aurelia snickered, taking a bite of her food. "That's too bad. She was pretty cute."

"That she is, but not quite as beautiful as you." Aurelia lightly rammed him with her shoulder. He chuckled. "What? It's true."

"If you keep flirting with me, you're going to make my sister think something is going on between us."

"Good," he said. "Or is that a bad thing?"

She glanced side-long at him but did not respond. He smiled, disarming her slightly. Any part of her that previously believed he was not flirting had been converted. He was without a doubt flirting with her shamelessly, and she didn't know how to feel about it. She wasn't sure if she should be flattered, scared, or tempted. Maybe she was a combination of all three.

"A bad thing for your miniature girlfriends, because I don't share. But I haven't decided what it is for me yet."

He fixed her with a curious stare and arched an eyebrow. "Is that so?"

She shrugged, trying but failing to look away.

He reached up and cupped her cheek. She unconsciously leaned into his touch. "What would it take to convince you it's a good thing?"

Her eyes flicked up to meet his gaze as he leaned in closer. She could feel his warm breath on her face. "I don't know. I guess I would like to know more about you and for you to know more about me. I want to know about what my future holds."

"No one knows what will come to pass, but we all make choices to shape fate the way we desire." He stroked the cheek he held gently with his thumb, his brilliant eyes so close as they bore into hers. Her eyelids fluttered shut as she nodded. His touch was a subtle hum of lightning against her skin. It vibrated throughout her body, striking and igniting the deepest places within her.

When she opened her eyes again, his gorgeous face was only an inch from hers. Breath caught in her lungs as she scanned his piercing blue gaze. Before she could turn away or second guess herself, his lips brushed against hers. His hand slid up to cup her other cheek, and he cradled her face ever so gently as he gave her another soft kiss. Liquid fire flowed through her veins at the first touch. His simple kiss was electrifying, but it wasn't enough. She wanted—*needed*—more.

He pulled away, and every part of Aurelia wanted to scream in frustrated protest. He scanned her face, looking for any objection—for any reason for him to stop—but found none. His eyes darkened, heating with a desire that rivaled her own. She smiled, feeling unexpectedly shy in the moment, and his responding look was sensual. He kissed her again, tangling one hand in her hair while the other wrapped around her waist to pull her closer.

A moan escaped Aurelia as his tongue traced her bottom lip. Her future was uncertain and there was a chance he'd have no part in it, but he was there now. They were together, and they liked each other. Maybe it was the tantalizing feel of his touch, or maybe it was his intoxicating scent, but that moment was all that mattered to her. She placed her hands on his shoulders and slid them up, wrapping her arms around his neck as her chest smashed against his. Her fingers wandered, stroking the dark wings she'd so longed to caress. He groaned deep in his throat, his fingers biting into her hips as their kiss grew more frantic.

The click and low squeal of the back-door opening forced their lips apart. Aurelia jerked back, immediately blushing, though no one could see them on the roof. Cristos placed a gentle kiss on her cheek before he scooped up their dirty dishes and jumped down. His wings flapped once in what was more of a graceful fall than actual flying.

"Thought you and Aurelia may want this," Variel said.

Aurelia could not see what the oracle handed to Cristos, but she heard the woman retreat into the cottage before Cristos returned with a flap of his wings. He held two steaming mugs in hand and passed her one before returning to his seat beside her.

"What can I say?" he said, blowing into the hot tea. "She's the best."

Aurelia smiled. It wasn't lost on her that Variel treated Cristos as a son. She was grateful for the wolf shifter taking them in and caring for them. They may very well be dead by now, if not for her.

Chapter Twenty-Five

Spectre Forest

Aurelia and Cristos searched the trees for nonexistent threats for the next few hours. He wrapped his arm around her shoulder, protecting her back from the cold breeze with his wing again. Between his warmth and the blanket draped across her lap, she was quite comfortable. They spent most of their watch silent in each other's arms, neither feeling the need to discuss their kiss or what it meant. They were in each other's arms until they weren't, and that was that. They had only known each other a short time, but Aurelia still did not want to think about the day when he was no longer in her life. The impending war made their future so tumultuous that she could not plan for it either way, so she decided to savor every moment of happiness.

When Taryn came to relieve them, Aurelia crept into the cottage. She expected to face Septima and Exie's stares upon entering, but her sister and the injured phoenix were already asleep on the sofa. Septima curled around Exie, her arm draped across the warrior's stomach. Aurelia smiled as she spotted them, taking a careful step over the neglected bedroll beside the sleeping women. Thanks to their quick decision to flee home, not only was Septima no longer going to be forced to be someone she was not, but she had the opportunity to find love. That alone made everything they endured worthwhile.

Variel slept in a reclining chair by the crackling fireplace and did not so much as stir as they passed her. Cristos silently gestured for Aurelia to follow him. She did, knowing they were entering the bedroom together to refrain from waking everyone else, but she also knew the looks they would get in the morning when they left the room together—again. She couldn't find it in herself to care. They could think she and Cristos had something going on, because they did.

Cristos placed new logs on the fire and left with the buckets in silence. He returned a few minutes later with fresh water. He heated it over the fire while Aurelia searched for clothes, hoping to find something that would fit her frame. All the Ekotorian females she'd met so far were much taller than her, taller than any of the women in the human realm. The trousers she found would have to be rolled up so they would not drag the floor, but they would have to do.

"I thought you would want a bath," he said as he poured the hot water into the tub.

Heat rose in her cheeks when he looked at her from across the room. "And what about you? Don't you want one?"

He grinned, and her heart flipped. "I do, but I'm more interested in knowing why you are so... I don't know... excited? My senses may be off. I'm trying to figure you out."

Aurelia's eyes widened in embarrassment at his words, her scarlet flush deepening as she rolled her eyes in an attempt to mask her initial thought. "I'm excited to take a bath. So, thank you for the water. Make yourself scarce for a little while."

He pouted playfully, but leaned over to press a lingering kiss on her lips and quietly left to give her the privacy she requested. She stood in the center of the room for several moments. She could still feel the ghost of his kiss and debated calling him back to join her as she had originally wanted to suggest, but her restraint won out. She regrettably removed her clothes and stepped into the deliciously hot bath alone.

The steaming water did nothing to lessen the warmth in her blood. The desire that began to fill her on their hunt had swelled as they bonded during their watch and now threatened to spill over. She was headed into uncharted territory with Cristos, but she would no longer try to stop it. She promised herself that she would move slowly with him, a vow that was hard to keep when he was in such close proximity, but she would move forward, nonetheless.

Sliding back until she was completely submerged, Aurelia closed her eyes and re-lived their kisses in her mind. It was a danger to her self-control, but she couldn't forget the feeling of his lips on hers. Memories of the way he ran his fingers through her hair, gripping her hip firmly as he devoured her, and the way he'd wrap his large arm around her waist and pressed against her taunted her. Sighing louder and far more frustrated than she intended, Aurelia grabbed the bar of soap and washed up. The longer Cristos spent in the living room, the more likely he was to wake the others. She was definitely not rushing just so she could see him again. At least that's the lie she told herself as she hurriedly dried and dressed before cracking the door open and waving him back inside.

Cristos slipped into the bedroom as she sat at the vanity to brush her hair. "I'll leave so you can bathe in a moment. I just need to braid my hair."

"You don't have to leave."

Aurelia's grip on the brush went slack. It dropped onto the vanity with a clatter that made her jump as she turned to face him. Cristos sat on the wooden chest at the foot of the bed, unlacing his boots. He wore that mischievous smile, the one where only the side of his lips quirked up, and she nearly melted into a lust-filled puddle.

"It doesn't bother me if you stay, Aurelia. I wouldn't want you to wake your sister, after all. Whatever you are comfortable with is fine with me."

His eyes were playful, contrasting with his flirtatious smirk.

Aurelia was completely speechless as she stared at him, but he continued to remove his boots and then his socks. He approached her, dropping to a knee in front of her as he grabbed her hand. Her breath hitched at his nearness.

"There are no expectations," he said. She nodded. "I just wanted to make that clear. You can stay while I bathe or you can go, but either way, I don't expect any more than what you want to give. I would like more of your kisses, of course, but that is up to you as well."

She didn't know what to say. She wanted to tell him he could have it all, have all of her, but she couldn't manage anything more than a smile and a nod like a love-struck fool. He must have sensed how she felt, because he smiled sweetly and rubbed a finger across the palm of her hand while he held it. Her breathing was shallow as she looked at him, but she could not look away.

"Can I have more of your kisses?"

She nodded. All she ever did was nod around him. He leaned over and grazed his lips against hers. Their kiss was slow, but heated. He parted her lips with his tongue, but still did not touch more than her hand. This kiss, where she sat on the vanity stool while he kneeled in front of her and held her hand, was leisurely and luxurious.

He snaked his arm around her shoulders and tangled his fingers into her damp hair as he kissed her deeply, so deeply she felt like she was falling. She was about to beg for more when he pulled away and began to unbutton his tunic. She sat there breathless as she watched him slowly expose his muscular chest, her eyes tracing the tattoo that enhanced his physique.

"I'm going to take a bath, so we can lie down and I can kiss you for the rest of the night—if you want me to. You can leave, or you can stay. It's completely up to you."

Cristos finished unbuttoning his tunic and let it slide slowly from his shoulders. Her eyes followed its descent, and she swallowed hard as the desire to reach out and touch him grew. He set his shirt aside and went to pour a fresh bucket of hot water into the tub, as Aurelia admired him in stunned silence. It occurred to her how unprepared she was to spend a night alone with a man like Cristos. The candlelight licked at his tanned stomach muscles, highlighting the definition, and she had to turn back to the vanity mirror before she gave into temptation. She braided her hair with trembling fingers, swallowing hard as she heard the sound of his trousers hitting the floor. He chuckled before she heard the splash of water that told her he had settled himself into the steaming bath.

"It's safe to turn around, Aurelia. I am fully covered by water."

She didn't think her face could get any hotter, but she turned around, regardless. There was no use in pretending she was unaffected, since he could sense what she was feeling.

Cristos leaned back in the tub with his wings draped behind him as the steam billowed around his face. He looked like a god. Aurelia had a hard time not ogling him. She lifted herself onto weak legs, walked to the bed, and laid down with her back to him to avoid peeking. She pulled the blanket up to her chin, trying not to think about the naked fae a few feet away. She could hear the water splash as he cleaned himself and struggled against the urge to roll over and watch. The more she looked at him, even if she couldn't see what was below the water's surface, the less likely she was to take things slowly.

"How's your bath?"

"Fantastic." His voice was way more sensual than she expected, or maybe it was her own desire messing with her head. She didn't know anymore. "I'm going to get out now."

Aurelia bit her lip at his warning and remained with her back to him. "Do you have other clothes?"

"I brought a few things in my bag. No stolen glances, Aurelia."

She fought a giggle as she snuggled deeper into the blanket and waited for him to tell her it was safe to look, but he never did. Instead, he crawled onto the bed and slid his warm body under the blankets beside her. He placed a delicate kiss on her forehead and laid on his side, draping an arm across her stomach.

"What are you doing, Cristos?"

"Going to sleep. What are you doing, Aurelia?"

She rolled onto her side to face him. "Apparently, I'm going to sleep."

"Can I kiss you goodnight? I don't think I could fall asleep without it."

She smirked. "If you can't sleep without it, then I guess I have no other choice. You'll need your rest if you're going to protect us."

"Please." He snorted. "None of you need my protection."

Cristos' lips were on hers before she could even consider his compliment. His lips were soft, almost silken, against her own. She ran her fingers through his lustrous hair and kissed him back. His lips lingered on hers for a tantalizing moment before he pulled her closer, her cheek pressed against his chest.

He kissed the top of her head, his voice a gentle whisper. "Sleep well, my beautiful Aurelia."

She smiled against his skin. "You too, my handsome Cristos."

Chapter Twenty-Six

Spectre Forest

Aurelia feared she'd be unable to fall asleep with Cristos in bed beside her, but it was the most peaceful she had slept in weeks. When she woke up, however, she was alone. She knew Cristos needed to relieve Taryn from watch in the early hours of the morning but had not noticed him leave. When she exited the bedroom, she found Septima and Exie were where they'd been the night before, but they sat up eating instead of snuggled up on the sofa. There was no one else in the cottage—not even Variel, who was usually bustling around the kitchen.

"Where is everyone?" she asked.

Septima pointed at the back door. "They saw something on watch last night. They are all outside talking."

Aurelia froze for a moment before mentally shaking herself and heading out to get the details of the sighting firsthand. Cristos, Variel, and Taryn stood in the backyard, talking quietly amongst themselves in a tight circle. Cristos pointed into the tree line and spotted Aurelia's approach. Their conversation ceased as she neared.

"Good morning, Aurelia." Cristos' smile was genuine as he reached for her hand. She didn't stop to consider her actions as she reached for him, letting him pull her in for a quick hug. Neither Variel nor Taryn seemed surprised by their show of affection.

"What happened?" She searched his eyes for any sign that they were in imminent danger.

"Everything is fine, don't worry. A few Warbotach scouts were out that way." He gestured at the same spot he'd been indicating to the others when she joined them. "They couldn't get through the wards, probably didn't even sense them, but I think it would be best to leave as soon as we're certain they're no longer in the vicinity and Exie is fit for travel."

"Are we in danger?" The comfort and security Aurelia felt when she woke up shattered. She no longer felt safe. She felt hunted.

"Those beasts won't get through my wards," Variel said. "The three of us will reinforce them, but you all are safe. There is no need to rush off, Cristos."

Cristos pulled her closer, his hand trailing up and down her back in comfort, as he kissed her softly. "Get some breakfast. I'm going to help Variel reinforce the wards, and then I'll come back inside."

Aurelia scanned their faces once more before she nodded and went inside. Exie and Septima no longer occupied the sofa, but she heard them talking in the bedroom. She did not dare enter uninvited for fear of walking in on them in a compromising situation. She knew her sister would give her the same courtesy if the roles were reversed. Before Aurelia could knock on the door,

Septima opened it with empty buckets in hand and bumped into her.

"Oh, hey, Lia. I'm just grabbing some water so Exie can bathe. She is feeling funky. She smells it, too."

"Tell everyone, why don't you," Exie groused from inside the room.

Septima giggled and squeezed by Aurelia to go fetch water. Aurelia peeked through the doorway and saw Exie sitting on the stool next to the tub. She looked so much better than she had when they first arrived. Her swollen eye and the bruises that mottled her skin visible to Aurelia were gone. Aesthetically, she appeared perfectly healed, but her slow, careful movements were unlike the energetic warrior. Her wounds clearly went far deeper than the flesh wounds that no longer marked her. Whatever Variel was doing, it was helping, but Exie still had a way to go before she was in perfect health once more.

"How are you feeling?"

The warrior smiled, but the dark circles under her eyes spoke to her exhaustion. "Better, but your sister is right. I do need a bath."

"I would have to agree. You reek, my friend." Aurelia pinched her nose, making a disgusted face before bursting into a fit of laughter.

Exie swatted her arm. "Hush you. Enough about my odor. What's going on with you and that fine winged male you keep sleeping with?"

Aurelia blushed at the phrasing and covered her face with her hands. "I told you two that nothing happened. Well, we've kissed since then, but that's it. What's going on with you and my sister?"

Exie shrugged. "She's been taking care of me. She's a good female."

Aurelia could not argue with that. Septima was the best woman in her very biased opinion.

"I kissed her."

Aurelia choked on her own saliva at the unexpected confession. She coughed uncontrollably, struggling to breathe as she gaped at the blond warrior. "I figured I should tell you, since you and Septima don't keep secrets from each other."

Aurelia knew her sister had a mountain-sized crush on Exie, but she was unsure of the Aegrician female's feelings. If Septima had kissed Exie first, she wouldn't have batted an eye, but the reverse had shocked her. She wanted to question the woman's intentions, like any older sister worth her salt, but she knew Septima would return soon. She decided to put the inquisition on the back burner and joked instead.

"You kissed her while smelling like *that*?"

Exie slapped her arm again, with a bit more force this time, as Septima reentered the room and hung the buckets over the fire.

"I'll ready her bath if you want to help her undress," Septima called over her shoulder.

"I can take off my own clothes." Exie's tone was firm as she pulled her shirt off and tossed it on the floor. The independent warrior was clearly not used to being babied. "Your sister is such a worrier." Exie complained to Aurelia as she stood and pulled off her pants, kicking them to the side. "Help me into the tub and then I'll take care of it from there."

Septima poured the water in and set a towel next to the tub before she wrapped her arm around Exie's bare waist and motioned for Aurelia to do the same. Exie was fairly steady on her feet, though still weak. They lowered their friend into the water and handed her a cloth. Septima added another log to the fire and then headed for the door, with Aurelia trailing behind her.

"Call me when you're finished. Do not try to climb out on your own." Septima lectured, giving Exie a firm glare before closing the door behind them.

Aurelia went into the kitchen and filled the teakettle, hanging it over the fire to boil while she prepared their mugs. Septima sat at the table in the chair closest to the bedroom, ears peeled for Exie's summons. Aurelia studied her sister for a moment, searching for signs that she had fallen in love. Aurelia didn't know what she was looking for, but her sister looked content, albeit a bit worried. She had not had the opportunity to truly observe Septima since the night they left home.

"Are you happy?" The question caught the younger Vesta sister by surprise. Her head tilted as she stared at Aurelia as if she was waiting for her question to make sense. Aurelia did not elaborate.

"Happy about what?"

Aurelia shrugged. "Exie said the two of you kissed. I was curious if it made you happy?"

Aurelia watched her sister's deep complexion flush. "I care about Exie, so I guess I am. I haven't had a chance to really process everything we've been through and encountered. Our lives have changed so drastically, and I haven't had the time to make sense of it. What about you? And don't you dare tell me nothing is going on with you and Cristos."

Septima knew her better than she knew herself, and Aurelia could no longer deny there was something between her and Cristos. She just did not know how to define what that was yet.

"He kissed me, but that's it. We are getting to know each other, but it's kind of hard to do when we don't even know where life will take us in a fortnight, much less after the war. If we survive, he will probably go back to his kingdom, but where will we go? I can't answer that question right now."

Septima nodded and considered everything she said. Before she could reply, Exie called out.

"Do you need some help?" Aurelia asked.

Septima's side-long glance was the only response she needed. If Septima and Exie wanted privacy, she had no intention of standing in their way.

Feeling dismissed, Aurelia washed her mug and decided to head to the backyard to see if she could help those that remained outside. She pulled on her cloak as she opened the door. The air was warm compared to days past, but it still had a chill to it.

Cristos and Variel approached the cottage from the tree line as she exited, and Taryn was perched on the roof in her phoenix form. The sun reflected off the crimson feathers, making them look as if they were aflame. Aurelia took a moment to admire her as the warrior tipped her head in greeting before she looked back out into the distance.

Cristos' smile broadened when he caught sight of Aurelia hovering near the home.

"Were you and Variel able to reinforce the wards?" she asked. Variel smiled as she walked past and went inside.

Cristos nodded. "Yes, they are secure." He reached for her cheek and she leaned into his hand. "Don't worry."

"How much longer until we leave?"

"That will be up to Exie. We will leave once she can shift. Hopefully, that will be sooner rather than later. We need to start building alliances before more people die."

"Do you think the other territories will help us?"

Cristos shrugged. "I don't know what to expect from Diapolis, since they have no vested interest in the war. Warbotach has no interest in them—at least not yet. They can be extremely helpful if they so choose. We can only hope that they decide to fight for both Ekotoria's future and the future of the human world. But their king is an isolationist. So, I really don't know what to expect."

"What are you going to do today?"

Cristos pulled Aurelia into a hug as he glanced around the clearing. She tucked her head under his chin and breathed in his sandalwood and spice scent. "I would like to spar a bit. I need some exercise, and to blow off some steam. I was going to ask Taryn when I got back."

Aurelia pulled away just enough to meet his eyes. "I'll spar with you. I need practice anyway."

He arched an eyebrow. "As long as you go easy on me."

She snorted out a laugh as she eyed his much larger frame. "I can't make any promises."

Cristos' long sword was already strapped to the center of his back, framed by his glorious black wings. A second sheath hung at his hip, encasing a shorter sword. He pulled out the polished titanium blade and offered it to her hilt first.

Aurelia took the weapon, weighing it in her hand as she examined it. It was heavier than her sword, but it would have to do since her blade was back at the war encampment. Kano prowled in her mind's eye as she thought of the camp. She knew he was probably wondering where she had gone and why she had not yet returned. She hoped the lanistas were taking good care of him while she was gone. Aurelia's heart ached for her loyal companion, but she forced the thoughts of him away as she turned her attention back to the sword she held.

Aurelia admired the intricate blade as she tried to steady her emotions before Cristos commented on them. The entire length of it was engraved with symbols and glyphs she did not understand. She passed her fingers over the engraving, careful not to touch the razor-sharp edge. She didn't know how sharp it was, but she figured Cristos would not carry around a weapon unless it could slice through skin and bone.

Cristos pulled the gleaming long sword from his back. The muscles of his arm flexed, straining against his fighting leathers. Aurelia did her best not to stare, but she could not help it.

The pair sparred as Taryn watched from the roof. Cristos taught her new maneuvers, focusing on how to best block against an opponent on horseback, although she hoped not to come face to face with one during the war. Hopefully, the people of Norithae would join them in arms once battle against Warbotach ensued, but it didn't hurt to be prepared, anyway.

Cristos refused to end their sparring match until she managed to disarm him. Aurelia, always one for a challenge, spun and kicked out to throw him off balance. When his focus was on her leg, anticipating another kick, she swung her blade. It collided with the center of his longer sword, and the impact wrenched the hilt from his hand. His blade landed with a thud in the grass, and she let her own weapon fall as she leaned over with her hands on her knees, panting. He chuckled as he bent over to retrieve his sword.

"Well, that was unexpected." Cristos lifted the bottom hem of his tunic and wiped the sweat from his face. Aurelia swallowed hard as she traced his defined abdominals. He dropped the fabric before he spoke again. "Who taught you to fight?"

She took a beat to answer, trying to forget the sight of his bare torso, to no avail. "My brother, Amadeus."

Aurelia snatched up her weapon without warning and took aim at the hard stomach that was burned into her brain. He expected the attack and blocked the strike with ease. The sound of their blades clashing rang throughout the clearing. They remained clinched; their eyes locked as she further explained. "We used to spar almost every day."

"Beautiful, strong, and a skilled fighter. You really are intriguing." Aurelia pondered his words, and Cristos took advantage of the momentary distraction. He swung his sword at hers, knocking it from her hands with ease. Her mouth fell open, and she narrowed her eyes in an offended glare.

"Hey! I wasn't ready."

He chuckled again and grabbed her blade. He handed it back as he lectured her. "You must always be ready. You never know when an enemy will strike, especially if they are running their mouth. It buys them time to find an opening."

Aurelia rolled her eyes and fell back into her defensive stance. "There are plenty of beautiful women who can fight. I've lived in an entire camp full of them." Aurelia swung her sword high, but Cristos parried.

"Oh, there are, sure. But you are a Vaekrosan human. From what I've heard, women are not taught or even allowed to fight in your homeland. Unless what I've been told isn't true?" His voice lilted questioningly, but he swung low. She jumped out of the way, dodging the strike, and he raised his eyebrows in surprise.

"No, you're right. Where I come from, women do not fight. We are expected to marry and breed. Maintaining a home and raising a family is indoctrinated into us at a young age, but my brother believed Septima and I should be able to defend ourselves."

"Sounds like a good man. Is he still in Vaekros?"

Aurelia handed her sword back to Cristos, her face falling as she thought of Amadeus. Her brother was probably beside himself with worry at their disappearance, but he would not have wanted them to be forced into a life they did not want to live. Still, she wished she could at least tell him they were alive and well. She settled on a bench near the tree line in silence. Cristos sheathed the swords before he followed and sat next to her.

"He is in Vaekros with my father." Aurelia avoided thinking about her family on the other side of the portal since they ran away. Once they arrived in Ekotoria, there was too much going on to ponder what she'd left behind, and—when she did have the time—it hurt too much. Now that Amadeus was on her mind, she couldn't bury the pain that missing him caused. The backs of her eyes began to burn as she clenched her jaw in an attempt to fight back the tears that threatened to fall. Cristos reached out and held her hand, no doubt sensing her internal anguish.

"I never did ask... Why did you and your sister come here? How did you even cross the portal?"

Aurelia swallowed around the lump rapidly forming in her throat and stared at their interlaced fingers that rested on her leg. "Septima and I ran away. Taryn and Exie found us in the forest and took us in. Without their sanctuary... well, I don't want to think what would have happened to us."

"Ran away? What made you leave your home? Your world?" Her entire body tensed at his words, making it harder to breathe. How was she supposed to explain why she abandoned half of her family to a man who had his brutally taken from him?

"My father promised our hands to two men we didn't even know. They seemed nice enough when we were introduced, but Septima...," she hesitated, licking her lips with a bone-dry tongue. "Septima didn't fancy the man she was to marry. She doesn't fancy men at all, but same sex couplings are not allowed in Vaekros. I couldn't let her be miserable for the rest of her life just because my father had laid out our futures for us. I'm the eldest sister. It's my job to protect her, and she is more important to me than anything in the human world."

Cristos nodded and squeezed her fingers gently. "You are so brave. Both of you. I'm sure Septima would have done the same thing for you."

The corner of Aurelia's mouth ticked up as she lost the battle, and the first tear fell. "She absolutely would have. Having to choose between Septima and my father, I chose her. I will always choose her. I miss my brother so much it hurts, but I can handle never seeing him again to save my sister. He is a man, and he has rights in Vaekros. He will be okay."

Cristos let go of her hand and wrapped his arm around her waist, pulling her in against his side. His embrace was so tight, Aurelia felt like he was the only thing holding her together at that point. "You made the right choice. After the war, both of you can build happy lives in Ekotoria. I won't let anything happen to you."

Cristos' words made an ember of warmth flood her chest as she wiped her cheek. It was becoming increasingly hard to picture a happy future unless he was in it.

"And your sister and Exie... they seem pretty close."

Aurelia nodded. "I just found out this morning that they kissed. I'm happy for her."

"Sounds like they are getting closer, just like me and you." Aurelia closed her eyes as he kissed her temple. The ember in her chest turned into a small fire, begging to be stoked into a blazing inferno.

"My father would be furious." Aurelia joked, but she knew the statement was true. Proteus would be furious, but luckily, he was too far away for her to be on the receiving end of his wrath.

"I do not doubt that. But you would have stayed in Vaekros if you were concerned about his opinion, so don't fret over it." He stood from the bench, their hands still clasped together as he gave a gentle tug. "I'm starving. Are you ready to eat?"

Chapter Twenty-Seven

Spectre Forest

Variel was already in the kitchen making sandwiches when Cristos and Aurelia entered the cottage. She gestured for them to sit at the table and placed a plate of food and a mug of tea in front of each. Septima and Exie were eating as they sat on the sofa. Septima flashed her sister a wry smile, wagging her eyebrows suggestively as she looked from her to Cristos. Aurelia did not want to know what went through Septima's mind as she stared at the post-sparring session sweat that still covered them.

The wolf shifter sat across from them with her own food and drink, setting her gaze on Aurelia. "You look so much like your mother did as a child," Variel said. Aurelia set her mug down with a thud as she struggled to make sense of the statement. How could Variel know what her mother looked like? Her mouth went dry as she stared at the elderly woman.

"My mother?" She felt ridiculous for even entertaining the shifter's words. There was no way Variel had known her mother.

She must be mistaken. "My mother is from the human realm. You couldn't have known her."

Variel's lip curved into a knowing smile. "Your mother lived in the human realm when you were born, yes. But, my child, your mother was not human."

The look on Cristos' face echoed how Aurelia felt. Her heart pounded loudly in her ears. She tried to calm herself so she could ask questions and actually hear the answers, but the thudding was persistent. Septima walked up behind her sister and joined them at the table.

"What do you mean our mother wasn't human?" Septima asked before Aurelia could remember how to speak.

Variel arched her brow as she looked from one sister to the other. "Your mother, Messalina, was from Aegricia. She left this realm when the disgraced queen, Joneira, took the throne. She did not tell you?"

Time slowed down as Aurelia turned statuesque. Her muscles felt weak and numb, like they'd atrophied over years rather than the seconds that passed. She stared blankly into the distance. She could feel Cristos watching her, probably waiting for a reaction other than shock, but she could not muster one. Septima's features fell into disbelief as she continued to converse with the oracle. "We never heard of Ekotoria before meeting Exie and Taryn. This makes little sense. She died when we were young, but she never appeared anything other than human... not that we knew what to look for to know she wasn't."

Variel nodded, her expression grim. "The queen before Otera killed anyone who challenged her to the throne. Your mother was chosen by the crown as the next queen of Aegricia, but Joneira stole the throne, anyway. The false queen held onto power until the rightful family, the Lumino family, rallied allies across the continent and forced Joneira out. The current queen, Otera, is your aunt—your mother's sister."

Bile rose in Aurelia's throat, coating her mouth in a bitter taste as she swallowed. "Could my mother shift?" She wasn't sure if she believed Variel, if she even wanted to believe, but the female had no reason to lie.

Variel shook her head and sipped her tea. "Your mother did not hail from a warrior bloodline, and she could not shift into a phoenix. Although she would have earned that ability the moment the crown was placed on her head."

Aurelia rubbed the base of her neck. "I thought the Aegrician people were nearly immortal. Our mother died from the plague. How could that have happened if she were an Aegrician? Would she not have survived?"

Variel's eyebrows scrunched together at Exie's question. Aurelia thought the shifter realized she had the wrong person, but nothing could have prepared her for what next came from her mouth. "Messalina Lumino did not die from some human disease. She was murdered."

Aurelia did not blink as her chest seized painfully. Her mind whirled as she tried to understand. Surely the oracle misspoke. "Who would kill her? Why would anyone kill her? She was just a Vaekrosan stay-at-home parent. Why would my father tell us otherwise?"

Cristos wrapped his arm around Aurelia's shoulders, pulling her in close as her entire frame trembled at the revelation.

"Before Joneira was overthrown, she planted rebels within the Aegrician military to kill your mother. Having the favor and protection of the Aegrician crown, they were able to cross between realms to reach your mother." Variel hesitated, scratching her chin. "I'd imagine your father told you otherwise because he thought you were too young to learn the truth."

"What happened to her?" Aurelia pursed her lips. The backs of her eyes burned. Had her father truly tried to protect them from the truth? Everything she knew about Proteus seemed to go against that theory. Did he truly care for his daughters? *No.* She had to stop thinking like that before she regretted her choice to leave.

"Who?" asked Variel, scooting up in her chair.

"The other queen. Joneira. What happened to her?"

Several moments passed in silence. Aurelia bit at her bottom lip in a vain attempt to lessen her anxiety. Variel peered so deeply into her eyes as she responded that Aurelia felt as if the woman was seeing her very soul. "No one knows. Most say she fled, but to where? There is no telling. I cannot even confirm if she is still alive, but the Elemental of Spectre Forest has foretold her return."

Cristos' eyebrows set into a worried frown as he leaned forward. "Are you talking about a prophecy?"

Turning to him, Variel nodded. "Raging fires will fade to gentle embers, and a new day will make a new dawn. When the throneless queen falls, the phoenix will be reborn from the ashes and rise again, bringing with it unity and peace once more."

Aurelia's stomach roiled and brought the bitter taste back. She tried to swallow, but her throat was too tight. She shook her head, unable, or maybe unwilling, to absorb everything being laid out before her.

"Could the throneless queen not be Otera?"

The shifter considered this, but she shook her head. "I don't think so. The throne will always be Otera's, at least until she dies. She will never be throneless."

"So, if our mother was not human...," Septima interrupted. She reached out to take her sister's hand. "Does that mean Aurelia isn't either? I mean, is Aurelia immortal?"

"Not necessarily," responded Cristos, looking to Variel for confirmation. The shifter nodded. He continued. "If a human mates with a fae, there is a chance their offspring will gain at least part of their fae parent's lifespan, but it isn't guaranteed. If Aurelia stops aging within the next few years, we will know. Unless Aurelia begins to exhibit powers before then. Your ears are human-like," he said as he traced the rounded tip of her ear gently. "But that could change if you came into any powers."

Aurelia reached up to touch her ear as she looked around the room, taking in the slightly pointed tips everyone except her and her sister had. Variel stood from the table. "I know this is a lot to take in, Aurelia, and I'm here if you want to talk more. I'm going to bring food to Taryn and work in the garden. There are some beans I need to harvest today. I'll be there if you need me." With a single dip of her chin, the wolf shifter grabbed the extra sandwich and a cup of tea from the counter and left the cottage.

Cristos rubbed his palm along Aurelia's arm, temporarily pulling her out of the downward spiral that was her mind. She glanced at him, completely numb inside. "I'm going to speak to Exie."

She heard his words, but could not quite grasp the meaning in her frazzled state. With parted lips and wide eyes, Aurelia watched him approach the warrior on the sofa. She was unsure of what to do with the bombshells Variel dropped on her. Septima held her hand as they sat together without speaking. Aurelia was too shocked to calculate something as trivial as time passing. Even when Exie and Cristos went out the back door together, her silence did not break.

"Do you want to get some air?" Septima asked after what could have been either an eternity or five minutes. She squeezed Aurelia's hand and pulled gently. "Come on. Let's go outside."

Aurelia glanced vacantly at the door and then at her sister before she reluctantly rose and let Septima lead her out the door. She was so young when her mother died that there was so much she didn't remember. She couldn't bring herself to doubt Variel's story, no matter how much she wished to. It was too much to comprehend all at once. It would take time that she wasn't sure she had for her to dissect and absorb everything she'd just learned.

They found Cristos beside the cottage, standing with a rainbow-colored phoenix that stretched its wings.

"I guess we will be leaving soon," Aurelia sighed as they approached the unlikely pair. Exie recovering enough to shift was exciting. She pushed the earlier revelations aside and focused on being reunited with Kano. She wasn't looking forward to the inevitable war that would follow their return, but at least she would see her feline friend again soon.

Cristos grabbed her by the hand and pulled her to him. Her head nestled below his chin. She watched the blond plumage atop Exie's head shine in the light of the setting sun as she dipped her head to Septima. "I'm going to take over watch soon, if you want to join me." Cristos' smile was innocent, but there was a mischievous glint in his eye when he glanced down at Aurelia again. She knew exactly why he wanted her to join him on the roof, and after the day she'd had, she looked forward to the distraction. His kisses may not be able to cure her melancholy, but she was more than willing to try.

"Possibly." Her voice came out sultrier than she intended. His eyebrows shot up at her tone and tightened his muscular arms around her. Aurelia forgot herself for a moment. Wrapped up in Cristos' hold, it was easy to ignore the fact that her life just irreparably changed. She even failed to recall that her sister and Exie were only feet away.

Aurelia returned her attention to Cristos, his ocean eyes deepening to an impossible blue before he leaned in and whispered in her ear.

"What must I do to convince you?"

Heat rose in Aurelia's cheeks as his breath blew against her neck. His usually smooth voice had a growling quality to it that made her shiver.

"I'll join you if you promise to keep me warm."

Cristos chuckled and gave her a slow kiss. "I promise to make you as hot as you'd like."

Each murmured word made his lips brush against hers. The flush in her cheeks flared into a fire at his words, but her eyes were where the heat truly shone from. She held his gaze, letting him see her desire. The unease her minimal experience caused her was still prevalent, but it was pointless to hide her face when he could scent her emotions.

"Do the two of you need some privacy?" She jumped at Septima's voice, her sister effectively shattering the moment. Aurelia buried her face in Cristos' chest, ducking her head to hide behind her curtain of crimson locks. She peeked at Septima through the veil of hair, absolutely mortified. Her mind had still not found balance after Variel's story, and that was the only reason she forgot about their audience. It was absolutely not because Cristos captivated all of her attention—at least that was what she told herself.

Aurelia steeled her nerves, preparing herself for the merciless teasing she knew her sister would unleash. Before she began to pull away from Cristos, his firm hold remained unyielding against her efforts.

"Yes."

She frowned up at him for a second, confused as to what he was affirming, before it dawned on her. Her face had never blushed so hard in her life. She was seconds from exploding from mortification. Did he seriously just ask Septima to grant them privacy? There was no way her sister would ever let her live that down.

Septima threw her head back and laughed before saying something about a test flight. Aurelia was too embarrassed to pay attention. Her face was buried in Cristos' chest as she saw her sister and Exie fly off in her peripheral vision.

Chapter Twenty-Eight

Aegricia

Otera's agitated footsteps echoed as she paced in her cell. She couldn't get Uldon's words out of her mind. The fact that his men had been able to capture her warriors concerned her. She was enthused over their escape, but they should have never been caught in the first place. Not being in the loop was slowly driving her mad. What were her people doing that led to their imprisonment? And how had they escaped?

The scabbed cut below her eye cracked open as she squinted in thought and sent blood dripping down her face. Uldon took his fury out on her after her commander had slipped through his clutches. It had only been a few days since, but she began to fear the deranged king. He was becoming more unhinged in his desperation, and it showed. If he discovered the crown in his possession was a fake... The very thought turned her blood to ice. He would kill her. He would kill her and all of her people.

When her warriors fled Aegricia, swapping the crown was an easy decision to make. She did not think he would find a way to bend it to his will, but it was not worth the risk. For now, her crown, the most powerful one in Ekotoria, was hidden away and safe. But she could not ensure it would remain that way from her place in the dungeon. It was only a matter of time before he discovered the truth. She just hoped to have it back on her head when that time came.

She changed her train of thought, afraid that even thinking of her deception would bring it to light. She brought the age-lined face of Bremusa to the forefront of her mind's eye. The elderly woman still lived. She was tasked with cleaning Otera's wounds after Uldon beat her. They were unable to speak much. The guard hovered close, but her friend was still alive and that was enough to ease at least part of her worries. Seeing Bremusa was the glimmer of hope she needed after her last encounter with the king.

The woman was sent to her cell as a common servant. She'd managed to tell the imprisoned queen that while Uldon knew her warriors had returned, he did not know Bremusa's true identity. While Uldon's men scoured the forests for the Elemental of Spectre Forest to help him take over the power of the crown, she was right under his nose, cleaning wounds and delivering meals, as a hunchbacked elderly female. When Bremusa finally unleashed her power, she would not be using it to help Warbotach. She would use her power to destroy them.

Chapter Twenty-Nine

Spectre Forest

B y the time Aurelia ate, bundled up, and joined Cristos on the roof of the cottage, Septima and Exie had already returned from their low-hanging flight and retired inside to bathe. Exie's ability to shift and carry Septima meant they would be returning to the Aegrician camp come morning—if they could find it.

Aurelia eyed the bow laying on the roof beside her. She hoped she would not have to use it on their journey, but knew that a time would come where she would have to use the weapon without hesitation. She needed more practice. Training would be grueling but necessary when they returned to the safety and routine of the war camp. Being prepared to fight in a war was unlikely, but she would improve as much as she could, anyway.

"What are you thinking about?" Cristos stretched his wing around her back as he wrapped her in a firm embrace. The chilly night air completely eclipsed the earlier warmth. Tiny bumps dotted Aurelia's skin, and she fought back shivers as she leaned into his warmth. "You seem worried. Is it because of what Variel shared today?"

Admittedly, she avoided thinking about the onslaught of familial information since she and Septima had stepped foot outside hours earlier. She focused on returning to the Aegrician camp and Kano, as well as her watch with Cristos on the roof, to distract herself. She shrugged.

"I'm just thinking about the war, and how unready I am to fight in it. I just wish I had more time to train. I don't have the mental capacity to delve into the thoughts of my mother yet. Realizing that I never truly knew her is... hard."

Cristos frowned and squeezed her shoulder gently. "I will teach you all that I can until we are out of time. But don't worry, Aurelia. I won't let anything happen to you."

She nodded, relieved he'd dropped the topic of her heritage, but his words did not comfort her. Exie had once said that one could never be fully prepared for war, and that statement resonated with her more now than before.

Pulling away from her just enough to look into her eyes, Cristos took her cheek in his hand and kissed her. It was brief, but the sensation of his lips upon hers lingered, creating a ripple of sensation throughout her body. When he pulled away again, his eyes were soft. "I promise you, Aurelia. I won't let any harm come to you. Even if I have to set you on a perch until the war is over."

The thought of being set in a tree to wait out the war was oddly funny. She snickered and leaned into his warmth. "I know what Variel told us is going to hit me, eventually."

"That's completely understandable. I still haven't accepted that I'm in the presence of a princess. How should I address you? Your

Highness, maybe?" She swatted at him, but he only held her tighter as he chuckled softly. "Okay, I'll stick with calling you princess."

"Please don't," she drawled. "Aurelia is fine. I'm not a princess. I don't know what I am, but I'm not that."

"Aurelia it is. I'm quite partial to that name, anyway."

They spent the next few hours cuddled together on the roof of the cottage, watching a few sprites dance along the tree line. Their bodies fluttered about, their glow shining through the darkness like a promise of better days to come. Taryn took over the watch, and the couple returned to the house. After quickly washing up, they crawled into bed and slept in each other's arms once more. Nothing happened aside from a few innocent kisses, but Aurelia did not want to imagine what her sister would say when they exited from the bedroom together come morning. They were returning to the Aegrician war camp, and that took precedence over entertaining her sister's curiosities—a fact she would be eternally grateful for.

The next morning, they all ate breakfast and collected their belongings. Everyone gathered on the front lawn, and the five took turns saying their goodbyes to Variel. Taryn and Exie stepped away and shifted. The temporary flames that engulfed them shined so brightly it made Aurelia squint. Septima climbed onto Exie's back, and Taryn dipped her head for Aurelia to mount her. Cristos reached for her as she approached the phoenix.

"I was hoping you would fly with me." Cristos hesitated as a flush bloomed in his tan cheeks. "If you want to, of course."

She grinned. "I figured you wouldn't want to carry me. It is a far flight. Your arms might get tired."

The corner of his mouth quirked up, and he tugged her into a kiss. Time seemed to stand still until he pulled his lips away. "I can handle it. I would consider myself lucky to be able to have my arms around you, uninterrupted, for a long flight. The longer, the better."

Warmth spread in Aurelia's chest, something that happened often since Cristos joined their company. Taryn launched from the ground before Aurelia had the chance to respond, flapping her large crimson wings until she had reached the tops of the trees. She perched there, waiting for the others to join.

Cristos scooped her up in his arms and kicked off the ground, followed by Exie. They rose in tandem through the canopy of trees and into the sky as the first rays of sunlight broke beyond the horizon.

The air was crisp, and Aurelia was thankful for Cristos' warm body against her. His sandalwood and spice scent was borderline intoxicating as it overwhelmed her senses. She could feel his smile against her forehead as every beat of his leathery wings carried them further from the safety of Variel's cottage.

"Are you warm enough?" Cristos tucked her cloak snug around her as they flew, trailing behind the phoenixes. Taryn led the group, with Exie and Septima close behind. Aurelia watched her sister lean her head back as she held Exie's reins, clearly enjoying the breeze on her face.

"I'm warm enough. You're like an oven." He chuckled.

"I'll take that as a compliment."

"Until it's hot outside, it is a compliment."

The thick trees gave way to sapphire water as they flew over the Elder Sea. Aurelia wondered how they would find the heavily warded camp, but Taryn seemed sure in her path. Aurelia assumed the commander must be able to track the camp that remained invisible to most. When they landed in the forest again, Aurelia knew they were close. She could feel it.

Taryn shifted back into her human form and stretched her limbs. She sipped water from her canteen before she spoke. "Camp is only a few miles inland. We should eat and relieve ourselves quickly. I don't want to be exposed for long. There could be Warbotach scouts around."

Aurelia followed Septima into the tree line to do as instructed. When they returned, bread and cheese, as well as berries from Variel's garden, were already being passed around. They all but inhaled the food while warily eying their surroundings. After putting away their empty food parcels, the group started hiking deeper into Spectre Forest.

The forest's wildlife made an orchestra of sounds as they passed through. The incessant noise was unnerving. Aurelia imagined what manner of creatures stalked them through the dense brush. The very idea frightened her, but she feared what sounds they could be obscuring even more. What if Warbotach had soldiers nearby? She moved closer to Cristos, clasping his hand in an attempt to calm her nerves. He responded to her nervousness and pulled her in close, disentangling their fingers to wrap a muscular arm over her shoulders.

The further into the forest they walked, the more the sounds of life died down, until an eerie silence surrounded them, scaring Aurelia even more than the cacophony had. It became so silent, the rustling of leaves sliced through the forest like an arrow flying directly at them. The hair on the back of Aurelia's neck rose instinctively, and she knew they were in trouble.

Cristos halted and scanned the forest as both Aegrician warriors unsheathed their swords. Cristos slid his own weapon out, shifting his stance to block Aurelia from the incoming threat. Exie thrust a dagger into Septima's hand, and Aurelia pulled her own blade from its holster on her thigh.

She broke into a cold sweat as they huddled together, watching the trees for signs of movement. Each held their weapons at the ready, waiting for the danger to reveal itself. Aurelia held her breath and listened.

A wet, guttural snarl pierced the uneasy calm and rumbled throughout Aurelia's bones. The forest darkened as if even the sun feared the creature that stalked them. Her hand trembled as she tightened her hold on the dagger.

Red eyes peered through the bushes. The creature tracked their every movement down to the terrified tremors that wracked her body. The creature's fur-covered body was a black void that swallowed up the surrounding forest. Its vicious, fire-filled stare was the only source of light.

"What is that?" Septima's voice shook. Aurelia wished she could reach out for her, but was too afraid to look away.

"Hellhound." Cristos' response sent a wave of dread crashing over her. Her knuckles went white as she gripped her weapon even harder.

The black creature was like an enormous, macabre version of a dog from the human realm. Its elongated canines gleamed as it snarled, the promise of a meal making it salivate profusely. The fluidity of its movements as it slowly prowled from the brush was startling. No creature that large should be able to move as silent and easily as it did.

The beast did not hesitate as it stalked closer, unphased by the size of their party. Her companions huddled close with their backs pressed together, creating an unbreakable center. They did not move as they waited for the hellhound to attack, but it did not strike. A second snarl filled the air and made Aurelia jump. Another hellhound crept out of the brush on the side opposite the original creature, hovering a few feet from them.

"They're herding us," Exie said. "There are probably more hiding."

Cristos pulled his wings tighter to his back as he cursed.

The hellhounds sprung forward in unison, snarling and barking as they snapped their massive jaws at them. Cristos swung his sword at the first dog's neck. The beast was too quick. It jumped back, Cristos' blade barely making its fur flutter. The second hound charged at Exie and Septima. They stood back-to-back with Cristos and Aurelia, and she dared a glance back at them. She could not tell if the creatures were trying to separate their group or force them closer to its companion. Exie struck out with such speed her weapon blurred. The animal crumpled to the ground; its maw opened in a yelp that never had the chance to escape.

Three more hellhounds darted from the brush and surrounded the group as they scrambled to regain their formation. Taryn pulled out a bow and let loose an arrow, hitting one of the creatures in the eye. It dropped where it stood, but its demise did nothing to slow the remaining hounds. They passed the carcass, one pausing to bite a chunk from its fallen friend. Aurelia could not look away from the blood that dripped from the cannibalistic beast as it neared. Cristos shoved his bow and quiver into her hands, forcing her to focus on fighting once more. He raised his sword and charged forward. He swung his blade, severing the head of the nearest hellhound from its shoulders.

The body hit the ground with a sickening thud, its head rolling a few feet away. Exie followed Cristos' lead and slashed at the beast in front of her. Her blade arced gracefully as she attacked, but she was too slow. The hellhound dodged her blow and wrapped its jaws around her arm. Exie screamed as a loud crunch echoed around them.

Aurelia's stomach roiled as she notched an arrow and waited for a clear shot. She watched in horror as Septima sprung forward. She hefted her arms above her head and brought her dagger down forcefully, burying it deep into the skull of the creature gnawing on Exie. The hellhound's jaw remained latched on the warrior's arm. Aurelia stared transfixed as she watched Septima grab the beast's maw and wrench it open to free her lover.

They fell back into formation as they eyed the final hellhound. Aurelia was sure it was going to attack, but it did not. The lone beast turned tail and ran so fast that in a matter of seconds, she could no longer see it.

Chapter Thirty

Spectre Forest

It took several painstaking hours of hiking through Spectre Forest before a clearing opened before them, and Aurelia recognized where they were. A slow smile spread across her lips. They had made it back to the camp.

She and Cristos took Taryn's hand while Exie held onto Septima, and the five of them entered through the ward that concealed the Aegrician war camp. The air that rippled around them was like a welcoming embrace as the barrier let them in.

The moment they stepped foot on protected grounds, Exie's knees buckled beneath her and she hit the ground hard. Septima kneeled beside her, cradling the injured warrior in her arms.

"I'll fetch the healer," said Taryn before she ran further into the camp.

Cristos and Aurelia watched over her sister and Exie as they waited for help to arrive. In a matter of moments, a rush of Aegrician warriors charged toward them—Blaedia, Taryn, Kason, and Holera among them. The healer, a woman Aurelia did not recognize, took charge of the situation. She pointed at the medical tent, a leather bag clutched firm in hand, and instructed Kason to carry Exie there. He obliged, lifting her gingerly before setting off at a brisk pace. Holera and Septima followed, the latter barking her own commands to ensure the man did not jostle the wounded phoenix as he transported her.

Cristos and Aurelia remained with the others that had joined them, unsure of what to do next. Blaedia approached them, looking far fiercer than she had ever seen her.

"Get cleaned up," Blaedia said, eyeing Cristos warily. She turned to Aurelia. "Bring him to my tent after, and we will talk. I'll have food waiting."

The general walked away, her commander trailing behind her.

"Please tell me there are hot showers here." Cristos grimaced as he looked down at himself. Aurelia was covered in grime herself, but Cristos had traded blows with the hellhounds. Dirt, blood, and an oddly gooey substance she refused to identify coated his clothing.

She giggled at his tone. "You are in luck. Come. I could use one as well."

Aurelia led them to her tent to grab a change of clothes and then showed Cristos to the showers. They cleaned up quickly and then made their way to Kano's enclosure. She knew Blaedia should be a priority, but she could not bear to wait any longer. She had not been separated from her feline friend for more than a few hours since her father brought him home. The need to be reunited with him was unbearable.

Tears stung the backs of her eyes as she neared the fence and caught sight of the great cat lounging near the trunk of a tree. His head perked up when he saw her approach. He sprinted to the fence and jumped onto his hind legs in an enthusiastic greeting.

"I'll go in first," she said. "He doesn't know you, and I don't want to take any chances."

Cristos grabbed her hand and pulled her back, catching her by surprise. "You're going to go in with the beast? You could get hurt."

Aurelia snickered, realizing she had never mentioned Kano to him. "Kano is my pet. He would never hurt me. I've had him since he was a cub."

His eyes were still unsure, but he nodded and released his hold. He stood back while she used her medallion to enter the enclosure and close the gate behind her.

Kano rubbed against her legs so hard Aurelia lost her balance. She fell to her knees and grabbed the tiger by the sides of his face, kissing him on the top of his head. Kano rolled onto his back, demanding belly rubs. Aurelia obliged, as tears wet her cheeks. She laughed as Kano batted at her arm when she stopped, acting like the average house cat. She wished to spend all night with him, but the general was waiting for them, and so was her bed. Aurelia stood and kissed her friend's furry head, reassuring him that she would return in the morning.

She exited the enclosure, smirking at the nervous expression on Cristos' face as she led the way to Blaedia's tent. She was amused by his unease. The man had no hesitation when fighting hellhounds, but her friendly tiger unnerved him. She refrained from teasing him as they made it to the general's quarters.

Aurelia could smell the rich stew that awaited them as the guard opened the canvas flap and allowed them inside. Blaedia sat at the table, sipping from a mug as they entered. She stood as soon as she saw them and waved them over.

Taryn slipped inside as they each took a seat across from the general. Her long black hair dripped water onto her fresh tunic as she hastened to join them. "I just checked on Exie," Taryn said. "She's stable and sleeping. Septima entered the shower tent as I left. She asked me to tell you she will stay with Exie in the medical tent tonight."

Aurelia nodded.

The pot of stew steamed in the middle of the table and its rich, herbal scent was mouthwatering. Aurelia's stomach growled so loud she flushed. They waited for Blaedia to fix her bowl before making their own, and thankfully, the general did not make them wait long.

"So," Blaedia said as she took her first bite of stew. "Tell me about the state of your kingdom."

Cristos set his spoon down and took a sip of his tea before he spoke. "What do you want to know?"

"Your king, is he dead?"

Aurelia saw a shadow of emotion pass over his face, but Cristos only nodded once. "Yes. Warbotach installed one of their generals to control the kingdom, but my people are waiting. They are ready to fight back."

"And your prince, is he dead?"

Cristos hesitated for a moment before shaking his head. "No."

Blaedia began eating again, and Cristos watched her, no doubt waiting for her to continue her questioning. She turned to

Taryn. "Meet with Kason and assemble an envoy to travel to Diapolis. Their help is imperative if we are going to take back our kingdoms." The commander bowed her head and rose from the table. She left the tent without another word. Blaedia returned her attention to Cristos. "Get some rest. We set up a tent for you. We will meet again tomorrow and plan your trip to Diapolis. I'm sure you know how much we need their warriors and dragons if we are going to defeat Uldon and his band of barbarians."

"Dragons?" Aurelia blurted the word before she could stop herself. She had come across all manner of magical creatures since she ran away from her cliff-side home, but the idea of dragons was something she could not wrap her mind around. Blaedia nodded.

Cristos pushed away his plate and turned his smile to Aurelia before he turned back to the general and spoke again. "Thank you. I can't tell you how much it means to me, and to my people, that Aegricia will fight with us."

Blaedia gave him a last nod before he and Aurelia exited the tent.

Aurelia shivered against the chilly air, and Cristos pulled her in close. "I suppose I need to find out where my tent is, but I can walk you back to yours first." Aurelia's chest felt heavy at the thought of being alone. The vicious snarls of the hellhounds haunted her. She didn't want to be alone. She nuzzled into his chest as he held her close.

"Cristos..." Her voice was low, but he heard her. He pulled away just enough to look into her eyes.

"What's wrong?"

She swallowed. "Do you think you could stay in my tent? There are two beds."

He smiled. "I'd rather sleep with you, but I am happy to sleep in your tent either way." One of his shoulders lifted in a shrug. "I don't want to be by myself either."

Aurelia's heart pounded hard enough to make her lightheaded as they arrived back at her tent. She had shared a bed with him before, but there was always someone else in the same cottage as them. The tent did not have solid walls and locks like the room at Variel's, but she knew no one would enter her tent and disturb them, either. Not that there would be anything *to* disturb. At least, that was what she told herself.

Aurelia grabbed a night dress and changed behind the divider while Cristos dressed into his nightclothes on the other side. After she'd finished, she joined him on the other side of the screen and froze. Cristos had removed his tunic and changed into looser trousers that hung obscenely low on his hips. She tried not to stare, but her eyes had other plans. As he looked at her, she swallowed hard. She forced herself to blink before she busied herself with the oven and set new logs inside and lit the fire with a candle that illuminated her room. She didn't rise from the oven until she heard water splash in the basin.

Cristos cleaned his teeth, seemingly unaware of just how nervous she was. Considering he could smell her emotions, she figured he was just being courteous, which she was thankful for. Aurelia waited until he finished at the basin before she closed the distance between them. The corners of his mouth lifted as he turned and noticed her behind him. He moved to the side so she could clean her teeth as well.

"What bed should I sleep in?" The question caught Aurelia by surprise. She had yet to decide if he would sleep in her bed.

If she were being honest with herself, she wanted him to sleep beside her. The more time they spent together, the more she wanted everything and anything he was willing to give her. But the practical side of her still worried about their future—or lack thereof. With the looming war, there was no way to know.

"That one." She pointed toward her own bed without thinking. He climbed into the bed, not knowing it was hers. She could always sleep in Septima's bed, and he would not know the difference. That was how she justified her choice as she thought over her options repeatedly. Aurelia swallowed hard as she settled on a decision and climbed into her bed, the bed where Cristos laid. His grin was wicked, and she knew she was in trouble.

Her heart turned into a fluttering butterfly as she slid under the covers. She could feel his body heat radiating, and her insides warmed at the sensation.

"I thought you wanted me to sleep in your sister's bed." Cristos rolled onto his side, his wings tucked tight, and rested his head on his fist as he stared down at her. Aurelia shrugged, trying to appear casual.

"I changed my mind. It's cold, so I figured your body heat would keep me warm. You are like an oven, after all."

Cristos grinned at her excuses, but played along as he pulled her against his chest and wrapped an arm around her waist. "How's this?"

Aurelia's cheeks grew so hot she thought she was going to burst into flames. She tried to calm herself, but his gaze seemed to see everything she was trying to hide. "This is good. I mean... I'm warm. Thank you."

He leaned in so close his breath skittered across her face. She bit her lip, but her entire body felt too sensitive. One minute they were looking at each other, and the next minute his lips were on hers, sending the fire in her cheeks exploding throughout her body. Cristos was everywhere at once. One hand was tangled in her hair, while the other gripped her waist. She opened her mouth for him, and his tongue delved inside, sliding against hers in luxurious sweeps. Her hands roved over his body, sliding up his arms and into his thick hair. Cristos dragged his mouth from hers and trailed his tongue up the side of her neck, eliciting a breathy whine from her. When he pulled away from her, they were both panting.

"Can I touch you?" His voice was full of desire as he gazed down at her. She nodded, digging her fingers into the muscle of his arm. "Is that a yes?"

Aurelia's breath caught in her throat. She licked her lips. "Yes."

Cristos' lips claimed hers again before returning to her neck. Her fingers threaded into his hair, tugging as he trailed his lips lower. He kissed every part of her neck as the hand in her hair slid down to cup her breast. She arched into his touch as she gasped.

Aurelia writhed beneath him, her body begging to be touched. The spreading heat that engulfed her pooled at the most intimate part of her. Cristos untied her tunic and pulled it over her head before he lowered his mouth to her breast, taking the taut peak into his mouth and sucking gently. She squeezed her thighs together, trying to soothe the ache that had developed there.

It was not her first time with a male, but she knew nothing she had experienced before could compare to him. He was nothing like the human stable boy she'd been with at her father's villa. Pleasure filled her, coursing through her like lightning, with every caress of his tongue on her breast. No human man could do that.

His hands gripped her thighs, spreading them open as he settled between them. He rolled his hips and the feel of his excitement against her core made her moan as she raked a hand down his back. He bit down on her nipple gently and the lightning surged stronger inside her. Aurelia opened her mouth to beg him for more, to beg him for everything, when a flash of light illuminated the tent. A throat clearing yanked Aurelia out of her lust-filled haze as Cristos rolled off her and yanked the blanket to her chin.

"Don't mind me," Septima murmured. She stared at the ground, her cheeks flush with embarrassment, as she shuffled over to the foot of her bed. Aurelia did not—could not—speak.

Her sister pawed through her wooden chest, grabbed something, and scurried from the tent without looking at them. Aurelia's heart thumped erratically as the tent flap closed, and they were left in the candlelit darkness once more.

Cristos' laughter shocked her senses and pulled her back into the present.

"Why are you laughing?" she demanded. The deep rumble of his laughter continued as she pulled the blanket over her face and let out a mortified groan. Cristos' laugh was infectious. Aurelia removed the blanket from her head and met his gaze before joining in.

Chapter Thirty-One

Spectre Forest

Septima's interruption doused the passionate heat that enveloped the couple, and after the extensive giggles faded, Aurelia rested her head on Cristos' chest and fell asleep. After her fitful bouts of unconsciousness in the Norithae dungeon, and in Variel's crowded cottage, deep slumber was a friend she missed dearly and welcomed with open arms.

Aurelia and Cristos slept through breakfast. Exhaustion muffled the bell that signaled mealtime, and no one came to wake them.

When Aurelia finally began to stir, she was disoriented. She couldn't remember where she was, but the warmth of Cristos' body stopped the panic before it had a chance to build. Waking beside him was a comfort she knew she could get used to. She rolled over and looked up into his ocean eyes. They were alert, full of a clarity her sleep-addled mind was not yet capable of.

Aurelia yawned and stretched, her body arching against the arm that wrapped around her bare stomach. Cristos' gaze darkened with a hunger that she knew had little to do with food. She bit her lip and looked down, embarrassed. During the night, she'd felt desirable under his caresses, but with the morning light came uncertainties.

She rolled away and slid from the bed, her nude back to him as she tugged on her tunic. She felt his stare boring into her, but she didn't look his way as she fluttered around the tent and got ready for the day.

Aurelia sat lost in thought at a small vanity, wrestling the last of her sleep-tousled locks into a braid, when his hands landed on her shoulders. She jumped, startled at the contact. Her inner turmoil distracted her so much, she hadn't noticed his approach in the looking glass she vacantly stared into. Cristos leaned forward and pressed his cheek against hers, meeting her eyes in the mirror as he murmured in her ear.

"No pressure, Aurelia. Remember, we will only do what you're comfortable with."

Her face flushed at his proximity, and she knew he had misinterpreted her unease. She didn't correct him, though. It was embarrassing to admit that she had limited sexual experience when it was clear he knew his way around a woman's body quite well. The stable boy she'd been with was just as much a bumbling virgin as she'd been. How many females, magical females, had he disrobed? She had never felt the need to compare herself to others before, but the insecurity was there now.

Of course, she'd rather die than say any of that aloud, so she nodded and kissed his cheek before standing.

"We should go. It should be lunchtime soon. We shouldn't skip a second meal."

He dressed quickly, and she followed him from the tent. The aching need Cristos had awakened within her still lingered, and she couldn't help but appreciate his form from her peripheral vision as they headed for the dining tent hand-in-hand. In a way, Septima had done her a favor and prevented her from doing more than she was ready for. Her body and mind ran at two separate paces when it came to him, the former much faster than the latter. Rational thought wasn't something she was capable of when he touched her.

She was pulled from her inner turmoil by the sound of her name being shouted. Exie and Septima sat on a bench near the training ring, waving. Cristos changed their direction and headed toward them with a sense of calm she hadn't expected him to have among the Aegricians. She had not forgotten the shadows that passed over his face when he spoke with Blaedia, but he seemed confident in their camp now. He knew his people would receive their help, and it had visibly lifted some of the burden he carried on his shoulders, in turn releasing some of her own worries.

Exie's wrist was wrapped in bandages, but she looked well. After everything the warrior had gone through over the past weeks, Aurelia was surprised she appeared so healthy and happy. Septima smirked at her as they approached. The look on her sister's face sent a wave of heat across Aurelia's that she could not hide, no matter how hard she tried. Her tight braid prevented her from hiding behind her hair, and suddenly she regretted not leaving it loose. She rolled her eyes, attempting to be nonchalant, but Septima's expression did not waver.

"Well, good morning! Did you get plenty of *rest* last night?" Exie's tone was neutral, but her shit-eating grin was enough to confirm Septima did not keep what she'd walked in on to herself. Aurelia's face matched the crimson of her hair as she fidgeted awkwardly and murmured a yes.

"We have a while until lunch, but they saved breakfast plates for us in the dining tent, if the two of you worked up an appetite."

Aurelia tried to walk away and save herself further embarrassment, but Cristos held her there. "How are you feeling, Exie?" he asked, changing the topic. Aurelia sagged in relief, grateful for the reprieve. She was so mortified she had not even considered inquiring about her friend.

Exie flourished her bandaged arm but smiled. "Sore, but good. I hope to not get injured again for a while."

Cristos chuckled. "That would be good. Will you be joining us in Diapolis?"

Exie shook her head. "Aello, the healer, forbad it. She demanded I take time to heal." Septima nodded in agreement, but Aurelia's heart dropped into her stomach. If Septima stayed with Exie, and Cristos left for Diapolis... The thought of being separated from either of them made her chest ache.

Cristos gave her hand a reassuring squeeze, and she knew he felt the shift in her emotions. He turned his attention to her. "Are you ready to grab breakfast?" She nodded her agreement, still lost in thought over separating from either of the two people who mattered most to her. Neither option appealed to her, but there wasn't much she could do about it.

They said their goodbyes and left Exie and Septima on the bench as they went for their food. Aurelia and Cristos grabbed the covered trays that awaited them when they entered the dining tent and sat at a table in the corner to avoid getting in the way as people dashed about the space preparing for lunch.

She lifted the lid and saw a bowl of porridge, eggs, and a strip of what looked like ham. It was no longer hot, but Aurelia did not care. She was starving.

The pair ate in silence, but their gazes kept finding their way back to each other. The awkward tension that had separated them since they woke lingered. Neither could deny how much they wanted each other. There was something unstoppable blossoming between them, but she wasn't sure if or when she'd be ready to take the next step.

The trip to Diapolis hung over them like a guillotine, and Aurelia wasn't sure what to do. She had a decision to make. Stay with Septima within the safety of their encampment? Or join Cristos and the diplomatic envoy on their quest to the seaside kingdom? If she were completely honest with herself, she wanted to go to Diapolis.

Septima did not seem to need her company anymore, and Aurelia did not want to be a third wheel. Her sister had someone else now, someone she may even be in love with. Aurelia swallowed hard and took a sip of her tea. If it were just a trip, free from the dangers of war, there would be no question. She would travel to Diapolis and explore as many unknown places as she possibly could. She would experience new things and learn more about the realm she would call home for the rest of her life. Adventure seeking was one reason they left home in the first place. But their reality was far grimmer than she'd imagined when they ran away.

There was a chance she would never see Septima again if she went beyond the wards, and that prospect terrified her.

Cristos reached for her hand, pulling her from her thoughts. "What's wrong?"

She shrugged and smirked slightly. "It's going to take some getting used to... you being able to sense my emotions. I can't seem to keep anything to myself."

Cristos chuckled as he squeezed her hand gently. "I don't need to rely on my senses to read you. You make faces when you're thinking—adorable faces."

Aurelia blushed, and she wondered how her face was not permanently stained red yet. "What kinds of faces?"

He reached out and touched her nose. "Well, for one, you scrunch your nose." She swatted at his hand, and he chuckled again. "What's on your mind?"

"I was just thinking about Diapolis."

Cristos' face softened, and he reached for the other hand, holding it across the table. "Are you trying to decide whether you will come?"

She nodded, fixating on their clasped hands to avoid his stare. His sun-kissed hands were so much larger than hers. "I want to be with you." She hesitated, threading their fingers together. "But I've never been away from my sister."

Cristos cupped her cheek and ran his thumb across it. She closed her eyes. "I'll understand if you stay."

Aurelia shook her head, trying to dislodge the burning sensation of unshed tears. "Septima has Exie now." She opened her eyes and met his gaze. "I want to go with you. I'm just afraid I'll never find my way back to her."

Her voice quivered at her admission, and she clenched her jaw as she fought to keep her composure. Cristos cupped her face gingerly, but his expression was filled with determination. "I promised I would protect you. If it's the last thing I do, I will make sure you return to your sister. I give you my word."

They stared at each other for a long moment as his words sunk in. She swallowed, shoving down her hesitation and fear. "I want to join you on the trip to Diapolis. I'm the only one, aside from my sister, from the human lands. Regardless of my mother's true heritage, they are my people, and the outcome of this war affects them as much as it does Norithae and Aegricia. It affects my family. Because of that, I believe I should be a part of the discussion."

Cristos tipped his head at her, still holding her hand across the table. "I agree with you."

"Thank you." Aurelia took the last sip of her tea and pushed her tray away. A woman swooped in and took their trays immediately before disappearing into the food preparation area. "We should probably find Blaedia and ask what their plans are. I imagine we will need to leave soon."

Cristos stood and walked around the table, pulling her into a tight hug. Aurelia did not object. The feel of his hard body against hers brought memories of the previous night to the forefront of her mind, and heat swept through her. She shoved her impure thoughts aside and accepted the comfort he was giving her. He did not speak, but the embrace said it all. *Everything is going to be okay.*

They found the general in front of her tent, speaking with three other phoenixes in their human forms as she looked toward the sky. They stood back, not wanting to interrupt, but Blaedia noticed them and waved them over. The warriors left as they approached, and Blaedia passed through the tent flap as Aurelia and Cristos followed.

"We sent a raven to Diapolis this morning to notify King Ailani of your group's arrival," Blaedia said, as she let the canvas fall shut. She led them to the large table at the center of the room and pulled the cloth that covered it off to reveal a map. Cristos leaned over for a closer look as Aurelia shifted her weight, unsure of what to do. "If you fly at least eighty percent of the way, it should take about three days to reach the capital city of Embershell."

Cristos scratched at his chin, obviously deep in thought, as he traced his finger along the path outlined in blood red ink as he spoke. "Any particular reason why you suggest only flying eighty percent of the way?"

Aurelia moved in to inspect the map, though nearly everything on it was foreign to her. Dense forests separated them from Diapolis. The thought of what lived within those trees made her stomach knot and her breakfast threaten to resurface. Images of the hellhound crunching down on Exie's arm flashed in her mind's eye, and it was nearly enough to make her change her mind about leaving the encampment.

"It's a safety precaution to ensure the messenger ravens make it there before you." Blaedia rolled her shoulders and leaned forward, bracing her hands on the table. "Dragons patrol their borders. Trust me when I say you do not want to come across one if they are not expecting you. The odds you survive the encounter... Well, let's just say it's very unlikely."

Cristos made a noise in the back of his throat that was halfway between a grunt and a gasp. "Point taken. I would rather not become a dragon's meal."

He flashed a smile at Aurelia, but she could not muster one in return. Her mouth had gone dry at Blaedia's warning as her heart broke into a sprint. Suddenly, hellhounds were the least of Aurelia's worries. She had been raised believing dragons did not exist, but there were legends about them to terrify her. Coming face-to-face with a dragon was not something she ever wanted to experience.

Blaedia chuckled as she covered the map again. "Take the day and rest. I'll have a map prepared for you, and my people will have packs ready for your journey. It would be best to leave at first light."

Cristos thanked the general, and they set out in search of Septima. Aurelia had made up her mind about traveling to Diapolis and wanted to spend the day with her sister and Kano before they were separated. She hated leaving her tiger again so soon, but knowing Septima would be able to spend time with him eased some of her guilt.

Septima and Exie were still sitting on the bench, watching two warriors spar inside the training ring. Septima stood as she saw them and slung her arm around Aurelia's shoulder, her sheepish grin letting Aurelia know she was done teasing her for now. "What are the two of you up to?" she asked, sounding happier than she had in days. It softened the dread building in Aurelia's chest.

Cristos responded before Aurelia could. "We just received instructions from the general about the diplomatic envoy setting out tomorrow." Cristos sat on the bench beside Exie and pulled Aurelia onto his lap. She yelped but did not resist.

"Are you going, too, Lia?" Septima sat on her girlfriend's other side as she waited for Aurelia's response, but her tone was resigned, like she already knew the answer.

Aurelia nodded. "Since you and I are the only two people here from the human world, I think one of us should be there. Since Exie can't go..." She trailed off for a moment before continuing. "Can you watch after Kano while I'm gone?"

Aurelia bit her nails, a habit she only fell back on in her most troublesome moments.

"Of course," Septima said without hesitation.

"The lanistas looked after him while we were gone, as they do with all of our animals," Exie offered. "I will return to that job tomorrow. I'll help Septima look after him. Don't worry. He's in excellent hands."

Cristos squeezed her shoulder gently, and she smiled through the tears that filled her eyes. "I hate being away from him, but I'm glad he will have you both. I look forward to the day when he can live with me again, like he has since he was a cub. I can't imagine what he's thinking now that he is stuck outside."

"Trust me, Aurelia. Kano is spoiled rotten by the lanistas. He may be used to being indoors with you, but he's meant to be in the wild. He's been given the opportunity to hunt and run around. I don't doubt he misses you, but he's not suffering." Exie smiled as she held onto Septima's hand.

The sight of their interlaced fingers warmed Aurelia's heart, easing the pain of leaving her sister behind. She voiced her concerns about Kano but could not do the same for her worries about Septima. Uttering the words would surely break her, but seeing the radiant look on her sister's face as she stared at her warrior helped strengthen Aurelia's resolve. All she ever wanted for her sister was love and acceptance, and she had clearly found that among the Aegricians.

She didn't expect either of them to find a partner so quickly, but she was happy they had. Now her only wish was that their hearts remained intact as they fought for a place to call a home. The transient camp was not a true home. Where they would live after the war, what kingdom they would settle in, weighed on her. Living a nomadic life was not for her. She just hoped they would survive long enough to be able to put down roots.

The lunch bell tolled, breaking the silence that fell between the four of them. The two females they watched sparring shook hands and left the sparring ring. People poured out from all over camp, converging in front of the dining tent. Aurelia had no appetite yet, but she and Cristos joined Exie and her sister, anyway. The only thing that mattered was spending time with Septima while she still could.

Chapter Thirty-Two

Spectre Forest

Cristos and Aurelia went to visit Kano after lunch while Exie and Septima stopped by the medical tent to get Exie's bandages changed. Aurelia urged Cristos to enter the enclosure when they arrived and introduced him to her tiger. Much to her surprise, the great cat immediately approached Cristos and nuzzled against his legs before flopping onto his back for a belly rub. They lazed around, showering Kano with attention for hours as they enjoyed the weather.

Aurelia wondered about the temperature outside the camp. She knew from experience that the wards made the weather within far more pleasant than it truly was. She shed her cloak and turned her face to the sky, letting the sunlight wash over her skin. When they left in the morning, she didn't know what awaited them, so she basked in the warmth while she still could. It was undoubtedly colder beyond the barrier, and she could only guess at the weather they'd encounter on their journey to Diapolis.

The enclosure's gate creaked open, and Aurelia's head whipped around to see who it was. The tension seeped out of her as she laid eyes on Septima and the freshly bandaged Exie. Kano leaped from his perch at her feet and raced over to greet the women. He clearly missed her sister as much as he had missed her. His reaction filled her with relief. It told her he would be fine with the pair while she was away.

They greeted Kano, giving him ample affection, before they joined Aurelia and Cristos on the ground. The tiger yawned, his giant teeth gleaming in the daylight, before he curled up in front of Aurelia. His heavy frame squished her feet, but she didn't mind. She ran her fingers through his fur, treasuring their time together.

The four sat in a comfortable silence for a while before Aurelia's curiosity got the best of her.

"What do you expect will happen in Diapolis?"

She faced Cristos, directing her question at him, as he scratched behind Kano's ears. Septima and Exie turned their sights on him as well, curiosity clear in their twin expressions.

"As in the alliance, or in general?"

"The alliance. Do you think King Ailani will side with us?"

Cristos stopped petting Kano and glanced up to meet each of their intense stares before answering. "I'm honestly not sure. The king of Diapolis tends to avoid any conflict that doesn't affect his territory. He may be all too willing to allow Warbotach through the portal. So long as they don't turn south and enter his kingdom, of course." Cristos hesitated and began to stroke Kano's fur again. "I could be wrong. The world has never been faced with danger of this magnitude before. He could very well decide to aid us in our plight to send Uldon and his people back across the Undying Valley."

"If he doesn't," Exie interjected, "then we may need to reach out to the Queen of Karinia."

Cristos nodded and met Exie's eye. "Yes, but she's even less likely to aid us. Her territories are so far removed from the conflict. The odds of Warbotach heading there are slim."

"Karinia?" Septima asked. "I thought the only territories here were Aegricia, Norithae, Diapolis, and Warbotach."

Cristos responded. "In Ekotoria, yes, but it is only one of the continents on this side of the portal. There are others."

Aurelia blinked. She had never considered how large the magical realm was, that there was more than Ekotoria. The vastness of this world both intrigued and unsettled her. There was still so much she didn't know about the place she intended to call home one day. "Are there many other continents on this side of the portal?"

Exie nodded. "There is Karinia; Queen Thalia is their ruler. There are also the Inferno Territories. I'm not sure who leads them. They are so far away that I have never been there."

"Nor have I," Cristos added.

The four spent the rest of the day in Kano's enclosure. The sun had just begun to set when the dinner bell rang. No one rushed to move from their sprawled positions on the forest floor. Aurelia laid on the ground with her head in Cristos' lap, watching as sprites began their nightly dancing ritual inside the tree line. She giggled to herself as she wondered if Dewdrop was nearby, along with her group of lovesick friends. Cristos gave her a questioning look, but she waved him off as she climbed to her feet.

Exie stood next and dusted off her fighting leathers before offering a hand to Septima. A bright smile lit up her sister's face as she let Exie help her up.

"Will you be sleeping in our tent tonight?" Aurelia was nervous about her response. She was not sure what she wanted the answer to be.

Septima shrugged, sending a sidelong glance at Cristos as she murmured under her breath. "I doubt I'm the one you want to have a slumber party with, Lia. I'll leave that decision up to you. Either way, I am fine."

Aurelia nodded, trying to play off her embarrassment, but she failed miserably. The blush that stained her cheeks was a dead giveaway. Thankfully, the two women had already headed toward the gate and did not see the rosiness that colored her face. Unfortunately, Cristos did. His grin was filled with a roguish mischief that made her flush darken. He grasped her bicep as she made for the exit, dragging his palm down the length of her arm in a slow practiced motion until he reached her hand. He intertwined their fingers as he spoke, gently pulling her toward the gate.

"Should I move my things to the tent Blaedia set aside for me?"

She could still feel the warmth of his touch radiating from her arm, and it made it hard to think. Aurelia bit her lip as she pondered her answer. "What would you prefer? I am unsure. It's hard knowing I'll be leaving my sister come morning. We haven't been apart since the day my father brought her home."

"That's completely understandable. I'm truly fine either way, Aurelia. We have a lifetime to be together…" He trailed off, his face darkening in an uncharacteristic blush. He tripped over his words as he rushed on. "I-I mean, if that's what you want. Anyway, it won't hurt my feelings if you want to spend the night with your sister." The mention of a future together caught her by surprise. Although she often pondered over the possibility, they never spoke about it. Planning did not coincide with war after all.

She ignored his comment about the future, unsure of how to respond. She simply nodded her head and focused on the matter at hand. "I'm leaning toward spending the night with Septima since I won't see her for a while. We'll figure it out after dinner. If she stays in our tent, we will find out where yours is."

Cristos squeezed her hand in acknowledgement, his shoulders tense as they traversed the camp in silence.

They lined up for dinner as soon as they reached their destination, and Aurelia looked around the tent for her sister. She spotted her and Exie sitting with Holera and Kason. Exie waved them over as soon as they grabbed their meal trays, motioning toward the empty seats at the end of the table. The group was fully immersed in their conversation when Aurelia and Cristos joined. Holera and Kason were leaning back casually in their seats, their bowls already empty. Kason had his muscular arm draped over the back of Holera's chair, his fingers absentmindedly fiddling with the ends of her hair as he spoke.

Exie, ever the extrovert, cut him off and enthusiastically introduced Cristos to him. The two males hit it off immediately, chatting about weapons and the upcoming journey to Diapolis. Aurelia tuned them out as she dug into her dinner. Kason was apparently a part of the diplomatic envoy and would set off with them in the morning. If their conversations remained as dry as the sword talk they were having, she was in for a boring trek. Although, from the way both of their eyes lit up as they went back and forth, at least they were enjoying themselves. Aurelia didn't understand their passion. As long as her arrows flew, her bow was taut, and her sword was sharp, she was satisfied.

As the men went on about the sort of hilt they preferred, she turned her attention to Holera. The warrior gave her details about their mission and travel companions. Their party comprised five people. She and Kason would join them, as well as a healer named Calista.

Dinner was filled with more talk of the impending war, and Aurelia kept to herself, for the most part, aside from speaking with Septima briefly to plan their night. The sisters decided to spend time together before bed, but Septima would sleep in Exie's tent. Since Aurelia and Cristos were set to leave at first light, her sister thought it made sense that they bunk together to make preparations easier.

Once everyone finished eating and cleared off their table, they made their way to the sparring ring. After their extensive discussion, Kason and Cristos decided they needed to test their weapons out on each other.

Exie sat on one of the nearby benches, her eyes gleaming with excitement as she watched the men fight. She bounced her leg and rotated her injured wrist, no doubt itching to join the fray. Holera handed Septima and Aurelia each a sword, insisting they brush up on their skills. After the time spent away from the camp and minimal training she'd managed at Variel's, Aurelia felt more than a little rusty.

She would much rather watch the two handsome men trade blows, but she knew Holera was right. They were about to set off on a dangerous journey, and she could not waste valuable training time. So, with the sound of clanging swords and grunts for background noise, the sisters practiced blocking, slashing, and footwork until the sun set disappeared behind the trees. The full moon shone through the treetops, joining the glowing sprites that gathered to watch the ongoing sparring match. They illuminated the clearing like little floating candles as they gawked at the now shirtless men. Aurelia chuckled to herself as she realized they were all female.

They headed for the showers shortly after, Cristos and Kason calling the match a draw. Her muscles felt like jelly from the overexertion, and she hardly had the energy to walk across camp.

After they washed up, Septima hugged her tight and told her to stay safe. Aurelia fought back tears as they held each other and said their farewells for the night. It was by far the hardest thing she'd ever done, and a part of her hoped Septima would not see her off in the morning. Aurelia already found it difficult to end the embrace, and she wasn't sure if she'd be able to leave if she saw her sister in the morning.

Cristos had promised to protect her, but there was a nagging voice in her mind that told her they were saying goodbye forever. Knowing they would be apart longer than they'd ever been made a knot form in her stomach. As they released each other and went in separate directions, it tightened so much she felt like her insides were a tangled mess. Every step she took toward her tent and away from her sister was like a knife to her gut. She knew she was being dramatic, but the sense of doom would not ease up.

Worries about leaving Septima and Kano behind, about venturing into the unknown, plagued her. She remained silent as she and Cristos entered her tent and packed for the trip. Even as they got ready for bed, doubt and fear continued to consume her.

She crawled into bed beside Cristos that night, all thoughts of the burning desire he'd previously awakened within her forgotten. They laid in silence, but Aurelia's mind had never been so loud.

She let out a loud huff and flopped onto her back to stare at the darkened ceiling. "Tell me I'm making a bigger deal out of leaving than I should." Cristos wrapped an arm around her waist, the small action comforting her.

"I'm not here to tell you what you feel isn't real or warranted. You've never been away from your sister, and that's scary. You left your world behind for her, and now your paths are diverging for the first time. It's a perfectly reasonable response."

"Thank you for being so patient with me." She murmured, his words easing some of her anxiety. He propped himself up on his elbow and gazed down at her for a moment before he pressed a kiss to her cheek. Her heart fluttered at both the action and the tender look in his eye.

"You don't have to thank me. I'm happy to support you in any way I can." His tone was casual, but his expression was intense as he kissed her forehead. "Thank you for letting me be here with you tonight. I would have missed you if I had to sleep alone."

Her trepidation was forgotten as she smiled at his words. She could not deny how much he meant to her at that moment. His fingers traced a lazy pattern on her hip as he stared at her with such affection that the butterflies he gave her took flight. "What would you have missed most? Tell me more."

His chuckle had a throaty quality to it as he rolled to hover over her. He braced himself with his hands and leaned down to kiss her.

It was a soft peck that left Aurelia burning for more. "I would have missed seeing your face as soon as I wake up the most."

He kissed her jawline next. "I would have missed being able to feel your smooth skin against mine."

Her heart thundered as she wiggled beneath him, trying to ease the pressure that his seductive tone was building between her legs.

He dragged his lips down from her jaw to her neck and gently bit the sensitive flesh. She moaned at the feel, her body instinctively arching into him.

"I would absolutely miss eliciting such delicious gasps and moans from you."

Aurelia couldn't breathe as he continued to trail kisses all over her neck. Every word, every touch, held her captive. He pulled away and before she could issue a complaint, his mouth descended on her. The kiss was hard and passionate, but he still hovered over her. His lips and tongue were the only part of him that touched her, and it was maddening. She didn't think, refusing to let doubt ruin this moment, as she wrapped her legs around his hips and pulled him closer. She ran her hands along the corded muscle of his back, sliding them up to stroke the base of his wings. They felt like the softest leather, but she didn't get to appreciate the feel for long. He groaned low in his throat and pulled away.

"My wings are... sensitive."

Aurelia smirked up at him, lust and mischief filling her expression. "Is that so?"

She caressed them again before he could respond, and they fluttered at her touch as he moaned.

He pressed his forehead against hers, his face pinched. "If you do that again, we won't get much rest before our journey."

"Good." Her response was breathy as she leaned up to reclaim his lips. She ran a hand along the space between his wings before dragging it over the base of one.

Their kiss grew more frantic as he ground himself against her. His hard length rubbed against her center, and she moaned at the friction. He pulled away and rose up on his knees between her legs.

Cristos slid his hands to her thighs, eliciting a tremor of anticipation from her. "I want to touch you." His voice dropped an octave, his tone so husky and seductive, she almost moaned again.

"Then touch me."

Her words were all the reassurance he needed, apparently. His mouth descended on hers, their tongues warring for dominance as his hands moved higher. He slid her night dress up slowly, breaking their kiss to pull it off and toss it aside.

He stared at her naked body like a starving man ready to devour her. The heat in his gaze set her aflame, and she pulled him down on top of her. Only he could douse the burning need that consumed her. They became a tangle of limbs as they rolled over.

Aurelia straddled his lap, rotating her hips as his hard length rubbed against her again. Bolts of pleasure shot through her entire frame as she pulled his tunic off. Being with Cristos empowered her in a way she'd never felt before. He worshiped her with every kiss. Every touch killed her reservations about moving too fast. She'd forgotten about how experienced he'd seemed compared to her. The only thing that mattered was the two of them. They didn't know what perilous road they'd head down tomorrow, but at least she had these stolen moments now.

He rolled them again and pulled his trousers off. The candlelight flicked softly in the tent, illuminating him as he hovered above her.

"Are you sure you want this?"

She met his stare, reaching out to wrap her hand around his cock as she answered. "I want you."

She stroked him; her grip uncertain as she took in the sheer size of him. Cristos was much larger than the man she'd been with before. A part of her was uncertain if he'd fit, but she was more than ready to try.

He groaned when she grasped him tighter, and it nearly undid her. The sound of his pleasure was all the encouragement she needed to guide him toward her entrance, tensing in preparation for the pain that was sure to come.

Cristos pulled his hips back, chuckling against her neck. "What is the rush?"

Aurelia frowned at him, but before she could speak, his hand was between her thighs. His fingers were deft as he teased her heated flesh. Her back arched as she moaned, her body trembling from the overload of sensations. Her desire built with every stroke, and she cried out as he pinched her sensitive bud. Before her scream of ecstasy had quieted, he shoved a finger inside her.

She writhed under his touch as he added another. Her climax built with his relentless movements. She opened her mouth to say something—anything—but all that came out was a breathy moan. She tried again, finally succeeding. "Cristos. More."

Full sentences were beyond her, but he understood. He kneeled between her thighs and grabbed her hips, yanking her down on the bed until their pelvises aligned. He reached between their bodies and rubbed circles on her most intimate part as he began to ease inside her.

Aurelia wiggled closer, trying to take more of him, but Cristos grasped her hips and held her still.

"I don't want to hurt you." He leaned forward and dotted kisses along her face and neck as he continued to enter her inch by inch. He returned his mouth to hers in a sensual kiss as he filled her, but once his entire length was buried inside her, he stilled. She could feel her body stretching around him. The pain was there, but bearable. After a moment, she lifted her hips beneath him.

Needing no further encouragement, Cristos lifted her from the bed and sat back on his heels, their bodies never parting as she straddled him.

Aurelia wasn't sure what to do in that position. She'd spent her time with the stable boy on her back. Embarrassment started to bloom, but before it could take hold and ruin the mood, he moved. He hoisted her up until he'd almost slid out of her and then pulled her back down. He threw his hips up to meet hers and stars exploded in her eyes. He repeated the motion, going faster with each thrust.

She threw her head back as she moaned, forgetting the uncertainty that just plagued her. She rolled her hips as she matched his motions, using her knees for leverage.

Her hands roamed his body, and she could feel his back muscles ripple beneath her palms. She touched the base of his wings, and this time she felt him twitch inside her. She continued to stroke them as their bodies slammed against each other. Her release came hard, and she clenched her fists as she screamed his name. She hardly noticed her nail biting into the leathery appendages as euphoria filled her, fogging her mind. Her body quaked as she rode the waves of her climax. Cristos groaned and buried his face in her neck as he thrust into her a final time. His wings flared out majestically behind him as he reached his own release, and Aurelia knew she'd never forget that moment for as long as she lived.

Chapter Thirty-Three

Spectre Forest

Waking up in Cristos' arms, his naked body curled around her, made getting out of bed even harder. She wished they could stay there all day, repeating the night before, but war waited for no one, and allies were important. Aurelia groaned as she sat up and stretched, hoping the action would motivate her some. Instead, the delicious soreness between her legs brought the memories of their tumble in the sheets surging back. She never knew how vivid her imagination was until Cristos crawled out of bed, his cock standing at the ready as he pulled on a pair of trousers. Oh, what she wouldn't give for one more round.

"Stop staring at me like that, or the envoy will leave without us."

She giggled at his words, but forced her eyes away as he adjusted himself. As appealing as he was, they had a mission. The pair rushed as they prepared to leave, already running late.

The camp looked deserted as they made their way to the dining tent, their weapons already strapped to them. After a quick breakfast, they would depart immediately. Their group would have to complete the flying portion of their journey before they camped for the night, so there was no time to waste.

Aurelia was still rubbing the sleep out of her eyes when they sat down at the table with the rest of their party. Their packs, prepared by the Aegricians, were already stacked in the corner when they entered the dining tent. Aurelia packed the knapsack she'd brought from Vaekros with a few changes of clothes and some essentials. She hoped the other sacks had the rest of their basic necessities inside.

They ate in rushed silence before they grabbed their gear and made their way to the edge of the wards near the sparring rings. Blaedia and Holera had solidified their travel plans with the group the night before, so after the ones responsible for flying looked over the map once more, they were ready to set off on the first leg of their journey.

Sliding one arm under Aurelia's knees and the other around her waist, Cristos lifted her like she weighed no more than a feather. Kason, the only other person in their envoy who could not fly, climbed onto Holera's back once the flames that ignited when she shifted forms faded.

The silver-haired woman was gorgeous in her humanoid form, but as a phoenix, Holera was stunning. Unlike the variety of crimson plumage Aurelia saw among the other warriors, Holera's feathers were mostly silver with delicate streaks of red highlighting her wings and tail. Calista rounded out their party. Her phoenix form had the signature fire-colored feathers of her brethren, but flecks of blue and green set her apart from the rest. Cristos, with his leathery wings and dark fighting leathers, was the least colorful in the group, but as Aurelia stared at his bronzed face, she decided he shined the brightest in her eyes. She tucked her tightly plaited hair into the hood of the cloak she wore, which matched her fighting leathers, and wrapped her arms around Cristos' neck as he prepared to kick off.

Kason took one last look at the map before securing it in his pocket. He nodded to the rest of them and pulled on Holera's reins. The enormous silver bird flapped her great wings at the signal and lifted through the tree canopy and up into the open sky. Calista followed, with Cristos and Aurelia close behind.

Aurelia stared down at the camp as they took off, her eyes fixated on the tent she knew her sister slept in. She was glad Septima hadn't come to bid them farewell, but it still hurt to leave without seeing her sister's face once more. She closed her eyes, willing the rapidly forming tears away, and buried her face into the crook of Cristos' neck for comfort. The protective barrier rippled around them as they crossed through, the feeling as unsettling as ever. She swallowed hard as she realized that this was it. She had officially set off on her first journey without Septima.

"How long do you think we will be in the sky today?" Aurelia asked in an attempt to distract herself. She pulled back from him enough to stare at the sapphire waters of the Elder Sea that glittered in the distance as the sun began to rise. The way rolling blue waves met with the dark green of the lush forest was a masterpiece that took her breath away.

"Probably about six hours. Are you already tired of me?" Cristos eyed her with an arched brow. She grinned.

"Not at all. I'm just concerned I'll make your back ache."

He chuckled and gave her a playful bounce in his arms as they traversed the skies. "You are not heavy. Besides, I've already told you before that it's an honor to carry you." He placed a kiss on her forehead, and the warmth of his affection washed over her. "I'm strong. I can handle it."

They fell silent after that, and Aurelia just savored the heat that radiated from him as it combated the chill of the wind that whipped around them as they cut through the air. As they traveled further south, the landscape morphed around them. Palm trees began to be interspersed throughout the evergreen and deciduous trees of Spectre Forest. The more distance they covered, the more common the tropical greenery became. Time passed quickly as she marveled at the beauty of Ekotoria.

As daylight waned, the mountainous coast leveled out and was replaced by sand. She watched as the Elder Sea took on a turquoise hue. Its rising tide licked at the shoreline as the rapidly fading sunlight reflected off the water, making the surface glow. Their party began to descend into the trees below as she admired the serene view—painting a mental picture to share with Septima when they returned. The dying rays of light cast dark shadows over the clearing they landed in. Although they could have easily exited the forest, they made the unanimous decision to make camp within the tree line, using the dense woodlands as an additional layer of camouflage. The men pitched the small tents that had been packed for them while Holera and Calista erected wards to shield their temporary base. Aurelia, unable to assist in either task, gathered firewood.

After the setup was complete, they all gathered around the now roaring fire and shared a simple dinner comprising dried meat, cheese, and bread. Aurelia nestled into Cristos' side; his wing extended behind her, blocking the wind. The temperature lost its frigid edge the further south they traveled, but without the sun, the air had turned brisk. Still, between his warmth and the heat from the flames licking at her face, she was more than content.

After they finished eating, Aurelia and Cristos retired to their tent, both exhausted. She longed for a bath, already missing the comforts of the phoenix encampment. She felt dirty from their hours' long flight, but Cristos did not seem to mind. He adjoined their bedrolls and snuggled against her; her back firmly pressed against his chest as his arm snaked around her.

His warmth permeated her thin nightdress, and the feel of his powerful body against hers made her yearn for his intimate touch. The visual of his wings erected behind him as he climaxed was still burned into her mind. The location was not the most romantic, and privacy was nonexistent, but she craved him, nonetheless. After experiencing the bliss that only he made her feel, it was nearly impossible not to desire him.

"Are you nervous to meet with the king of Diapolis?" Aurelia rolled over and pressed her cheek against his chest as she sparked the conversation in an attempt to redirect her lustful thoughts. He shrugged.

"I'm not nervous to meet him, but I am concerned that he won't help us. I've heard enough to know how little he involves himself in the affairs of other kingdoms. He may decline to align with us, but we will never know unless we try."

Cristos rolled forward, pressing her back against the bedroll with his body. "Let's not dwell on uncertainties. We will have our answers soon enough, and I can think of far better ways to occupy ourselves."

His hand slid between her thighs, effectively ending all talk of Diapolis.

Cristos was already gone when Aurelia woke the next morning. She could hear him chatting with the others outside, but she did not rush out of bed. It would be a long day, and she was not looking forward to it. The only light at the end of the dreary tunnel was the prospect of a bath when they rested in Diapolis before their audience with the king.

She was trying to convince herself to get up when a head of shaggy black hair and bright blue eyes peeked through the tent flap. She covered her face with a blanket as she grumbled, "I'm still sleeping."

Cristos chuckled as he crawled inside and pulled the pillow away just enough to slide his head under it. "No, you are not."

She stuck her tongue out at him. Instead of being offended by her gesture, he leaned in and caught it in his mouth. As he sucked at her tongue, Aurelia found that while she had no interest in getting ready for the day, she had plenty of energy to kiss Cristos. Their lip lock grew increasingly heated, but as she tried to untie his trousers, he pulled away. "I would love to stay here with you all day, but we really need to get going. We would like to make it to Starcrest by lunchtime. We should be able to find horses somewhere in town."

Aurelia rose from the bed begrudgingly and pulled on her boots. If she wasn't able to stay in bed with him, she might as well get a move on. The sooner they left, the sooner she could bathe and sleep in a proper bed. That was her motivation for the day.

Holera and the others were fastening the last of their gear as she stepped out into the blazing sun. They began to take down her tent before she was more than a few feet away. Cristos handed her a sandwich before he fastened his weapons to his body. He caught her watching him and grinned, but she did not look away. The fighting leathers left very little to the imagination, and she enjoyed the visual as she hurried to finish her breakfast.

They left a few moments later, quickly passing through the rest of Spectre Forest. Even after exiting the woods, trees still dotted the rolling hills as they walked over. The group traveled in silence to avoid drawing any unwanted attention to themselves. The second leg of their journey was uneventful. The only other person they came across was a lone man pulling a cart. Aurelia was bored out of her mind, but relieved the weather was tolerable. Unlike the forest that surrounded the war encampment, the sky was clear, and there was no possibility of snow. A cool breeze blew from the sea and ruffled her loose crimson hair, but it was not cold enough to warrant a cloak.

By the time the sun reached its zenith, empty fields gave way to fenced pasture land, and the grass was bisected by a roughly cleared road.

"Looks like a few more miles until we reach Starcrest," Kason said as he examined the map. "From there, we should have time to pass through a few more towns, especially if we can purchase a few horses. If we stop in Claywind, we won't make it to the capital today. Still, I'd rather stay at an inn than sleep in a tent again. Plus, it wouldn't hurt to wash up and look presentable for our meeting with the king. I'm uncertain they'll allow us time to do so when we arrive at the palace."

Cristos agreed with Kason, and the women nodded their assent as well. Everyone was tired of walking and being covered in dirt and sweat. Where there was an inn, there would be a tub, and that fact put a spring in Aurelia's step as they pressed on.

Chapter Thirty-Four

Diapolis

Starcrest was a small frontier town that bustled with activity. From what Aurelia could tell, there were no divisive neighborhoods. There was just a plethora of ranch-style homes spread out across the plains. The hastily cleared road they traveled smoothed out as they passed through the town's main strip. It seemed like the heart of the town and contained everything the residents would need. A small corner store, a tavern and restaurant, and an infirmary were open for business, townspeople coming and going without giving their group a second glance. Going unnoticed was a welcomed experience for Aurelia, and one she hadn't experienced often since coming to Ekotoria. Even in Norithae, where the citizens were too scared to stare at their mobile jail as they were paraded through town, people stole looks when their captors weren't watching.

She studied a few other establishments as they made their way to the tavern, but their signage was not in a language she knew.

They entered the restaurant and chose a corner table near the door, since Cristos and Holera's warrior training would not let them sit in a vulnerable position. They had been walking for hours, and Aurelia did not care where they sat as long as she got off her feet. Her legs felt like they were going to fall off, and she needed to rest, if only for a little while. Cristos offered to carry her, but she was too stubborn to appear weak to the rest of their party. It was a decision she regretted with every throb of her muscles as she collapsed on a wooden chair. Kason didn't join them immediately. Instead, he approached the bar and asked where they could find horses to purchase and a messenger raven to send word back to camp.

When he finished his inquiry, he rejoined them. They ordered as Kason filled them in on what the barkeep said. According to the man, Claywind was five hours due south on horseback, and if they followed the main road another mile south, they would find a ranch that sold horses. He had also helped Kason send a message back to Blaedia. With the next step of their plan solidifying itself, they waited for their lunch to arrive as they chatted amongst themselves.

Unlike the stews that Aurelia had grown accustomed to since joining the Aegricians, the food they were served comprised grilled fish served over rice and a side of steamed vegetables. She did not typically enjoy fish, but whoever prepared it had done a superb job. The white fish was unlike any she'd had in Vaekros. It was mild and so perfectly flavored; she thought it may have been the best meal she'd ever eaten.

After they finished their food, they wasted no time heading south, as they had been instructed. The rancher was already outside, conversing with a woman as they approached. At least a dozen horses, in a variety of colors, grazed on the long grass inside a corral. The man smiled and met them halfway up the long lane that led to the only house on the property. He reached his hand out to Kason, who shook it firmly.

"I take it you are looking for horses?"

Kason nodded. "We need three horses to take us to the capital. Lokela sent us your way when I inquired at the tavern. Bane, is it?"

The man smiled and glanced over his shoulder. "Yes, I am Bane and that is my wife, Kai, over there. I can certainly send you on your way with three horses. Follow me, and we can get you all set up."

They trailed behind Bane as he led them to the stables, and Kason paid him for the animals. Aurelia did not know how much money Blaedia had sent them with, but hopefully Kason had enough for the inn and whatever they'd need on their way back to camp.

When they left the ranch, they did so astride some of the most beautiful horses Aurelia had ever seen. The healer, Calista, rode a black mare named Scoudra, the smallest of the three. Holera and Kason shared the largest steed, a black and white stallion named Tasu. The hulking beast did not seem strained even under the large, muscle-bound weight he carried. Aurelia and Cristos mounted a red stallion called Teoron. He was so large, Cristos needed to help Aurelia climb into the saddle. Even after she was seated, she could not reach the stirrups. She held onto the saddle horn like her life depended on it, which it probably did. She did not want to find out how she'd fare if she fell from that height.

As they headed for Claywind, Aurelia grew more comfortable on the massive animal. She leaned back against Cristos, nestled between his thighs. She hadn't expected just how intimate riding together would be, but that intimacy only increased as he slid his hand under her cloak and rested it on her thigh. His fingers drew small circles across the leg of her pants, moving higher with every rotation, and she had a hard time focusing on the path they traveled. It took everything in her to refrain from grabbing his hand and placing it where she really wanted him to touch. The others did not seem to notice where his hand was, and if they had, they did not care. It was not a secret that they were lovers.

"I sensed your excitement when Kason brought up staying at an inn tonight. Don't tell me you are already tired of camping. I have pretty fond memories of tents as of late." Cristos' breath brushed against her ear when he spoke, sending a shiver down her spine.

"If I never spent another night in the tent, I would not complain. We can create memories under a real roof as well." Aurelia smiled and leaned her head back against his chest. "But I suppose you're right. It's not that bad. You really should stop what you're doing to my leg, though. It's quite distracting."

Cristos moved his hand, brushing against the part of her that ached for his touch, and her hips bucked. "Distracting you from what?"

She threw her elbow back and hit him in the stomach, and he chuckled. "You're distracting me from maintaining my seat. You are going to make me fall."

He cupped her womanhood and pulled her flush against him, his hard length pressing against her backside. She gasped and bit her lip to stifle a moan as he teased her through her trousers. "Don't worry. I won't let you fall."

Calista glanced at them, and Aurelia's cheeks reddened. The healer was not talkative, but Aurelia did not doubt she was perceptive enough to know what was going on beneath her cloak. She swatted Cristos' forearm, and he moved his hand, flatting his palm atop her thigh. He did not behave for long, and the more he secretly touched her, the more desperate she became to get to an inn. Her self-control was already pitiful when it came to the handsome winged man, and it was rapidly waning.

They passed through two other small towns, only stopping to relieve themselves and stretch their legs. They wanted to reach their destination by nightfall, so they continued southward at a brisk pace. Aurelia attempted to admire the landscape as it became increasingly tropical, but focusing was hard thanks to Cristos' relentless teasing. The rolling hills led to a more chaparral landscape as clay and sand replaced lush grass and dirt.

The temperature grew warmer as they covered more ground, and Aurelia shed her cloak. She draped it over her lap, which only encouraged Cristos to stroke her more. He brought her to the edge of release, retreating just before she climaxed, over and over as they journeyed. By the time they arrived in Claywind, Aurelia had gone molten, and she was sure she would combust at any moment. Her legs were numb and tingly, and she wasn't sure she'd be able to stand when they dismounted.

When they reached Claywind, their party headed straight for the clearly marked inn. A white-haired young male met them outside the stables beside it. He approached Scoudra first and helped Calista off the mare before he grabbed the reins.

"What brings you all to Claywind?" he asked. "Will you be staying with us long?"

"We will be leaving tomorrow," Kason said as he climbed down and went inside to secure their rooms. Holera guided Tasu as she followed the stable hand while Cristos wrapped his arms around Aurelia and hopped off Teoron, his wings fluttering as he slowed their descent. They made sure the horses were secure before joining Kason inside. By the time they entered, he had already rented three rooms and secured a table for dinner.

From the outside, the inn looked well maintained, enchanting, and cheerful. Plaster walls and stone pillars made up the outer structure. It was tough to see much through the small, curtained windows, but the pleasant atmosphere could be felt outside. As they entered through a thick, metal door, they were welcomed by aromas of roasted food and cheerful singing.

A tavern occupied the first floor, and it was filled with an enthusiastic assortment of patrons. The bartender offered them with a short wave as he filled glasses with ale. The establishment was just as enchanting inside. Aurelia could see the stairs that led up to the inn, and tables were scattered throughout the rest of the space.

They were served plates of grilled fish and vegetables, just like in Starcrest, but with a side of flavored rice. Cristos left for the bar and returned with five glasses of whiskey. The alcohol burned Aurelia's throat when it went down. They unwound from their journey as they indulged themselves. By the time they paid their tab and retired upstairs, she was one glass away from stumbling.

The rooms above the tavern were small but cozy. Aurelia was not sure she and Cristos would fit on the little bed because of his wings. Even with them tucked to his back, they would have no choice but to sleep close together. Not that she was complaining.

Aurelia opened a small door in the room's corner, assuming it was a closet, and nearly cried when she found a tiny bathing room with an actual tub. It was small, but she did not care. As long as she could soak in the hot water and clean herself, she was happy.

Cristos warmed the water over the fire for her and poured it into the small tub.

"Would you like me to wash your hair?" he asked as he stood behind her and brushed his fingers through her loose waves. The whiskey, coupled with hours of him bringing her to the brink of climax, made her crave for more of his touch. She unbuttoned her tunic while he ran his fingers through her hair, carefully trying to untangle the knots. She let her eyes fall closed as every nerve ending seemed to come alive under his fingers.

"I would love that. I'm so tired."

Cristos turned her around and took over, unfastening her tunic. His eyes were heavy lidded, his exhaustion clear after the long day in the sun, but he made quick work of the remaining buttons. When the last one was unclasped, he slid the fabric off her shoulders and let it fall to the floor as he cupped her cheeks and kissed her. She leaned into him on weakened knees and wrapped her arms around his back as she undid the cloth panels of his tunic that surrounded the base of his wings. His lips left hers just long enough to pull it off, and then he yanked her to him once again.

The kiss was ravenous, their pent-up desire bubbling over. Cristos pulled away first and their bare chests heaved as they both struggled to catch their breath. Sliding her trousers off, Cristos led her to the tub. He helped her climb in, and her eyes nearly rolled when the hot water touched the most sensitive parts of her. Cristos used an empty glass to pour the water over her exposed chest and shoulders until her entire body was dripping.

"Lean back," he murmured as he kneeled behind her. They could not fit in the tub together, but she wished they could. The only thing that would make that bath better would be having a naked Cristos pressed against her. "He kissed the back of her neck, and she moaned but did as he asked. Warm water flowed down her head as he brushed the hair away from her face.

Cristos massaged lavender scented shampoo into her hair, and it was one of the most sensual moments of her life. By the time he rinsed her hair and helped her to dry off, she thought she would explode if he didn't take her soon. Aurelia did not bother with clothes. There was no need for modesty with him. She sat on the edge of the bed and watched as he shed his trousers and bathed, her desire ever increasing as she admired his muscular form.

As soon as Cristos finished drying off, he came over and eased her down on the bed. He pulled her forward until her hips reached the edge and spread her thighs, falling to his knees between them. He buried his handsome face between her legs, and she bit a pillow to stop from screaming as he finally drove her over the edge. By the time he sheathed himself inside her, the pillow hit the floor. When they came together, she couldn't care less if anyone heard their pleasure.

Chapter Thirty-Five

Diapolis

Cristos' face was the first thing Aurelia saw when she opened her eyes, and it put a smile on her face. He slept on his back with one wing unfurled and the other tucked beneath him. She couldn't imagine trying to lie comfortably with wings, but he had clearly perfected the skill. One of his arms draped across her stomach while the other hung limply off the bed.

She watched him for several moments, both admiring the view and afraid to wake him. When she finally attempted to slip out from under his arm, one brilliant oceanic eye popped open. Before she could fully slide off the bed, he tightened his arm and pulled her close again.

"Where are you sneaking off to?" His voice was raspy from sleep. She grinned and brushed his black hair from his eyes.

"I was just going into the bathing room. I will be right back."

He released her, smacking her bare backside as she scurried from the bed. She gasped and leveled him with a playful glare before she grabbed her clothes and made her way into the bathing room.

They joined their companions in the tavern an hour later. All five of them were a sorry sight. One glance was all it took to know they stayed up too late the night before. Aurelia hoped the bags under her eyes faded before their audience with the king. She pinched her cheeks, hoping to bring some color back to her lifeless complexion as she eyed the others.

Holera's silver hair was disheveled, but she attempted to wrestle it into a rough braid as they sat down at the table. Kason, who consumed more whiskey than the rest of them, did not even bother to button his shirt before coming down to breakfast. Even Calista looked like she had been up late, and Aurelia wondered what she'd been doing and with who. Calista was beautiful. Her red hair fell in a straight, silky curtain around her shoulders and her green eyes shined bright. Aurelia was certain any of the tavern singletons would have happily entertained the healer for the night. She did not know Calista well enough to ask, but she could not stifle her curiosity.

After a quick breakfast, the group set out. They did not look much better after the meal, but at least Holera's hair was somewhat contained, and Kason was fully dressed. The stable hand that greeted them when they arrived was there and retrieved their horses immediately. After reviewing the map and having a word with the barmaid, Kason said they had a four-hour ride ahead of them before they reached the capital city.

According to Cristos, Embershell was situated on the southernmost coast and said to be the most beautiful city in

Ekotoria. A high wall separated Diapolis from the Undying Valley, a spreading desert that consumed everything in its path. The king of Diapolis, Ailani, and his male consort, Makoa, ruled the kingdom. She knew he did not involve himself in the business of other kingdoms, but learned he did not worry himself much about the inner workings of his border towns either. Still, from what she'd heard around the tavern, the king was well loved by his people.

They began the final leg of their journey under the palest blue sky Aurelia had ever seen. The temperature was warm enough to ride without cloaks, and she pushed her sleeves up to expose more of her skin to the brilliant sunlight. Wispy clouds drifted across the sky as they pressed on, bringing with them a refreshing breeze from the sea. They could not see the coast from the road, but she knew it was not far away as she smelled salt in the air.

There had been no time for Aurelia to enjoy the sea since they crossed the portal. It was always too cold, too dangerous, or too far away. The villa she was raised in was set too far above the sea, and much too treacherous, even if she could reach it. She spent plenty of her time in Vaekros longingly watching the waves as they crashed against the rocky cliff side she'd called home. She hoped they would be able to visit the water while they were in Diapolis, if only just once, so she could feel the sand in between her toes.

Cristos leaned forward, resting his chin on her shoulder, and distracted her from her inner musings. She studied his face out of the corner of her eye. If Cristos was nervous about their visit, he did not show it. His blue eyes glistened in the morning light as they rode, a smile hinting at his lips. His fingers caressed her thigh, and she wondered if he was thinking of their night together. The number of times he'd made her scream his name while impaled by his-

"Have you ever been to Diapolis?" Aurelia blurted out, desperate to derail her train of thought. He shook his head and sat up straight.

"I have not, but my father has... had. He used to tell me stories about it."

Aurelia could hear his smile falter as he answered. "I'm sorry." She felt guilty for reminding him of his loss.

He leaned forward again and kissed her on the cheek. "For what?" His hand left her thigh and wrapped around her waist, squeezing slightly. "What happened to him was not your fault, so there is nothing to apologize for." She leaned back against him, savoring his proximity. "Plus, I don't mind thinking of the good memories."

She felt his smile return as he pressed his cheek against hers and tightened his hold around her. She nodded, unsure of how to continue the conversation, and said the first thing that came to her. "I hope we get to go to the beach."

Cristos returned his hand to her thigh and chuckled. "Do you, now? I think we can work that out."

A flutter of excitement filled her at the thought. Just her and her bare-chested fae enjoying the sea and sun sounded like the perfect day. For a moment, she felt like there was no war looming overhead, and they were not going to Diapolis to beg the king for an alliance. They were just a new couple planning an outing.

They continued to push south as Aurelia imagined their date. The dense evergreen forests of the north were long gone, giving way to a mixture of oak and massive flowering shrubs. As they neared the sea, the plant life became even more distinct. The flowers were even larger and grew more vibrant than any other she'd ever seen, yet they complimented the surrounding trees rather than overshadowing them. Sugarcane fields and fruit trees replaced the plains that had greeted them when they entered Diapolis.

They took their last rest in the town of Armaday. Aurelia had the opportunity to try a mango for the first time, and it quickly became her new favorite fruit. She was certain she could eat mangoes every day and never grow sick of them, even though it was difficult for her to peel.

The general mood amongst their party shifted as soon as they departed Armaday. A cloud of wary hesitance descended on them, and the unease of her companions increased her own exponentially. No one knew what to expect from King Ailani, and that uncertainty plagued them. He could align with them or tell them they were on their own and make defeating Warbotach and protecting both realms nearly impossible. He could lock them in a dungeon as soon as they arrived or feed them to his dragons. Different scenarios of varying degrees of peril continued to flood her mind and ramp up her fears. She'd been lost in what-ifs until she caught sight of the colossal wall that enclosed the city of Embershell. She knew the protective barrier surrounded the city and extended the western border of Diapolis, but the sheer size of it astounded her. She craned her neck to stare up at it as they drew closer, and she was certain it nearly reached the clouds. Aurelia hadn't expected a wall to keep nature at bay, but she could see no sign of the expanding dead lands from where she sat.

As they reached the city's entrance, she all but forgot the wall. Statues stood sentinel on either side of the road that led into the city. They reached higher than the Norithaean palace, and she could not help but marvel at them.

The statue on the left was a beautiful female holding a large fish in her hands, but she did not have legs. Instead, the entire bottom half of her body was a jewel encrusted tail, like that of the fish in her hands. Her deep violet hair was flowing, and her eyes looked like pure amethyst. Iridescent patches of color speckled her skin like scales, and the effect was enchanting.

On the right stood the statue of a male. He had legs, but that was the only ordinary thing about the sculpture. A massive dragon perched atop his shoulders, its mouth open in a ferocious snarl. The dragon was covered in emerald scales and glistened in the midday sun. The male's massive muscular arms pointed into the distance, toward the direction from which they came. His hair was a vibrant bronze that rivaled the beauty of his sun-kissed skin.

Aurelia was overwhelmed. She could not decide where to look. Everything was bright and elaborate. She closed her eyes and breathed deeply.

"Wow."

Cristos held her close as he murmured in her ear. "The sight is almost as beautiful as you are." Her face warmed, and it was only partly because of the sun.

Kason and Holera led them to the entrance, walking a dozen or so steps in front of them. Six men approached on horseback, blocking their path as they neared the gate. Cristos stiffened behind her.

"What's happening?" she whispered.

Cristos leaned closer to her ear, his voice so low she could barely hear him. "I think they are the welcoming committee."

Chapter Thirty-Six

Diapolis

The Diapolis welcoming committee, as Cristos called them, was like no males Aurelia had ever seen. Their tanned bodies were so sculpted they looked like they were carved from stone. Just like the statues nearby, their skin had scattered iridescent patches. She was not sure if the patches were tattoos, or a part of their complexion, but she was dying of curiosity. They were all dressed in matching sleeveless tunics and loose-fitting trousers that reached their knees, with leather sandals that wrapped up their muscled calves. Between the identical clothing and the swords that hung from their belts, Aurelia assumed they were guards.

Cristos guided their horse forward, pulling him to a stop as they reached Holera and Kason's side. Calista flanked the other side, and they stood as a united front before the blocked path. A guard with shoulder-length golden hair broke from the rank and approached them at a trot.

"King Ailani is expecting you." His accent was unlike any she heard before. It lilted as the words rolled effortlessly from his tongue. "I am Kimo, Captain of His Highness' Guard. I've been sent to escort you to the palace."

Kason nodded, taking on the role of their leader, and followed as Kimo turned his horse and led them through the gate and into Embershell.

Cristos' hold on her remained firm as they silently trailed behind Kason and Holera. The Elder Sea bordered two sides of the city. Its bright turquoise water sparkled in the sun to their right. That side of the road consisted solely of sand and was filled with beach goers. Aurelia envied the carefree attitude of those who basked in the sunlight and splashed in the gentle waves. She pulled her attention away, trying to stifle her longing, and focused on the left side of the road. It was lined with a variety of businesses that were filled with patrons. She knew little about Embershell, but from the number of people who strolled in and out of the shops and eateries, she knew it was prosperous.

As they continued on, the palace came into view. Eight thin, round towers of the massive castle dominated the skyline and were connected by tall, narrow walls made of silver stones that glittered in the sun. The castle had a plethora of floor-length windows, and Aurelia imagined how beautiful the view of the sea would be from them. Effigies of kings from the past, carved from the same silver stone, lined the castle gates.

"This city is amazing," she said, trying to keep her voice low.

Cristos nodded and squeezed her waist.

Kimo slowed to a stop as they approached the castle's gates, his people halting a few paces behind him. An archer saluted

Kimo from atop the wall before disappearing behind the stone. Moments later, the enormous wooden gates that closed the castle off from the city opened, and the group entered. A violent wind whipped Aurelia's hair as they passed through the castle's gates, and a piercing squeal sounded over her head. She resisted the urge to cover her ears as she looked up. The sight sent the breath rushing from her lungs.

Fierce jade eyes burned into her from the sky as a dragon flapped its magnificent wings and flew higher as it headed toward the water. Scales the color of a darkened forest covered the whole of its massive body. Everyone who'd traveled with her from the encampment turned their attention skyward to the beast. The guards, and even the horses, were unimpressed by the airborne creature, but Aurelia could not tear her gaze away from it.

They walked through the courtyard and curved left, aiming toward a cluster of buildings. Guards lined the top of the wall and filled the palace grounds. They all watched their procession, and the intense stares were enough to pull her focus from the dragon disappearing in the distance. A knot of unease formed, tightening in Aurelia's stomach.

Once they reached the array of buildings, Kimo and the other guards dismounted and signaled for them to do the same. A young male, appearing no older than sixteen, ran out of an open door and grabbed onto Kimo's horse's reins. Cristos climbed off Teoron slowly, and grasped Aurelia around the waist, lifting her with ease and setting her down beside him.

Kason was next to leave his saddle. He glanced warily around the courtyard. It was clear Aurelia wasn't the only one affected by the unwavering attention of the guards on duty. The Aegrician females dismounted on their own, and Aurelia wished she had that ability. She felt so exposed, so out of place, and she despised showing such weakness in such an uncertain situation. Variel claimed she was part Aegrician, but nothing about her felt like that was true as she observed the confidence the phoenixes exuded, even in their humanoid form. She felt pitifully mortal and frail at that moment, a little mackerel in a shark tank.

Memories of her last palace visit gnawed at her frazzled mind as they were led inside the massive castle. Aurelia tried to reassure herself with the fact that she wasn't in chains this time, at least. Cristos held her hand, their entwined fingers helping to soothe her raw nerves. She knew he could sense her nervousness and intimidation, but there was little she could do to calm her emotions. They followed Kimo down a long marble corridor and through a golden set of double doors. She peeked over Kason's shoulder as she tried to steady her rapid breathing.

Great braziers surrounded six marble columns, lighting the entire throne hall. It bathed the entire area in a welcoming orange glow that eased some of the tension in her shoulders. Mosaics of legendary creatures decorated the stone walls. The lanterns illuminated the stained glass, casting warm flecks of color on the floor. Massive windows framed by ivory drapes stretched to the ceiling, a perfect display for the shimmering sea below.

They walked along a plush ivory rug that lined the aisle from the entrance to a grandiose golden throne. It was set before one of the tremendous windows, and the sun shone through, causing the gold to glint so bright Aurelia needed to squint to see it properly. It had intricate engravings, but she could not focus long enough to make them out. The gorgeous man who occupied the throne captured her attention the instant she laid eyes on him.

King Ailani was the physical embodiment of the sun. He wasn't rugged like Kason, nor did he have chiseled features like Cristos. The only way she could describe the king was beautiful. His features were soft and inviting. His hair flowed freely over his shoulders all the way down to his chest in loose, sunshine-colored curls, and his dazzling turquoise eyes rivaled the sparkling waters of the Elder Sea. His short-sleeved jacket was a brilliant shade of eggplant, and the shimmery silk fabric had dragons embroidered in golden thread on each bicep. His jacket and fitted black trousers were clearly tailored with great care and flattered his slender figure. His delicate face split into a radiant smile full of perfect teeth as they were ushered closer to him.

A dark-haired male stood beside the throne. His raven hair was straight and silky. It perfectly complimented his deep tan skin and emerald eyes. His dark tunic and trousers looked like they were made of wet ink and hugged his lean yet muscular frame. Both men appeared joyful as Kimo led them into the chamber. The guard bowed low and backed away, leaving them before the king and his consort.

King Ailani's eyebrows furrowed. A look of confusion descended over his face before it cleared, and his smile returned. "When I received a raven from the Aegrician general, it said nothing about the king of Norithae visiting as well."

His genial tone seemed like a good sign, but he made little sense to Aurelia. The Norithaean ruler had been slaughtered by Warbotach when their kingdom fell.

She felt Cristos stiffen beside her at the king's words, his grip on her hand tightening. She frowned as she turned to look at him, confused by his reaction.

"I am no king, Your Highness," Cristos said as he bowed his head.

King Ailani huffed a chuckle. "A king without a throne is still a king. You look just like your father. He was a great ruler and an even better man."

Aurelia's eyes bulged as they fixated on Cristos. His gaze remained pointedly fixed at his feet. The dots began to connect themselves in her mind as she stared at the guilty look on his face. Anger and hurt coursed through her veins as she ripped her hand from his. Betrayal joined the negative cocktail of emotions that consumed her as Cristos thanked the king for the kind words about his father.

She turned her back on him and moved to stand beside Callista, putting as much space between her and the Norithae king as possible.

Chapter Thirty-Seven

Diapolis

King Ailani studied their group with a sharp eye that belied the carefree exuberance he projected. His gaze followed Aurelia as she stormed away from Cristos.

"Oh my. It appears you did not share your identity with the Aegricians, after all."

She heard Cristos' teeth grind together before he spoke. "My lineage holds no importance in this war. All that matters is freeing Norithae and Aegricia from Warbotach's hold." His tone was amiable, but she could hear a tinge of bitterness in his words.

King Ailani rose from his throne, waving his hand dismissively.

"Enough about war for now. Did you witness the statues that line the palace wall?"

She watched Cristos bob his head in her peripheral vision. Just glimpsing his face made the anger burn stronger in her chest. He knew everything about her, and she hadn't even known who he truly was. She could understand him not telling her immediately, but there had been plenty of opportunities over the last few weeks. They had grown so close, and now that all felt fake to her. He was no longer her handsome winged lover. He was the king of Norithae.

Her eyes watered as she fixed her sight on the Diapolis ruler. She wasn't sure if sadness or fury caused the tears, but she refused to let them fall. A small part of her wished she'd remained in the encampment with Septima and Kano, continuing to live in ignorant bliss, but it was far too late for that. It was better to know the truth. She had fallen for him, and all the while, he lied and concealed things from her. She had no interest in being with a liar and knew it was better to cut ties now, rather than have him destroy her heart later. That realization didn't make it hurt any less.

"Those effigies are my family. Those statues—those men—were beloved rulers and a symbol of hope for our people for centuries. Lineage holds far more importance than you can imagine, especially in times of unrest. You are not just the king of Norithae. You are the promise of a better future for your nation."

King Ailani's jovial tone turned passionate, and his eyes bore into Cristos as if he was trying to drill the words into the depths of the Norithaean's soul. The man who stood beside the throne stepped forward and placed his hand on the king's shoulder as he addressed Aurelia and the others.

"It is growing late. You have all traveled far. Kimo will escort you to the guest chambers. Get cleaned up and rest. Servants will bring dinner for you. We can discuss the purpose of your visit tomorrow."

The king placed his hand atop the other man's, his intense gaze softening with affection as he stared at him. Her stomach pinched at the sight. She hoped Cristos would look at her with that kind of love in his eyes one day, and now that prospect was dead. She envied the men and their happiness.

When the king turned back to them, the fire that burned in him as he lectured Cristos was gone. He smiled as he nodded in agreement. "This is my consort, Makoa. He is a far more gracious host than I. Please rest, and we will continue tomorrow evening."

Kimo approached from the entrance and bowed to his rulers before gesturing for the group to follow. They trailed behind him in silence, and Aurelia stayed as far from Cristos as possible. She couldn't even enjoy the intricate décor of the palace they traipsed through, her mind still roiling at the royal revelation. Kason and Holera marched on either of her sides, helping her maintain the distance. She assumed they were also upset by his secrecy, but she couldn't bring herself to care about anyone else's feelings at the moment. Her own were far too overwhelming.

The captain of the guard came to a halt in the center of a long hall. Polished oak doors lined the walls, and torches illuminated the space. She could feel the warmth of their flames licking at her skin, but her heart was too frigid to thaw.

"How many rooms do you require?" Kimo asked.

"Three," Cristos answered before anyone else had the chance.

"Four," Aurelia spat. Venom filled her tone as she pointedly ignored the look her former lover gave her.

"Aure-"

Kason cut him off, confirming that they needed four rooms.

Kimo shifted uncomfortably as he showed them which chambers were theirs. Based on his size and physique, she was certain he was an excellent warrior, but he seemed at a loss when it came to dealing with the tension that plagued her traveling party. He nodded awkwardly as he let them know servants would bring dinner within the hour and left immediately after.

Kason whirled on Cristos as soon as they were alone.

"You had no right to hide this from us. Your title changes everything. We could have requested more aid, knowing the whole of Norithae would back you as their king. Instead, our general planned our negotiations around the fact that you were a warrior who could round up an average number of soldiers to fight."

Cristos' eyes were hard as he stepped forward. "I told you my people were ready to fight and only waited for an opportunity. Never did I say it was only a fraction of my people. It is not my fault you drew your own conclusions."

Kason growled low in his throat, but Holera placed her hand on his arm. "This isn't the time nor the place. We need to write Blaedia."

He nodded and shot Cristos another glare before claiming the chamber nearest him. Holera followed as Calista entered a room across the hall.

Aurelia balked at the rapidly emptying passage, unprepared to be left alone with Cristos. She darted to the nearest door, trying to escape, but he grabbed her forearm before she could retreat.

"Please talk to me."

His pleading tone was a knife in her chest. She felt torn in two directions. Half of her wanted to listen to him, to learn why he'd concealed his identity. The other half wanted to rage at him for lying to her. No matter which side won out, she would have to hear him out, regardless. She yanked her arm out of his grasp and gave a single nod before entering the room. She left the door open, the only invitation he'd receive from her.

The guest chambers were massive. The same floor to ceiling windows lined the far wall, the sun's dying rays bathing the room. A four-post bed took up a large portion of the area, its size rivaling the one she had in Vaekros that comfortably fit her, Kano, and Septima. An ivory down comforter and pillows covered the mattress, and she admired the hand carved frame. Intricate swirls decorated the posts, and the footboard depicted a fish-tailed female with a serene expression. Aurelia desired to feel the level of tranquility the woman expressed, but her emotions continued to whip violently around inside her.

She turned her attention to her left and spotted an unlit fireplace. Two armchairs sat before it, with a small table between them. She took a seat in one of the ivory chairs, absentmindedly noting that the color seemed quite popular in Diapolis. She glared at Cristos as he sat opposite her. He looked dejected as he leaned forward with his head hung low and rested his arms on his knees.

His melancholy enraged her. How dare he act as if he was the one who was wronged?

"How can I help you, Your Highness?"

He flinched. She wasn't sure if it was the ire in her tone or the title that affected him, but she was glad it did either way. Lashing out at him helped to bury some of the hurt that threatened to overwhelm her.

"Please, Aurelia, don't be angry. I didn't tell you at first, because I was not sure if I could trust you. Once I knew you were truly on my side, there was never a good time to tell you." His ocean eyes were dull as he gazed up at her.

"Never a good time? What about when we spoke about your father having visited Diapolis before?"

"What was I to say? 'Ah, well, I've never been, but my father visited frequently to negotiate trades. The work of a king is never done'?"

His sarcasm grated on her nerves. Her nostrils flared as she exhaled angrily, jumping to her feet.

"That would have been better than lying to me. I shared my bed with you. I shared my body with you. All you gave me was half-truths. There is nothing about me that you do not know. I kept nothing from you, and you hid something so incredibly important from me."

He responded to her harsh tone, shooting out of his seat. He shoved the small table aside with his foot, his wings twitching behind him as he stepped into her space. Both of their chests heaved as they glared at each other.

"I did not lie to you. I told you about my parents and told you exactly how I feel about you. Yes, I hid the fact that I am the new king, but I never *lied*. My father was just murdered. I still do not feel like I even deserve the title."

His superior height served as fuel for her already fiery temper. She refused to back down as he crowded her.

"Concealing the truth is just a pretty way to frame a lie. Even if you are not ready to claim the title, you were still the prince, and you said nothing of that either. Even when asked if the prince still lived! You were audacious enough to speak about our future together, all the while knowing you'd return to rule Norithae after the war. We have no future anymore."

Pain filled his features as he took a step back, like he'd been struck. Regret tinged her anger, but she didn't take back her words, for they were true. He would return to Norithae, and she would travel Ekotoria with Septima until they found a place to call home.

"Aurelia," his voice was small as his morose eyes stared at her. "Is that truly how you feel? That we have no future together?"

His question stole the wind from her sails as she slumped back down into the armchair and buried her face in her hands. "I do not know anymore. You have a responsibility to your people."

He kneeled in front of her, gently wrapping his fingers around her wrists as he pulled them away to gaze into her eyes. "I have a responsibility to you, too. Why can you not join me in Norithae?"

She snorted derisively. "Ah, yes. That sounds lovely. The king's human lover is not an appealing title."

"You're not solely human, Aurelia, and even if you were, I would not care. Your lineage means nothing to me. Only you do, and I care for you far more than just a simple lover. Why is my title so important to you?"

Her anger reared again. She pulled her hands from his grasp and stood, walking around him to pace about the room.

"Because you lied, Cristos. You lied, and you let me foolishly fall for you. It's not as if we can live happily ever after with one another. You are the *king*."

"Then be my queen."

"You are being ridiculous."

"I do not know how else to get through to you. We have not known each other for long, but you are the most important person in my life. If you cannot forgive me, then I will live with that regret for the rest of my life, but I will not beg for forgiveness. I kept my position a secret to protect the interest of my people. What if the Aegricians sacrificed me to Warbotach to form a treaty?"

"They would never do that."

"And how was I supposed to know that at first? There are so many lives that depend on me. I have to be cautious."

Aurelia stared at him, betrayal clear in her eyes. "Fine. Let us say I understand why you did not confide in Blaedia, but why did you not trust *me*?"

He sighed and stood, walking over to her. "I do trust you. There was never a good time, and I did not want to burden you with the knowledge. How would you have felt if you had to hide the truth from Blaedia? From Exie? From Septima?"

His words made her recoil like he'd slapped her. "Was it never a good time? Or are you going to insist you lied for my own good? Make up your mind."

He groaned, throwing his hands in the air. "You are the most frustrating creature I've ever met. Both. The answer is both. I could not find the right time to tell you, and I did not want to cause you unnecessary stress. I just want to make you happy."

"Well, Your Highness, that is not how reality works."

"Stop calling me that."

"Would you prefer King Cristos?"

"Aurelia." He growled her name, and even in her angry state, the sound sent a shiver up her spine.

"Yes, King Cristos?" They both leaned in, fire in their eyes.

"What will it take for you to believe me? I must take care of my people, but I want a future with you. I am sorry that I did not confide in you of my own accord, but the truth is out there now, and I cannot change the past."

"If you ever lie or hide things from me, I will not forgive you again."

His eyes brightened, a cautious optimism filling his features. "Does that mean you forgive me now?"

"No. I have not forgiven you yet."

His face started to fall at her words, but she grabbed his tunic and yanked his face to hers before the sad look could color his entire expression. The kiss was hard and passionate as they poured everything into it. Their tongues warred with one another in a bid for dominance. Aurelia poured the hurt and anger she felt into it, amplifying her desire. She hoped he could taste her bitter emotions.

She tangled her fingers in his hair and pulled at the strands as she leaped up. He caught her, his fingers digging into her backside as she wrapped her legs around his waist. Her back slammed into the wall beside the bed a second later, and he rubbed his hard length against the junction between her legs. She threw her head back and moaned at the sensations that zipped through her entire frame.

Cristos' mouth descended on her exposed neck, his teeth biting into the sensitive flesh before he sucked roughly. Her pulse quickened as she rolled her hips against him. The clothing that separated them was a frustrating barrier, and she pulled at his tunic as he ripped the fabric of her trousers and tore them from her body.

Aurelia slid her hands between them and pulled at his trousers' fastening before she shoved them down to his thighs. They were both feverish in their movements, and as soon as Cristos' stiff cock sprang free from its leather confines, he slammed into her. She arched her back as she screamed in pleasure. His thrusts were punishing, but she met each powerful stroke as she braced her hands on his shoulders. The anger that consumed her from the moment she'd found out about his secret fed into the force of her movements. He pulled out of her and set her on her feet.

"Wha-"

Before she could finish a word, Cristos spun her around and placed his palm between her shoulder blades. He pushed gently and bent her over the bed, her chest flat against the mattress. She looked back at him, watching as he widened her stance. He held her gaze as he slammed into her once more from behind, and Aurelia's legs buckled beneath her.

Aurelia soaked in an oversized clawfoot bath with Cristos behind her, his arms wrapped around her. They spent the better part of the night and most of the morning releasing their pent-up aggression, and the space between her legs ached in the most delicious way. They hadn't talked much, but she'd made a conscious decision to forgive him. Until the war was over, she would enjoy her time with him. Her heart would certainly shatter into a million pieces when he took the throne and left her behind in Aegricia, but she'd concluded it was too late, anyway. Though she hadn't told him, she knew she loved him. Whether she rejected him now or lost him after the war, she would hurt. At least they could make more memories together before then.

"Why are you so sad?" Cristos asked as he sniffed at the air.

"Stop doing that."

"I cannot control what I smell."

"Then stop breathing."

Cristos snorted and leaned forward to kiss her shoulder. He dragged his nose along her flesh until he reached her ear and whispered in it. "But your scent is intoxicating."

His fingers dipped below the water, trailing over her legs as he reached between her thighs. He brushed against her sex, but a knock on the bathing chamber door interrupted him. Aurelia slouched in the water, hiding her breasts below the surface as she called out. The heavy oak cracked open as Leinani, the servant, charged with delivering their meals since last night, peeked inside.

"His Highness was not sure if the two of you had clothes suited for a royal party, so he sent some, just in case. I'll hang them in the armoire." She glanced down at them awkwardly, her eyes shooting upward almost immediately. "They should fit."

Cristos caught Aurelia's eye and lifted one eyebrow before he looked at the servant over his shoulder. "Please pass along our thanks."

Leinani flushed as Cristos looked at her and bowed before closing the door.

Aurelia laughed quietly and rolled her eyes as she leaned back against her lover.

"What?" He asked as he twirled the ends of her hair.

"It's like Dewdrop all over again. Females are weak when it comes to you."

He chuckled and pressed a kiss to her cheek as he poured soap on a cloth. "It doesn't matter. You're the only one for me."

"How quickly you forget your sprite harem."

His deep laugh made her back vibrate as he pulled her arm from the water and began to wash her skin. "Well, you said you do not share, so I had to disband the harem."

They finished their bath and continued to banter back and forth. His title still weighed heavily on Aurelia, but they both carefully avoided broaching the subject. She exited the bathing chamber first and headed for the armoire as soon as she entered the bedroom.

She threw the heavy wooden doors open, dying to see the dress King Ailani provided, and gasped the moment she laid eyes on it. A stunning emerald dress spilled out. The silken bodice sparkled as the light from the room fell across it. It was sleeveless with a flowing chiffon skirt.

Aurelia ran her hands over the fabric and smiled. The shimmering masterpiece was nothing like the party dresses she'd worn in Vaekros, and she was excited to wear it. The gathering itself made her nervous, but as she caressed her luxurious armor, she was certain she could handle Diapolis' high society. A small, anxious part of her whispered in her mind, telling her she was nothing more than an average human playing dress up, but she shoved that away. Ekotoria would fracture and the human world would crumble beneath the barbaric weight of Warbotach if they did not succeed in their mission. Doubt had no place within—not when the stakes were this high.

"Do you like it?" Cristos' voice interrupted her thoughts. She lifted the trim that escaped the armoire back inside and closed it before turning to him. His wet hair dripped, leaving trails of water over his defined torso. Her eyes fixated on the deep v of his waist that was interrupted by the plush ivory towel hanging low on his hips. She swallowed hard and averted her gaze as she wondered when the effect he had on her would lessen in intensity.

"Very much so." She sat at the vanity in the corner and began drying her hair. The emerald gown would be her chainmail tonight, and the cosmetics that filled the space in front of her would be her war paint. Convincing King Ailani to come to their aid was a different kind of battle, and it required intellectual weapons to win. The better she looked, the more confident she would feel, and that could make all the difference.

"I look forward to seeing you wear it."

"I'm sure you will steal all the attention. I can hear hearts breaking already."

Cristos snorted. "We shall see, won't we? I hope the tailor took my wings into account or I'll be going in trousers." Aurelia was certain no one would mind too much, but it was probably best if the king of Norithae did not show up half naked.

Her stomach flipped uncomfortably as she thought of his title. She was trying to accept it, but it bothered her far more than learning her own royal status had. Yes, she was technically a princess, but she did not feel like one. Besides, outside of a few Aegricians, Variel and Cristos, none of the fae knew her lineage, so it was easier to ignore. But her lover had a throne that waited for him to claim, and it was a concept she struggled with.

Aurelia watched Cristos' reflection in the looking glass and saw his smile falter as her temperament fluctuated. She found herself frequently wishing he did not have the power to scent her unsteady emotions.

He pasted a forced smile on his face as he held her gaze. "We still have some time before we have to get ready. Would you like to go visit the beach?"

Aurelia beamed at the suggestion, agreeing in an instant. She plaited her wet hair and rushed to pull on an ordinary tunic and trousers. Cristos was ready before her, and as soon as she pulled on her boots, they exited the guest chambers.

The palace corridors were brimming with servants that rushed about, no doubt preparing for the night's events. With people darting in and out, it did not take Aurelia and Cristos long to find to find the courtyard. The sun hung high above them, and a cool breeze blew from the sea. The smell of saltwater filled her nose as the wind ruffled the little hairs that had escaped her braid.

The men patrolling the area did not stare when they approached the gates of the palace, which was a welcomed change from their arrival. The gate guard gave a quick greeting nod and let them pass. As they headed down the main road to the sea, Aurelia hoped they would be allowed admittance upon their return.

The brilliant turquoise water crashed in stunning waves on the pale, golden sand. The contrast was intense, but also complimentary. Cristos slipped off his shoes, and Aurelia followed suit before they crossed the road, hand in hand. The feel of the warm sand between her toes mingled with the saltwater scent, creating the perfect cocktail of tranquility.

Aurelia closed her eyes and tilted her head back to bask in the warmth of the sun's rays. She was reminded of the summer trips her family took to the eastern coast of Vaekros. She lowered her head and looked out over the water as she shoved down the happy memories. She missed her siblings so much, but nothing good would come from dwelling on experiences she could never repeat.

She watched waves crest and crash over a shipwreck just off the shoreline and admired the rippling effect that it sent dancing across the surface. Cristos rubbed the back of Aurelia's hand with his thumb, tightening his hold when she nearly lost her footing as they neared the water. They sat in the sand, just out of the tide's reach, and everything felt perfect in that moment.

"It's beautiful," he said as he wrapped his arm around her waist and pulled her in close. She nodded and leaned her head against him.

"I could get used to this view. It almost makes me forget the war."

She smiled as a mother, father, and their two young sons splashed about in the sea. What she wouldn't give to have a happy family like that one day. The youngest child splashed his feet once, twice, and then Aurelia gasped.

"Cristos, look! He has a tail!"

Cristos chuckled at her enthusiastic surprise and kissed her cheek. "Most Diapolisians can shift forms in order to live in the water."

Her grin was so wide that her cheeks ached as she continued to watch the child. His expression was the epitome of joy as he used his tiny tail to splash his family, who laughed good-naturedly at his antics. It was a beautiful moment, and she felt so fortunate for having witnessed it.

With the lovely Diapolisian family playing before them, and the massive dragons that flew through the air above them, Aurelia snuggled into Cristos' side and enjoyed the small reprieve from the horrors their future held.

Chapter Thirty-Eight

Diapolis

They returned to the palace after two hours. Aurelia would have loved to remain on the beach until sunset, but they had to prepare for their evening with the king. Kason leaned against the door frame of his bedchambers as they turned down the long corridor. She stuttered to a halt, her fingers tightening on Cristos' nervously. The Aegrician had been as livid about Cristos' secret as she had, and she feared a confrontation was brewing. They had to be on their best behavior while they tried to secure the alliance, but her worries were for naught.

"Holera and Calista are waiting for you inside," Kason said as he nodded toward his room. "Holera brought your dress over. They want to get ready for the party together."

Aurelia smiled, but her eyes darted to Cristos and back to Kason. "Where will you get ready if we're taking over your room?"

"We'll dress in your chambers. Holera put my dress clothes in there already. Besides, I believe Cristos and I need to talk."

His tone was devoid of the anger it held the night before, and the rugged man looked almost sheepish as he scratched the back of his neck. She couldn't help but laugh quietly to herself at Holera's manipulations. It would be for the best for the men to make up, but the fact that the warrior left them little choice in the matter amused Aurelia.

Cristos kissed her forehead and watched her join the women before he led Kason into their chambers. Holera's lips curled in a mischievous grin as she peered over Aurelia's head and watched the two disappear behind the heavy oak door. She commended the phoenix's plan as a knock sounded behind her. Calista let Leinani and Akela into the chambers. The king sent the two servants to do their hair and makeup before they donned their dresses. The easy atmosphere reminded her of the times she prepared for elaborate Vaekrosan balls, and she wished her sister was there.

The three women were painted, poked, and prodded into perfection. The entire process took several hours, but when they finally stood before the massive looking glass, Aurelia knew the effort was worth it. Diapolis' tropical culture was woven into their appearance from the flowers laced into Holera's long silver braid to the crystal dolphin pendant that rested against Calista's exposed collar bone.

The Aegrician women were stunning, but Aurelia's eyes kept drifting back to her own reflection. Her heavily painted lids were dark and smoky, making her blue eyes shine, and her lips were stained by the juice of native berries, making them appear far more plump than usual. Her crimson hair had been tamed into loose curls that hung loose down her exposed back.

The gown King Ailani provided fit like a glove. It fastened over one shoulder, held in place by a jeweled brooch shaped like a dragon. But it wasn't her dramatically enhanced makeup nor the crystalline beast that held her attention. It was the elegant circlet adorning her hair that she fixated on. Emeralds and seashells seamlessly blended together and highlighted the single pearl that glimmered in the center. The intricate design reminded her of a tiara, and for the first time, Aurelia actually felt like a princess.

The only thing missing was Exie and Septima. She missed her sister so much it hurt, and no celebration would be complete without Exie, because no one partied quite like the warrior did. Diapolis would have been blessed with her karaoke after a few drinks, no matter how inappropriate the lyrics. Her infectious exuberance might have single-handedly convinced the king to side with them.

Aurelia smiled to herself as she followed the others into the hall, imagining how the night would have gone if the two women were there.

Kason and Cristos were already waiting as they exited the guest chambers. The Aegrician male looked dumb struck as he caught sight of Holera's cobalt blue gown with a sparkling cinched waist that emphasized her already magnificent curves. Aurelia hardly caught a glimpse of the suit he wore as he crossed the wide hall in two strides.

She averted her eyes from the passionate kiss he gave his lover and looked at the healer beside her. Calista was equally stunning in a cherry red gown that flowed around her, a crown of white flowers gracefully adorning her hair. There was little doubt that the only uncoupled person in their group would garner an excess of attention when they joined the party.

Aurelia shifted her attention to Cristos and swallowed hard. He looked magnificent. His obsidian suit was exquisite. Between the dark fabric and his leathery wings, his ocean eyes were even brighter than usual. Aurelia could not look away from his breathtaking visage as he approached her.

His smile was radiant as he scanned her body from head to toe. He cupped her face and a flush heated her cheeks. For a moment, she forgot they were not alone. The rest of the hall faded away, and they were the only ones there as his mouth descended on hers. By the time he pulled away, their companions were gone. She was so wrapped up in Cristos that she hadn't even realized they'd left.

"You look absolutely beautiful."

She returned the compliment with one of her own as they made their way through the maze of palace halls. Cristos pressed his palm flat against the small of her back. The gesture probably appeared sweet to the Diapolisians they passed by, but they didn't know that her lover used it as an opportunity to caress her bare skin. She knew he was trying to drive her mad, and she was frustrated by his success.

His hand crept lower, until he cupped her bottom, and she smacked his stomach. He let out a grunt to appease her, but she knew it did not hurt him. She rolled her eyes as she grabbed his arm and threaded hers through it.

"Are Norithaean males not taught to behave like gentlemen?"

Cristos barked out a laugh before he pressed a kiss to the side of her head, careful to avoid the seashell tiara. "Apologies, my lady. It is easy to forget oneself when in such ravishing company."

She giggled at his words, but her reply died on her lips as they stepped into the opulent ballroom. Crystal chandeliers dominated the ceiling, and tall white candles were scattered around the room, creating a warm and romantic ambiance. King Ailani sat at the center of an incredibly long dining table that looked out over the vast dance floor. His consort, Makoa, sat beside him, and they chatted amongst themselves. Holera, Kason, and Calista had already joined them.

Aurelia and Cristos hastened to do the same. Cristos pulled out her chair and sat between her and the king. A servant swooped in with filled champagne flutes before they'd even finished taking their seat.

To her surprise, the king lifted his glass to them in a cheer before clinking glasses with his consort. She smiled at the matching adoration in the Diapolis rulers' eyes. In her world, a king could never marry another man. Ekotoria truly was different, and it filled her with happiness. If a ruler was free to love who he pleased, it gave her hope for Septima's future.

Dinner was served almost immediately. The feast spread across the center of the long table, and the sight made her mouth water. Grilled fish, several stews, fresh fruits and vegetables, and a variety of shellfish Aurelia could not identify were beautifully plated on crystalline platters.

The rest of the table waited for the king to serve himself out of respect before fixing their own plates. Cristos cleared his throat a few minutes later and caught the king's attention.

"Since you are well aware of the reason behind our visit, we should discuss it."

The king raised an eyebrow and dabbed his mouth with a napkin. "About my aiding you in the war against Warbotach?"

Cristos nodded once. "You have a history of remaining neutral, and I have always found that admirable. But Warbotach's invasions, and their desire to cross into the human lands, affect us all."

King Ailani's face was impassive as he countered Cristos' statement. "It affects all of you, but it has no impact on us. If Uldon wanted my territory, he would have come here instead of going north, but he did not. He bypassed my lands in his quest to conquer the portal, and the crown that controls it."

"Just because he has not set his sights on you yet does not mean he will not attempt to invade Diapolis in the future. If he cannot exert control over the crown and venture into the human lands, there is no telling what chaos he will unleash throughout Ekotoria. You and I both know his territory is dying, and he will not stop until he has claimed every bit of prosperous land he can. With the aid of your men and dragons, he does not stand a chance. Please. Help us defeat him once and for all."

King Ailani glanced at Aurelia before turning back to Cristos. Her heart sank at his apathetic expression. "If I prematurely thrust this war upon my people, then what is to stop you from requesting my aid in future conflicts? Diapolis' neutrality is what keeps us safe. If I change my stance now, then it will be expected again in the future, and I cannot commit to that."

Cristos ran his hand over his eyes and Aurelia could feel the anger seeping from him as he struggled to keep his tone level. "Hundreds, maybe even thousands, of people have already been slaughtered. Norithae and Aegricia have fallen. If Uldon crosses into the human realm, millions more will lose their lives. If he cannot get through the arch, then what? He has more than two-thirds of the continent under his control. Do you think, if trapped here, Uldon will leave Diapolis in peace? If you decide to watch this war unfold, you will have the blood of countless fae and humans on your hands at best, and your own blood and the blood of your people flowing freely through your neutral streets at worst."

The king's indifferent mask cracked, anger burning in his eyes as he glared daggers at Cristos. Aurelia's heart broke into a sprint as she grasped her lover's hand beneath the table. Had he gone too far?

Makoa brushed the back of the king's hand with his own, and just like that, Ailani recomposed himself. He smiled, but it did not reach his eyes as he addressed the entire table. "I will give it some thought. I may not have a decision before you leave tomorrow, but I will consider it. I give you my word. For now, enjoy the party. The path you travel is long, and there is no telling when you will find the opportunity to have fun again."

The table slowly resumed eating as King Ailani effectively ended the conversation, but Cristos fixated on his plate, his hand squeezing Aurelia's almost painfully. Her heart broke for him, and she longed to wipe the sullen expression from his face. He had lost more than anyone else among them. He lost his father and his kingdom in one fell swoop. She could not imagine how much pain he was in, and she was filled with guilt over their argument the night before. He had the weight of a kingdom on his shoulders, and she had added to his burden with her anger.

Dinner passed in silence. Servants cleared the table when the last fork was set down. The opulent chandeliers dimmed as a five-piece band began playing an upbeat melody. Aurelia had never heard music with such a tropical flair before, and it was infectious.

Cristos stood and offered his hand. After the disastrous conversation, she did not think he would be in the mood to dance, but she was excited, nonetheless. Dancing was a pastime she'd often indulged in with Septima in their room in Vaekros, and she missed it dearly. He led her around the ballroom floor in a flawless waltz. He was much more graceful than she imagined. The way he moved, the way he held her close, made her heart flutter.

Holera and Kason joined them on the dance floor. As they strolled past, Kason grinned at Cristos and murmured under his breath. "Blood flowing through his neutral streets, eh? I am sure that line will echo around in his mind all night. Good one."

Cristos smiled, but the couple had already moved on to the center of the ballroom before he could respond. Aurelia flushed as she saw the way they moved together. They were not doing anything inappropriate, but sensuality oozed from them. She wondered how long they had been together. She still did not know how they categorized their relationship, but it was clear they cared deeply for each other.

Cristos spun her, and she caught a glimpse of Calista floating past them in Kimo's arms. The captain of the guard gazed adoringly at the healer as they twirled around the dancefloor. Aurelia grinned broadly up at her lover as he pulled her close once more. She made a conscious decision to ignore the state of their diplomatic affairs for the night. There was nothing more they could do. It was all up to the king now. It seemed the rest of her companions were of the same mindset. They spent hours on the dance floor, reveling in the lighthearted music that flowed through the air.

By the end of the night, Aurelia's feet ached, and she had consumed far too much champagne. They left the ballroom first, and Cristos carried her back to their chambers after she almost stumbled into a flaming sconce in a deserted hall.

.

Cristos tried to help her out of her dress, but she twirled out of his reach as if they still occupied the grand ballroom.

"Aurelia, hold still. Let's get you into your night dress and wash your face."

"No," she said as she continued to hum a tune and dance around the room.

He groaned as he reached for her again. "We head back to camp tomorrow. You need to rest. Let me help you change."

She heaved an exasperated sigh and reached for the broach on her shoulder. She unpinned it, and the bodice peeled away from her torso and fell to her waist, resting on the full skirt. "Satisfied?"

"Very." Cristos' eyes darkened as he reached for her, and even in her alcohol-soaked mind, she knew sleep was no longer a priority.

Chapter Thirty-Nine

Diapolis

Aurelia's head pounded viciously as their traveling party prepared to take to the sky the following morning. The sun had barely begun its ascent, but the meager light was enough to make her squint. She thoroughly regretted her overindulgence. The champagne had been delicious, but the hangover was excruciating. Her stomach flipped dangerously as Cristos lifted her up and cradled her in his arms. While she was not looking forward to the flight, she was glad they were leaving their horses in Diapolis. The uneven road and bumpy gait would have been the death of her.

The mood was somber as Holera's powerful wings cut through the air, and she led the way with Kason astride her back. King Ailani had promised to consider their request, but both he and his consort were absent as they left. Aurelia found his lack of farewell a foreboding sign. She gazed over Cristos' shoulder, watching as the palace grew smaller in the distance. Her hope shrunk alongside the disappearing structure. Despite his reputation, she thought he would aid them in their desperate plight, if only to protect his kingdom's future. If the passionate speech Cristos' gave him at dinner did not sway his stance, she did not think that anything could.

They traveled hard throughout the day, hardly stopping for more than a few minutes to relieve themselves. They arrived in Claywind just as the sun set over the distant hills. They would reach their camp the following day if they kept up the grueling pace. She felt bad for Cristos and Holera. Calista, at least, could fly unhindered, but Aurelia and Kason were useless in the air. She wondered if it bothered the Aegrician male as much as it upset her.

They stopped at the same inn they'd visited on the way to the capital, and Kason purchased three rooms for the night. They ate dinner in the tavern before retreating to their chambers. The optimism that filled them on their first visit had been replaced by defeat, and no one seemed to have the energy for drinks and lighthearted conversation like last time.

The morose cloud followed Aurelia and Cristos to their room. He prepared her bath in silence as soon as they entered and sat on the bathing chamber floor as she washed up. The heavy sense of dread stole the joy that soaking in hot water usually gave her. She finished quickly and climbed out.

Cristos bathed as she pulled on her nightdress and braided her hair. The pair climbed into bed shortly after and held each other in the shadowed room. They avoided speaking about King Ailani and the war, but that left little to converse about. Diapolis' indecision increased the likelihood of their failure, and it was hard to think of anything else.

A small, wistful part of her hoped a raven would beat them back to camp carrying the promise of aid, but she knew that was unrealistic. Still, the idea of telling Blaedia they had not secured additional forces was far from appealing.

Her disheartened spirit zapped the life from her body and exhaustion consumed her. She stared at the dark ceiling for hours, listening to Cristos' steady breathing, before unconsciousness pulled her under and relieved her of the burden of failure.

A piercing scream ripped Aurelia from her dreamless sleep. She shot up in bed, her heart hammering, as she whipped her head from side to side in an attempt to identify the source. The extinguished candles and small strip of moonlight that peaked through the curtained window did little to illuminate their room.

Cristos was already out of bed and fastening his trousers before she realized that the shouts that continued to shatter the silence of the night were coming from the streets below.

"Something's wrong. Get dressed. Quickly." The urgency in his tone spurred her into action. Her hands trembled as she pulled on her fighting leathers. He'd already strapped on all his weapons by the time she laced her boots.

Frantic thumps sounded at their door as Holera yelled over the cacophony below.

"Warbotach soldiers are attacking. Get outside now!"

Aurelia's blood ran cold at her words. She froze, eyes wide, as she watched Cristos grab her bow and quiver.

"Hurry!" He shouted as he yanked the door open and dashed into the hall. She rushed after him and stuttered to a stop as she caught sight of the expressions on her friends' faces as they waited in the hall. They hastened down the stairs, shoving past patrons who darted about, trying to gather their belongings and flee the establishment while they still could.

When they finally pushed their way through the tavern exit, they saw a dozen Warbotach soldiers mounted on scarlet horses. They galloped toward the inn and fire spewed from the crimson beasts' mouths, setting the town ablaze as they went. Men, women, and children stumbled through the streets as the rampant inferno forced them from the safety of their homes. Some of the civilians wielded weapons in an attempt to defend their city, while others fled across the open fields that bordered the town in a mad dash to disappear within the tree line of Spectre Forest.

"Their horses breath fire!" Aurelia gasped. The terrified faces and pain-filled screams of those who fell victim to Warbotach overwhelmed her senses, and she focused on the beasts to prevent her tears from falling over the devastation that surrounded her. The peaceful town of Claywind was unrecognizable as flames and chaos reigned.

Cristos thrust her bow and quiver into her hands. "Kill as many as you can and keep your distance. Stay safe, love." He kissed her hard and quick. He was gone before she could reply, and the endearment that fell from his lips felt far too much like a goodbye. She watched as he drew his long sword and charged the nearest Warbotach beast. She'd never known fear as great as what consumed her when the horse reared back and unleashed its flames the moment Cristos tried to dismount its master. She didn't breathe as he took to the skies to avoid the blast.

Kason's expression hardened as he began barking commands. "Calista, warn King Ailani. Go!"

Calista erupted into flames without a word and shifted into her Phoenix form. Her massive wings kicked up dust and debris as she took off and headed toward Embershell.

"Aurelia, Holera! Go high. Somewhere with better aim."

Holera darted around the back of the tavern at his command. Aurelia ran after her, glancing back to see Kason, sword in hand, join Cristos, who was single-handedly battling three Warbotach soldiers.

She felt better about letting him out of her sight now that she knew he had backup. Holera had already used a cart parked alongside the inn to climb onto the roof. She reached down to help Aurelia up, her shorter frame making the ascent impossible alone.

They ran along the rooftop until they reached the edge. They both notched arrows as they stared at the horror unfolding below. The blazing buildings illuminated the road, and Aurelia scanned the carnage for a target. Her heart stuttered to a halt as she saw an enemy sword arching through the air toward Cristos' neck.

Afraid to distract him from the incoming threat, Aurelia bit back a scream. She froze in horrified silence as time seemed to slow. The wicked blade gleamed in the firelight as she fixated on her lover. Cristos ducked the swing at the last second and thrust his long sword up. She watched as the weapon pierced the Warbotach soldier's abdomen. The beastly male collapsed against Cristos as the blade exited his back. Cristos pulled his sword free and threw the corpse to the ground as another enemy bellowed in the distance and charged at him.

Holera elbowed her roughly to get her attention.

"Focus, Aurelia. Aim for those still atop their horses and then take the fire breathing beasts out. Our men can handle the ones already on foot. Be careful not to hit anyone on our side. There are a lot of Diapolisians down there."

Aurelia nodded and took a breath to steady herself. She pulled back the string on her bow and exhaled as she launched an arrow at one of the mounted soldiers in the distance. Her trembling hands threw off her aim, and she missed.

"Damn it," she hissed and notched another arrow. Holera shot, hitting the same male in the eye.

"Got him."

Aurelia had only ever shot animals, and even that had ladened her with guilt. How was she supposed to kill a person? She warred with herself internally as she tried to steel her nerves. She pulled her bowstring taut once again and searched for another target.

All doubt she had about harming someone disappeared as she watched a Warbotach soldier gallop toward a lone child in the street with his sword held high. She unleashed her arrow, not daring to breathe as it whistled through the air. It hit home, burying deep into the man's back. He fell from his steed but managed to climb to his feet. She notched another arrow, but a Diapolisian woman ran him through with a spear before she could fire.

Aurelia watched the woman usher the child toward safety before she set her sights on another enemy.

"Good job," Holera shouted as she downed another soldier with ease. The warrior's accuracy was startling in its magnificence, and Aurelia was envious. Would she have failed to save that small child if the townswoman hadn't interceded?

She shelved her doubts and continued to rain arrows down on the barbarians below. The violent bloodshed carried on for several long minutes before they downed all the Warbotach attackers, but it felt like a lifetime.

Aurelia and Holera watched as Cristos and Kason tied up the lone survivor and dragged him back to the inn. The soldier had tried to escape when their defeat became obvious, but Cristos had chased after him. He had thrown a dagger at the deserter and impaled his thigh to stop his retreat, but she wasn't sure why he had not killed the coward.

"Let's go," Holera said as she grabbed Aurelia by the arm and led her to the edge of the roof.

They climbed down and ran over to where Kason and Cristos stood, the injured Warbotach soldier firmly bound at their feet.

The townspeople did not waste time reveling in their victory. They gathered buckets of water and formed an assembly line as they battled the raging fires that threatened to destroy their town.

Cristos held the injured man's lead, so Aurelia maintained her distance as she scanned his body for injuries. She heaved a sigh of relief when she found none. Other than a soot smudge on his cheek, he looked the same as he had the night before

She turned to Kason and saw that his arm had been sliced, but the cut did not look deep. He seemed unfazed by the pain as he ripped the hem of his tunic and tied it around the wound. After he finished, he kneeled and began wrapping the Warbotach soldier's leg in another strip of his tunic.

"Why are you dressing his wounds? Just end his miserable existence. He doesn't deserve to live." Holera's voice was hard as her eyes shot dangers at the fettered male. Kason glanced up at her before he continued his ministrations.

"Because he's coming with us. It's only fair we return the treatment Warbotach showed you."

The hard edge in Kason's voice left no room for argument. His fierce expression was enough to tell her how he had fared while Holera had been captured and locked away with her companions in Norithae.

Chapter Forty

Spectre Forest

Aurelia pitied the Diapolisians who fought to save their home as the flames continued through their small town, but her party couldn't stay to help them. There was no time to waste. They couldn't even wait for Calista to return.

Holera and Aurelia rushed to gather their belongings and stopped to leave a message for the healer with the innkeeper while Kason finished binding the enemy's wound. As soon as the women rejoined the others, Holera shifted. The flames that surged as she changed forms drew the attention of those who battled the never-ending blaze, but as soon as they realized it wasn't a fire they needed to fight, they returned to the matter at hand.

Kason threw the tethered soldier across Holera's back and climbed up behind him. He didn't utter a word as he exerted his strength to still the Warbotach man, who struggled to break free. Aurelia wrapped her arms around Cristos' neck and buried her face in its crook as he cradled her. He kicked off the ground and followed Holera into the night sky. They traveled at a brutally fast pace as they raced back to their encampment. Violent winds thrashed against their bodies, making the flight bumpy and unstable, but they didn't slow. Aurelia was afraid to speak with the rushing air threatening to steal the breath from her lungs. All she could do was continue to cling to her lover, deeply inhaling his sandalwood and spice scent for comfort.

The sun rose as they dashed over Spectre Forest. The now illuminated trees were a blur of green below them. She could not help but wonder if Calista had reached King Ailani yet. She fervently hoped that the weight of the kingdom would come to the townspeople's aid.

Aurelia could not stop replaying the horrifying events in her mind. She could still hear the terrified screams, smell the singed flesh and burning homes. She could still see their faces as they feared for their lives. Even worse, she could still see the lifeless eyes of the Diapolisians that had not been lucky enough to survive. The visages of the soldiers she'd felled with her arrows began to flit around, mingling with the images of the atrocities they created. They were barbaric, and there was little doubt the world would be a better place without them, but she still struggled with the fact that she had killed someone.

Cristos held her tighter as he followed Holera's rapid descent into the forest. She wasn't sure if he'd scented her shame and heartbreak, or if he was simply securing his hold as they went in for their landing, but either way, she appreciated his comforting touch.

They landed just outside the barrier that surrounded the camp. Though Aurelia could not see the protective layer, she could feel its power buzzing through the air. They joined hands, Kason holding onto their Warbotach prisoner, and passed through the wards. The feeling of traversing the magic was far less uncomfortable than the mass of staring eyes that greeted them. The camp was alive with warriors on their way to breakfast, but they all halted as the group made their appearance.

Silence descended upon the busy clearing, and it unsettled her. She shifted her weight awkwardly before the general came to her rescue. Blaedia ran toward them, with Taryn less than a foot behind her and several other guards bringing up the rear. As the spectating warriors focused on their leader, Aurelia anxiously scanned their faces. A glimpse of ebony braids streaking through the air was her only warning before a body collided with hers, sending the breath rushing from her lungs.

"Lia!" Septima shrieked as she tackled her. Aurelia hugged her sister tight as she half-laughed and half-sobbed into her shoulder. They had only been apart for a few days, but it felt like a lifetime.

"I missed you so much." Her voice cracked as she murmured to her younger sister. Septima rolled off her, and they both sat up, dusting off their clothes. "How's Kano?" She was genuinely curious about her pet, but she also was not ready to share the recent events. It was always best to head Septima off before the interrogation could begin, or she'd never be able to escape her questioning.

Exie crouched beside them. "That cat is a big old baby," said Exie, flourishing her hand. "He is spoiled, absolutely rotten."

Aurelia smiled softly at her words, aching to see her furry friend.

"Ready to get something to eat?" Cristos asked as he approached them. She looked around him, watching as the general ordered a few men to haul the prisoner away for safekeeping. Blaedia patted Holera on the back and followed behind the prison transport.

She nodded. "What are they going to do with him?"

Cristos helped her to her feet and wiped the tear tracks from her face before he answered. "Blaedia is going to find out why they were in Diapolis, and then use him to send Uldon a message."

Septima and Exie joined the four returnees as they made for the dining tent. They hadn't eaten since the night before and had severely overexerted themselves in the time after, especially Holera and Cristos. They grabbed their plates and claimed a nearby table as they devoured their meals. Aurelia was so ravenous that she did not even taste the food before she swallowed.

She habitually glanced around the tent as they ate, waiting for the healer to arrive, but Calista had not made it back to the camp yet. Aurelia worried over both her safety and King Ailani's decision. If the events of Claywind were not enough to convince the king to aid them against Warbotach, then there was nothing that could sway him. Just as Cristos had said, their neutral blood ran in the streets of Diapolis, and now they waited to see how he would react to the attack. They had no way of knowing until Calista returned.

Holera and Kason finished first and left the tent, probably to interrogate the prisoner or possibly shower. They were all covered in grime and blood, so it wasn't an unlikely option, but the look in Kason's eye as he said they were taking the prisoner with them led her to believe it was probably the former. Cristos filled Exie and Septima in on the details of their disastrous trip throughout the meal. Aurelia remained silent, not wanting to speak about her experiences.

After they emptied their plates, Aurelia and Cristos showered quickly and set off in search of the prisoner. He was not hard to find. A newly erected tent stood beside the sparring ring with two guards posted outside its entrance. Blaedia strolled out, wiping her hands as they approached.

"Oh, hey. Did the two of you get something to eat?"

Aurelia nodded.

"We did," Cristos answered, before motioning toward the tent. "Did you find out anything from him yet?"

The general's face twisted into a fierce grimace. "They were sent to Claywind to send a message."

"What message?" Cristos moved in closer to Blaedia.

"That nowhere is safe. Uldon wanted to make sure King Ailani knew Diapolis was next. Apparently, he wants the entire continent under his thumb before he crosses the portal."

Aurelia gasped, her heart stuttering as she listened. "What if other towns were attacked?"

Cristos spoke at the same time. "Has word been sent to the king?"

Blaedia nodded. "A raven is being sent now. I would not doubt if they targeted other towns. Hopefully, they can respond to the attacks quickly with the aid of their dragons."

"What's the plan moving forward?" She heard Cristos questioning the general, but it was hard for her to focus on the conversation. All she could imagine was the scene that had unfolded in Claywind, unfolding throughout the rest of the peaceful, tropical kingdom.

"We march on Norithae next and unseat Uldon's general. I hope your people are ready to fight, as you said, because we can't take back Aegricia on our own."

"They will fight. I will send word to my spies. They will make sure my people are prepared for our arrival."

Blaedia gave a curt nod and headed for her tent. Cristos pulled Aurelia into his arms as soon as they were alone and crushed her to his chest. He had undoubtedly sensed her crippling anxiety, and his firm hold helped ground her as the world spun beneath her feet. He waited until she'd calmed down to pull away. The absence of his warmth was almost painful, and she fought the urge to cry. Cristos leaned his forehead against hers. "I must go send a message to my people. You should visit Kano, and I'll meet you there as soon as I finish."

She nodded hesitantly, her frazzled nerves making her unwilling to part with him. Still, Aurelia stiffened her spine and started toward Kano's enclosure while Cristos went in the opposite direction. The air hummed around her as bumps rose along her arms. She shivered as she glanced around the camp, but no one else seemed to hear the vibrations that set her teeth on edge. She knew it had to be her own anxiety playing tricks on her, but she struggled to breathe as trepidation overwhelmed her. Her brisk walk turned into a mad dash across camp. Seeing Kano would calm her—hopefully.

The magnificent tiger sat at the edge of his enclosure and stared in her direction as if he was waiting for her to arrive. As soon as he spotted her, he stood on his hind legs, and the fence groaned under the weight of his massive paws. She pulled her medallion out and rushed to greet him. She only managed to take a few steps inside before Kano leaped on her. They toppled to the ground. He nuzzled her forcefully, pulling a giggle out of her throat. His rough tongue left a slimy trail up her face as she pushed his giant head out of licking range.

"Calm down, boy!"

Kano growled low in his throat, his version of pouting, and flopped onto his back for a belly rub. Aurelia laughed under her breath as she caressed him. She was more grateful for the opportunity to do so than she ever had been before. She probably appreciated petting him more than he enjoyed receiving the caresses. Just hours before, she wasn't sure she'd ever see her precious cat again, and she reveled in their time together.

The uncertainties of the future, the endless possibilities, bombarded her. How would the war affect the gentle giant? Kano's impressive size and ferocious bite would be helpful in battle, but she did not want him to get hurt. Kano was loving, but protective. She had little doubt he would tear anyone who tried to harm her to shreds, but how could she take advantage of his unwavering loyalty and put him in harm's way? If the entire camp was to march on Norithae and then Aegricia, did the phoenixes expect him to join the attack? They needed all the help they could get, but it was her job as his guardian to ensure his safety.

Aurelia continued to argue with herself, her thoughts going in a vicious circle. Both sides were valid, and she couldn't decide what to do. She leaned back against the trunk of a massive tree and closed her eyes, pulling the fresh forest air into her lungs with deep breaths to steady herself. Kano plopped his head in her lap, and she stroked behind his ears as she continued to struggle with her indecision.

Warm lips pressed against her cheek, startling her awake. She hadn't even realized she fell asleep, but when she opened her eyes, the sun was lower in the sky. Cristos smiled as he leaned over her. She wondered how he had gotten inside Kano's fenced in home, but the question answered itself before she got to ask as her sister and Exie sat on the ground by her feet. Cristos took the spot beside her and wrapped his arm around her shoulders, pulling her close. "I saw you were asleep, so I went to talk to Blaedia."

Her eyebrows pinched in confusion as she rubbed the sleep from her eyes. Hadn't they gotten all the information they needed from her earlier? "About what?"

"I thought it was time to tell her who I am. Then I ran into Septima and Exie, and I told them as well."

Her eyes grew wide. "What did she say?"

Cristos chuckled. "Apparently, the general had already received Kason's message and knew. Septima, on the other hand, smacked me." Septima smirked at him. "But we've since made up." Her sister rolled her eyes and chuckled.

Aurelia tilted her head as curiosity reared inside her, but she let it go for now. She would hound her little sister for the details later. It wasn't like the youngest Vesta sibling to be so forgiving. "Well, I'm glad. I think your secret is safe with them."

He nodded and kissed her temple. "I think so too."

They remained in the enclosure for another hour before the lunch bell rang. They all said their goodbyes to Kano and headed for the dining tent. A line was already forming when they arrived, but the camp was still bustling with activity. It was an unusual sight. Usually, as soon as mealtime was signaled, all goings-on halted as everyone rushed to eat, but that wasn't the case today.

Dozens of warriors, male and female, were paired up both inside and out of the training rings. The sparring matches were intense and unyielding as clanging weapons rang throughout the clearing. Blaedia must have informed them of the impending battle. Aurelia watched as they honed their impressive skills, and she never felt more unprepared.

Aurelia and Cristos retired early that night. Now that the adrenaline of the attack had completely worn off, their long day had caught up to them, and sleep was imperative. Even as exhaustion tugged at her consciousness, Aurelia could not stop thinking about Uldon's plan to conquer the continent. Blaedia and Taryn had been so certain that he would stop at nothing to cross the portal and make the human realm his domain. No matter how she looked at the situation, it just didn't make sense. Why did he suddenly decide to attack Diapolis? If anything, it just ensured that the tropical kingdom would join up in arms against him and add dragons to his enemies' ranks. His course of action baffled her. She curled up into Cristos' arms, tucking her head beneath his chin.

"Do you think Uldon is working with someone else? I mean, could someone be backing him in his bid to conquer Ekotoria? I just don't understand why he circled back to Diapolis if the human world is his end goal."

Cristos shrugged. "It's possible that he allied with someone from off the continent." He released a breath. "That's a scary prospect.

Uldon is unstable, at best. If he has the power of another nation behind him... I sincerely hope that is not the case."

She agreed. Just dwelling over the possibility made her chest tighten uncomfortably. "It is quite terrifying. Did Blaedia tell you when we will head for Norithae?"

"They're still handling the logistics, but it sounds like we'll set out in a week or less if they can iron out all the details. We are going to move closer first. Once we're in position, scouts will advance ahead and release the prisoner to deliver a message."

She tilted her face up to stare at him with a furrowed brow. "What's the message?"

His blue eyes sparkled in the dim candlelight as he looked down at her. "Surrender or die."

The words sent a foreboding chill ripping through her body. Once the prisoner delivered that message, there was no turning back. Not that they could turn back, anyway. Ekotoria could not carry on as it was. War needed to wage before peace could reign—if they won, that is.

Her sense of dread kept growing as she fixated on the danger looming in their near future. Cristos lifted her chin and leaned down to kiss her gently.

"Don't worry, love. I won't let anything happen to you."

She smiled softly at the endearment, but his words did not assuage her fears. She had far more to lose in this war than just her own life.

Chapter Forty-One

Spectre Forest

The next morning came and went, and Calista had still not returned from Diapolis. They had not received any word from her, and the entire camp worried about her absence. Aurelia hoped she was delayed because she was going to return with members of the Diapolis military. The southerners would have no hope of finding the encampment without her, but it was probably just wishful thinking. There had not been any messenger ravens from King Ailani, either.

The camp's atmosphere completely changed as they prepared to march on Norithae the following morning. People tended not to linger as much. The training rings were always occupied, and there was less socializing after dinner. Before they'd been captured in the forest, ending the night drinking and playing card games in Exie's tent was the norm, but now all their spare time was occupied with war preparations. She imagined the same went for the rest of the camp. Now that the promise of battle was on the horizon, fun and entertainment were neglected, replaced with sparring and sharpening weapons.

Aurelia and Cristos spent hours in the clearing outside their tent with Septima and Exie in an attempt to hone their skills. Even as Aurelia pushed herself, sweat soaking her tunic, she could not match the intensity with which the phoenix trained. Exie seemed to have no lasting damage from her injuries, and the viciousness with which she swung her blade intimidated Aurelia. She almost pitied her sister for being on the other end of the strikes.

Septima and the blond warrior went public with their relationship while Aurelia and the others were in Diapolis. They continued to share Exie's tent and seemed incredibly happy together, but that affection was nowhere to be seen as they circled each other with swords held high. As she watched them spin and slash in a violent dance, Aurelia could not help but think about their future. One day, Septima would age, and Exie would maintain her magical youth. The worry over their future mirrored one of the biggest fears in her own relationship, but at least she had some hope of having an extended lifespan thanks to her mother's fae blood. Still, there was no guarantee that she'd live longer, and she honestly wasn't sure what she dreaded more: losing Septima by not aging or losing Cristos by growing old.

When the dinner bell rang that evening, her exhaustion was bone deep. Her fatigued muscles screamed as she forced herself to lift each spoonful of stew. The meal tent was filled with the same seriousness that consumed the rest of the camp. There was no light-hearted conversation as they devoured their food.

When the couples went their separate ways afterward, a firm knot took root in Aurelia's stomach and refused to dissipate. With every passing moment, the move grew closer, and the pit of her stomach grew tighter. She tried not to dwell on what morning would bring as she and Cristos headed for their tent hand-in-hand and instead focused on the promise of washing away the day's stench.

Aurelia opened the tent flap, intending to fetch a set of clean clothes before heading for the shower tent, but she stumbled to a halt as Cristos lit a candle. The soft glow danced along the surface of a metal basin large enough for her to soak in. Her eyes darted over to her lover in shock, and he smiled at her.

"What?" It wasn't even the question she wanted to ask, but her brain refused to function properly as he cupped her face tenderly and kissed her.

"Surprise. I thought a bath would help ease some of your stress."

Her heart swelled at the gesture. How could she not fall for such a thoughtful man?

"How did you get this in here? When?" she asked as he grinned and kissed her again. They'd been training outside their tent's entrance all day, and she could not figure out how he'd managed to pull it off.

"I begged Kason to help me. He snuck it in while we were at dinner."

She looked from him to the massive basin once again. The steam rose from the water in swirling ribbons that beckoned her. She felt the tension begin to lessen in her sore limbs as she pulled off her shoes and unbuttoned her tunic. She slid the top off and let it fall in a heap at her feet as she began to unfasten her trousers. Cristos' hungry gaze followed her every move, but he did not touch her as she stripped bare.

"I can't believe you did this. I had not even dared to wish for a bath since we returned." She was certain he could scent the overwhelming love she felt for him in that moment, but she was still not brave enough to say the words. "You're too good to me."

His eyes flashed with an unreadable emotion before he walked over to the soaking basin and offered his hand. Aurelia took it and stepped in, slowly sinking into the hot water. She let out a pleasure filled moan as she fully submerged her aching body. The basin was too small for them to both fit, but Cristos didn't seem to mind as he pulled a wooden stool over and sat behind her.

He used a glass to pour the gloriously heated liquid over her. "How's the temperature?"

She hummed, sinking further. "Delicious."

"Do you want me to wash your hair?"

She nodded as she stifled a yawn, feeling incredibly lucky to call such a man hers.

His strong fingers massaged her scalp, and the smell of lavender filled her nose, creating a relaxing yet sensual experience.

"You look like you're about to fall asleep." His voice was like velvet, low and smooth, and the deep cadence lulled her heavy eyelids shut as he rinsed the shampoo.

" I just might. Thank you for taking such great care of me."

"Anything for you." He kissed her temple and set the glass aside before he lathered up a cloth and began to wash her body tenderly. He rinsed the parts that were not submerged as she sighed happily. There was nowhere in the world she would rather be right then. "Are you ready to get out?"

She frowned as the pampering came to an end, but agreed. They were setting out for Norithae at first light, and they needed to rest.

She expected Cristos to bathe after her, but after he helped her out, he grabbed a towel and began to dry her off. As he thoroughly rubbed the plush fabric over her body, her eyes fluttered shut once more. When his lips followed the path of the towel, she had never felt more cherished.

Kneeling at her feet, he spread her legs, tossing the damp fabric aside once he wiped away the last of the water droplets. His mouth found her core, and her knees buckled, but his firm hands gripped her waist. He supported her frame as he gave her slit a slow lick. Her thighs twitched, and he smiled against her heated flesh. She gasped as he hooked one leg over his shoulder. Another torturous swipe of his tongue had her tangling her fingers in his hair and yanking roughly. Her calf brushed against his wings and they fluttered in response as he buried his face between her thighs.

She arched her back in pleasure, moaning his name as he ravaged her. He sucked on the sensitive bundle of nerves at her center, and she almost climaxed right there. "Bed. Please." Desire laced her voice, making it unrecognizable as she issued the command.

Cristos obliged, lifting her and carrying her across the room. He pulled away and lowered her onto the fur blankets that covered their mattress.

She sprawled on her back, the smooth fur caressing her bare skin as she held his gaze. He was still fully clothed, and she leaned up to unbutton his tunic, but he pressed her back down gently. "Tonight is about you, love."

He bent her legs and pushed them up until her knees were even with her shoulders, then he spread them apart and lowered his head. Stars exploded in her vision as he worshiped her with his tongue. The pleasure he gave her was second to none, but she wanted more. There was no telling what the attack on Norithae's invaders would bring in the morning. Though she hated to focus on the negative outcomes, it was entirely possible that this could be their last night together. She wanted to satisfy him as much as he satisfied her.

"Go wash up. I'll be waiting."

Cristos' ocean eyes darkened at her words, and he hastened to follow her directive. She'd never been sexually demanding before, but he had a way of filling her to the brim with confidence. She rolled over and watched him as he shed his clothes. He bathed in record time, but his hands lingered as he washed his hardened length and stared intently into her eyes.

Aurelia bit her lip as she enjoyed the view, squirming to relieve the tingling pressure that began to build between her legs once more. After rising from the tub, Cristos dried off quickly and returned to the bed, but it felt far too slow as the need coursed through her. His warm body slid along hers as he crawled onto the bed and claimed her lips in a deep and luxurious kiss.

The slow swipes of his tongue made her feel like they had all the time in the world. She ran her fingers through his silky black hair as his hands slid up her arms, gently pulling them above her head and holding them in place. She was left panting as his lips left hers and trailed down her neck, leaving sensual kisses in his wake. He shifted, adjusting his grip so that he held both of her wrists in one hand, pinning her to the bed as his other hand traced down the outline of her body until he reached her chest. Bowing his head, he cupped her breast, kneading it in his palm before gently easing it into his mouth.

She pulled at his hold, her hands aching to roam his muscular form, but he tightened his grasp and pressed her harder against the bed. He continued to suck and nip at her breast as his hand trailed downward, sliding over the plane of her stomach until he found that sensitive bundle of nerves at her center. His fingers circled it lightly, increasing in pressure until she panted. She undulated under him, her body on fire as it filled to the brim with lust. He slipped two fingers inside her, pumping and twisting vigorously as he wound her body up like a tightly coiled spring.

Her body craved the feel of him deep inside her, and she couldn't handle any more of his teasing. She begged him to impale her with his stiff cock, and her dirty words did the trick. He pressed her hands so hard against the mattress that it almost hurt as he slammed inside her. His pace was brutal and punishing. Electricity surged through her body, and her torso bowed off the bed with the force of her climax as he pinned the rest of her body down. Aurelia screamed herself hoarse, his name on her lips, as she rode the intense waves of her pleasure.

When she came back down from the high, he released his grip and hovered above her. His pace slowed dramatically, their bodies sliding against each other like smooth silk as he made love to her. The frantic energy was replaced with emotion as he languidly kissed her.

When he pulled away and rested his forehead against hers, his eyes shined bright in the dim candlelight as he murmured quietly.

"I love you."

"I love you, too."

The dangers they'd face tomorrow fueled the passion that ignited between them. If this was their last night together, she was going to savor every last second. They took their time, enjoying each other's bodies until they were exhausted and sated, and when Aurelia fell asleep, she did so in the arms of the man she loved.

Chapter Forty-Two

Spectre Forest

Fog crept between the trees, swirling ominously throughout the camp, as if Spectre Forest mourned the violence that awaited them as they journeyed north. Warriors energetically flitted about as they packed their tents and prepared to leave. They seemed to vibrate with anticipation, but Aurelia was somber as she headed to breakfast. She could understand their excitement. This was the first major step they'd made toward reclaiming their home and rescuing their queen. But she was not eager to experience war, and she did not feel prepared enough to fight. Even Septima seemed hesitant as she assisted Exie with her lanista duties.

After they ate, Aurelia and Cristos grabbed their weapons and satchels from their tent before a warrior came and used her magic to shrink it down to traveling size. Aurelia was curious about how that particular magic worked, but she hesitated to ask as the warrior moved on to the next canvas structure and repeated the process.

The moon had begun its slow descent beyond the horizon, but not a hint of daylight was to be found. She couldn't shake the sense of foreboding that seemed to follow her as the eerie mist licked at her ankles.

According to Blaedia, a majority of their forces would travel on foot through the forest to avoid detection. The element of surprise was imperative to achieve rapid success with minimal damage.

The general sent a few phoenixes ahead to Aegricia, so they had an idea of the state of their territory and civilians. As soon as they ousted Warbotach from Norithae, they were going to reclaim their home. Not only were the scouts tasked with gathering information, but they would also have to spread the word quietly among their people. When the time came, Aegricia needed all able-bodied citizens to take up arms—even those who were not warriors. Most importantly, the people who were subjugated by Uldon needed to know there was still hope, and that their army had not abandoned them.

Though most of the warriors of the encampment were to march on Norithae, Blaedia staggered their departures to avoid the risk of mass casualties if Warbotach set upon them as they traveled.

There would also be a flying squadron who would reach Norithae first to monitor the positioning of Warbotach's soldiers and make camp to the northwest as they waited to attack. They planned to send one of the more unassuming females into the city undercover as a merchant, and covertly notify the citizens of their approach. Cristos also sent a raven to one of his most trusted spies the night before, but it was impossible to know if the message had been received.

As the first of the phoenixes set out beyond the wards, Cristos and Aurelia went to fetch Kano. The great cat would join their trek through the forest on a leash. She worried that her beloved pet would get hurt on their travels, but he would be an invaluable source of protection. There was no way Warbotach soldiers and their fiery mounts could ambush them with Kano present. He would hear any signs of ambush and alert her. Still, she feared the animal she had sworn to love and protect would get hurt more than she worried about herself.

Exie and Septima finished fastening the leather leash and harness to him as they arrived. The harness wasn't necessary since Kano would never break the leash and run, but many of the warriors were still wary of his massive size and powerful canines. He was certainly strong enough to free himself from the tether, but he would never do so unless it was to defend Aurelia or her sister. It was a small concession to make in order to give her traveling companions peace of mind.

Aurelia wrapped the leather lead around her hand, and the group of four made their way to the sparring rings with the tiger in tow. Most of the remaining warriors had already gathered and were talking amongst themselves as they arrived. Travel packs and other personal belongings littered the ground at their feet as they waited to set out.

The grim skies began to lighten as Blaedia lifted her fist in the air, and dozens of warriors burst into colorful flames as they shifted into their firebird forms. They launched from the forest floor in unison and flew high above the canopy of leaves that sheltered the camp. Aurelia watched as a kaleidoscope of vibrant phoenixes headed for Norithae.

Taryn approached the invisible barrier that surrounded them with a few other females. The air in the clearing hummed around them as they removed the wards, the thick fog stirring as their magic swirled around them. Aurelia felt the moment the shield dispersed, and her anxiety surged as they were left exposed to enemies and the elements alike.

The temperature was frigid, but she was thankful that there was no snow as they began their long march. They had to traipse through the dense trees and foliage when their journey began, carefully avoiding gnarled roots that threatened to slow their progression. The thick canopy blocked most of the sunlight, only letting narrow slivers of sunlight shine through like dying spotlights on the forest floor.

The harsh weather and minimal illumination had little bearing on the lush trees that seemed to follow their own set of nature's laws. In the Howling Forest of Vaekros, winter left branches barren while leaves littered the ground and slowly decayed to enrich the soil that once gave them life. But in Ekotoria, the trees held tight to their vibrant greenery like prized possessions they could not bear to part with.

The absence of natural debris helped to keep their footsteps stealthy as they trekked through the forest. Blaedia planned to march north until nightfall. Once the meager rays were replaced by the moon's soft glow, they would erect their protective wards once more and set up a temporary camp for the night. At daybreak, they would set out once more for a much shorter journey. The group would halt a few miles outside of Norithae's borders and make a more permanent camp as they waited for word that the undercover warrior had succeeded in alerting the citizens. Aurelia didn't think she would be able to breathe easily until the protective magic surrounded them once more.

The general had methodically planned the positioning of both their camp and the northern camp of the flying squadron. When the time came, they would hit the invaders fast and hard. With the Elder Sea extending along the eastern coast, Aegrician warriors coming from the northwest and southwest, and Norithaean civilians amassing their forces in the center, Warbotach would not be able to flee nor request more forces. Blaedia left nothing up to chance now that they were finally making a move against the barbarians that had captured her queen and sent her warriors fleeing to the human world.

The large group never wavered or slowed their procession as they marched. It was the first time Aurelia did not worry about being attacked by hellhounds or any of the other dangerous creatures that called the Spectre Forest home. Hundreds of phoenixes moved purposefully toward their destination, with dozens of males mixed into their ranks. Even with safety in their vast numbers, they held their weapons aloft like they were prepared to strike down any threat foolish enough to challenge them. Their show of strength gave Aurelia a small semblance of comfort. They may very well be marching to their deaths, but she was unlikely to reach her end before the battle raged—hopefully.

Cristos' expression matched the steely resolve of their companions as he held Aurelia's hand firmly in his. Her other hand gripped Kano's leash so tightly that her knuckles blanched. They traveled in silence to avoid attracting unwanted attention. While they were unlikely to come across a force strong enough to intimidate their warriors, they did not want to lose the element of

322   CROWN OF THE PHOENIX

surprise by alerting Warbotach of their approach. Cristos would gently squeeze Aurelia's hand on occasion or lean over to kiss her temple, and his small gestures assured her in place of the comfort his words normally gave her.

She kept stealing glances at Septima and Exie, who were bringing up the rear astride a large black mare. The warriors did not have many animals among them, aside from Kano, but the few they had remained under the lanistas' care as they traveled.

After Aurelia turned back from staring at her sister, she caught sight of a wide grin gracing Cristos' lips. He watched her intently as they trailed behind the phoenixes, who led their party. It was hard not to blush as his stare remained fixed on her.

"What are you looking at?" she whispered.

His broad smile only grew. "You."

She nudged him with her shoulder, careful not to stumble as they zigzagged between thick trunks and verdant greenery. "I can see that, but why?"

Cristos leaned in and whispered in her ear. "Because you are so beautiful."

His breath caressed the shell of her ear and made her tingle in unmentionable places. She bit her lip to hide her smile as warmth spread throughout her body.

They continued their trek in silence. As the sun retired for the day, the group began to set up camp in a large clearing that placed them within a day's hike of the kingdom of Norithae. Though the open space was vast, it was miniscule in comparison to the one they had previously occupied. They were forced to erect fewer tents and double up in order to provide shelter for everyone.

Exie, Septima, Aurelia, and Cristos had to bunk together. While there would be no way for Aurelia and Cristos to have any alone time, she was happy to spend time with her sister and her friend.

After they placed their satchels inside their tent and deposited Kano in his temporary enclosure, the couples headed for the shower tent. The camp's original set up held dozens of curtained stalls, but the makeshift bathing area only contained small basins and cloths to wash up with. It was cold and uncomfortable after their jaunt through the freezing forest, but at least they had access to fresh water. Aurelia was grateful for that luxury now that war loomed just beyond the horizon.

The smell of roasting meat wafted through the air as they exited, clean but shivering as the cool night air rushed against their skin. The succulent aroma would have attracted every carnivore within a few miles, if not for the wards, and Aurelia was thankful to be safely behind the magical barrier once more. The four made their way to the center of camp where a giant, freshly built fire roared. Aurelia had not noticed hunters gathering game as they marched on, but when she caught sight of deer and rabbit roasting over the large flames, she was grateful they had.

She rushed to stand near the blaze, desperate for its warmth as she wrapped her cloak tighter around herself. Cristos came up behind her and pulled her into a tight embrace. His natural warmth encompassed her, and she snuggled into him as his wings curled around them, blocking the chilled breeze.

Aurelia scanned the clearing and saw warriors surrounding smaller bonfires that were scattered amongst the tents. The only times she saw the camp's occupants en masse were when they'd gathered to move locations. Their numbers were as intimidating as the controlled strength they'd moved with, but she could not help but wonder if it would be enough to defeat Warbotach and their malicious king. If everything went according to Blaedia's plan and they managed to take Norithae, would there be enough survivors to reclaim Aegricia? Her fears were relentless and all-consuming as she returned her empty stare to their roasting meal.

Aurelia watched the flames lick at the darkness, a small light trying to conquer the night. Was that what they were? Cristos leaned forward and pressed his cheek against hers.

"What are you thinking about?" he asked.

She shrugged, and her eyes fluttered shut as she let the warmth of his face permeate her, hoping it would thaw her icy trepidation. "A bit of everything, but mostly about the war and who will survive the next few days."

He pulled away, and she instantly missed his heat until he spun her around. His gaze was fierce, shining with determination. "I've told you that I will let nothing happen to you, and I mean it." Cristos cupped her face gingerly and gave her a soft kiss. The gentleness of his lips reached the depths of her heart.

When he pulled away, she stared at him for a long moment as she tried to commit every minute detail to memory. The way his blue eyes sparkled as brilliantly as the Elder Sea when he was happy. The way his thick, dark hair always stuck up in odd directions when he woke up. The way his chiseled bone structure softened when he smiled. The way he had looked at her as he told her he loved her. The sound of his voice when he said her name. His laugh. She wanted to lock every single thing about him into a war-proof box inside her mind.

"Even fighting side-by-side, you will not be able to watch me every second. I know you will do your best to keep me safe, but there's no guarantee that I will remain so. If so-" Her voice broke, but she soldiered on. "If something happens to me, I do not want you to blame and punish yourself. I would be sad if I were the reason you stopped smiling."

The passionate fire in his eyes softened as he stared at her. "What would there be to make me smile if I did not have you?"

Aurelia brushed her fingertips along his cheekbone. She didn't have an answer to his question, because if he were to die, then her happiness would die along with him.

He hugged her so tight she could hardly breathe as he whispered in her ear. "Please don't fight. Stay in the camp."

She smiled at his words, but it did not reach her eyes. Aurelia knew she was far from the best warrior, but she could not remain safely tucked away while the two people she loved most in life risked their lives. It wasn't even just Septima and Cristos she worried about. The faces of her friends flashed through her mind's eye. Exie. Taryn. Holera. Kason. Even Blaedia. No, she could not let them put their heart and soul into the coming battle while she hid like a coward. "I can't do that. This war only has one outcome I can live with and to achieve it, we will need every weapon raised against Warbotach. I am able-bodied, and I will fight for the freedom of Ekotoria and the human world. I may have left my father and brother behind, but I must do my part to protect them from magical subjugation."

Cristos cupped her face as he stared into her eyes, and his features fell at whatever he saw looking back at him. As much as she knew he wanted to keep his promise, there was no guarantee, and she was determined to join their ranks in battle. "Then please keep Kano by your side. I trust he will protect you if I fail."

Aurelia's heart sank at the thought of dragging her beloved tiger into battle. She was supposed to protect him, not put him in danger. She kept silent, unable to agree with his suggestion. The rational part of her knew Kano would rather die protecting her than live without her, but the emotional part was not willing to allow it.

Dinner being served brought their conversation to an abrupt halt, and Aurelia was glad for the reprieve. She needed time to think before she made her decision. On one hand, the tiger would have no one if she and Septima both perished in battle. On the other hand, she had cared for him since he was a cub, and she loved him like family. For the first time, she regretted the day her father brought him home. Kano should have happily lived out his days as King of the Jungle, far from the war that wasn't his to fight.

They ate in silence before heading to bed alongside Exie and Septima. With an early morning ahead of them, the four blew out their candles and crawled into their beds.

With Cristos' arm draped over her and his warm body pressed against her back, Aurelia tried to silence her racing mind enough to sleep. Her old life had been safer, but it was also empty. Even as she prepared to stare death in the face, she had no regrets. Still, she longed for the day her new life became just as safe and predictable as the old.

Chapter Forty-Three

Spectre Forest

*T*he chill of the isolated stone cell permeated Otera's bones as she
curled up on the dank floor in a futile attempt to warm herself.
*The wind whipped harshly through the tiny window overhead as the
moon's soft beams taunted her. Its gentle glow served as a reminder
of her dreary situation. The night was free to come and go while she
remained stuck in time, never leaving her confines.*

*The wounds Uldon inflicted the last time they met had healed,
but she had yet to see the Warbotach leader since. Bremusa was also
absent, her last vestige of hope disappearing alongside the elderly
woman. Otera spent her monotonous days wondering where her
army was and if they were okay. Would they come for her and
free their people? Or would she remain forgotten in that dreadful
dungeon until she turned to dust? Uldon's men had captured her
commander once. Was he able to hunt her down again? And what
if her general fell? Without Blaedia and Taryn, their forces were
bound to crumble.*

Doubt and fear mingled in a toxic cocktail that plagued Otera. She wanted to believe in her worries, but she had been trapped for so long. The endless days and nights blended until she could no longer track the passage of time. She closed her eyes, trying to muster up the will to carry on when all hope seemed to be lost.

Faint breathing reached her ears, and she startled upright. Her eyes snapped open as she whipped her head around, trying to locate the source. She heard it. She knew *she heard the soft cadence of air being inhaled and exhaled. Or was the solitude starting to warp her mind?*

"Hello? Who is there?" The door had not opened, but still she could not shake the feeling that another presence lurked somewhere in her lonesome cage.

"Hello?" Otera climbed to her feet, and her atrophying muscles shook violently from disuse as she scanned the poorly lit room. The foreign breaths sped up, and her own increased to match the rapid chilling her blood, but the room was empty.

Aurelia jolted upright, chest heaving violently as she looked around the dark tent. Cristos still slept beside her, not so much as twitching at her sudden motion. Exie and Septima occupied the other bedroll and remained blissfully unconscious as she tried to stifle her anxiety.

Her dream haunted her as her shadowed surroundings took on the desolate chill of Otera's cell. It had felt so real, like her spectral form was really beside the imprisoned Queen. The first time she'd dreamed of the Aegrician ruler, the illusions were foggier, but this time Otera knew she was there. Aurelia knew it was just a dream, but she could not shake the ominous feeling that had embedded itself in her chest.

Aurelia had never actually laid eyes on the woman before, but she'd visibly changed between the two unconscious sightings. Her frame was far more sunken as starvation and inactivity took its toll. Was her subconscious really strong enough to fabricate those minute details? Still, there was no way she'd actually visited the dungeon as she slept.

She continued her internal argument as she tried to steady her frantic breathing. She wondered if maybe this was what Variel had warned her of. Maybe her mother's fae blood was manifesting within her. Was this magic? Were those encounters actually visions? No. It was only a dream. It had to be a dream, because if it wasn't, she would have to watch as Septima aged and died while she maintained her youth. Fate was so cruel. She did not want to be a helpless spectator as her sister withered away, nor did she want Cristos to witness her own life fading.

The impossibility of their future weighed on her heart as she settled back down in bed. *It was just a dream.* The words became a mantra she repeated as she tried to will herself back to sleep. Cristos pulled her close, snuggling into her as a soft snore escaped his parted lips. She closed her eyes and firmly set her feet in denial as she drifted off into a blissful, dreamless slumber.

A raven arrived the following morning as the camp rushed through breakfast before preparing to set out on another long hike through

Spectre Forest. Blaedia received the message and shared its contents with their forces. The prisoner had reached Windreach, the capital city of Norithae, and delivered their warning to Warbotach. Their enemies now knew to be prepared for battle, though they did not know when the Aegrician forces would strike. Though sending the prisoner back gave away an element of surprise, the usurpers did not know that Norithae would raise their weapons alongside them. Blaedia felt the taunting news would draw the Warbotach soldiers out from under the palace walls. Hopefully, fighting out in the open would be enough to protect the innocent civilians that still filled the territory. She did not want to sacrifice any who were either too young or unable to fight.

They still had seen no sign of Calista yet. The longer she was gone, the more worried Aurelia became. There was a chance that King Ailani would send his dragons and men to aid them, but there was also a chance that he blamed their presence in his kingdom for the attack.

She tried not to dwell on the negative possibility, because they would need their help in order to reclaim Aegricia. Norithae was guarded lightly compared to the phoenixes' northern territory. Aegricia had the crown, the queen who wielded it, and the portal. Uldon and the bulk of his forces guarded the kingdom and the power they so desperately desired with an intensity that would make it almost impossible to reclaim without Diapolis' help.

After Blaedia shared the message with the camp, the warriors packed up with renewed vigor, and they continued their journey to Norithae with weapons held high and a ferocity in their eyes that made Aurelia's heart pound nervously. This was it. The foretold war would rage soon, and time was moving far too quickly.

This leg of the trip was shorter than the previous one, since they were stopping several miles away from the city to remain unseen by Warbotach. Blaedia was certain patrols would comb the forest for signs of their approach. In order to avoid being spotted, the most powerful phoenixes would erect a protection barrier that moved with them as they grew nearer to Norithae's border. Aurelia was stunned to learn that a mobile ward was possible and asked Cristos why they hadn't marched under a shield the day before. He explained it required an excessive amount of energy to perform and maintain the magic, so it was something that wasn't used unless absolutely necessary.

The warriors were silent as wraiths as they floated over the underbrush, ready to exact their revenge. The probability of encountering Warbotach soldiers was high as they neared their destination. They advanced with such stealth that not even a felled twig snapped as they moved through the dense trees.

Even Kano stepped carefully as he walked beside Aurelia. His warm flank pressed against her leg protectively while his ears twitched as he focused on the natural sounds that filled Spectre Forest. The tiger may not have understood what was happening, but he had always been sensitive to the emotions of those around him. The way he treaded lightly and hovered close to her side was his usual response to her unease. She reached her leash-wrapped hand down to stroke his head. The action was meant to soothe him, but it also helped lessen the weight on her own heart. It was impossible not to think back to her conversation with Cristos the night before, as her feline protector prowled beside her. He would hate to be left behind as she ran headfirst into danger, but she would hate allowing him to accompany her into it.

She stifled a sigh, too afraid to make a sound, as Cristos' gripped her free hand in his. The pommel of his sword was held high in his other hand, prepared to defend or attack at a moment's notice. Aurelia had her bow and quiver strapped to her back. Holding onto Kano's lead made it impossible to hold her weapon at the ready, but it was easy to reach if she needed to.

Spectre Forest transformed drastically as they progressed. It felt like the terrain became more rugged with every step they took. Aegricia, the northernmost kingdom in Ekotoria, rested high in the Aegrician mountains, and Norithae was surrounded by the rocky ranges. Windreach, Norithae's capital city, was nestled in a deep valley that was only accessible by boat or by a relatively narrow pass that cut through the mountainside.

The air thinned and grew colder as they continued to press on, and the fragrant scents of the forest's plant life were overpowered by the salty aroma of the Elder Sea. Their hike turned treacherous as the flat forest floor morphed into a steep incline littered with rubble that had cascaded down from the rough peaks above. Aurelia focused on her feet, afraid to stumble and draw attention to their party. When she glanced up from the haphazard stone that threatened to trip her, she saw warriors methodically spaced around their perimeter with their arms outstretched.

Though she could not see the wards they fabricated, she could feel their continuous magic hum in the surrounding air. The barrier muffled the sounds of the forest, and the frigid chill of the mountain air became tolerable once more. The knot of anxiety that had twisted in her gut since the morning began to loosen. Her breaths came easier now that they were cloaked from their enemies.

She was still filled with dread about the upcoming battle, but the temporary sense of security still calmed her some.

They reached the site that would serve as their permanent camp just as the sun reached its zenith in the sky. A host of warriors casted lasting wards around the perimeter before the ones tasked with maintaining the temporary barrier released their magic. Unlike their other camps, the space that was chosen for their encampment was not a large clearing. It could hardly be called a clearing. The small open glade had just enough space to hold the downsized bathing and dining tents. The rest of the tents had to be staggered within the trees, but they were able to pitch more than the previous.

Aurelia and Cristos were given their own tent again. Kano still had his own enclosure, but it was far smaller than the one he occupied when they first arrived in Ekotoria. She was just thankful that it was sizable enough for him to be comfortable.

A solemn and serious mood descended over the camp after the initial setup was finished. The warriors did not converse amongst themselves and few lingered around the fires. A handful trained, and several more sharpened their weapons out in the open, but most of them disappeared into their tents. Aurelia and Cristos ate lunch quickly and went to spend time with Kano in his new home. Kano lounged with his head in Aurelia's lap, and Cristos sat a few feet away as he sharpened his blades with a rough stone. Septima and Exie joined them a short time later. Her sister approached her while Exie pulled out her sword and joined Cristos in his ministrations.

"How are you feeling?" Septima asked as she sat cross-legged on Kano's other side. She stroked his fur as she stared at Aurelia.

"Honestly," Aurelia answered. "I'm a bit scared."

"Same." Septima's face was more serious than usual. Her beautiful face crinkled as she frowned and blatant worry filled her features. Aurelia studied her younger sister's face just as she had done many times before, searching for doubt. Though her fear was apparent, there was not a hint of regret in her expression. "But I think that's normal."

Aurelia considered her words and nodded. Exie said the same thing to them weeks earlier. The sisters looked toward the blond warrior as she and Cristos were deep in conversation. If Septima was not distressed over their decision to flee Vaekros and run headfirst into a foreign, magical feud, then Aurelia was resigned to whatever their future held.

She sighed heavily before she responded. "Blaedia said we will march on Norithae tomorrow."

"Exie told me. War is inevitable—I know that—but I wish we had more time." Septima took Aurelia's hand and squeezed it within her own. "We need to watch out for each other. I cannot handle life without you, Lia."

The backs of Aurelia's eyes burned as she fought against the tears that desperately tried to fall. She squeezed her sister's hand back and cleared her throat in an attempt to hide the overwhelming fear and love she felt as she glanced around the enclosure at the only family she had in Ekotoria. "I feel the same. That is what makes tomorrow so scary. I am more scared of losing any of you than I am of dying."

Exie and Cristos joined them before Septima could respond. Cristos sheathed his sword and sat beside Aurelia, placing the weapon on the ground beside him. He pulled Aurelia into his lap and nuzzled her neck in a move far too similar to the great cat that now slept at her feet. She giggled and swatted him playfully as he planted a kiss on her cheek.

"What were you two talking about?" Exie asked as she interlaced her fingers with Septima's.

"Tomorrow." Septima's usually chipper, and sometimes snarky, tone was glum as she answered her girlfriend.

Cristos wrapped his arms around Aurelia's waist and rested his chin on her shoulder as he addressed the group. "I think the war is on everyone's minds. It's hard not to think about it, but take it one step at a time. Focus on tonight. Tomorrow, focus on the battle. If you dwell on the enormity of war, it will swallow up the future happiness that we are fighting for." Exie nodded. "We should probably grab dinner and wash up. We have a long day ahead of us. The more sleep we get, the better off we will be."

Aurelia could not argue with his logic, so she stood and said a long goodbye to Kano. She still wasn't certain she'd let him join the warriors' ranks tomorrow. If she did not, this was likely the last time she would see him until after the battle—*if* she even returned. The others rose to their feet. Exie pulled Septima into a hug, and Aurelia tried to give them some semblance of privacy as the phoenix whispered in her sister's ear.

Cristos led the way out of the enclosure to the camp's epicenter. The familiar scent of stew met Aurelia's nose as her stomach grumbled impatiently. She did not know if she would be able to quiet her anxious mind long enough to sleep, but at least she was hungry.

Warriors had already formed lines when they reached the dining tent. The meal bell hadn't even rung, but she assumed they had the same idea of an early dinner and an early bedtime. Aurelia hoped the bathing line would not be as long. Although, if the tiny basins were replaced with their usual stalls, a magically warmed shower was worth the wait.

Holera and Kason occupied a large table inside the dining tent as Aurelia's small group entered. After everything rapidly transpired upon their return from Claywind, they hardly even saw the pair and had not spoken to them in days. Exie walked straight to their table and sat down without hesitation. The other three trailed behind her and claimed seats of their own. Aurelia looked forward to chatting with them. After spending so much time traveling together, she'd genuinely grown to like and respect the Aegrician couple.

"Has anyone heard from Calista today?" Aurelia asked as she sat across from Holera. Cristos settled into the chair beside her as Holera glanced at Kason. He shook his head, his jaw clenched.

"Not unless Blaedia is keeping the message quiet," Kason said as he sighed. His stiff posture relaxed, and his furrowed brow relayed the worry he didn't voice. "I'm hoping she is traveling with a Diapolisian fleet and will meet us in Norithae."

Aurelia held onto the same hope, but unless the healer showed up in the middle of the night, they would not know until the last hour was upon them. Even if Calista searched for their new camp, alone or with Diapolis' dragons and warriors, there was no promise that she could even find them behind the strengthened wards.

Even though Aurelia was hungry, she ate slowly. She knew that sustenance was important, especially since she would have to fight for her life come morning, but the normally savory meal was sawdust in her mouth. Her mind continued to reel, conjuring terrifying visions of possible outcomes. She looked up at the faces she loved so much and forced herself to finish her stew. She needed to be strong for them.

After dinner, Aurelia hugged her sister goodnight. It was a long, tight embrace she had a hard time breaking. Once their extended farewell concluded, she and Cristos headed to the bathing tent. She almost cried actual tears when she entered and saw the divided shower stalls. She lingered under the hot spray for longer than necessary, letting it wash away some of her nerves. She did not know when she would have the opportunity to shower again, so she made sure to enjoy it.

When they climbed into bed that night, Aurelia hoped they would have more nights together. The fact that she could not count on that particular fate made her chest ache so much that breathing was a struggle. Cristos pulled her close and pressed his lips to hers and suddenly sleep was the last thing she desired. This could be their last night together, and she intended to make it count.

His tongue slid across her lips as he asked for permission and Aurelia threaded her fingers in his damp hair, tilting her head to deepen the kiss.

Their kisses became feverish. His hands were everywhere. They slid across her back and caressed her breast. His light touches made her moan as his calloused palms glided along her bare skin, igniting her body with the same electricity he always invoked. His hard length rubbed against her sensitive bud as he ground against her. The thin cloth of their sleepwear was a maddening barrier between them. She slid her hand beneath his waistband and wrapped her hand around his stiff cock. She stroked him, running her thumb along the tip as she tightened her grip. He groaned deep in his throat, and the sound sent delicious tingles up her spine as it empowered her movements. She bit his bottom lip and sucked it into her mouth before he pulled away with another groan, more frustrated than aroused.

"If you keep doing that, I'm going to bury myself inside you."

She released his hard length and playfully pulled at the fabric of his sleep trousers. "I was counting on that, so take these off."

Cristos shrugged a single shoulder as he grinned. "If that is what you want, I aim to please."

He made quick work of his pants, tossing them on the floor, before he pulled her nightdress off. His hands ran along her flesh as he slid the thin fabric over her head, and she hadn't realized removing clothing could be so sensual. He leaned in to kiss her again, and she felt the tip of his cock at her entrance. She opened her thighs to give him better access, but he did not enter her. Instead, he reached between them and gripped his length and rubbed the tip in her wetness. Once. Twice. Three times. She was ready to scream in frustration, but before she could, he began to slip slowly inside her, one delicious inch at a time.

Aurelia appreciated his gentleness, but it wasn't what she wanted. She wanted him undone. She wanted all of him, raw and uncensored. She slid her arms around him and began to stroke the wings that were folded against his back. That was all it took for him to throw caution to the wind and slam into her. His hard thrusts and firm grip on her waist made her shriek in pleasure. The sound was somewhere between a scream and a gasp as he pounded into her with reckless abandon. The entire camp probably heard her, but in that blissful moment, she did not care.

Chapter Forty-Four

Spectre Forest

Time stopped for no one, and morning came too quick. A warning bell tolled through their hidden camp and ripped Aurelia from her blissfully dreamless sleep. The melodic gong was a deep, somber sound that sent a wave of dread washing over her as she rolled out of bed. Cristos followed her from the comfort of their warm fur blankets, and they pulled on their fighting leathers in silence. This was it. Their fragile peace was going to shatter before high noon, and they were going to be thrust into the chaos of war.

Aurelia could not shake the trepidation that compressed her chest. Battle was messy, and lives were sure to be lost even if they succeeded in reclaiming Norithae. She exited the tent with Cristos in tow and glanced around the already busy camp. She focused on the resolute expressions that surrounded her and wondered who was living their final day. Would it be one of the cooks who was hurrying to finish preparing breakfast? One of the lanistas that were tending to the horses? Would it be one of her friends? Her family? Was it her last day?

They ate as soon as the food was ready, and Aurelia didn't taste one bit of the porridge she forced down her throat. Every bite threatened to resurface as her knotted stomach protested against the meal. Her macabre thoughts continued to amplify with every second that passed, cycling viciously as her anxiousness hit new highs.

After they finished eating, Aurelia and Cristos joined the warriors that had congregated at the heart of the camp. They were all strapping armor over their fighting leathers, and Aurelia stared in surprise. She had assumed the Aegricians would take to the sky first and press their advantage, but it looked like they were planning to attack on foot instead. Hopefully, Warbotach held the same expectations and would prepare for an aerial assault. If there were more long-range fighters than swordsmen, maybe their chances of survival and success would increase.

Holera waved the couple over once she finished donning her protective gear. The silver-haired phoenix looked fierce and deadly in the ebony Aegrician armor. It appeared to be composed of feathers, but it did not so much as ruffle in the stiff wind that tore through the open glade they occupied. Aurelia inspected the impressive design as she greeted the warrior. The breast plate was made of the thickest leather she'd ever seen. It flared out at the shoulders and had long panels that draped just past the groin to protect both sides of the body.

Exie, Septima, and Kason joined them almost immediately. Kason handed Cristos a set of armor while Holera and Exie fitted Aurelia and Septima with the undersized replicas of the

Aegrician war garb. Their human statues were far smaller than the fae warriors, and their petite protection looked almost doll-like in comparison. Aurelia felt like a young child playing dress-up rather than a soldier preparing to take up arms.

The Vesta sisters were handed a slew of weapons as soon as their armor was properly secured. Aurelia was not the worst with a sword, but she was far more gifted as an archer. She was given a filled quiver and bow that she strapped to her back. She was also given a short sword and two daggers so that she was not left defenseless after her cache of arrows ran out. Piercing the enemy from a distance weighed heavily on her conscience, but the idea of running a sword through another living being—of having their blood coat her hands—made her stomach lurch.

She peered down at herself, surprised by what she saw. She was not mentally nor physically prepared for war, but she certainly looked the part. Septima stood beside her, her grim expression echoing Aurelia's as she was outfitted with multiple blades of her own. Cristos had already fastened his long sword vertically down his spine. He wore his short sword at his hip, a dagger sheathed on each thigh, and three more small blades attached to a belt that rested atop his armor.

Aurelia's heart thundered in her ears when she took in her battle-ready friends and family. Tears filled her eyes as she tried to come to terms with the fact that they might not all return to camp after all was said and done.

Blaedia approached the gathered warriors in long, confident strides. Outfitted with a slew of deadly weapons and the prominent Aegrician armor, she looked invincible as she stood before them. Her powerful voice boomed throughout the camp, and Aurelia felt the telltale tingles of magic in the air as the amplified words echoed around her.

"Today we fight to reclaim what is ours. Saving our queen and restoring our continent starts here. First, we free Norithae from the Warbotach scum. With the aid of their people, we will advance north and save our homeland."

The general scanned the crowd. It felt like she met each and every eye as she raised her hand and placed it against her heart. The passion and determination in her tone sent shivers down Aurelia's spine. "It is normal to be afraid, but do not let it still your hand. We must overcome our hesitations because we fight for what is just. We fight for freedom. Defending the future of our people is the most noble cause. Whether you fall in battle or live to tell the tale, you are a hero, and your kingdom will forever be indebted to you. Fight hard, fight smart, and we will conquer the enemy."

Blaedia paused as she eyed her warriors again. She raised her fist in the air as she let out an impassioned bellow. "TODAY, WE WILL BE VICTORIOUS!"

Cheers erupted throughout their ranks, and the crowd repeated her words in a fervent chant. Fists shot into the air around her as the crowd roared. Blaedia normalized feeling scared and encouraged conquering it instead of condemning the uncontrollable emotion, and the speech moved Aurelia just as much as the spirited warriors that surrounded her. She thrust her arm up and raised her voice to join the emboldened chorus.

Cristos stared at her as she shouted. She smiled over at him, and his eyes sparkled as he grabbed her waist and pulled her to him. He kissed her deeply, and for a moment, she forgot about the impending battle as their surroundings faded. His passionate embrace held all of her attention. He pulled away far too soon, and the cacophony filled her ears once more. His ocean-blue stare held hers as he pressed his forehead to hers.

"I love you so much. Be careful and stay safe. I cannot live this life without you."

Her heart seized at his heavy words, and she pressed her lips to his once more. Aurelia broke the kiss and cupped his cheek as she responded.

"I love you, too. Life without you isn't an option, so you are not allowed to fall in battle."

He gave her a crooked grin, but it did not reach his eyes. She wanted—needed—to see happiness fill his features before they ran headlong into danger. She kept her tone light and shot him a playful wink. "Let's go get your throne back, Your Majesty."

He barked out a laugh and unleashed the heartwarming smile she craved.

"What am I going to do with you?"

She shrugged a single shoulder as she smirked at him. "You should have thought of that before. Now you're stuck with me."

"I have no complaints."

Their easy banter did not last. The Aegricians began to fall into lines along the invisible wall of the camp. Aurelia glanced in the direction of Kano's enclosure, still warring with indecision. Septima pulled away from a passionate embrace with Exie and turned to her.

"Go get him. He would want to be with us, no matter the outcome. Don't take away the opportunity to protect the ones he loves."

Her sister's words resonated deep within her. She was right. If she remained in the camp like Cristos had asked, she would hate not being able to fight alongside her family and friends. Survival be damned. She raced over to the enclosure and released the great cat. She considered leashing him and setting him loose at her side once the time for battle was upon them, but she let him roam free for two reasons. She wanted the Aegrician warriors to trust he would not turn on them as they fought for their lives, but mostly, she wanted him to join her of his own volition. The tiger may not be able to understand the dire situation they were heading into, but she still wanted it to be his choice. When weapons clashed and the war raged on, she wanted him to be able to decide if he fought or fled. It was the only way she could think of that gave him some semblance of power over his role in Ekotoria.

With Kano and Cristos flanking her, Aurelia hurried to catch up with Septima and Exie as rows of warriors marched through the warbling air of the wards and out into the Spectre Forest. They advanced on Windreach in silence, determined to free Norithae and move north to free Aegricia, fueling their powerful strides. Every single person held a weapon at the ready as they scanned the woodlands they traversed.

Kano let out a low warning growl as a small Warbotach patrol approached. Before Aurelia even processed the enemy's sudden appearance, several phoenixes broke away and dispatched them before they had a chance to sound an alarm. Their forces pressed on, and those leading the group began to maneuver the treacherous mountain pass that would take them straight into the heart of the capital city.

Aurelia stretched up on the tips of her toes, straining to see if any of their people had been hurt. Her inferior height made it impossible to see over the mass of lanky warriors that marched in front of her, but she spotted the vibrant flames of a phoenix shifting through the throng of bodies. A firebird took to the sky, teal and crimson feathers clashing beautifully.

The intense coloring looked like water and fire fighting for dominance over the impressive creature, but Aurelia's awestruck gaze turned horrified as it landed on the massive talons. Two bloodied bodies hung limp in the phoenix's grasp. She couldn't see well enough to identify them, but the dark Aegrician armor held her attention captive like an ominous omen. Powerful wings carried them overhead in the direction of their camp, and Aurelia's stomach clenched painfully as she silently hoped the injured would survive.

The warriors did not dally as their comrades raced toward their base in search of medical attention. They continued on, weapons never faltering from their readied position. As their forces continued to funnel into the narrow passage, Aurelia drew nearer to the point of conflict. She passed six scarred bodies left to rot on the forest floor, their sightless eyes fixated on the thick greenery above. The bright sunlight that streamed through the canopy served as a morbid spotlight as the rays illuminated the wounds that ended their lives. Her insides lurched, and she fought to hold down her breakfast as she tried to pull her gaze from a slit throat. The deep gash exposed interior tissue and bone that she never wished to see.

Cristos reached over and covered her eyes, turning her head to face forward as they continued to traipse through the forest.

When they moved past the grisly sight, he removed his hand and intertwined their fingers. He gripped her hand so hard it throbbed, but she did not ask him to loosen his hold.

The dull ache, the feel of his strength, and the warmth radiating from him all served to reassure her. The prickles of pain reminded her she was still alive. Cristos was still alive. Kano. Septima. Exie. Taryn. Blaedia. Kason. Holera. Her eyes flitted around their ranks, focusing on each of their faces. At least for now, all the people she cared for in this world still soldiered on, and that would have to be enough.

A vicious snarl tore from Kano's throat. The unexpected ferocity made her heart slam into her chest as she jumped and whipped her head around in search of the threat. Several of the nearby warriors stepped away in fear of the tiger, but Aurelia knew better. He would not react so viscerally unless they were in imminent danger. His ears were flat against his head, and his lips were pulled back, exposing his sharp canines. She slowed to match his deliberate steps as she forced herself to stop staring at the great cat and scan their surroundings. He was behaving far too fierce, and she was certain he sensed something they could not.

Nothing seemed out of place as they continued forward, but once half of their forces had entered the mountainous pass, she spotted the first Warbotach soldier astride his fire-breathing steed. Before the Aegricians could react, dozens more appeared out of thin air and descended on them from all sides.

Her thundering heart and gasping breaths were at odds with her oddly calm mind. As her body tried to convince her to flee, her mind cataloged the violence that erupted around her. The enemy had to have been hidden by wards, but they were not enough to fool Kano. They attacked almost as soon as he reacted to their presence. They'd effectively cut the phoenixes' forces in half as they blocked the rocky path that led to Windreach.

Sounds of battle echoed from the mountain's narrow pathway as chaos reigned inside Spectre Forest. Aurelia raised her bow, not allowing herself time to hesitate as she fired at the throng of invaders that tried to break through the wall of warriors. She did not know what would happen if they managed to infiltrate their ranks and fragment their formations, but she could feel the need to prevent that from happening deep in her soul.

Her arrows whistled through the air, accompanied by the other archers among their forces who shot at the enemy. The sounds of swords clashing and pain-filled screams overwhelmed the dense woods.

She notched her last arrow and let it fly. It buried itself into the eye of a Warbotach soldier who was swinging his sword at Kason's turned back. Kason disposed of his opponent and turned to see the man she'd pierced with her shot. He nodded his thanks as she pulled her sword and turned her attention elsewhere.

Aurelia felt strangely empty as the fighting raged on. After it was over, she would have time to process the carnage her hands dealt, but for now, she needed to survive. Most of the Aegrician archers traveled at the front of their procession and were trapped by the soldiers that attacked the pass. When the few that remained ran out of arrows, the battle began in earnest.

Warbotach reinforcements continued to appear without warning to join the fray. Her allies were divided, their tight grouping destroyed. Cristos slashed at a swordsman that advanced on him as she raised her blade to deflect an attack. Kano sprang from her left, knocking her assailant to the ground before their blades could meet. He tore the man's throat out in an instant and returned to Aurelia's side.

They were surrounded by enemies, but her furry friend never left her side. He only attacked the ones who advanced on her. When another soldier advanced on horseback, the tiger pounced. The man was thrown from his mount, the creature dead before it could expel the flame that had started to form in its mouth.

The rider hit the ground hard, rolling from the impact. His confused expression hardened into a rage filled mask as he set his sight on her beloved pet. Aurelia lashed out with her sword, tearing open his gut with the strike. She pivoted as an angry roar sounded behind her. Pain exploded in her left arm as a blade bit into it.

Still, she felt detached from herself, as if she was merely an observer in her own body. Her instincts ruled as she lifted her sword with her right to engage with her attacker, but she never got the chance. She dove to the side to avoid being impaled by the man's broadsword as Kano tackled him from behind.

She and her tiger dealt unyielding carnage as the enemy continued to press them from all sides. She tried to catch sight of Cristos and Septima, but everyone was a mass of bodies. The Aegrician armor made them all look the same at a quick glance, and she could not offer more than that as she continued to fight against the seemingly endless stream of attackers. It was impossible to make sense of what was going on around her.

Kano unleashed a vicious growl behind her as he coiled his hind legs, poised to pounce. Aurelia reacted to his ferocity and ducked as he launched himself over her head. She turned in time to see the tiger topple another Warbotach soldier that had tried to sneak up on her. He tore at the man's face, shredding it to ribbons as they hit the ground.

"Thanks, boy." She turned to search for her next opponent as she said the words, but there were none. The attacks had ceased. She wasn't sure if they had killed them all or if Warbotach had retreated, but she didn't care. There were more pressing matters. She strained her eyes, searching for Cristos, Septima, Exie, any of her loved ones, really.

Now that the danger had abated, she took in the horrifying scene before her. Dead bodies littered the ground. Aegrician, Warbotach, and fiery horses alike in their stilled chests and blank stares. Injured cries filled the forest as dozens of phoenixes took to the skies, undoubtedly scanning for more threats. Aegrician warriors walked among the bodies, searching for their survivors. If any Warbotach soldiers survived, they retreated because not a single scarred face scattered on the forest floor held any life.

A familiar face appeared in the tree line, and Aurelia felt like she could breathe again. Cristos was saturated in blood, but stood tall. From a distance, he did not appear wounded, and she sighed in relief as she rushed to his side. He smiled brilliantly as he ran to meet her and reached out to pull her into a hug before his smile faltered.

"Your arm!"

Aurelia glanced down. Her eyes widened as she stared at her blood-soaked fighting leathers and the long gash on her forearm.

"Are you hurt anywhere else?" Cristo's panicked voice was unnatural as he scanned the rest of her body.

"I am okay. It was not my sword arm, and Kano protected me. He took care of the attacker before I even laid eyes on him."

"Not your sword arm," he scoffed. "How in the realms did you go from being terrified of war to reassuring me that your sword arm is fine?"

His voice was hysterical as he fretted over her, and she could not fight the grin that graced her lips. Cristos was always so calm and collected in times of strife. Seeing his blatant worry and obvious love for her warmed her heart. She placed the palm of her uninjured arm over his heart as she stretched to kiss him gently.

"I am okay, I promise. Have you seen Septima? Exie? Holera? Anyone?"

Her smile faded as he gave a grim shake of his head. "I will look for them as soon as we get you to a healer."

"I. Am. Fine." Her tone brokered no room for argument as she stalked through the sea of bodies in search of her sister and friends.

"Aurelia! Cristos!" She spun as she heard Exie's shout, but the joy that had surged disappeared just as fast when she caught sight of the warrior. Exie was covered in blood and what looked suspiciously like organ tissue. She limped slightly as she hastened toward them, but the unsteady gait and excessive gore wasn't what stopped her heart. It was the panic and absolute terror coloring the phoenix's expression that made it impossible to breathe.

Exie sobbed as they rushed to her side. She pulled herself together enough to speak and shattered Aurelia's world. "Septima is gone! I can't find her anywhere! We have to find her."

"What do you mean 'gone'? Where did you get separated?" Cristos was the voice of reason as Aurelia stood frozen in place, the desolate horror consuming her.

Another cry escaped the warrior as she tried to explain. "No, she is gone. I saw one of those barbarian's hit her over the head and carry her away on his fire beast. I tried to stop them, to get to her, but I couldn't. I was fighting too many at once and-" Her words turned into an anguished wail. "I could not save her. We have to find her."

The world spun violently as Aurelia tried to wrap her mind around the phoenix's words. There was no way. It couldn't be. She couldn't be, but...

Septima is gone.

To be continued...

CROWN OF THE EXILED

CROWN OF THE PHOENIX
BOOK TWO

COMING SOON

About the Author

C. A. Varian was raised in Lockport, Louisiana, into an often-low-income household. She spent a lot of her childhood fishing, crabbing, and playing school. She loved pretending to be the teacher and assigning work to her cousins. Her love of reading started very young, where she used to complete several books per week in elementary school so she could earn a free personal pizza from Pizza Hut. Even once  free pizzas were no longer an option, she still steadily read novels, usually above the reading level for her age group, and loved visiting the library to stock up on books. She started writing poetry and short stories while still in junior high through high school, although she stopped writing, at least for fun, once she had children and went to college. Thankfully, her writing hiatus has ended.

She earned a Bachelor of Arts degree in History, as well as a Master's degree in History. She also worked towards getting her teaching certification. She did almost all of her college education while also being the mother of two children. After graduating from college, she began teaching public school, a career that she continues to this day, currently teaching special education at a local middle school.

She's married to a retired military officer, so she spent many years moving around for his career, but they now live in central Alabama, with her youngest daughter, Arianna. Her oldest daughter, Brianna, no longer lives at home and is engaged to be married. She has two Shih Tzus that she considers her children. Boy, Charlie, and girl, Luna, are their mommy's shadows. She also has three cats: Ramses, Simba, and Cookie, as well as five chickens and two ducks.

Follow C. A. Varian

Sign up for C. A. Varian's newsletter to receive current updates on her new and upcoming releases, sales, and giveaways: **https://se ndfox.com/cavarian**

You can also find and follow her here:

Facebook: @C.A.VARIAN1
Tiktok: @authorcavarian
Twitter: @cherievarian
Instagram: @C._A._Varian_author
Website: https://cherievarian.com/

Also By C. A. Varian

Hazel Watson Mystery Series

Kindred Spirits: Prequel
The Sapphire Necklace
Justice for the Slain
Whispers from the Swamp